PRAISE FOR PATRICK S TOMLINSON

"A murder on a spaceship is the ultimate locked-room mystery, and debut author Tomlinson has a lot of fun dragging his detective all over the ship as he investigates who killed Laraby."
Library Journal

"There is so much good stuff wrapped inside *The Ark*: a locked-room murder mystery, bare-knuckle action, and the kind of hard-boiled science fiction that will make your brain pop. Climb aboard."
Adam Rakunas, author of Windswept

"The stakes are high in this thrilling debut."
Kirkus Reviews

"Deftly plotted, The Ark is an excellent work of science fiction. I eagerly await *Trident's Forge*, the next novel in the series."
Mutt Cafe

"Another amazing story with all the twists and turns I've come to expect from Patrick S Tomlinson. With a great mix of science fiction, action and mystery it is wonderfully written and it's not 'world' building but as the author said it's 'race building', so don't miss out on the turbulent ups and downs that had me undeniably hooked throughout the entire thing."
Books in Brogan

"This book is fresh, new, clever. I loved everything about this book, it ambushed me with amazing prose, and compelling characters. I read it in one sitting. I cannot remember when a book was this captivating, this enthralling. More Mr Tomlinson, please."
Book Drunkard

"The generations of isolation in the controlled society of the Ark have left them in a setting that makes this novel different. I also enjoyed the twists that were alluded to in this book that will bring some interesting turns in the a⎯⎯⎯⎯⎯⎯⎯⎯⎯⎯⎯⎯⎯⎯⎯⎯⎯⎯⎯⎯⎯⎯⎯eries. I give this novel a 4.4 out o⎯⎯⎯
John's

PATRICK S TOMLINSON

TRIDENT'S FORGE

CHILDREN OF A DEAD EARTH II

ANGRY ROBOT

ANGRY ROBOT
An imprint of Watkins Media Ltd

Lace Market House,
54-56 High Pavement,
Nottingham,
NG1 1HW
UK

angryrobotbooks.com
twitter.com/angryrobotbooks
Kexx appeal

An Angry Robot paperback original 2016
1

A catalogue record for this book is available from the British Library.

ISBN 978 0 85766 486 0
EBook ISBN 978 0 85766 488 4

Map by Stephanie McAlea
Set in Meridien and Digital Serial by Epub Services.
Printed and bound in the UK by 4edge Limited.

This novel is dedicated to my wonderful, loving, supportive, talented, beautiful girlfriend, Niki, because her mother seemed quite concerned that I didn't dedicate the last one to her.

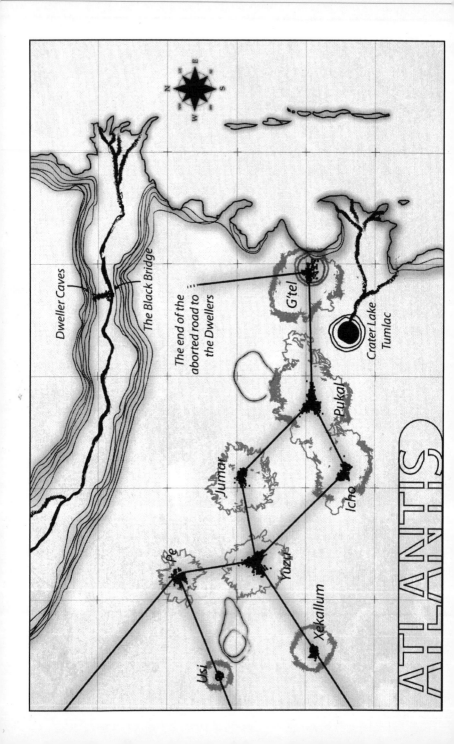

ATLANTIS

Dweller Caves

The Black Bridge

The end of the
aborted road to
the Dwellers

G'tel

Crater Lake
Tumlac

Pukal

Jumat

Icho

Pe

Yozu

Xekallum

Usi

CHAPTER ONE

The stars shone brightly. Especially the new ones.

Those were the ones that held Kexx's attention, and why ze'd left G'tel's protective halo of trees so late at night. Out here, the glare from the campfires didn't interfere with the sky. Ze watched the two new pinpricks of light and pondered their meaning while the heat of the village fires slowly leached from zer body.

A young, inexperienced ulik bumbled into the clearing, betraying the presence of its pack. Kexx let a ripple of light wash over zer skin, both to let the uliks know ze was watching them, and to let them see the half-spear stuck into the ground next to zer.

The offending ulik was apparently young enough to have gotten caught, but experienced enough to know what an adult of G'tel could do with a spear point. It gave an answering wave of soft blue light down its front legs. The pack headed for the beach to forage in the tidal pools for much less dangerous prey.

Kexx watched them go, eight in total. It was large for an ulik pack, but most of the members looked scrawny. Perhaps the castoffs from healthier packs had banded together for safety. In truth, if the pack had decided to attack zer, Kexx probably couldn't have killed them all before being brought down zerself. But ze would've gotten more of the uliks than the pack could afford to lose and still hope to take down tomorrow's prey. So they passed. Such was the simple math of living on the surface. Kexx wished the pack luck in its wanderings and returned to watching the new stars.

7

Three years ago, the dimmer one arrived. Varr made three passings, then the brighter one appeared. They hadn't been named yet, mostly because the elders were convinced that they were Seeds of Cuut, preparing to rain fire down on them like the legends from the deep times. More than one family had fled the village that first night to try to return to shelter in Xis's womb underground, only to find the Black Bridge blocked and fiercely guarded by Dwellers in no mood to welcome refugees. Which shouldn't have come as a surprise to anyone. Dwellers barely tolerated traders, much less new mouths to feed.

Kexx couldn't blame them for their fear, but ze wasn't convinced of the danger. Sure enough, the new stars fell into a rhythm in a matter of days. Now they sat side by side, motionless in the night sky, but that was hardly the strangest thing that had happened. First, there had been the hard-shelled emissary sent to watch over them through its crystal eyes. Which of their triumvirate of gods it was watching for was a matter of some intense debate that persisted to the present. Nevertheless, the elders ordered it brought into Cuut's temple so that offerings of food and prayer could be made to it, and to make sure it only saw what they wanted it to see.

Then, nearly a year later, a strand of light, long and straight as the cleaved edge of a crystal, descended from the smaller star, connected with the larger, and slowly made its way down until it touched the ocean far to the east.

Try as they might, the elders could find no reference to such a happening anywhere in the songs or scrolls. Desperate for answers, they'd even sent an envoy to consult those Dwellers who commune with Xis in the deep below, but even *their* wizened ones squabbled over the meaning of the omen. Some believed it was Cuut coming to finish zer long battle with Xis for all time. Still others argued that the new stars were heralds of Varr, and that the ray of light was an invitation to leave Xis's womb behind forever. Of course, Kexx's village and the three fullhands like it had done that generations ago, venturing out from the Dweller caves, never to return. A gathering of village elders insisted the omen was meant for them alone, Dwellers be damned.

Kexx was no elder of the faith, and didn't feel qualified to question their proclamations, but ze still couldn't shake the feeling that there wasn't enough known about any of this for anyone to make such exacting, contradictory conclusions with the unflappable confidence the elders so often displayed.

A cool ocean breeze blew across Kexx, sending a small shiver through zer body. The skin on zer arms and in the folds of zer flattened headcrests was still damp from the water of the evening's cleansing ritual. A new storm front was moving toward the village, ze knew the feeling in zer air bladders. Kexx held zer hands up into the wind and spread zer fingers to let the salty smell of the ocean play through them.

Something on the wind caught zer attention. An unfamiliar smell mingled with the aroma of the sea. Kexx spread zer arms wide, trying to get an indication of the direction the strange smell was coming from, but the wind had churned it up too much to get a bearing. It didn't matter. A moment later, a warning howl pierced the night's quiet. One of the uliks had spotted something, and it didn't like what it saw one bit.

Kexx sprang up from the ground and grabbed the shaft of zer half-spear. The pack was a short run down the beach, flashing undulating waves of light over their skin in a typical threat display. Whatever the source of the smell was, it had spooked an entire ulik pack. Cautiously, Kexx crouched down and stalked off in their direction, the soft blue lights in zer skin shrinking down to pinpricks. The pack had arranged itself in a straight line on the beach facing the ocean, trying to make itself look as large and intimidating as possible.

Ze scanned the waves, looking for whatever had frightened the pack. Kexx spotted the hole in the water a moment later. A black void as dark as a cloudy night floated on the surface. It was easily as large as a bulo carcass. An enormous translucent triangular crest sprang from the creature's back and billowed in the wind.

The pack leader's skin-glow changed abruptly as the creature continued to approach without slowing. Its nerve broken, one ulik spun around and darted for the cover of the crop fields with the rest of the pack in hot pursuit. Kexx's instincts screamed at zer to follow their example, but curiosity kept zer feet planted to the sandy beach. As long as ze stayed out of the water, the enormous creature was no threat.

That's what Kexx kept saying to zerself as the creature plowed straight into the shore with enough force to gouge out a furrow in the sand. Thoroughly beached, the mysterious creature leaned onto its side with a shuddering gasp like creaking wood. With the muscles in zer legs tensed for a quick escape, Kexx watched the creature intently, quietly praying to Xis, or even Cuut, that it didn't suddenly sprout legs and run zer down. For its part, the enormous nightmare remained motionless.

Animal calls drifted across the night air. Soft at first, confused, like someone waking up, but they grew in both volume and number. They were high pitched, almost like children. Even more bizarrely, they seemed to be coming from *inside* the beached creature.

Swallowing a gasp, Kexx gripped the shaft of the half-spear tightly as the first figure emerged from the creature. Silhouetted against the night sky, the figure looked too short to be an adult. It was more the size of an adolescent, much like the voice, but the proportions and the way it moved were... unnatural.

The single figure was quickly joined by two more, then four. Soon, more than a fullhand of them stood atop the creature's back. Was it a creature at all? Before Kexx had time to ponder the question, a brilliant light erupted from one of the figure's hands, so bright that Kexx had to shift zer gaze to avoid night blindness. Three others joined in, white light streaming from their hands like tiny suns, brighter and purer than any campfire. They swept the beams of light up and down the beach as if searching for something. Beams, Kexx realized, that looked very much like the thread of light reaching down from the new stars to the west.

Kexx dropped prone, making zerself as small as possible. No animal's skin-glow was that bright. Whatever the strangers were, they weren't G'tel, from another village on the road network, or even Dwellers. The realization raced through Kexx's mind, leaving a wake of bone-gripping fear as it went. Too terrified to move, yet too curious to look away, Kexx studied the small creatures as they jumped down to the sand and made their way down the beach.

Now and then, one of the creatures shone its light on another while they talked, giving Kexx a clear view of them. Their skin was smooth and pale, like corpses, empty of the shifting patterns and colors of living flesh. Absent too was any skin-glow, except for the lights coming from their hands. They had two arms and two legs, but they were knobby, stiff. Their hands and feet were broad and flat. Long black strands covered the tops of their heads where display crests should be.

The group moved closer to Kexx's hiding place. Had ze been spotted? Kexx held up a hand cautiously to sample the air. The strange smell that had drawn zer down to the beach was strong on the breeze, wafting off the creatures like a dux'ah at the height of mating season. They moved strangely on their rigid legs, haltingly and without fluidity. Everything about them screamed foreignness.

One of the creatures stopped suddenly and pointed their light beam directly into Kexx's face. It was like staring into the midday sun. Kexx winced and threw a hand over zer eyes out of reflex. The creatures shouted at each other in alarm. Now there was no question that ze'd been spotted. Zer muscles shaking with panic, Kexx jumped up to zer full height and shook zer half-spear menacingly, hoping ze terrified them half as much as they did zer.

The one that had spotted zer stepped forward and hushed the rest, then signaled for them to spread out into a semicircle with Kexx at its center. Their coordination sent a trembling quake through Kexx's muscles and joints. These were not merely clever animals like the ulik that had scattered into the night, their crests tucked tightly to their skulls. Nor were their sounds mere animal calls. The strangers were talking to each other, just as G'tel did, but in a tongue unlike any Kexx had ever heard. They were intelligent, and therefore, infinitely more dangerous.

The trading scale in Kexx's mind tilted decisively from curiosity to retreat. Ze spun around toward the cover of the yulka field and took off at a dead run, but as soon as ze took the first step, one of zer toes caught on a root protruding from the sand, sending zer toppling onto the back face of the dune. Kexx reached out to break zer fall, but the ground rose up and knocked the wind from zer air sacks like a well-landed punch.

Kexx watched in horror as zer half-spear rolled down the dune and out of reach.

Footsteps surrounded zer. Kexx flipped around and sat up just in time to see the strangers swarming down the dune from all directions at once. Even on the shifting sands and with their jerky gaits, they moved unnervingly fast. Kexx lunged down the dune and made a wild grab for zer spear, but one of the strangers had apparently moved to flank zer and snatched it up first. The circle closed around zer. Kexx held up zer hands while a pattern of slow glowing waves radiated across zer skin from zer chest out to zer fingers in the universal sign of submission.

At least Kexx hoped it was universal.

The stranger with Kexx's spear stood at the ready, but didn't point it at zer. That had to count for something. The one who'd discovered zer walked up slowly. Ze was smaller than the others, and softer somehow. Ze moved with more care and grace than the others, despite zer strange legs with their knobby protrusions. Ze stopped just short of where Kexx sat and held out an open hand. In zer other hand, Kexx saw a yellow cylinder and realized it, not their hands, was the source of the light beams. It was a… a tool?

Awe welled up inside Kexx's chest in a way ze hadn't felt since zer first cleansing ceremony, barely a year out of zer larval phase. These strangers had been sent by Varr, they must've been. Who else had the power to capture a piece of the sun? Kexx put zer hands flat and dropped zer forehead to the sand and started to chant a prayer, but this seemed to confuse and upset the strangers more than anything.

The small stranger standing in front of Kexx shook her head in a gesture Kexx didn't recognize, then held out zer open hand again.

"Watashin onamae ha Mei Nakama desu. Onamae wa?"

Kexx stared up at the stranger uncomprehendingly. Ze wasn't even sure zer mouth could mimic the sounds. The stranger's face twisted up in an expression Kexx couldn't interpret. Then, ze pointed a single finger back at zer own chest.

"Mei," ze said simply.

"Mmm," Kexx struggled to wrap zer mouth around the

unnatural sound. "Mmuaeee?"

The stranger's mouth tugged up at the corners. "Hai! Mei." Ze tapped a finger on zer chest for emphasis, then pointed back at Kexx and paused expectantly.

A name. "Mei" was the stranger's name. And now ze was asking for a name in return.

"Kexx," ze said quietly.

"Kex," Mei repeated, clipping the end and changing the meaning to a reddish, inedible fungus, but it was probably closer than ze had gotten to saying Mei properly on the first try.

"Kexx," ze repeated back to Mei. The corners of the stranger's mouth tugged up again, wider this time. Wide enough to make creases in zer cheeks. Then, without warning, the pale little stranger lunged forward and wrapped zer arms around Kexx's shoulders. A hug. Ze was being hugged.

Kexx hugged the peculiar little creature named Mei back, and laughed in relief. Mei joined zer. They laughed together for a long time.

CHAPTER TWO

Tau Ceti G, (Human designation: Gaia),
Local Standard Year 3 pl (Post Landing)

Benson blew his whistle, then stepped onto the field. "Pass Interference. Defense. Number twenty-one."

"What?" Korolev yelled. "I just pushed him out of the way."

"Yeah," Benson shouted. "That's pass interference. You can't interfere with an eligible receiver if they have a chance to make a fair catch outside of the first five meters."

"But I'm *supposed* to keep them from catching the ball. That's my whole job!"

"Yes, but... just not like that."

"That doesn't make any sense, chief."

Benson threw up his arms. "Hey, I'm just reading out of the rulebook, OK? I didn't write it. Now are we playing football or not?"

The twenty-two men wandering around the makeshift "field" murmured general agreement that they were in fact playing football and reset for the next down.

"OK, put the ball at the spot of the foul on the twenty seven-meter line," Benson said.

"The twenty-seven?" Korolev objected. "That's like a thirty meter penalty!"

"That's the rule."

"So I can get a late hit on the quarterback or drill a guy out of bounds and only get fifteen meters, but if I touch him in the open field before he touches the ball, it could be *ninety* meters?"

"I suppose, if your quarterback has a laser for an arm," Benson admitted.

"That's dumb."

"That's the game. Now c'mon, we've only got three more practices before we play the Dervishes."

"I miss Zero," their middle linebacker, Lindqvist, muttered. He was a Nordic mountain of a man who would have been better served by the universe if he'd been born in an age when breaking a wooden shield with a single ax swing was a highly prized skill.

"We all do," Benson snapped. "But the Zero stadium is a little busy right now shipping food and supplies to keep all of us fat and happy, OK? It's either this or soccer, kiddies."

A chorus of groans let Benson know what the consensus on *that* possibility was.

"That's what I thought. Now c'mon, line up on the twenty-seven!"

Coach Benson tucked the tablet he'd been referencing under an arm and watched the scene unfold. Tau Ceti G's... *Gaia*'s first organized sports league was only five days away from its opening game, and American-style football was about to come roaring back from a two-and-a-half century hiatus. Sure, the old player stats and records from the days of the NFL and IAFL weren't any good on a new planet with only ninety-five percent Earth gravity, but they'd decided to jettison the anachronistic imperial yard in favor of the slightly longer meter for the field, which would hopefully account for the lighter gravity to some degree.

After two weeks of practice, one thing was abundantly clear. Even in the lighter gravity, they had a long way to go before the old records were in any danger. Benson only hoped the coaches of the Dervishes, Yaoguai, and Spartans were experiencing similar setbacks.

Not that their trials should have come as any great surprise. Each of the four teams was only afforded an hour of practice per day on the single playing field. Acreage inside humanity's rapidly-growing colony of Shambhala came at a premium, and Benson had called in more than one favor to get the field built in the first place. Professional players back on Earth drilled and trained as a fulltime job. Benson's players were former Zero players, farm hands, construction techs, and one skinny-ass software coder who had somehow been graced with a leg that could kick a football through the uprights from almost sixty meters out, so long as the wind wasn't blowing, which it nearly always was.

The play clock resumed, and the quarterback started his snap-count.

"Blue forty-two. Hut, hut. Hike!"

He'd barely dropped back into the pocket before Benson blew his whistle again.

"Holding. Offense. Number thirty. Ten meter penalty."

"That's bullshit," Hoffman, playing number thirty, said. "Why is it ten meters when the offense gets called for a hold, but only five when the defense holds?"

Benson shook the rules tablet in the air angrily.

"I don't fucking know, OK? It's football, it's not supposed to make sense! Now just move the ball back, we're burning daylight."

Forty-five sweaty and profanity-laden minutes later, the Mustangs' practice was over, just in time for the Spartans to take their turn on the field. Benson slapped shoulders and gave a round of congratulations to his new team, then turned down the path toward his home. The setting sun hung low on the horizon, shining ever so slightly more brightly in his left eye.

The vat-grown eye, courtesy of Doctor Russell, was just a bit more sensitive than his right. It, along with extensive burns on his hands and face, as well as a lungful of plutonium dust, were the keepsakes he'd earned fighting an utter madman named David Kimura and his patron among the crew, Avelina da Silva. The lunatic had detonated one of the small implosion-triggered nukes the Ark used for propulsion. Only a stray bullet from Benson's gun denting the explosive shell surrounding the plutonium pile inside had prevented it from going nuclear, throwing out a huge fireball of conventional explosives and a cloud of vaporized plutonium in the process.

However, considering he'd saved all of humanity in the process, Benson considered the injuries a fair trade. Like his eye, Dr Russell had expertly healed his burns and lungs. Only an occasional itching under the skin of his left cheek where the nerves in his clone skin grafts hadn't quite lined up remained to remind him of the damage he'd sustained in the fight.

Still, some nights, it was enough. Certain kinds of wounds ran deeper than flesh.

He shook off the thought as he turned onto the city's central boulevard. Not for the first time, Benson marveled at how quickly Shambhala had grown. It wouldn't be long before walking from one end of the city to the other wouldn't be feasible. Public transit would be needed before long. The politicians were already fighting over the whats and wheres.

Benson glanced into the Bay of Landing where the space elevator's anchor station floated. Its thin, carbon-nanotube ribbon shimmered in the deep red-orange hues of sunset as it reached tens of thousands of kilometers up to the Ark floating in the null-g of geosynch. Benson's beloved Zero stadium had reverted to its original purpose: a dock and maintenance bay for elevator cars, as well as a warehouse and staging area for all the people, material, and supplies that continued to move back and forth between the Ark and the planet on a near-daily basis. Continue up some tens of thousands of kilometers more and the Pathfinder probe sat, now serving as the elevator system's counterweight.

Humanity's home for the last two and a third centuries had undergone a metamorphosis since it arrived in orbit around Gaia. Its three kilometer-long pleated conical meteor shield had been ejected just before decelerating for the Tau Ceti system. Only a handful of helium-three tanks still studded the outside of the reactor bulb, enough to fuel the ship's fusion reactors for another fifteen years, at most. Only five thousand people remained behind to maintain its systems and tend the farms. Its stockpile of nuclear bombs all but exhausted, it would never move again, save for the occasional station-keeping thruster firing. The Ark had been reborn as a space station.

However, this new role was no less important than its original one. While the majority of mankind had moved down to Gaia's surface over the last three years, Shambhala was still dependent on the immense ship's fusion generators for power, her navigational lasers to deflect the Tau Ceti system's population of asteroids, and what remained of its farmland for food.

As a posthumous gift to mankind, Avelina da Silva, the genius geneticist who had been in charge of the team adapting food crops to Atlantis's biosphere and the woman who had nearly succeeded in killing every last human alive, had sabotaged the first batches of staple crop seeds with time-bombs hidden in their DNA that turned the plants into black sludge less than a month after germination. Their best scientists were still busy cleaning up the mess, damn her.

Benson took a moment to admire human tenacity. Despite possibly the best example of Murphy's Law since the phrase had been coined, in less than three years their beachhead on Gaia had grown from a handful of tents and latrines huddled around the first landing shuttles to a fully functional and expanding city of twenty-five thousand people, complete with power, running water, sewers, networked data systems and a desalinization plant, all with a workforce that had been cut by two fifths just a month before they'd arrived.

Not that humans had done all, or even most, of the building. The majority of labor came courtesy of the army of machines that had spent the last two and a half centuries locked away in the Ark's cargo bays. The explosion of activity only served to reinforce to Benson how much humanity had sat on its hands during the long road to Gaia. What he witnessed now was nothing short of a force of nature at work.

As he walked down the wide boulevard, nearly everyone paused to acknowledge his passing with something bordering on reverence. Benson had known celebrity in his life aboard the Ark as a Zero champion, but it was nothing compared to the legend that had grown around him as the savior of all mankind. It probably wouldn't be long before they started pushing to put up some gaudy bronze statue of him in the city center.

A piece of litter caught his eye. A crumpled piece of paper, laying on the side of the road where it had been scrunched up and carelessly dropped. An old ache gnawed at him as Benson picked the trash up.

Trash. It was a word mankind hadn't used in centuries. Nothing went to waste on the Ark. There, he'd have used the surveillance net to backtrack the culprit and slap them with ten hours of community service for breaking Conservation Code Seven.

But here in Shambhala, only three years into the experiment, humans were already falling into old habits. Bad habits. Benson carried the paper and dropped it into the nearest recycling bin, shaking his head as he did so.

One last turn and Benson was at the doorstep of the house he shared with Theresa, his wife of almost three years and the city's first chief constable. It was a quaint yet comfortable affair straight out of the housing catalog, printed in a day flat by extrusion gantries. The rounded red roof tiles gave it a Mediterranean architectural flavor, but the flare did nothing to hide the fact it was still a standard unit. Not that Benson cared. It had Theresa inside it, so it was home.

The door recognized his plant and opened automatically, inviting him inside.

"Esa, I'm home!"

"Kitchen," came her reply.

Benson hung his jacket and whistle by the front door, set his tablet down on the small entryway table, then took a deep, cleansing breath, letting the day's stresses and frustrations leak back out of him on the exhale.

"You smell like a jockstrap," Theresa said from the dining room.

"I love you, too."

"I thought you're just coaching the team, not rolling around in the dirt with them."

"There's a lot of yelling and running up and down the sidelines involved." Benson stared up at the ceiling for several seconds.

"What's wrong?" Theresa asked.

"Hmm?"

"You're counting ceiling tiles again. That's weird."

Benson pulled out a chair and sat down heavily. "I'm not counting, I just... like having a ceiling."

"What do you mean?"

"I don't know. It just feels more secure. I guess I'm still not entirely comfortable with the sky. Sometimes I get caught up looking at a cloud or something and feel like there's nothing keeping me from falling off the planet."

"Only gravity," Theresa teased. "You know, one of the four fundamental forces of the universe."

"Yeah, yeah."

"Mmm," Theresa hummed. "I love the skies here, especially at night. The stars make me feel like I could stretch my arms out forever."

"You could, and still never find something to grab onto, that's the problem. I spent enough time out among the stars a few years ago, thank you very much. I'd still be out there floating through them if it hadn't been for a safety tether."

Theresa hugged him lightly from behind. "Don't worry, you're not floating away from me that easily." She gave him a peck on the head, then pretended to spit it back out. "God, you're as sweaty as a jockstrap, too. You're taking a shower."

"After dinner. I'm starving. Speaking of dinner, what did Jack send down the beanstalk today?"

Theresa held up a finger and turned for the small kitchen, then returned with a steaming plate of–

"Algae and mushroom casserole."

"Again?"

"Hey, I slaved all day in the kitchen–"

"Heating up the package the casserole came in. The door told me you got home ten minutes ago."

Theresa put up her hands. "All right, guilty, but it's not like I'm choosing the menu. And it wouldn't kill *you* to prepare dinner once in a while."

"I've been busy coaching, you know that."

Theresa sat down and cut herself a piece of casserole. "Oh yes, the work of our director of recreation and athletic preparedness is never done. Who could blame him for failing to perform his share of the household chores?"

"Have you seen some of the people coming down the elevator? A lot of them can barely lift anything heavier than the contents of their forks or chopsticks, much less do any physical work like, say, building the colony. They should have given me this job years ago."

Theresa shrugged and set a piece on his plate. "Well, seeing as that means I'd have made chief years ago, I'm hardly going to argue the point. Now, can we eat?"

Benson picked up a fork. "I'm hardly going to argue the point."

He had just enough time to get the first bite on his tongue when the call came in through his plant.

<Mr Benson. My name is–>

"I know who you are, Merick. Your name comes up in the corner of my vision, remember?" Benson said out loud as well as into his plant interface. "What I don't know is why nobody down here knows how to ring first. I've just sat down to dinner."

<Apologies, sir, but I–>

Benson stood up from his chair. "At least put yourself up on the screen in the living room."

<This is a sensitive communication.>

"The only other person here is the chief constable. Now please get out of my head."

The link cut off, replaced by a gentle chime and an *Incoming Call* icon glowing on the far wall. Benson answered it.

"Ah, Deputy Administrator Merick. How are things in the Beehive?" he said, voice dripping with sarcasm.

"Busy, to say the least. I'm sorry to intrude, Mr Benson, but Administrator Valmassoi has called an emergency council meeting."

"Ah, well then you're talking to the wrong Benson. Esa, phone for you."

"No, I was asked to contact you, personally. Your presence has been requested for the meeting."

Theresa walked into the living room holding two beers. "What's going on, Bryan?"

"Secret agent stuff, apparently."

"Cool. I'll get my coat."

"I'm sorry," Merick's face tried and failed to hide his nervousness. "But the chief constable's presence is not necessary at this time."

"Hold on," Benson took the lager Theresa offered and sipped

it. It was crisp, without the skunkiness of last month's batch. The brewmaster was getting the hang of things, finally. "Ah, that's nice. Now, what sort of 'emergency council meeting' requires the Athletics director and not the chief constable?"

Theresa put a hand on Benson's shoulder. "Did you forget to pay the deposit on your equipment rental?"

"I could have sworn…"

"Mr and Mrs Benson, if you're finished, this is a serious matter that requires Mr Benson's immediate presence. The meeting is starting in ten minutes, as soon as Captain Mahama is able to join us from the Ark."

That got Benson's attention. "Mahama's coming all the way down here?"

"No, but she will be joining us by holo link. Administrator Valmassoi will be most grateful if you can join him and the rest of the council in the capital building."

"Can we finish dinner first?"

"If you can eat it while you're walking down here. Merick out." The link went dark.

"This better be good." Benson stood and chugged the rest of his beer. "I'm still starving."

Theresa grabbed her jacket off a rack in the entryway. "It'll reheat."

"Yeah, because algae reheats so well."

CHAPTER THREE

Theresa crossed her arms close to her body against the brisk night air. With so little cloud cover, temperatures dropped quickly after the sun set. The capital was a short walk downtown from their duplex in Shambhala's suburbs. Less than a block from home, they passed the new museum. The curator, Devorah Feynman, now officially past mandatory retirement age, showed no signs of slowing, and even fewer signs of trusting anyone else with the task of transferring *her* exhibits from the Ark to the surface. Not even the crew dared to broach the subject of stepping down with her. No one wanted to risk it.

Theresa smiled at the thought of the diminutive tyrant riding roughshod over not only her subordinates, but her superiors as well. Few people in the history of the species had ever been so perfectly suited for the role life had provided them.

"Any guess what's gotten up Valmassoi's backside?" Theresa whispered as they approached the Capital's steps.

"You mean generally, or for this meeting in particular?"

"The late-night emergency meeting with the football coach. Isn't it a little early for a performance-enhancing drug scandal? You haven't even played the first games yet."

"Honestly, I think my linemen could benefit from a few rounds of PEDs."

Theresa answered him with an elbow to the ribs. "Be serious."

"I don't know, Esa." He paused to nod to the two door guards, who waved them both through without the customary search. "But we'll find out in a minute."

The capital building's inner rotunda was enclosed by a six-sided dome. The floor tiles came from locally sourced marble that had been quarried about five kilometers up the New Amazon river, the mouth of which spilled out into the Bay of Landing. The tilework was also hexagonal, as were many of the rooms surrounding the rotunda. Officially, the capital was dedicated as the Westminster Building, but everyone had quickly taken to calling it the Beehive.

Theresa and Benson reached the cabinet chamber where Deputy Administrator Merick waited for them.

"I thought we'd agreed that the chief constable wasn't needed at this meeting," he said tensely as they approached the door.

"You *thought* that, yes." Theresa had little regard or time for the chairman's lapdog.

"I'm sorry, but I must insist that–"

Ever the peacemaker, her husband put an arm around the smaller man's shoulders. "Merick, c'mon. She's chief constable, *and* my wife." He pointed at the door. "Anything I hear in there is just going to be pillow talk in a couple hours anyway. This way, she doesn't have to hear it secondhand."

Theresa shrugged her shoulders. "He's right, you know."

Defeated, Merick opened the door with a theatrical sigh and announced their arrival to the council room at large. Administrator Valmassoi already sat at the nominal head of the hexagonal, twelve-seat table, flanked by the other council members, who doubled as his ministers of finance, health, agriculture, labor, and civil engineering. As far as Theresa could see, the ministers of education and the interior either hadn't arrived yet or hadn't been invited.

Standing off to one side, Theresa locked eyes with Chao Feng, formerly First Officer Commander Chao Feng. Certain improprieties had led to his being relieved of that title shortly after the Ark arrived at Gaia. Mainly his ham-handed attempt to protect himself from suspicion in a murder investigation by concealing his romantic relationship with the victim, leading Theresa's husband on a wild goose chase while the real killer's plot very nearly succeeded in causing the extinction of the entire human race. Instead, they only managed to slaughter two fifths of it.

In spite of his short-sighted and selfish behavior, Feng was far too capable and well-connected to discard entirely. He'd settled into the role of coordinator and liaison between the colony's civilian government and the crew still running the Ark high above.

Feng nodded to her. Theresa nodded back. He didn't make eye contact with her husband, however. There was still an awful lot of baggage between the two of them. Enough to ground a shuttle.

"Ah, Detective Benson…" Administrator Valmassoi said. "And our chief constable…"

"Is there a problem, administrator?" Theresa asked sweetly.

"No, of course not. I just hadn't been expecting your presence for this meeting."

"Neither had I," Merick said from the doorway.

Theresa was about to snap at him, but Valmassoi waved him off. "It's fine, Preston. We'd be honored to include our chief law enforcement officer's insights in our deliberations. That will be all for now."

Merick bowed. "I'll be just outside if you need anything." The door clicked shut behind him.

"Now then." Valmassoi held a hand out to two unoccupied chairs. "Detective, chief, please have a seat."

"Thank you," Benson said as he sat down. "But it's actually just coach, or if you really must be formal, director of athletic preparedness and recreation. My wife is the detective now." Benson reached over and squeezed Theresa's hand.

"Of course you're right, coach. Your reputation precedes you."

"What's this all about?" Theresa said.

Valmassoi held up a hand. "We're about to start. We're waiting on one more guest." As he said it, a flickering, translucent image of Captain Mahama filled the seat next to the administrator. Her dark complexion stood in stark contrast to the drab gray and brown of her command uniform. Even from thousands of kilometers away and looking like a ghost, the woman effortlessly commanded attention.

"Can we clean that up at all?" Valmassoi leaned back to ask a holo tech hidden in the shadows.

"Sorry sir, there's some high-altitude particulates interfering with the com laser. Probably from that wildfire on the other side of the continent."

Valmassoi nodded curtly. "Can you hear me, Captain?"

After an almost imperceptible delay, Mahama's ghostly figure turned to face roughly where the administrator sat and nodded. "Indeed I can. How do I look?"

"Like something haunting Scrooge's house," Valmassoi said.

Mahama smirked. "I'm afraid I neglected to bring any chains. Is the room secure on your end?"

"Yes."

"Good, is everyone present?"

Valmassoi nodded in Theresa's direction. "And then some."

Mahama's holo glanced over and smiled. "Ah, I'm sorry we didn't think to include you on the list, Chief Benson. It was an oversight, I assure you."

"Thank you, captain." Theresa appreciated the courtesy, even if she doubted its veracity.

"All right." Mahama laced her fingers together and cracked her knuckles theatrically. "It's essential that everyone understands that this discussion is of the utmost sensitivity. Anything said here stays here for the time being."

Benson adjusted himself in his chair. "I thought we were done keeping secrets. Sir."

Mahama looked squarely at him. "It's good to see you again too, detective."

"Why does everyone keep calling me that?"

"Apologies, Mr Benson. Force of habit. I'm not making everyone swear an oath of secrecy. However, I am asking for a certain level of... discretion while we decide how best to respond to today's events."

"And what are these *events*, madam captain?" The question came from another familiar face, Dr Russell, who'd been named health minister just in the past year. She'd been the one to treat Bryan's extensive burns and other injuries he'd received in the final showdown with Kimura three years earlier. Her plastic surgery work in particular was excellent. Few people knew his face well enough to spot the subtle scars left over from the skin grafts. Theresa could, but she never let him know it. If anything, the fresh skin had taken a few years off his face. She didn't mind.

"I was just coming to that. Administrator, the video if you please."

Valmassoi pointed at the holo tech and made a "get rolling" gesture with his index finger. A moment later, the lights in the room darkened as one of the walls lit up, displaying a scene that everyone in the room, indeed everyone in the city, had already spent hours watching over the last three years.

Video feed streamed from inside the temple on the continent of Atlantis the natives had built around the first of Pathfinder's rovers they'd discovered. The rover itself was powered by a radioisotope thermoelectric generator with a half-life measured in decades, which was why it was still operating three years after being captured.

Aside from a couple of scientific instruments that had glitched or fallen victim to the natives' curiosity, it was still fully functional and had been gathering information on their new neighbors the entire time. Much had already been learned about their physiology, culture, and even language thanks to the happy accident of the rover's capture.

It appeared they were watching another of the Atlantians' frequent offering ceremonies, where the village elders tried to earn favor from the rover with bribes of tubers, fungus, piles of seeds, and the occasional animal. The rover would show its gratitude by taking measurements, collecting and analyzing samples, and even dissecting certain specimens, all under the control of an exuberant exobiologist sitting in a lab aboard the Ark. They could only guess at what the natives made of its odd behavior.

Theresa watched intently as the rover's binocular camera mast panned through the collection of aliens, their bioluminescent skin glowing in rhythmic patterns synchronized with the haunting melodies of their prayer songs. The scene was utterly foreign, yet compellingly beautiful. The sheer number of individuals jumped out at her. There had to be three hundred of them crammed into the circular room, well above normal. Attendance at these ceremonies had slacked off over the years, falling into a pattern resembling the spikes for Christmas and Easter Mass at the Catholic cathedral, and relative calm the rest of the year. But today didn't fall into that pattern of holy days for the Atlantians.

Something had happened to bring a lot of faithful back into the fold. It was only then that Theresa pulled back from the video enough to look at the time/date stamp in the bottom right corner of the image.

"This isn't a live stream?" she said.

"No," Mahama answered. "This was recorded this morning, just after midnight local time for their village."

"It's certainly a big turnout. But what are we looking for, specifically?" Benson asked.

"The answer is coming right about... now."

A wave of activity spread through the crowd, starting at the temple entrance. The natives parted to either side, allowing two figures to pass into the center of the room. It took a moment for the rover's cameras to adjust on the pair of dark faces, but once the faces resolved–

"Mei Nakama," Theresa said breathlessly as the rest of the room erupted in shouting.

"Order," Valmassoi said sternly. "Quiet down, please."

"She's supposed to be dead!" This came from Gregory Alexander, latest heir to a very long line of bigwigs stretching all the way back to the construction of the Ark itself. His family name still graced the tallest residential building in Avalon module, and now he was the owner of the only custom construction company in the city. Since landing, his wealth and sense of entitlement had both grown at roughly similar rates.

Everyone was entitled to a home. But if you had the money and wanted something more than the standard, cookie-cutter layout, Alexander Custom Builders was where you went. And although his power and influence were substantial, he wasn't a council member per se, even if it was rumored that several of them were deeply indebted to him in the form of exceedingly generous upgrades to their home designs, provided free of charge with a wink and a nod. Theresa found his inclusion at a "secret" meeting troubling, but pressed on.

"We were obviously mistaken, Mr Alexander," Valmassoi said.

"And I'd remind you that you've been included in this meeting as a courtesy, so please try to contain yourself."

Alexander glowered, but returned to silence for the moment.

Theresa leaned back in her chair and smirked. The Unbound, or what remained of them after the trials of David Kimura's coconspirators had thinned their ranks, had struck out for themselves and established a small fishing village twenty kilometers north of Shambhala. Close enough to trade with the rest of humanity when necessary, but far enough away to maintain privacy and independence, which had been the hallmarks of their hermit society even while they had eked out a living hiding in the sublevels of the Ark.

A sudden and powerful hurricane had leveled their village a year earlier and swept the bodies out to sea. Or so everyone had been led to believe.

"Well," Benson put his arms behind his head. "That explains why we never found their bodies. There weren't any bodies to find."

"Then how the hell did they get across the ocean?" Alexander barked.

"Isn't it obvious?" Theresa said. "They've been living as fishermen for two years."

"Are you saying they crossed several thousand kilometers of open ocean in fishing canoes at the height of hurricane season? That's preposterous!"

"It's either that or the breaststroke," Theresa replied.

"Actually, it's neither." Benson circled something on his tablet. "Can you give my pad access to the big screen, please?"

The tech in the corner glanced over at Valmassoi, who nodded his acceptance. Two keystrokes later and a satellite image appeared of the Unbound's village from a day before the hurricane hit with a big red circle around one of the buildings by the shore.

"Everybody see that 'barn' right on the shore? Does it look suspiciously like an upside down boat to anyone else?" He zoomed in on a pair of large triangular tents. "And those are sails, if I'm any judge."

"What are you suggesting, detecti... Mr Benson?" Mahama's image asked.

"Simple. The Unbound planned out this whole thing. They built a boat that could handle the ocean right under our noses, then used the hurricane to cover their escape."

"No way," Valmassoi shook his head in protest. "We'd have spotted them. The satellites we have in orbit have centimeter resolution, for god's sake."

"Not necessarily," Theresa added. "We don't have anything near complete real-time coverage of the surface. We only had the eighteen platforms Pathfinder dropped into orbit when it arrived, minus the four we've already lost to breakdowns. There are gaps. We have to prioritize surveillance targets, and the open ocean isn't high on the list. One of our birds can see if you're holding a tablet. But we have to know *where* to point it."

Alexander scoffed. "Are you telling me that a bunch of low-tech fishermen evaded the Ark and her illustrious crew?"

Theresa's husband couldn't help but laugh at that.

"Something humorous, Director Benson?" Mahama asked politely.

"Yeah, you. All of you. The Unbound spent their entire lives hiding inside a tube sixteen kilometers long with a million cameras inside it. Hell, they ran a damned farm without us knowing for thirty years. They know our systems, our protocols. They've been evading the crew for decades. You really think we could keep a lid on them down here, with an entire planet to hide on?" He snorted. "You're dreaming."

"But how did they navigate straight to the rover site over thousands of kilometers of ocean?" Mahama said. "That's quite a feat."

"That's the easiest part to explain," Benson said. "If you have the rover coordinates, just take a tablet and hack the GPS software and flip it to receive only. Then you're passive and we have nothing."

"You have a criminal's mind, Mr Benson," Mahama said.

"Thank you?"

"How far behind are we here?" Theresa asked.

"What do you mean?" Mahama asked.

"When did they land? When was actual first contact made and how long have they been in situ talking to the Atlantians?"

Mahama shrugged. "We don't know. We only know they entered the temple for the first time yesterday."

"How can we not know that?" Alexander asked with a huff.

"Don't get so worked up, Greg," Benson said. "You look like you could use some time outside. Why don't you come try out for the football league? I'm sure someone could use a center of your... stature."

"Over my dead body."

"That's the perfect attitude for a center."

"If you're quite finished, gentlemen?" Mahama scolded. "To answer your question, Mr Alexander, we're searching back through archived images and data as we speak looking for clues we may have missed."

"Well look for their damned ship parked on the shore. That should tell you."

Benson tapped the table. "If they were smart, they'd have made landfall in the middle of the night and scuttled the ship before daybreak. The sats would never have the chance to catch them."

"Awful lot of planning there," Valmassoi added.

"And that surprises you?" Benson shifted in his chair. "These folks are survivors *among* survivors. Maybe it's time to stop underestimating them."

"So there's no way to know how much of a head start they have?" Valmassoi asked.

Theresa held her hands open. "Maybe not. Well, actually..." She swiped her tablet a couple of times and the picture of the old village came up again with the suspected boat circled. "If that's really the boat they used, and I'm almost sure it is, then it's around what? Twenty, twenty-five meters long? Last census we took, the Unbound were right at thirty-six people, including four children that had been born since we landed. Between people and supplies, they would've been packed in tight. Fresh water isn't a problem if they took that solar desalinization machine with them, but food would be a real issue."

"But they're fishermen, on the ocean," Mahama observed.

"Yes, that's true," Benson jumped in. "But they were barely above subsistence levels before the storm, and that was using tidal traps and multiple boats with nets. None of which are going to work on the open ocean if they're trying to get somewhere, because the nets create drag and slow you down, adding time to the journey. They could use hooks and lines, but you can't pull nearly the same volume of game that way, especially out away from the more fertile coastal waters. So yeah, they may've been able to catch enough to supplement their stores to some degree, but they had to bring most of their food from the start. So that limits how much time they could've spent on the open water to, I don't know, a couple months? Three months?"

"You sure seem to know a lot about fishing," Dr Russell teased.

"He loves nature documentaries," Theresa said. "Drives me nuts with them."

The village on the screen shrank to a pinprick, then shot to the right side as Mahama took control and zoomed the view out to encompass a flattened representation of the entire planet.

"There are a few archipelagoes along the way where they could've stopped and replenished."

"That's possible," Benson added. "But I think we're shooting for a worst-case number right now, yes?"

Mahama nodded.

"OK, so how fast can a sailing ship average over water?"

Theresa consulted a database in her plant. "Call it five knots."

"What the hell's a 'not'?"

"Right, sorry, about nine kph."

Benson nodded. "OK, is that an Earth standard?"

"Broadly speaking, with a ton of variables, yes."

"All right, average wind speed here is a little higher, so call it twelve kph, just under three hundred kilometers per day in ideal conditions."

"Hold on," Valmassoi jumped back into the conversation. "Are you saying they made the crossing in *two weeks*?"

"No, I'm saying they *could* have, if everything went perfectly. Which, as you know, it usually doesn't."

"But that still puts them on site for more than a local year!" Alexander said.

"A *year*," Mahama corrected. "Earth's year doesn't have any meaning anymore."

"Yes, fine, a year. That's still enough time to learn the language and say all sorts of things. We could have a real situation here."

"And that's why this meeting was called," Mahama tried to regain control of the conversation. "The question is what to do about it now that they have made first contact with the Atlantians for us."

"Yes," Valmassoi added. "Who knows what stories they've been telling the natives. We'll be lucky if they don't teach them how to build an invasion fleet to sail right over here and wipe us all out."

"Can't happen," Alexander jumped in. "The Ark's navigational lasers would burn any ship to ash before they got within a thousand kilometers of Shambhala."

Theresa rolled her eyes, but Feng was the first to respond to the needless bravado. "First of all, the prevailing winds blow east to west. They'd have to sail right on around Gaia, then cross our whole continent overland. And second, I suspect Captain Mahama would prefer to find a solution that doesn't involve wholesale slaughter of the people we're trying to share this world with."

"Too true," the captain said. "The task before us now is basically public-relations damage control. The Unbound have forced our hand here."

"Should've spaced the lot of them," Alexander mumbled, but Mahama ignored him and continued.

"We have to either contain or counter whatever biased information they may have given the Atlantians about our presence and intentions."

"How do we do that?" Valmassoi asked.

"We move up our timeline and send the diplomatic mission to introduce ourselves to the Atlantians."

"When?"

"Last year would be ideal," Theresa quipped.

"Snarky," Feng said, "but entirely accurate. Maybe we got lucky and they stopped at a particularly beautiful tropical island for a few months and really did only get there two days ago, or maybe they've been there for a year already and only now got around to attending church. Either way, we need to get our people there immediately."

"We're not close to ready," Valmassoi objected. "Waiting for a good translator program was the entire point of delaying first contact. We've only just started to get a handle on the natives' language."

"Because our linguists and translation algorithms have only had the audio/visual feeds from the captured rover to work with," Mahama said. "And a lot of *that* has been repetitious prayer ceremonies instead of back-and-forth conversations. No, the best way to do this is just to drop right into the thick of it. We probably should have done it sooner anyway."

"Indulging in a little Monday morning quarterbacking, captain?" Benson asked.

Mahama looked at him quizzically. "I'm afraid I don't get the reference."

"Sorry. I mean you're exercising hindsight."

"Perhaps a little. But either way, we need to regain control of this situation as quickly as possible, before the Atlantians start hearing stories about conquistadores, smallpox blankets, and slave ships."

Benson shook his head. "It won't come to that."

"What makes you so sure?" Valmassoi snapped. "Why else would they have faked their deaths just to go running straight to the natives?"

"I don't know, to be out from under our yoke? They're human beings, maybe they're just curious. Maybe they wanted to explore and learn new things, push past their own horizons instead of trading a fishbowl for a fortress. People used to do that, you know."

"You almost sound proud of them," Alexander said, putting in no effort to conceal his mocking tone.

"Maybe I am. I'm certainly proud of *her*," Benson swapped the screen back to the paused image of Mei's face. "Or did you all forget that this girl literally saved the whole fucking human race when she turned on Kimura?" Benson shook his head slowly. "I haven't."

Theresa couldn't help but feel a swell of pride at her husband's passion. He could get so... animated. Righteous. Bryan never went looking for fights, it wasn't his way. But when presented with one, he didn't know how to back down either. It was the boy in him. The one with a chip on his shoulder. Theresa found herself smiling.

Captain Mahama's ghostly image laced her fingers and smiled herself. "Which is why, Mr Benson, you will accompany the delegation."

And then there were the days her husband's passion got him into trouble. Benson sat up in his chair. "Me? Why?"

"Because the Unbound trust you, especially this Mei girl. You have a relationship with her."

"I wouldn't go that far." Benson glanced over at Theresa and tugged on his collar.

"A mutual respect, then," Mahama corrected. "Mei seems to be a hit with the locals. You can talk to her, see what they've been saying and see what their intentions are, maybe even persuade her to make introductions to the Atlantians for us."

"I'm no diplomat."

"*That's* a massive understatement," Theresa added with a smirk.

"Not helping, my love."

Mahama stepped in to diffuse the brewing domestic incident. "While *Chief* Benson's assessment of your diplomatic acumen is almost certainly accurate, you're not going to be the main act, as it were. Your responsibility will be limited to dealing with our wayward flock. The rest of the delegation will handle the Atlantians."

"Well that's a relief," Benson said sarcastically.

"For all of us," Feng added helpfully.

"I don't think this is a good idea," Benson said.

"Noted. If there are no *other* objections," Mahama cut him off. "I introduce the motion for a vote. Is there a second?"

"I second the motion," Alexander said. *Voting now*, Theresa noted.

"But, wait…"

"Motion is seconded," Valmassoi took over. "All in favor?"

A wave of "ayes" went around the room before Benson knew what was happening.

"Opposed?"

"Me!" Benson said.

"You have to say 'nay,' Director Benson."

"Nay!"

"That's better. Of course, the *ayes* have it regardless. Motion carries."

"Wonderful," Mahama said. "Mr Feng, you will make the arrangements?"

"Of course, captain."

"Excellent. Now, I must excuse myself."

Valmassoi stood up and gave a small bow in Mahama's direction. "Of course, captain. Thank you for coming."

"In a manner of speaking." Mahama smirked as her image faded to black.

The meeting concluded, the council members stood up to leave. Benson sank into his chair. "What just happened?"

"You were volunteered for a high-profile mission, dear." Theresa patted his forearm, trying and failing to hide her amusement.

"So it seems."

"I don't know why you're upset, you got to vote on it."

"Democracy is two wolves and a sheep voting on who's for dinner." Benson twisted around to look at Feng. "And exactly what *arrangements* are you going to make?"

"Transportation, obviously. We're going to need to fit this little trip into the shuttle schedule. Unless you want to build your own boat?"

"I just might."

"Bryan," Theresa moved behind Benson and put her arms around his shoulders. "What's wrong? Aren't you excited to meet the neighbors?"

"It's not that." Benson reached up to squeeze her wrist. "I just *really* hate flying."

CHAPTER FOUR

Kexx sat next to Mei on the banks of the small lake at the center of the village, watching in rapt attention as the children swam, splashed, and squealed in the water. The *human* children, as the visitors called their race were, to be blunt, simply terrible swimmers. Even the youngest among the G'tel village were comfortable moving through the water as soon as they entered the world.

But whatever they lacked in competency, the strange, pale little creatures more than made up for it with sheer, screaming excitement. Their joy was infectious, quickly spreading among many of the village children who had come running down to the lake to see what all the noise was about. Without a second thought, and much to the surprise of the horrified parents who came looking for them, many of the G'tel children jumped in and started splashing the visitors, spraying them by blowing water through hollow stems, and challenging them to see who could stay underwater the longest. In this last category, the human children inevitably lost, but giggled anyway.

Kexx couldn't remember seeing anyone have so much fun while being so profoundly awful at something. But more importantly, it was the first time ze'd seen any of the visitors and zer own people interacting so freely. For the children in the water, all of the fear, mistrust, and apprehension of the last three Varrs had simply disappeared. They played like they'd all been friends since their naming. Even the ring of nervous parents standing around the shores of the lake, both G'tel and human, soon lost interest and sat or laid down to enjoy the afternoon sun. Even a pair of bearers, usually nervous and fearful, had come out to enjoy watching the frivolity.

Leave it to the innocence of children to set fear aside in favor of an afternoon free of their daily chores. Glancing around at the adults sunning themselves, Kexx realized that maybe that spark still burned in everyone.

Ze looked over at Mei's face, trying to gauge zer expression. It wasn't easy. The visitors' skin was, well, dead. It was a single color, uniform and unchanging like the sunbleached flesh of the recently departed. Even Kexx found it unnerving at times.

The humans couldn't produce either the contrasting patterns that G'tel used during the daytime, or the waves of gentle blue light they used at night. In fact, the only change in the human's skin Kexx had seen at all was a slight reddening, but that seemed to have more to do with too much time in the sun than trying to communicate anything. Instead, the visual cues for their language were hand gestures, shifts in the tone and volume of their childlike voices, and frustratingly subtle, rapid movements and changes to their strangely contoured faces.

Right now, for example, Mei's soft mouth was turned up at the corners, small creases had formed on zer cheeks, and zer eyes were half shut. Kexx had come to recognize this arrangement as either contentment and happiness, or squinting against a bright light. Which one was it now? Was it both? There was no way to know.

Before the visitors arrived, it never occurred to Kexx to think of the spoken and visual parts of their language as separate components, but now it was foremost on zer mind. Mei was proving to be a fast learner, but even as ze mastered the words, they were flat, devoid of emotion, intentions, and all the tiny social and hierarchal nuances that Kexx had always taken for granted.

Mei was equally aware of the problem and trying fast to come up with zer own solutions. Conversations with zer were held back by zer limited vocabulary, but that was changing with shocking speed as ze picked up new words by the handful daily, much faster than even the brightest G'tel child. But her progress with the visual part of G'tel language was just as slow and plodding as Kexx's was with zers.

Mei noticed Kexx staring and zer expression changed once more. Ze'd tried to explain to Kexx that among zer people, staring at someone was considered rude. But among G'tel, watching someone intently was polite. It meant you were paying attention to what they were thinking, saying, or feeling, clues to all of which were on the skin for everyone to see.

"What, Kexx?" Mei said in zer mouth's best approximation of the words. Then, she slowly ran three fingers widely spaced up her arm. Ze was trying to mimic the pattern of stripes G'tel would make to convey the emotion behind the question. Stripes radiating out from their chest and down their arms was a signal that the person was trying to push away defensively, or in annoyance. But stripes moving from their hands toward their core was an invitation to come closer out of curiosity or concern. Mei was trying to say she wasn't offended and wanted to talk.

Very clever, this one.

"You are happy?" Kexx asked.

Mei exhaled fully, then laid back on the ground with one of zer strange, ridged arms tucked behind zer head and closed zer eyes.

"Yes. Many," ze whispered. Kexx assumed ze'd meant to say "very" instead of "many," but the distinction was a small one and zer meaning was conveyed regardless. It was a drastic change from the days after Mei and the rest of zer people had washed ashore. They were all on the verge of starvation and sick as uliks caught out in the sun. Six of them had already died by the time they arrived from… wherever they'd come from. It was nearly a full Varr before they recovered, and two more of them died in the process.

Through the grace of Xis, all of the children had survived, including Mei's own child, Sakiko. What had happened to the child's other parent, or the bearer, ze hadn't said. Maybe there was nothing to say, maybe it was too painful. Kexx couldn't begin to imagine what the survivors had been through out on the open ocean for so long. There was a reason G'tel swam and fished in the shallows near the shore. The deep ocean held dangers colder and darker than anything living under the stars. To build their "boat" to float out among those dangers seemed like madness. But Mei was not mad, none of the humans were. They just saw things differently, as if they saw... more. Kexx didn't understand what, but ze desperately wanted to.

One of the children squealed in a way that seemed designed specifically for rupturing eardrums, drawing the attention of every adult of both peoples. But a burst of laughter followed, confirming that all was well. How fortunate it was, Kexx thought, that the one thing they all shared and understood was laughter. Maybe it needed no translation. Maybe it was Xis's way of reminding them all of what was most important.

Without warning, Sakiko came running up on the two of them, still dripping wet from the pond.

"Mama!" ze screamed, "Fula splashed me!"

Mei sighed heavily, then propped zerself up on zer rigid arms. "So splash zer back, Sakiko. Ze's playing with you."

"But it got in my eyes!"

"Can you still see?"

Sakiko pawed at the ground with zer feet. "...A little."

"Then you're fine. Go play. Kexx and I are talking."

Sakiko's tiny face and soft, pliable features turned towards Kexx. In just the six Varrs since the humans had arrived, ze could already recognize the changes in the child's face, to say nothing of zer speech.

"Hi Uncle Kexx." Sakiko waved zer hand in a human gesture of greeting, the imagined slight by Fula forgotten.

"Hello, Sah-Key-Coo," Kexx said, still struggling with the name, much to zer embarrassment. Kexx still didn't understand the "uncle" title. Mei had tried to explain it as a kind of family relationship that Kexx also didn't understand, but ze felt honored regardless. Kexx returned the greeting wave and approximated a human smile.

The relative calm of the day was broken by the sounds of argument coming from the temple. Kexx sat up to get a better look at the commotion and saw three of the elders standing outside the temple shouting and waving their arms. Their patterns passed wildly between anger, confusion, and near panic.

Most unlike elders, who were less prone to emotional outbursts after their transition. It did not bode well.

Mei noticed too and moved to stand up, but Kexx put a gentle hand on zer shoulder. "What?" ze asked.

"Stay here, Mei." Mei nodded zer head, a gesture Kexx knew meant acceptance, even if zer face looked sour, somehow. Kexx left Mei by the lake and jogged up to the group arguing outside the temple.

"Elders," zer skin flashed deferential patterns. "What's wrong?"

"Truth-digger Kexx," Tuko, the village chief, grabbed zer forearm. "We have a new problem."

Ze was the youngest chief in a century, only a year past zer transition to elder. There was still much color in zer crests, and the heat and strength of a young warrior lingered in zer bloodways. Even after the transition, the attributes of youth clung more tenaciously to some than others.

Kexx returned the grip. "What is it, elder?"

"It's the *rovor*." Zer mouth twisted awkwardly around the unfamiliar human word for the emissary. Kexx looked at Tuko expectantly until ze continued. "It's talking."

"Let me get Mei, ze can help to translate for–"

"No, you don't understand. It isn't speaking human. It's speaking *our* language."

The mood inside the temple was hushed, guarded. All but a handful of village elders and a couple of important guests had been unceremoniously herded out of the dome and ordered not to reenter or speak about what they'd heard until the elders had decided what to do about it.

Tuko stood at the center of the assembly, gripping the ancestral spear of the village chief. The rover, for its part, sat at the center of the floor as passively as it ever had, except for the bizarre, mouthless voice filling the air. Over and over, it repeated the same message:

–Greetings. We long to know your people in friendship. We come in calm. Watch the sky for our great bird. –

"What in Cuut's name does *that* mean?" The question came from Kuul, a young, ambitious fighter many years yet from zer transition. Ze'd succeeded Tuko as head of the village's warriors after Tuko's transition and ascension to chief. Kuul made no secret of the disdain ze had for the humans, or zer disapproval of their continued presence in the village.

"I was hoping our truth digger would know," Tuko said. "Kexx has spent more time with the humans than anyone."

Kexx ignored the accusatory undercurrent of Tuko's statement. "Have you tried asking it?"

"Of course we did, but it just repeats the same words. It's stupid. It can't think," Kuul spit back.

Kexx's skin pattern changed, dialing back from confusion and alarm and returning to a slow pulse showing deference. "Chief Tuko, Mei has explained to me that this..." ze swept a hand toward the rover, "...isn't alive like an animal, or even a plant. It is a tool, like a spear or a plow."

"Plows and spears don't move and talk by themselves!" Kuul objected.

Kexx bowed slightly. "I would like to ask permission to bring Mei into this conversation. Ze can explain this better than I can."

"Ze can barely speak our language," Kuul said.

"Ze is learning very quickly. Faster than I did as a child. Ze can answer our questions. We just have to have the wisdom to listen."

Tuko flexed zer fingers in a signal of annoyance. "You give your pets an awful lot of praise. Maybe too much."

Kexx lowered zer bow a fraction more. "You appointed me as this village's truth-digger. My task is to learn that which can be known, and to share it without distortion so that your wisdom may be built on bedrock instead of sand. You've never expressed doubt in my work before."

Tuko put a hand under Kexx's chin and pulled zer back upright. "Just remember who your people are, and where your loyalties belong."

"I haven't forgotten, elder."

"Fine. Bring your pet so we may ask our questions."

Kexx said zer thanks and went to retrieve Mei from by the lake, but the humans had already packed up and left. Kexx asked one of the G'tel children where their new playmates had gone. Ze pointed uphill to the outskirts of the village where the humans' shelter had been hastily built near the halo tree's inside edge. Several of the adults saw Kexx approaching and moved to block zer from entering.

Kexx reached the shelter and slowed to a walk as ze neared the line of humans. "I need to see Mei," ze said, but if anyone understood, there was no sign of it on their stony faces.

"Mei," Kexx called out, hoping ze would be heard over the growing sounds of alarm echoing through the rest of the village. Something was happening back down the hill.

Kexx spotted one of the G'tel children who'd been playing in the water. Ze cupped zer hands and shouted as loud as ze could. "Cho! What's wrong?"

Cho stopped and turned to face zer. "The elders say the emissary's message changed. It's counting down to something."

"To what?"

"I don't know."

"They come," came the small voice from right beside zer. Kexx nearly jumped out of her skin from the shock. Ze looked down to see Mei standing a step behind zer, holding and staring at some sort of flat, shiny rock Kexx had never seen before.

"Who, Mei? Who comes?"

"The rest of us." Mei turned the rock around and held its perfectly flat, polished surface so Kexx could see it. Ze nearly pushed the ornament away to press Mei for an answer, but then something on the surface of the rock caught zer eye.

It was a picture, like a simple painting, except it was *moving*, as if it was trapped just below the surface. But the rock was thin, impossibly thin. Kexx reached out in bewilderment to touch the moving painting, but jumped back as the image changed entirely again in response to zer finger, replaced by rows of small squares containing their own simple pictures in bright contrasting colors.

Kexx was mesmerized. Zer question entirely forgotten, ze moved to touch the enchanted rock again, but Mei slapped zer hand away.

"No toy play," she said, getting the word order wrong, but close enough.

Kexx pointed a wavering finger at the rock. "What is *that*?"

"Tool," Mei answered simply, apparently not wanting to waste time explaining.

The moment passed and Kexx remembered the immediate crisis. "What do you mean 'the rest of us,' Mei? There are more of you?" The human nodded. "How many?"

"Many, many. Greater," Mei paused, struggling with a word, "Greater two hands villages."

Ze meant to say two *fullhands*, Kexx was certain of it. They'd only started on numbers in the last few days. Ze swallowed hard. Two fullhand villages of humans? With numbers like that, they weren't just a wayward tribe that had washed up on the shore, they were as numerous as the entire village network, maybe more. The sudden realization blanked Kexx's skin with fear.

"And they're all coming right now?" ze said carefully, afraid of the answer.

Mei shook her head, a negative signal. "No. Maybe, ah…" Ze looked around, then pointed at the human shelter and made a big, all-encompassing circle motion, "…two hands of this, multiple."

Kexx nodded, borrowing the human expression. Mei was trying to express multiplication, if Kexx was to judge. There were just over thirty humans in the village. Thirty times two fullhands, around six hundred on their way. That was at least a number their warriors could deal with, if it came to that. Which, glancing down at Mei's "tool", Kexx sincerely hoped it wouldn't.

"If there are so many of you," Kexx spoke slowly, trying to give Mei time to digest the words. "How do you know so few are coming now?"

"That only fit in shuttle."

Kexx grimaced at the unfamiliar word. "Shuttle?"

Mei squinted her eyes, frustrated. "Ah… bird. That only fit in bird."

Bird again. The rover used the same word, not that it made any more sense the second time around. Kexx hovered near incredulous.

"What kind of bird carries six hundred people?" The moment the question left zer mouth, a low rumbling sound came from the ocean. Quiet at first, more felt than heard, but it grew quickly. Every face in the village turned to try to spot what came from the horizon. The sound grew like an approaching storm, but impossibly fast.

Then, all at once, the sound exploded into a fullblown hurricane. Thunderous winds buffeted everyone caught outside as an enormous wedge, black as the deepest cave, soared just above the halo trees, blotting out the sun as it casted a shadow over fully half the village. G'tel left in the open ran for the safety of their homes, dropped to the ground and covered their heads, or simply froze in abject terror. As quickly as it appeared, the black triangle covered the length of the village and disappeared on the other side of the trees.

Horrified and operating at the very edge of zer wits, Kexx looked down to see Mei pointing at the nightmare.

"That kind of bird."

CHAPTER FIVE

It took all of the three days preparing for the mission before Benson finally committed himself to actually getting on the shuttle. Whoever had been in charge of assigning the seating arrangements had given him a place of honor near the front of the shuttle's passenger compartment in a window seat. Whether the choice was out of ignorance of his discomfort with flying, or a devilishly cruel sense of humor, Benson couldn't say.

The shuttle's enormous interior was almost completely empty. To keep things simple, the diplomatic mission to meet the Atlantians had only a half dozen members, another half dozen support staff, and a four-member security detail. Add in the pilot, copilot, flight engineer, and com officer, and the entire compliment only reached twenty people out of the shuttle's full capacity of just over five hundred.

It was, in a word, overkill, but it was also the only viable option. Shambhala had a small fleet of quad-rotor helicraft among the equipment delivered by the Ark, but they were small, four-seat affairs powered by quick-discharging capacitor banks in place of traditional fuel-burning turbine engines. This made them phenomenally efficient and pollution free, but severely hampered their range before they had to be plugged back into the city's electrical grid for a recharge. They were built for scouting and surveying duty, not transoceanic voyages.

So a shuttle it would be. By pure happenstance, the *Discovery* was picked for the mission, as she had the fewest flight hours on her clock. She was the same bird Benson and Theresa had ridden down to the surface three years ago. She was named after one of the original quartet of NASA space shuttles from the late twentieth century, and one of only two that hadn't met an unfortunate and fiery end.

Benson counted that as a good omen, but still took great care to strap himself into his flight web so tightly that he could only breathe through his stomach. Then he shut off the false window panel and closed his eyes.

"What's the point of the window seat if you can't enjoy the view?" The voice was Korolev's. Benson looked over as the young constable sat down in his own seat on the aisle with an empty chair between them. The mission's entire compliment couldn't even fill the first two rows.

"The only view I'm going to enjoy is the outside of this beast while I'm standing safely on the ground. If you want my seat, you can have it."

"Thanks chief, but you look like you'd explode if anyone hits the release on your harness."

"I'll risk it. I'd rather be sitting all the way in the back anyway."

"Why?"

"It's the last part to crash."

Korolev snorted at that. "What is it with you and flying, anyway?"

"The only other time I went flying, I had a maintenance pod blow up with me inside it."

"But you spent your entire life flying through space at fifteen thousand kilometers per second. It doesn't make sense."

"They don't call them *phobias* if they make sense, Pavel."

His friend smiled and shrugged, then strapped himself in for takeoff. Korolev had been Benson's only choice in the composition of the expedition's personnel. He'd lobbied hard to borrow the constable from Theresa's force and get him assigned to the security detail. Korolev was a good kid, and he had a history of loyalty and an aggressive streak about a kilometer wide that had only grown since he started playing defense for the Mustangs' infant football team. It was probably the Russian blood in him boiling up to the surface.

He'd even saved Benson's life during the Kimura incident by

ignoring orders to stay out of the bomb vault where the final showdown had taken place. Korolev took a few lungfuls of plutonium dust in the process of dragging Benson's unconscious ass out of the irradiated compartment before he started glowing. All things considered, Benson was relieved to have him along.

The expedition's leader, on the other hand, filled him with somewhat less confidence. Administrator Valmassoi was a decent enough politician. He'd maneuvered the colony through several domestic crises ably enough, including the quasi-uprisings among the group fighting to leave the surface and go back to living on the Ark. They were called Returners, but they weren't going anywhere.

Valmassoi was already campaigning for Shambhala's first actual elections coming in the next year and was polling very well. That was mostly a matter of knowing which squeaky wheels to grease to keep the whole rickety contraption hobbling forward. But that required an intimate familiarity with the players involved and the intricate web of relationships, favors, patronage, jealousies, and vendettas that bound them all together.

What Benson had trouble with was seeing how that skillset dovetailed with the task at hand, where everyone was basically walking in blind.

"You look preoccupied. Still nervous about the flight?" Korolev whispered.

"Hmm? Yes, but no, just thinking about how ridiculous this whole thing is."

"Again?" Korolev smirked. "Aren't you bored with that yet?"

"It's hard to ignore, and our leadership isn't inspiring a great deal of confidence."

"Any particular target today?"

Benson cocked his head back to where Valmassoi sat two rows back and on the other side of the aisle.

"What's wrong with him?"

"Apart from shanghaiing me into this mission? I'm concerned about how he's going to kiss alien ass when we don't actually know where their asses are."

Korolev nodded sagely. "A valid concern."

"That and he's leaving Merick in charge of the colony for

however long this expedition lasts."

"Merick is deputy administrator, you know."

"He's a glorified personal assistant, at best. What if something happens while we're gone? Like the Returners start up again?"

"Those whiners? They want to go back to the Ark because life is too hard down here. Not exactly the building materials for a violent mob. Theresa can handle whatever comes up, you're worrying too much."

"I hope you're right," Benson said and looked at his feet.

The sudden banshee cry of the shuttle's six immense turbine engines spinning to life cut their conversation short. An airliner of old Earth would have bothered with sound-deadening insulation for the cabin and efficiency-sapping modifications to the engines and contours of the fuselage to reduce noise over populated areas. The Ark's shuttles weren't built for such delicate sensibilities. They were constructed to be light and powerful workhorses, with no regard for the comfort of either their passengers or the people living outside.

The flight engineer emerged from the cockpit and checked the crash webs of every passenger in turn, tightening straps where needed, then giving them a thumbs up before moving on. Once she was sure her cargo was secure, she announced one minute until takeoff and disappeared back behind the flight deck door.

Benson shut his eyes once more and tried to pretend the rest of the world didn't exist. The brakes released, and the shuttle rolled forward, gently at first as the pilot centered the immense craft on the runway. Amazingly, the shuttle was capable of vertical takeoffs using a network of ducts that diverted engine thrust to nozzles at its three corners. The maneuver burned a staggering amount of fuel, of which there was precious little surplus to begin with. There wouldn't be an opportunity to refuel during the trip, and chances that the Atlantians had built a serviceable runway on the other side of their destination seemed remote. They were cutting close to the shuttle's maximum range as it was, so every drop counted.

The engines throttled up as the shuttle charged down the runway. Really, it was just a straight patch of hard-packed dirt that had been scraped level with interlocking metal strips laid across it to improve traction. It was far from smooth, but the shuttle's undercarriage had been designed with improvised fields in mind.

Benson's kidneys and spine, however, had not. The vibrations grew as the *Discovery* picked up speed, causing his teeth to clatter together and sending his eyes bouncing around in their sockets. Relief and anxiety fought it out in Benson's stomach when the lumbering giant finally did lift off from the ground and take to the air. Anxiety won as the shuttle pitched upward and threw him into his seat, clawing for altitude.

"You're looking pale, chief," Korolev said. "Need a bag?"

Benson shook his head and squeezed his eyes tighter. A small tremor passed through the fuselage as the shuttle slipped past the sound barrier and continued piling on airspeed.

The hull creaked a bit as the turbines were spooled down and the scramjets came online. This was followed by another round of acceleration. Even through his nervousness, Benson couldn't help but be impressed. The only other time he'd been strapped into the bird, it had been for the reentry flight. There was no acceleration then. Indeed, the shuttle's engines had only been powered up during the descent to the landing strip in case of emergency.

The shuttle was immensely powerful. The only thing in his experience that matched it had been the month they'd all lived through after the Ark had flipped over to decelerate for Gaia, a pulse of atomic explosions going off every other second for weeks. The entire population had lived crowded onto the surface of Avalon module's forward bulkhead. Thirty thousand people stumbling around on 3.14 square kilometers, living in overcrowded apartments set ninety degrees in the wrong direction, eating nothing more glamorous than algae and tofu rations and fighting lines at the toilets during the trio of hour-long breaks they were afforded each day.

It wasn't a fond memory for most.

The weight pressing on Benson's chest eased as the shuttle reached its cruising altitude and speed. Soon thereafter, the pilot got on the intercom and announced that everyone was free to unbuckle their webs and move about the cabin. Benson pulled out a tablet and passed the time watching highlights of old NFL games, looking for new plays and defensive arrangements for the Mustangs to try out in practice.

[Important Implant Software Update, Fixes Audio Integration Bug #3947-B-56. Install Now?]

The alert floated in the augmented reality environment in Benson's field of vision. Audio bug? Was that the infernal ticking sound he'd been hearing for the last week?

<Yes. Install now,> he thought. The update downloaded, and the slight but persistent tick disappeared.

The flight was short. Almost as soon as Benson's anxiety had returned to a manageable level, the pilot got on the PA system and announced that they were beginning their descent and to get back in their webs. The engine whine dulled as the pilot throttled back. Benson's stomach lurched with the shuttle as it pitched into a shallow dive.

"Nothing to worry about, chief." Korolev cinched up his lap belt. "We'll be on the ground in ten minutes."

"That's a little vague, don't you think?"

Korolev just smiled and shook his head. "No pleasing some people."

Benson gritted his teeth and focused on his breathing, his mission with Mei and the Unbound, his team's troublesome third-down conversion rate in practice, basically anything but the rapidly approaching ground.

"Can you turn on the window panel?" Korolev asked.

"No."

"C'mon, chief. You're keeping your eyes closed anyway."

"Are you going to continue pestering me like a poorly disciplined five year old until I relent?"

Korolev pondered this. "That seems probable."

"Of course it does." Benson reached over and switched the virtual reality display back on. The shuttle's hull had no real windows, aside from those in the cockpit put there in the extremely unlikely event the pilots lost instrumentation and had to make a dead-reckoning landing. Instead, the inside walls of the cabin were coated top to bottom with displays so hi-def, it wasn't like looking out a window, it was like there was no window at all.

Benson had enough trouble dealing with the mere existence of the sky. Flying through it brought a whole new world of dread. But neither could he really tear himself away from the view. The shuttle glided over the vast, sapphire ocean. The color was breathtaking. Benson had spent some days at the beach with Theresa and seen the ocean, of course, but the vantage from up here was totally different. He could see the white caps of waves, but the expanse of water was so vast it was impossible to get a sense of scale. Benson wasn't even sure how high above the waves they were.

It reminded him of floating in the space outside the Ark, except here, infinity had shape and form.

The shuttle slowed as they passed the first barrier island. A smattering of scrub brush among the dunes gave Benson some idea of altitude. They were coming in low, no more than a hundred meters. The hull groaned gently as the exhaust from the turbines was redirected through ducts in the fuselage and took the shuttle's full weight. They were hovering. The landing site had to be very close by.

Gaia was, as a general rule, a flat world. It was over a billion years older than Earth had been. The core was still molten enough to maintain a weakened magnetic field, but volcanism was rare, and plate tectonics had slowed to, well, even slower than plate tectonics usually were. The world's mountain ranges weren't being built back up nearly fast enough to keep up with the erosion and gravity dragging them down. Canyons and valleys, however, were the opposite. Rivers had been cutting through the landscape for hundreds of millions of years longer than on Earth. Canyons were deeper, wider, often reaching all the way down to solid bedrock. One such enormous canyon snaked through the high plains a few tens of kilometers north of where they were now.

"There it is," Valmassoi said loudly from the other side of the cabin. The seatbelt light forgotten, Korolev unbuckled himself and scooted over to the other side to get a better look.

"Hey. Get back here," Benson shouted. "You'll unbalance the shuttle."

"Chief, there's twenty of us. She can handle it."

"Ugh," Benson said, embarrassed by his anxiety-fueled outburst. Temporarily pushing his fear to the background, Benson unfastened his webbing and joined Korolev and the others getting a look at their destination.

"That's a big hole," he said, and indeed it was. The village where the temple to the human's rover had been built sat in a bowl carved out of the ground, but not by hands, human or alien. And not by water or wind, either.

It was a crater, an eroded remnant of a meteorite impact eons ago. The surface of Gaia was covered in them. The Tau Ceti system held ten times the density of protoplanetary material compared to Earth's solar system, despite Tau Ceti itself being a metal-poor star from an earlier generation of star formation than Sol. There were competing theories as to why, including a lack of Jovian-class gas giants to hoover up much of it, but no one was really sure why the dust and asteroids were so thick.

But the why didn't matter. The practical effect for Gaia was a period of heavy asteroid bombardment that still hadn't entirely run its course more than five billion years later. It was why the discovery of the Atlantians had come as such a huge shock to everyone. With a dinosaur-eradicating impact event averaging once every few million years, no one expected complex life would've had a chance to evolve, to say nothing of an entire civilization.

Yet as the shuttle cruised low and slow over the alien village, a civilization was exactly what spread out below them. A perfect ring of thick trees grew around the lip of the crater, acting as both a defensive wall and a barrier to the fierce winds constantly blowing in from the ocean. Inside the tree barrier, multiple concentric rings of adobe and brick buildings encircled a small lake at the very bottom of the crater.

Everywhere he looked, Benson saw the native Atlantians openly gawking up at the shuttle with their noseless, alien faces. Many ran for the safety of their homes. A few fell to their knees with arms spread wide in open worship. Some simply froze in place like statues. A very few shouted and shook spears at the monster invading their sky.

As the shuttle cast its long shadow over the village, Benson's suspicions about the rationale for taking the immense craft grew. Maybe it *was* the only practical way to cross the ocean with twenty people, but had a direct flyover in broad daylight really been necessary?

Benson dropped that thought and returned to the view. Outside the village, acres and acres of farmland reached deeper into the continent, interrupted by irrigation canals and cart paths. But the most obvious feature was a wide, perfectly straight road sticking out from the west side of the village and continuing past the horizon. It went another forty-odd kilometers before reaching the next village, then branched out to three more, then another twenty from there. No one knew if this particular village was the first to build roads, or only the most recent to be added to the network.

"At least don't set us down in their crop fields," Benson said. "Our exhaust might start a wildfire and cost the entire season's harvest. And that wouldn't be good for diplomacy."

Valmassoi nodded. "Where would you suggest we set down, then?"

Benson scanned the landscape until he spotted a clearing. "There. It looks like a crop processing area. Can our pilot set us down in there?"

"Looks like a tight fit, but doable. But it's four kilometers from the village."

"Which gives us plenty of time to think up clever opening lines before our guests arrive."

The administrator chuckled and looked to Sergeant Atwood, his hand-picked head of the security detail. Atwood was the Beehive's sergeant-at-arms, commanding three other guards. Her force operated as an independent arm of Theresa's constables, focused on personal protection instead of law enforcement, so even though Korolev technically had seniority over her, Valmassoi had insisted on putting her in charge.

Benson didn't mind. Madison Atwood had been a hell of a Zero player in her day. She was smart, tough, competent, and adaptable.

"What do you think, sergeant?"

Atwood tied her dark hair back into a short ponytail as she

surveyed the scene. "We're pretty exposed out there, but that's true for at least ten klicks in any direction. And the terrain is flat enough that we can see anything coming from a long way off. We'll have plenty of time to dig in or dust off."

"You're assuming there'll be trouble," Benson said.

Atwood shrugged. "It's my job to assume there'll be. I don't like surprises."

"Not even surprise parties?" Benson asked.

Atwood shot him a warning glance. "Especially not those."

"So, you're comfortable with Mr Benson's landing site?" Valmassoi asked. Atwood nodded. "OK, tell the pilot that's our LZ. Sergeant, get your team ready."

Without another word, Atwood got up and walked toward the rear of the cabin, followed closely by her two team members. Korolev shrugged at Benson and chased after them.

Valmassoi continued. "The rest of us are going to wait inside until the security team has signaled the all clear."

A tremor rippled through the floor as the shuttle touched down. Benson let out a breath he hadn't realized he'd been holding in. Not seeing anything more important for him to do, he walked to the back of the cabin and watched the security team as they prepared.

Atwood already had two big crates pulled from storage, and the team busied itself spreading their contents all over the deck. The riot suits were familiar to Benson from his days running Avalon module's police force. They'd been designed for low-to-moderate threat environments and were rated against physical blows from fists or clubs, and slashing or piercing attacks from knives or other edged weapons. In theory, they would be more than adequate to protect them from anything that could be produced by late stone-age technology.

In theory.

The other crate held the other half of their kit, which was not at all defensive. Benson reached in and grabbed one of the rifles, careful to keep his finger well away from the trigger. It was a short, blocky design meant for use in the tight confines of an urban environment, but it would work equally well inside a dense forest. It was black and utilitarian almost to the point of ugliness. It was part of the very first batch of guns manufactured in over two hundred years. Most people had believed mankind was better off without them, and indeed they were still banned for civilian ownership. But the scars of David Kimura's attack on Shangri-La ran deep. Losing twenty thousand people in minutes did that to a society.

Complicating matters further was the footage of the final confrontation with Kimura, where Benson had used the last gun in existence, the same FN M1910 .380 auto that had killed Archduke Ferdinand and triggered World War I, to thwart the bombing that would have blown off the back half of the Ark and left everyone to freeze or starve to death.

Between that and the shock of moving to the surface and having to fight for the top spot on the food chain for the first time in a few thousand years, Shambhala's leadership had been forced to be a little more practical on the matter of firearms prohibition.

Korolev saw him holding it and walked over. "We're a little past stun-sticks, huh chief?"

"You can say that again."

"Mr Benson," Atwood's sharp voice snapped from behind them like a board breaking. "Are you qualified in the use of the P-120 personal defense weapon?" It was more accusation than question.

Benson held up a hand, but Korolev jumped in before he could answer. "Are you kidding? Chief Benson is the *only* person qualified. Unless you think a couple of hours on the range is the same as being in a real gunfight."

Ah, Korolev. Reliably loyal and predictably hotheaded. Atwood was about to blow her stack, and rightfully so, but Benson averted the eruption by setting the rifle back in its case. "It wasn't much of a gunfight, constable, considering I was the only one with a gun. Sergeant Atwood is right, I haven't been trained on this particular weapon. And you should really show more deference to your superiors, Pavel."

"Yes, sir." Korolev squared his shoulders. "Sorry, ma'am."

If Atwood stepped any closer to Korolev, she'd have stood on his toes. She was a good five centimeters shorter than him, but she hardly seemed to notice. "You may have been assigned here as a favor to Mr Benson, but you're under my command for the duration of this expedition, and until you are relieved, you *will* respect my authority. Do you understand?"

"Yes ma'am. Won't happen again."

"I expect not. Now get in your gear. If you're not squared away when that door drops in three minutes, you'll stand the rest of this watch naked. Move!"

Korolev saluted crisply, then fell back and hurriedly got into his riot gear. Atwood glanced up at Benson and motioned toward the front of the cabin. "Walk with me."

Benson stopped once they were out of earshot of the rest of the security detail. "Would you really make him stand a shift naked?"

"Damn straight I would. Lessons need to be memorable if they're going to stick."

"Don't judge him too harshly. Pavel's a good kid, dependable. He's just young and full of testosterone."

Atwood nodded. "Why do you think I want to see him naked?"

Benson chuckled. "You're an attractive lady. I'm sure you could just ask nicely."

Atwood put a hand on her chest, feigning shock. "Fraternize with a subordinate under my chain of command? That's unethical. I'm sure you agree."

"I'm not sure I do, considering I married someone from my chain of command. Then again, I'd never considered simply ordering her to get naked on the clock."

"I find it streamlines the process."

"It's certainly cheaper than dating, I'll give you that." Benson stopped and leaned against a seatback. "He's not wrong, you know."

"About what, exactly?"

"Gunfights. I'm the only person in more than two centuries who's been in one. No amount of training or practice will prepare you for it, not even an honest-to-goodness fist fight. Your hands sweat and shake, your heart pounds out of your chest, your body does everything it can to fuck up your aim. And no one was throwing things back at me."

"Not unless you count nuclear bombs."

"Point," Benson admitted.

"I hear you," Atwood conceded. "Any advice you can offer?"

"Yeah, don't get cornered into a fight."

"And if it can't be avoided?"

"Distance is your best friend."

Atwood digested this. "Hey, listen, we picked the P-120 blueprints out of the archives because it's ambidextrous and dead simple to operate. We packed backups. If you download the drivers, I could link one to your plant and train you up in half an hour."

"Why would you want to do that?"

Atwood shrugged. "You've already said it. You're the only person with real experience. I only have four people against lord knows how many hundreds or thousands of potentially hostile natives. Boosting my combat strength by twenty-five percent is a no-brainer."

Benson rubbed the back of his neck. "I see where you're coming from, and I appreciate the offer. But I'm here as a diplomat. Giving me a gun sends entirely the wrong message."

"I understand. I'd at least like to add you to the plant link my detail uses for coordination, if that's all right?"

"That's fine."

"OK, just keep it clear except for emergencies. The training offer is open if you change your mind."

"Thank you, but to be honest with you, sergeant, I hope I never have to fire one of those damned things again."

CHAPTER SIX

By the time Kexx brought Mei back to the temple, the infighting had already broken out with a vengeance. Long-simmering divisions and arguments had been given new life when Mei and her people landed six Varrs before. The arrival of the humans' giant metal bird boiled them over. The elders and their attendants quickly split to opposing sides of the temple while the rover sat in the middle and impassively observed the two bickering camps.

Tuko's voice was the loudest, as usual, but even ze was having trouble being heard above the din as Kuul, Chak, and the rest tried to outshout and flash one another. Eventually, Tuko's patience reached its end. Tuko spun zer ceremonial spear once, then brought it crashing down on the outside of the rover hard enough to crack the shaft. That spear was over three hundred years old. It had been held by an unbroken succession of chiefs for that entire time. The sound of the ancient halo tree wood snapping bordered on heresy, but successfully shut every mouth, dimmed skin, and turned every face in Tuko's direction.

For a long, uncomfortable moment, Tuko turned the broken spear shaft around in zer hands, inspecting the fracture as one would a wound. "Friends." Tuko's voice was even, measured, quiet. But it carried through the sudden silence of the temple like a hurricane. "Our people await our wisdom. Is it too much to ask that we agree on some?" Their shamed silence dragged on as Tuko's eyes passed over every one of them in turn.

"My chief," Kuul moved to the front of the crowd and took a knee, averting zer eyes from both Tuko and the rover, as was proper. Zer skin, however, glowed brighter than Tuko's. It was either a calculated insult, or an honest oversight from an ambitious young warrior. Kexx tended to believe the latter, but Tuko's position mandated that ze assume the former.

Tuko's skin flared bright as a torch. With a flick of the wrist, the spear in zer hand rested on the back of Kuul's neck, right on top of the bloodways that fed zer brain.

"Shall I cut, Kuul? I don't see why not, you don't seem to be using your head."

The room froze. The threat was theatrical... mostly. But, even with a broken shaft, Kuul felt the immense weight of authority of the spear at zer neck. Kuul's skin dimmed and changed to the quick, inward-flowing dots of embarrassment and total submission. Tuko held the broken haft in place for a time, driving the lesson home before lifting the spear.

"You wished to say, Kuul?"

Kuul's skin brightened, but did not match Tuko's. Not a complete idiot, then. "My chief." Zer eyes darted over to the now-silent rover at the center of the room. "The emissary can talk. It stands to reason that it can also *listen*."

Tuko looked over at the rover with suspicion, then pulsed zer agreement. Without another word, everyone followed Tuko out of the temple and back into the afternoon sun.

"Thank you, chief," Kuul said. "Our early scouts tell us there are less than thirty of them. My warriors alone are ten times their number. Let us go out to show these raiders the futility of their invasion."

A chorus erupted in support, but a flash from Tuko silenced them. "You call it an invasion?" Ze held out a hand in Mei's direction. "Our guests have been here for many Varrs. Have they not been civil? Why just today I watched their children playing with ours. Is that typical of an invasion?"

"How can we know what's 'typical' of these people?" Kuul pointed at Mei. "We have no idea why they're here. Maybe they're criminals. Maybe they're scouts. Maybe they were sent here, meant to look and act harmless so we would drop our guard."

"That's preposterous," Kexx angrily said before catching zerself.

Tuko turned to face zer. "You have something to add, truth -digger?"

Kexx straightened zer back and placed zer hands on Mei's shoulders before continuing. "Mei and I have had several conversations about their choice to come here, to meet us."

"And you've kept these 'conversations' to yourself?" Kuul demanded.

"A truth-digger may keep anything they learn private until their examinations are complete."

"So we're just supposed to take your word for it, then?"

"No," Kexx shook zer head without realizing it, a uniquely human gesture. "You're supposed to take zer's." Kexx gently pushed Mei forward into the circle. "It's all right, Mei."

Tuko took a step closer. "It's all right, child. You don't have to be afraid."

Mei squared her shoulders and went even more rigid than normal. "Not afraid," she said in passable G'tel, "And not child. Have child."

Kexx grimaced, afraid of Tuko's reaction, but zer skin just fluttered in amusement. "Of course. Forgive me. Why did you come to our village six Varrs ago?"

"To learn. To see. Live whole life in a… cave. Wanted to explore. Tired of waiting."

Tuko considered this for a long moment. "You lost people during the travel on your…" Ze glanced up at Kexx, looking for the unfamiliar word.

"Boat," Kexx provided.

"Yes, your 'boat.' Many of you didn't survive." Mei's lower lip quivered just the slightest bit, but she remained defiant. Tuko continued. "Why didn't you just take this great bird instead? The one the other humans took?"

"Not ours. We from different village. No great birds."

"There's more than one human village?"

Mei shook her head, then caught zerself and wiggled zer hand in the G'tel way. "Only one now. Ours empty."

"And is this other village as big as yours was?"

Mei wiggled zer hand again. "Bigger. Much bigger."

"Where is this village?"

Mei smirked. Kexx recognized the gesture, but doubted anyone else understood it. Ze raised a hand and pointed to the ocean, pointed up to the mysterious line in the sky, faintly visible even in daylight, then traced zer finger back down to the horizon.

"There."

A chilled silence ran through the crowd. There had been rumors of course, suspicions that these new visitors were linked to the strange happenings in the sky. Most had seen them as omens for either good or ill, but without confirmation, rumors were all they'd been. Two of the elders dropped to their knees in prayer, while a third seemed frozen in shock. The rest resumed arguing among themselves.

Kexx had to admit, Mei had a flair for dramatic timing.

"Varr has returned to us," one of the elders, Chak, whispered solemnly. Ze referred to an old story. The oldest, actually: of Varr, the long exiled mate of Cuut and Xis. "We must open our doors to the humans and prepare an appropriate sacrifice."

"Is that true, Mei?" Tuko asked. "Have your people been sent to us by Varr?"

Mei stumbled. "I… um."

"You see?" Kuul pounded a fist on zer chest. "Ze is no child of Varr. Ze can barely speak!"

"How well do you speak human, Kuul?" Kexx bit back.

"I don't," ze announced proudly. "Why should I fill my mouth with their mud?"

"Because Mei has honored us by learning our tongue as best and as quickly as ze can."

"As ze should. Learn to speak like a civilized person."

Chak pushed back into the circle. "Varr has been in exile for thousands of years. How do we know zer tongue isn't the human tongue? We can barely speak to the nomadic clans."

"Because the nomads are little better than animals." Kuul barked. "And we should drive them off just as we would those raiders!"

Chak pressed zer small frame as close to Kuul's body as propriety would allow. "You would spit in the face of our salvation? You are a spear with no mind to wield it."

Tuko stepped up and physically pushed the two of them

apart. "So, as I understand it, our difficulty lays in whether we should worship the humans," zer eyes darted over to Mei and back again, so quickly Kexx nearly missed it. "Or slaughter them, yes?"

A general murmur of agreement made a lap around the circle of elders.

"A stark choice." Tuko paused. "A depressingly familiar choice. Isn't this the essence of every choice we face? Isn't this always your *wisdom*?" The slowly falling bands on zer skin froze and broke up into flickering dots, a sign of extreme frustration. No one dared answer.

Tuko absently rubbed at zer left shoulder, an old complaint from a long-ago fight with a tribe of raiders. "Mei, what do your people want? Why have they come now?"

Mei shrugged. "I don't know. We have not talked, two years."

"I see."

"But you won't beat them," Mei hurried to add.

"Nonsense," Kuul bristled. "We could beat you easily."

"Once, maybe. Not twice." Mei pointed back at the line in the sky. "Because they come back. More birds, more people, and many bigger spears."

Kexx stepped in. "Mei has told me the great birds can hold many hundreds of humans. They chose not to bring that many today. Whatever they are and whoever sent them, they came to talk, not to fight."

"You're sure of that?" Tuko said. "Sure enough to risk our village?"

"Yes," Kexx answered without hesitating. "With an unburdened soul."

Tuko's hand worried away at zer shoulder. "Well, I am not so fortunate, or certain. Kuul will take two fullhands warriors and–"

"Finally, wisdom!" Kuul shook zer hands in triumph while excited ribbons danced across zer skin.

"And," Tuko's voice took on a sharpened edge, "escort our new guests into the village, where we will perform the evening cleansing and make the appropriate sacrifices. Meanwhile, Chak and a fullhand of warriors will take our bearers into Xis's temple below where they will be out of sight and safe. If that is agreeable to everyone?"

It wasn't really a question, but as Kexx looked around at the skin patterns and posture of all present, it seemed that everyone at least found the proposal equally *disagreeable*. And what was compromise, if not that?

Kuul stormed off with several warriors in zer wake, while Chak meandered away to moan with two of the other elders. The rest of the circle of elders returned to the temple. All except Tuko, who stood zer ground. Resolute, but agitated.

Kexx approached. "My chief."

"Truth-digger. You wish to say more?"

"I wish to go out to greet the new humans and keep an eye on Kuul. As you've said, I've spent more time with them than anyone else."

Tuko let out a short laugh. "You might return with a spear in your back." Ze sighed, a long, heavy sigh, as if deep water squeezed at zer air sacks. "No. A truth-digger's job is to observe. I need you to keep your distance and report what you see. It may have been a mistake letting you get so close to Mei and zer people."

"Fullo trained me to see what others cannot, or what they don't wish to see."

"And did Fullo wish to see the inside of an ulik's belly?" Tuko snapped. "Fullo was a good truth-digger, but ze had a warrior's soul. Always getting too close, too narrow. Too..."

"Too focused?" Kexx asked pointedly.

"Perhaps," Tuko said after a pause. "The other elders are focused enough in what they see. I need your mind to remain broad, open to different possibilities, different perspectives, if your counsel is to have value. Do you understand?"

"I understand that Kuul is scratching for a fight and will look for any excuse to start one."

Tuko waved an arm in annoyance. "That's been true since ze first balled a fist and threw zer first punch. Chak is right about that one, ze's a spear in need of a strong hand to wield it. If Kuul starts a fight with the humans, on zer hands it be. Might be just the excuse I need to replace zer."

"If any of us are still alive." Kexx folded zer arms. "You've seen the rover. It's magic, Tuko. But to them, it's just a tool. If that's their idea of a plow, imagine what their spears must be like. You heard Mei, ze wasn't worried about Kuul and zer warriors in the slightest."

"Ze may be bluffing."

"Mei has never given me reason to doubt zer before."

"You put a lot of faith in your pet," Tuko said. Kexx laughed and flashed annoyance. "What's funny?"

"You saw their great bird darken the sky over our village. Are you really so convinced that *Mei* is the pet?"

CHAPTER SEVEN

"We're all clear out here, administrator."

Sergeant Atwood had been thorough. It took her detail fifteen minutes to clear a patch of land barely larger than the shuttle that had touched down on it. All things considered, however, her caution was probably warranted.

"Any sign of the Atlantians?" Valmassoi called down the stairwell.

"No. Nothing moving out here except these damned bugs."

"Thank you, sergeant. We're coming out now." The administrator turned to the rest of his flock while Benson leaned against the bulkhead with his arms crossed. "OK everyone, we're going to exit in a calm and orderly fashion. Once you're outside, stay inside the perimeter established by the security detail. No wandering off to look at a plant. No stepping away for a little privacy. And no ducking behind a tree when nature calls. Use the facilities on the shuttle or hold it. We move together as a single group. OK?"

There was a general murmur of agreement, enough to assure Valmassoi that his message had been heard, or enough to set up the I-told-you-so and shift culpability to the eventual offenders. Benson had done the same many times in his day and couldn't help but admire a fellow practitioner of the art.

The line of dignitaries walked down the single flight of stairs like a line of cattle being herded out of a barn. Cattle. Benson hadn't thought of the old epitaph for at least a year. With the crew of the Ark tens of thousands of miles up in the sky, and nearly everyone else busy building new lives down here in the dirt, the old labels had fallen out of use. Maybe they didn't really apply anymore.

Benson tucked into the end of the line and waited patiently for everyone to shuffle out into the light. Warm air from the outside blew up the stairwell and mingled with the stale, cool air of the cabin. The breeze was heavy with pollen from the fields outside. Someone further down the line sneezed once, then again, then finally hard enough to pop a lung. Allergies were new to everyone. The air on the Ark had been so thoroughly scrubbed of particulates, by the time it reached one's nose, there was nothing to sneeze out again. For a small but unfortunate percentage of the population, landing on Atlantis had been an unexpected adventure in mucus.

He reached the bottom of the stairs and set his right foot onto the ground. Benson fought a sudden urge to kiss the dirt. Everyone milled about underneath the shuttle to stay out of the noonday sun. They were a few hundred kilometers south of the planet's equator, but still well inside the tropics, and local summer was approaching its height. Atwood's team stood at the shuttle's three corners with weapons held at low ready while she busied herself assembling a small quadcopter drone.

Benson left her alone and walked over to the edge of the clearing. The crops grew tall in the sun. They were a bleached lavender and shaped like branching ferns. He ran a hand under the leafy stem and felt knobby growths. He flipped the plant over and saw three rows of what he assumed were seeds growing down the entire length of the stem. It didn't look like any of the native plants from their continent, but then corn didn't look a damned thing like its undomesticated ancestors either.

He pinched off a few seeds and walked back to the group under the shuttle. "Think these are safe to eat?" he asked Valmassoi.

"For Atlantians, or for you?"

"For me, obviously."

"How the hell should I know?"

"Didn't we bring a botanist?"

Valmassoi looked at him like he'd grown a second head. "We didn't come here to hit the buffet line, Mr Benson. We're here to talk to these people."

Benson's already tenuous opinion of the administrator took another hit. "And what are we going to talk to them about? We have crop failures back in Shambhala."

"Because they were sabotaged."

"Why does that matter? These fine folks are growing food by the square kilometer. If this stuff is any good to us, we can learn from each other. Swap ideas and methods. We've only been here for three years. They've been here for tens of thousands. Do you really think they don't have anything to teach us about living on this planet?"

To his credit, Valmassoi glanced down at the seeds in Benson's palm with a newfound appreciation for their potential. "Well, what do they taste like?"

Benson looked down at the seeds in his hand with suspicion, then looked around. "Hey, Korolev. I dare you to eat one of these—"

"Get bent, coach."

Benson nodded. "Smart man. Well, painted myself into a corner, I suppose." He jiggled the small kernels in his palm, then popped them into his mouth and chewed, ready to spit them back out at the first sign of bitterness.

"Well?" Valmassoi asked. "How are they?"

"Like… beans."

"Beans?"

"Yeah, texture-wise. Except they taste like tofu and caramel."

"Is that bad?"

"No, just weird." Benson risked swallowing the seeds. For science.

"Was that wise?" Valmassoi asked.

Benson only shrugged. "Somebody had to eat the first apple."

"That didn't turn out so well, as I recall."

"I don't know. The Garden we left *is* at the bottom of a black hole."

"And if you keel over dead in an hour?"

"Then you'll know that we don't need to bother asking for help growing it."

Valmassoi smiled. "Sounds like a win-win when you say it like that."

"What's our next move?"

The administrator nodded in Sergeant Atwood's direction. "As soon the good sergeant gives her thumbs up, we'll lock down the shuttle and start walking for the village."

"And then what?"

"And then wait outside for someone to come out and greet us."

"Which probably would have been on friendlier terms if we hadn't buzzed their village, you know," Benson said.

Valmassoi squared his shoulders at the comment. "We're on a scouting mission just as much as a diplomatic one. It's nice to know what we're facing before we set down, don't you think?"

"The satellites already told us anything we could've learned from a flyover. This little display was a show of force."

Valmassoi shrugged and patted the underside of the shuttle. "I must admit your disapproval confuses me. You never used a 'show of force' during your career as Avalon's chief constable, Mr Benson?"

"Of course I did, when people needed a reminder." He pointed a thumb out behind him. "But they haven't done anything to provoke us."

Valmassoi's hands made a placating gesture. "And now they never will. No harm done."

Benson had to fight back the urge to slap the smug little shit. "Did it ever occur to you that just maybe a stunt like that might *provoke* them? These people evolved on a planet where giant rocks from the sky have been trying to kill them for billions of years. So what do they do? Build their damned houses in the craters. Something tells me they don't stay scared for very long."

"We'll see." Valmassoi waved him off dismissively. Their conversation was interrupted by a mosquito-like buzzing as Atwood's quadcopter drifted by.

"We're all set, administrator," she said. "Ready to move out on your word."

"No time like the present."

The shuttle's hatch closed and locked behind them. Everyone formed a double-file line with Atwood and Korolev at the front and the other two security officers at the rear. The quadcopter shot up out of sight as they moved further away from the shuttle.

The expedition got its first surprise when the simple worn cart path quickly joined up with the main road. It had been assumed that the road network between the different villages was nothing more complicated than packed dirt periodically cleared of vegetation. But one foot on the hard surface told another story.

"It's concrete," Atwood said. "Or something very much like it."

"How industrious," Benson said. "I bet their huts aren't just sticks and mud either, then."

The group walked along chattering among themselves for the next kilometer until a distressed shout brought everyone to heel.

"Aaaah..." Atwood's free hand shot up to her temple and began rubbing frantically. Benson had seen it before; Atwood's plant was getting corrupted data that her brain couldn't make sense of. He'd never had it happen, but Theresa had. She described it almost like having a seizure.

Benson put a hand on her shoulder. "What's wrong?"

"The drone. It's—"

The quadcopter crashed into the road not far from Korolev. One of its rotors kept spinning, then sparked once and ground to a halt. Korolev kicked the smoldering wreck. "Ah, chief?"

The other two guards shouldered their rifles and started hunting for targets before Atwood could put up her arm. "No! Stand down. It's OK. It was just some damned birds. They knocked it down."

Benson bent over the smoking wreckage of the drone and out of one of the ducted fan assemblies he picked an iridescent scale the local bird analogues used for feathers. "They must have been attracted by the sound. Mistook it for a bug."

"Pretty big fucking bug," Korolev said.

"Maybe they're hungry." Benson looked up and scanned the sky for the birds, blocking the noon sun with his hand. He spotted them, a lazy circle of three. Their altitude was hard to guess, but they were large animals with a wingspan at least as wide as Benson's arms. Carrion eaters? After a couple more slow rotations, they all peeled off and headed almost due north in a "V" formation. "That's weird."

Valmassoi stepped in. "Do you have a replacement?"

Atwood shook her head. "Not onboard the shuttle. I didn't think it would be necessary."

"Can we proceed without it?"

Atwood took on the distant stare that signaled she was consulting her plant. "I can link up with our satellite feeds. There'll be about a second of delay, and we'll have gaps every hour or so."

"Why the gaps?"

"Because the birds aren't dedicated surveillance platforms, they're GPS sats. Their telescopes don't have wide enough aperture for total, full-time coverage of the surface. And even if they were, we're down a few from malfunctions."

Benson stepped in. "It's that or we go back to the shuttle and scrap the expedition."

The administrator sighed as he weighed the options. "It'll have to do. Let's get going. Contact the Ark and see if they can retask some of the sats and shrink those gaps."

Atwood saluted. "Yes, sir."

"And someone remind me to tell Captain Mahama that a full-coverage surveillance net is getting bumped up in the manufacturing queue."

Benson opened a private link to Atwood's plant. <Hey, you OK?>

<Yes. Just a strange data echo, but it's fading.> Atwood glanced down at the remains of her drone. <Still sure you don't want to get trained up on a rifle, Mr Benson?>

<Not as sure as I was half an hour ago.>

<I hear that. Let's get the line moving. I don't really want to stand still for too long out in the open like this.>

Benson nodded and started down the road again. The group continued on the next two kilometers in alert silence only occasionally punctuated by a wry joke and nervous laughter, or a command from one of Atwood's detail. Benson passed the time talking to Theresa through a plant link, updating her on their progress and reassuring her of his safety in equal measure.

Along the way, they passed three stone markers placed within view of the road. Each had a slightly different glyph of a simple, curving design. It was a good bet the glyphs represented Atlantian numerals and that the stones themselves were mile markers. Benson tagged the GPS coordinates of the second one, then compared them against the third. Lo and behold, the Atlantian distance measure tagged in at roughly 735 meters. Benson uploaded the finding and images of the glyphs to a research database for linguists and exobiologists and flagged the files for further review.

"There it is." Korolev pointed down the road as they crested a small hill. The circle of tree tops that marked the outer edges of the impact crater the village had been built into were plainly visible.

Atwood scrutinized the view with a small pair of binoculars. "The road seems to lead into a set of gates built into the trees."

"Is that necessary?" Valmassoi asked. "The forest can't be *that* dense."

Atwood let the binoculars hang around her neck. "It looks pretty overgrown to me. You could probably get through it with a machete, but it's definitely enough to slow you down. What now?"

"We go knock on the front door, of course." Valmassoi turned to address the rest of the group. "OK, everyone enable your translators, but leave the talking to me for the moment. Stay together, and don't make any moves that could be seen as threatening."

"What do aliens find threatening?" someone asked.

"Oh, pointing spears at people, for example," Benson said in a quiet but strained voice as he stood near the edge of the crop field with his back turned to the rest of the party. Directly in front of him, a tall, slender figure stood hunched over so as to stay concealed in the crops and use Benson's own body for cover. In its hands was a spear almost two meters long tipped with a black, napped-stone spearhead, probably made of obsidian and therefore sharper than a surgeon's scalpel. It wouldn't do much against the armor the security team wore, but for Benson's light shirt and unprotected abdomen, it would do the job all too effectively. Even with his eyes focused like a laser on the alien in front of him, Benson could see several more figures moving silently through the crops, flanking the entire party.

Carefully, slowly, he put up his hands. Korolev looked in his direction and gasped, then brought his rifle up to his shoulder, but Benson waved at him to stand down. By then, the rest of the expedition realized what was going on and started screaming at each other in alarm.

Benson turned his head as far as he could without breaking eye contact with the alien and yelled at the group. "Will you all kindly shut up? No sudden moves. There's more of them out here."

<Contact left!> The voice came through the link Atwood had set up for her security detail. Atwood shouldered her own weapon as a dozen more Atlantians emerged from the crops on the other side of the road.

"Well," Benson looked over at Valmassoi. "They've *greeted* us. Now what?"

CHAPTER EIGHT

"OK." Benson forced calm into his voice. "Everyone just take it nice and easy."

"Tell that to the people pointing spears at us," Valmassoi said.

"I'd be delighted to if I had the first idea how."

"You *would* know if you'd turn your damned translator on."

If Benson's hands hadn't been busy being held at arm's length looking nonthreatening, he would have slapped himself on the forehead. In the heat of the moment, he'd forgotten to activate the translation matrix that had been uploaded to his plant as part of the expedition preparations. He dug through his plant's internal menu tabs and flipped it on, then paused.

"Wait. Why am I talking to them? You said you should be the one to talk."

Valmassoi gave him an incredulous glare. "Are you serious?"

"I'm just the director of recreation and athletic preparedness, remember?"

"Is it really the time for this?" Atwood asked.

"I'm just trying to follow my orders," Benson said.

"I've never had to talk with a weapon pointed at me before. You have."

"Aw, you haven't lived," Benson said. "Last time it happened to me, it was a nuke."

"I *am* living," Valmassoi squeaked, "And I'd like to keep on living. So if you wouldn't mind, Mr Benson?"

The Atlantian holding the spear to Benson's navel barked something at him with a deep, wet voice. The matrix in his plant lagged for a moment while it digested the sounds. Then, in a calm, monotone female voice utterly divorced from the reality of the two meter-tall, spear-wielding alien shouting in Benson's face, the matrix said "Submit to/Follow us."

"Well that's not very helpful, is it?"

"Keep him talking," Atwood said. "Give the matrix more to work with."

Benson nodded and thought, Hello, my name is Bryan. A moment later, the matrix spoke the translation in his head as a best-approximation phonetic spelling of the words floated on the left side of his field of vision.

"Ah… Kulay. Bryan, see coe."

The alien's smooth skin rippled with rapidly shifting contrasting bands of light and dark. Its face also changed, going darker, while the frilly layers of crests on the top of its head rose. Benson didn't need a translator to tell him it was a threat display. The Atlantian repeated its order, more loudly, and punctuated the order by poking Benson in the stomach hard enough to rip a small hole through his shirt and break the skin beneath.

"Hey!" Benson shouted back at him.

<Fuck this, everybody stay cool,> came Korolev's voice through the security detail's com. Benson glanced over to see Korolev tighten his grip on his rifle.

<Pavel…> Benson thought. <What are you doing, buddy?>

<Mr Korolev,> Atwood's commanding voice burst in. <Stand–>

Bang!

The spear shaft in the alien warrior's hands exploded as the five point seven millimeter bullet from Korolev's rifle struck it at over a thousand meters per second. The wood was reduced to an expanding cloud of splinters as the outer layers of the bullet casing peeled off and dumped the majority of its kinetic energy. The Atlantian shouted something short and loud even before the obsidian spearhead had hit the road at Benson's feet.

"Excrement," said the calm, feminine voice of the translator matrix, missing some important context. Benson didn't need to speak a language to recognize a curse word when he heard one.

The alien's strange, wavy pupils grew until they nearly filled their oval eyes, while its skin, so dark just a moment before, went white as a sheet.

Korolev yelled something off to Benson's left. His translator quickly added, "Drop it." Much to Benson's surprise, the warrior in front of him glanced down at its decapitated spear and threw it at the ground.

"Now the rest of you," Korolev shouted. The apparent leader of the warriors stood tall and defiant, but fluttered its head crests. All around him, Benson heard the immensely satisfying sound of spears clattering on the road.

"Excellent." Benson probed the small tear in the front of his shirt with a finger, then put on his best smile. "Now then, let's try this again. Kulay. Bryan see coe."

The alien's eyes darted around the scene, still struggling to understand what had just happened. "Kuul see coe," it said in a more muted, cautious tone. "My name is Kuul."

"Nice to meet you, Kuul. Take me to your leader."

"Seriously," Valmassoi whispered to Benson as they waited outside the village's gates. "'Take me to your leader?'"

"Isn't that what you're supposed to say?"

"No, that's what the aliens say in tacky scifi movies."

"We *are* the aliens here. I've been waiting to say that my whole life."

"Well I'm glad we could make a little boy's dream come true. Speaking of boys, what do you suppose I should do about Korolev?"

"Give him a medal?"

"That's not exactly what I had in mind. Sergeant Atwood is livid and wants to send him packing for the shuttle."

"But?" Benson could hear the word coming.

"But, I asked her to hold off until I talked to you."

"I thank you for that, but I don't see as Pavel did anything wrong."

"He disobeyed her stand-down order and fired on the people we're supposed to be introducing ourselves to."

"Well, technically, she hadn't finished giving the order yet when he fired."

"That's an awfully fine hair to split."

"I keep my razor sharp. Besides, he didn't strike first." Benson pointed to the small rip in his shirt and the tiny stain of blood next to it.

Valmassoi scoffed. "Hardly a fatal wound."

"No offense, but that's easy for you to say. That jerk Kuul wasn't backing down without a lot of convincing."

"You have to admit, defending Korolev flirts with hypocrisy for a man who was lecturing me against shows of force earlier today."

Benson shrugged. "Not really. If you'll remember, I said we only flexed our muscles when people needed a reminder. Kuul needed a reminder, or in this case to be taught the lesson in the first place. He didn't recognize our guns as weapons, so he thought he had us dead to rights. Korolev's solution was... novel, but it did drive the point home rather effectively. It was almost a lot worse. Another couple seconds, and one of Atwood's people would've had to shoot him, and they would have lost a lot more than just a spear."

Valmassoi waved his hand, conceding the point. "Still, Mr Korolev has a history of ignoring the chain of command. He has to be reprimanded."

"The last time Pavel ignored orders, he saved me from being cooked by plutonium dust from the inside out and wound up in sick bay for a week for his trouble. I've been his boss and now I'm his coach. Sometimes you have to trust your players to change the play on the field if they see something you missed. Otherwise opportunities slip away. What you call 'ignoring orders,' I call taking initiative."

Valmassoi shook his head. "Peas in a pod, you two. Anyway, there isn't much to do right now. Our security detail can't really afford to be down a man."

"I wholeheartedly agree."

"We'll sort it out when we get back to Shambhala. But for the rest of this expedition, I would strongly caution Mr Korolev against showing too much more *initiative* if he doesn't want Sergeant Atwood to shoot him."

"I'll pass that along."

"Be sure that you do." Somewhere on the other side of the tree line, a horn bellowed. Valmassoi clapped his hands together. "Ah, it's almost show time. Please excuse me."

"Be my guest." Benson watched him go, an actor eager to climb onto his stage. Korolev inched over to where he stood and leaned in to talk privately.

"He looks happy."

"As a pig in shit," Benson agreed. "This is a politician's natural environment."

"Chief," Korolev pitched his voice lower. "Am I in trouble?"

The corner of Benson's lip curled up. "Oh, most definitely."

"But I did the right thing."

"That's the most reliable way to get into trouble, in my experience." Benson put his arm around the younger man's shoulder. "Don't worry, we'll sort it out when we get back. And by the way, that was a nice fucking shot."

"Thanks, but I can't take much credit for it." Korolev patted the top of his P-120. "These things are gyroscopically stabilized and the scope automatically compensates the reticule for range. If you take even a second to aim, it's damned near impossible to miss out to five or six hundred meters."

"A little more complicated than my old handgun, huh?"

"Yeah, just a little. Are you all right, chief? You look a little flush."

"Hmm? Oh, a little lightheaded, probably just nerves."

"Something bothering you?"

"Well I was almost run through with a spear a few minutes ago."

Korolev shook his head. "That's not it."

"It's not?"

"No. You've been in enough scrapes to manage the adrenaline crash. Something else is on your mind."

Benson nodded. "The birds."

"Birds?"

"Yeah, the ones that took out Atwood's drone. Didn't that seem just a little strange to you? Convenient, even?"

"Seemed pretty damned inconvenient to me. It would have spotted that Kuul prick and his minions in the field way before they could sneak up on..." Korolev's face lit up with understanding. "Oh."

"Now you get it."

"You think they were trained birds, and someone sent them to knock out our surveillance?"

"I'm just saying I don't put much stock in coincidence. Especially when I'm on the pointy end of it."

"But how would they know about it. Unless..."

"Unless what, Pavel?"

"Unless Mei or one of the other Unbound told them what it was."

Benson let out a long breath as he considered the possibility. "She risked her life once to save us. I can't believe she'd willingly help lead us into an ambush now."

"What if it wasn't, you know, willingly?"

Benson's eyes hardened and glanced down at Korolev's rifle. "Then we'll have a real problem, won't we?"

"What should we do?"

"Nothing at the moment. I think you cured Kuul of his overconfidence, for now at least. Just keep your eyes open, yeah?"

Korolev nodded. "You know I will."

The immense wooden gates guarding the only opening in the village's thick ring of trees swung to the outside, groaning and creaking like an elderly giant unwillingly roused from its bed. Benson found himself moving toward the front of the crowd through pure Brownian motion.

Light streamed between the doors as the crack widened. The crowd of humans pressed forward, propelled by anxious curiosity, straining to get a look at whatever was about to come out of the gates. The crack quickly grew until it was wide enough for the first members of the welcoming party to begin streaming out. Eight Atlantians walked out, tall and proud, dressed in elaborately woven skirts and forearm sleeves that shimmered in the sunlight like iridescent sequins. At first glance, Benson guessed they were made from the same scales he'd picked out of the drone wreckage.

The Atlantians were all bare chested, which was unsurprising considering half or more of their communication was done through their skin. It had to be awfully handy during a hunt. Each member of the retinue carried a spear nearly twice as long as the ones Kuul's warriors had tried to ambush them with. They didn't look terribly practical, and the ornate, fragile-looking spearheads all but confirmed their function was purely ceremonial.

On their heads, decorative plumes served to accentuate the crests and frills nature had already provided. But the strangest thing about their appearance wasn't the decorations, their noseless faces, or even their ever-shifting skin. It was in the way they moved, fluid and loose to the point that their bodies seemed as if they were on the verge of falling apart. On an intellectual level, Benson knew it was because the planet's version of vertebrates didn't have a calcified skeleton. Their internal support structure was cartilage suffused with a lattice of fibrous keratin to give needed rigidity in the long bones, while their joints were merely softer areas. The arrangement gave them immense flexibility, but without rigid bones or locking joints, their strange, wobbly gaits just screamed *wrong* to Benson's lizard brain.

He pushed the thought to the back of his mind. The procession of eight came to a stop, then split into two lines to bracket the road with parade-ground precision. Behind them, the largest broom-head Benson had ever seen stepped through the gate. The immense biped towered at least three meters at the shoulder.

Wild broom-heads roamed the prairies near Shambhala. The herbivores scraped together sustenance by running their baleen-like mouthparts through the endless fields of wild plants, ingesting seeds and pollen. But none of them were nearly so large as the bruiser standing proudly outside the gates. Apparently, domestication had suited him.

Standing on the broom-head's back, with all the subtlety of a peacock, a single Atlantian blew an enormous horn. The alien's skirt, forearm sleeves, and head crest enhancements were the brightest of the group. Benson had no doubt this was the village's king/chief/high priest, whatever term they used.

A last warbling blast from the horn and the village's chief jumped down from his mount. Benson worked his tongue, trying to get some moisture back into his suddenly dry mouth.

Was it getting warmer out here? Valmassoi approached the chief, his arms held out and his palms open, showing they were empty of weapons. Something behind the broom-head caught Benson's eye, or more specifically, someone.

Standing just inside the gate among a crowd of taller Atlantians, Mei watched the proceedings. Benson's spirit soared. From what he could see, she looked healthy and unharmed. And he could see quite a bit, considering just how little Mei was wearing. Her hips and forearms were covered with the same skirts as the natives, and her hair was adorned with similar decorations. Her shoulders, chest, and waist, however, were completely bare. Judging by her tan, she hadn't been wearing much else for quite a long time.

She'd never been very modest, but she'd been little more than a teenager when they'd met, still in her adolescence. Motherhood had done much to settle her fully into her adult body, but Benson still thought of her as a girl.

<Christ, is that Mei?> Korolev asked.

<Yeah,> Benson answered.

<Well, she's certainly, er, grown up.>

<Zip it up, Pavel.>

Mei's eyes lit up as soon as she noticed him. Benson wanted to run over and hug her, but it would have to wait. Valmassoi was working his way through some boilerplate introduction speech, chewing on the foreign words his plant translator was feeding him. The chief's expression and posture was hard to read, but seemed noncommittal.

Benson's stomach churned uncomfortably as a chill ran through his body. He really wasn't feeling well. His first thought was heat stroke, but it hardly seemed warm enough for it. Had he been drinking enough water?

Valmassoi finished his speech, and the chief took his turn to make his welcome announcement. Benson's plant spit his words back out in English, but he was starting to feel a little dizzy and had a great deal of difficulty concentrating. Apparently, the chief went by Tuko and was really going on about Cuut, who as best as anyone could guess was one of their trinary of major gods, the smitey one with a nasty habit of throwing asteroids whenever he wasn't happy about something or another.

Tuko held out both of his four-fingered hands to Valmassoi, palms out, and waited expectantly. The administrator looked like he'd missed a beat, unsure of what to do next. Hesitantly, Valmassoi fell back on habit and mirrored Tuko. The chief touched their palms, laced their fingers, then leaned in and pressed their foreheads together. Once it was over, Valmassoi forced an admirably convincing smile, not that Tuko would be able to appreciate it. Then again, Mei and her people had been here for months already. Who knew how much the villagers had learned about their guests in that time.

Valmassoi, appearing to be back on firmer ground, extended his right hand. "You honor me with the greeting of your people. Let me honor you in return with the traditional greeting of ours."

With the same trepidation Valmassoi had just shown, Tuko put his hand out. The administrator took it and shook it firmly.

<Well thank god they have hands and not tentacles,> Korolev said through the security detail's private line.

<Cut the chatter, Korolev,> Atwood snapped. <Keep the line clear.>

Valmassoi started escorting Chief Tuko down the line, making introductions. Each person in turn went through both the Atlantian two-hands-and-a-forehead-rub, then a good oldfashioned human handshake, but Benson wasn't paying attention. He was beginning to feel dizzy. It felt like a swarm of fish were doing hot laps inside his stomach.

Before he knew it, or was in any way prepared, Tuko was standing in front of Benson with outstretched arms, waiting for him to do the same. A bead of cold sweat rolled down the side of Benson's temple.

"And this is Bryan Benson," Valmassoi said in questionable Atlantian. "One of our, ah, warriors."

"I, um, don't feel so well," Benson pleaded.

Valmassoi ignored him. "Don't be rude to our host, Mr Benson."

Benson swallowed hard. The saliva slid down the back of his throat like a wad of peanut butter before dropping into the boiling cauldron that had become his stomach. Weakly, he reached out his arms and held up his palms. Tuko leaned in and pressed his clammy, four-fingered hands into Benson's and squeezed. His fingers felt boneless, like shaking hands with sausage links, or wriggling worms. The momentary flicker of revulsion Benson felt at the alien's hands was all the excuse his weakened constitution needed.

He turned away from the chief just in time. With a mighty heave, Benson's guts inverted themselves, sending a powerful stream of vomit and bile onto the pavement. Another wave of nausea followed just to emphasize the point before Benson collapsed to his hands and knees and continued retching onto the ground until he was dry as a desert well.

With an unreadable expression on his face, Tuko turned and spoke at Valmassoi.

"Is this also part of your traditional greeting?"

CHAPTER NINE

After the… memorable happenings of the afternoon, everyone retreated inside the gates to settle in and prepare for the evening meal. The sick human, Benson was zer name, had been taken off to the human shelter at the edge of the village where Mei was busy looking after zer. Mei apparently knew this Benson quite well. Even with Kexx's limited knowledge of human expression and range of emotion, ze could tell that Mei was very upset by Benson's sudden illness.

With the rest of the fresh arrivals tied up with the evening meal, Kexx stopped by the human's shelter to check on Mei and zer new ward.

"How is ze doing?" Kexx asked as soon as ze had Mei's attention.

"The idiot?" Mei snapped.

"Your friend, Benson?"

"Yes, the idiot." This was accompanied by quickly opening and closing zer free hand, imitating the flashing pattern that showed anger.

"Do you know what's ze's sick with?"

"Not sick. Ate yulka seeds without cooking them first. Who does that?"

"Some of your people, as I recall."

"*We* were starving. *Ze* was snacking."

It was true enough. In the days after they'd landed, Mei's people were hungry enough to try anything once. The yulka seeds hadn't been a problem for the humans at first, cooked as they were into breads, soups, and the like. But there was something about the raw seeds that really didn't agree with the human stomach, as poor Benson was the most recent to learn.

"How do you know for sure it was yulka seeds?"

"I saw little bits of them on the road where Benson threw up."

"Will ze be all right?"

Mei shrugged. "Nothing strong tea and sleep won't fix." Mei started pulling the decorations out of zer, ah, *hair*. The long, black filaments were at once exotic and beautiful. A new fashion among some of the village's adolescents was to mash up yulka stalks, then dye the fibers with ink and weave them into their head crests to imitate the human look. The style was met with great disapproval by the village elders, which of course only enhanced its appeal for the young.

Hair. Kexx tossed the human word around inside zer head. When Mei and zer people appeared six months earlier, they'd been treated by most of the village as a curiosity. Strange castaways from across the ocean, but lost, almost utterly out of their element, dependent on the charity of the G'tel, and easily managed.

The day's events had changed that calculation rather dramatically. Apart from a short report to Tuko, Kuul had been quiet ever since zer confrontation outside the village, which was itself an unprecedented occurrence. Kexx was intensely curious to know just how they'd managed it.

"Mei, can I ask you something else?" Ze gave Kexx a little nod and a *go ahead* hand gesture. "Kuul told us about a weapon one of your people used. Ze called it a thunder club. Kuul said it shattered his spear with just a sound. Do you know anything about it?"

"Not just sound." Mei shook zer head. "And it's not a club. It's a *gun*."

"A... guun?" Kexx attempted the new word.

"Gun," Mei corrected. "It throws tiny, ah, spears. Smaller than my finger. We call them *bullets*. Noise is just side effect."

"All right. But how can such small spears do that much damage? And why didn't Kuul say ze saw them?"

"Ze couldn't. Bullets go very fast. Faster than eyes can follow.

Farther and more accurate than any spear, too."

"How many of these... bullets?" Mei nodded approvingly. "How many bullets can these guns throw?"

"Fullhands, or fullhands of fullhands. Depends on what kind. And they reload fast."

"How can our warriors defend themselves from your guns?"

Mei laughed, but there wasn't much humor in it. "Take them while they're asleep and pray no one wakes up."

"And are these guns your most powerful weapons?"

Ze was silent for a while before answering, like ze was remembering something. "No," Mei said finally. "Not even close. Very good at killing each other."

Mei's tone sent a shiver running through Kexx's body. Ze hadn't been bragging, or boasting, or bluffing when ze'd told Kuul that zer warriors couldn't beat the humans twice. It wasn't even confidence Mei had shown. It was fear. Ze knew exactly what zer people were capable of, perhaps had even seen it, and it haunted zer.

"But they didn't," Kexx said gently.

"Didn't what?"

"Didn't kill anyone. They shattered Kuul's spear, but that's all. If what you're saying is true, and you've never lied to me before, then they could have killed Kuul and every last one of zer warriors and taken control of the village already. If their advantage is so overwhelming, why didn't they?"

Mei took a moment to collect herself before answering. "We've tried to be better." Mei looked back over zer shoulder at Benson sleeping off the sickness on a cot. "And Benson-san wouldn't stand for it anyway."

"You trust zer that much?"

"With my life," Mei said without hesitation. "With all our lives."

"But ze isn't their leader."

"That doesn't stop Benson."

Again, not a boast, just a recitation of a self-evident fact.

"Thank you, Mei. I should get back to the temple before the evening cleansing. Take care of your friend. I might have some questions for zer when ze's ready."

Mei waved zer hand. "Go take your bath."

Kexx bowed slightly, then jogged back down the hill toward the temple. It was a little joke between them. Coming from anyone else, calling the ritual of purifying the body and soul of the day's dirt before communing with Xis at night a mere bath would have been deeply offensive. Spears had been thrown between tribes for much less. Coming from Mei, however, there was an innocent naiveté that made it funny and endearing.

At twilight, the entire village arrived at the shores of the pond and disrobed. Xis had decreed from deep time that Zer people should enter the dream plains with clean bodies and clean souls. So, just after Cuut dipped below the horizon, but before zer light had entirely faded, the entire village would congregate, child, youth, and elder alike, and wash away the day's oils, dirt, and regrets. Soon, the elders said the words to start the ceremony and everyone took the cue to slip into the water.

Normally, trios of lovers would rinse and tease one another in preparation for the evening's more private festivities, but not tonight. The village's bearers were still being watched underground until Tuko was certain there was no danger to them, the poor creatures. Without the rigor of youth or the wisdom of elders to look after them, the bearers would be as defenseless as infants before their naming. They were rare, with only one or two born to a clutch. And like anything rare, they were precious and required protection.

Several of Mei's humans had taken up the cleansing ritual over the months as well, even though it wasn't required or expected of them. Tuko invited their new guests to attend the ceremony as observers, but their leader, Valmassoi, volunteered to participate. Ze hesitated a bit when Tuko explained that the cleansing could only be undertaken while completely naked, but relented under pressure from the rest of zer people and disrobed to a chorus of hooting and hollering from the assembled humans. Ze complained about a chill in the air, which was met with a round of laughter from zer people, however the joke was lost on Kexx. Mei had explained their discomfort with public nudity once, but Kexx just couldn't get a grip on the concept. They were a strange people.

The warmth trapped from the heat of the sun relaxed the day's stress out of Kexx's tired back and limbs. The rote repetition slipped Kexx into the comfort of the familiar. Aside from a few days spent fighting a fever in zer youth, Kexx had never missed the evening's cleansing. It was a part of the rhythm of the day, as dependable as the sunset itself. It was a signal that the day's labors were over and it was time for rest and reflection.

But even as Kexx repeated the chants and scrubbed zer skin clean, ze couldn't help but feel… hollow, as if something had been misplaced. A horn blew, the sign to wash another's back. Feuding parties washed each other's backs to repair the community bonds broken by the day's arguments. Kuul grudgingly accepted a scrub from Chak, who performed the rite in as perfunctory a manner as was required before returning to the other side of the pond. Kexx, without any great foes at the moment, grabbed a partner at random and tried to let the water rinse away zer unease, but it was a stubborn stain.

Before the sun had started its journey the next morning, a runner appeared in Kexx's hut and gently shook zer awake. Cold and stiff, Kexx blinked and groaned at the disturbance.

"Ugh, what?"

"Chief Tuko wants to speak to you."

"Now? Before breakfast? My head is too cool to think."

"'As soon as is convenient,' were zer exact words," said the young messenger. "There are fires going in the temple. You can warm up there."

Not in a position to refuse, Kexx thanked the runner and rose from zer cot. Ze hurriedly dressed, then grabbed some yulka bread to snack on. Truthfully, the cold wasn't nearly the disadvantage to Kexx that it was to most. Ze'd spent many nights in the wilds and was used to working cool. Of course that didn't mean ze liked it. There were only a hand of years before zer transition to elder, and while ze still felt the heat of youth in zer bloodways, it took longer to flow than it used to. Still, the increased calm and wisdom that came with the transition would be a welcome addition for zer work as truth-digger, even as it sapped some of zer strength and vigor. And enough exercise could counter much of that loss, or delay it at the very least. Maybe ze'd even think seriously about mating as an elder. So far, there just never seemed to be time.

Kexx stepped into the predawn air and listened. Sounds of argument floated up from the temple further down the bowl. Kexx followed the voices and entered to find the elders in a spirited debate, which was a very strange thing for them to be doing while the rest of the village slept. Tradition maintained that the elders' deliberations could be witnessed by all. The door hadn't been barred, so the meeting was technically still open to anyone, except of course no one else was awake to know it was going on.

But stranger by far than the time was the new dome of mudstone at the center of the temple, which two mudstone formers were even now finishing around the rover.

Kexx turned zer attention back to the squabbling elders and made eye contact with the chief. "You asked to speak with me, Tuko?"

"Truth-digger," zer title, Kexx noticed. It was to be a formal occasion. Kexx's suspicions floated higher. "Thank you for coming. I hope we didn't wake you."

Kexx pointed at the new construction. "What's with the hut?"

"Ah, I see you've noticed the inner sanctum we've built to protect the emissary."

So that was the polite fiction they were going with. The hut was built with haste, since last evening's cleansing at the earliest. The mudstone formers looked exhausted, and their usual precision and craftsmanship were not apparent in the finished product. The job had been rushed, hardly appropriate for an "inner sanctum" of such an important relic.

"It's kind of hard to miss. And I doubt very much it's for the *rover*'s protection."

"Watch your tongue," Kuul snapped. "Remember your place here."

"I am remembering my place, warrior," Kexx snapped right back, flashing a challenging burst of light from zer skin. "I am the truth-digger. What good am I if I can't speak plainly what I see right in front of my face? You don't want the rover listening in on us anymore. I can't say I blame you for it, either. But don't insult my intelligence."

Kuul's skin flickered in disbelief, stunned into silence. Ze wasn't used to being addressed in such a manner, and it showed. All things considered, it had been a rough couple of days for the warrior's ego.

Tuko was the one to break the silence. "Too right you are. We decided after the cleansing last night that some privacy for our deliberations about the human question would be best."

"From the humans, I can understand, but this?" Kexx waved a hand around, encompassing everyone standing inside the temple. "When did we start holding meetings while the rest of our people sleep?"

"Have you forgotten we have not one, but now two groups of humans staying within our halo trees?" Kuul recovered enough to ask.

"I haven't. And I call many of those humans friends. Mei's people have been here for six Varrs already peacefully and have taught us much. We should be inviting them to contribute an elder of their own, not running secret meetings to exclude them."

"And Valmassoi's group? What of them? Are you so eager to throw away our sovereignty to them as well?"

Kexx prepared to throw out a nasty little insult about Kuul's impotence to do anything to defend the village's sovereignty, but held back. It was true enough, but hardly Kuul's fault. The sheer power the humans wielded was beyond anything anyone had dreamed possible just the day before. No one could have been adequately prepared for it.

"Why was I called here?" ze asked instead.

Tuko took a step closer to where Kexx stood. "If you had advice for your elders, what would you say about the other villages? Do we keep the human presence here secret, or do we call a gathering?"

Kexx wasted no time considering the question, the answer was obvious. "We can't hope to keep them secret. It's just not possible."

"We've kept our group secret enough," Chak added. "We built their shelter on the far edge opposite to the gate and kept traders outside our walls for that very reason."

Kexx shook zer head in the human gesture. "That was in the lull between harvests. We've only had a handful of traders from the other villages in that time, and the nomads have been strangely absent. Harvest is in less than a Varr. Traders will be swarming the roads. Secrets never stay in one place during harvest season. And besides, the humans *fly*. You're still pretending like we can control anything they do. We can't. If they want to announce themselves to the other villages, there's nothing we can do to stop them. Better to call a gathering and get it over with."

Tuko gripped zer spear a little tighter, a new shaft, Kexx noticed, then turned around to face the rest of the elders. "And this is why we have a truth-digger. Trained from youth to see and say those things that we choose not to. We will call a gathering."

"When?" Chak asked.

"Immediately. Wake the signalers and have them send a message with Cuut's first light."

The decision made, the elders filtered out of the temple and left the mudstone formers to finish their work. Some drifted back to their cots to regain a little lost sleep. Tuko remained behind to pray. It was unclear to whom. A frustrated Kuul roused zer warriors from their beds and led them on a forced run down the road. Judging by Kuul's sour mood, they wouldn't be back until the midday meal, at the earliest.

Kexx, for zer part, made zer way through the halo trees to the signal tower facing west. Kexx climbed it and waited for the sun to rise, passing the time listening to the wind playing through the trees, watching the subtle shifts in the lights of the dux'ah herd as they quietly grazed on the rows of yulka stalks. The youngest dux'ah were always the loudest, flashing their skin with the reckless ignorance of youth, much to the annoyance of the adults. Over time, some of their young friends would fall to an ulik pack and they would learn not to draw so much attention to themselves. Cuut's lessons were harsh, but ultimately strengthened all.

The sun came up and the signaler joined Kexx at the top of the tower.

"Hello, Kexx," ze said. "You have a message to send?"

Kexx waved zer hand in confirmation. "From the chief zerself."

"Well, you're in luck. The new signaler over in Pukal actually wakes up on time."

The signaler translated the message into flashspeak on a scrap of leaf, then aimed the polished crystal shale straight down the road to the next village and flashed the "Ready to send" signal. A short while later, zer counterpart more than a day's walk away acknowledged the signal with three flashes of zer own to say ze was ready to receive the message. From there, it would spread throughout the road network. By midday, every village on the roads would know about the gathering.

It was an amazing, hard-fought accomplishment. Just settling on a single flashspeak every village could agree on had taken more than a year of argument. But even as the signaler spread Tuko's message across the plains, Kexx couldn't help but think about the young dux'ah, brightly flashing their lights for all the world to see, utterly unaware of the peril they invited.

CHAPTER TEN

Benson spent another day and a half "learning his lesson" under Mei's care before he felt well enough to start moving around the village again. Although, to be honest, he was milking it a little by the second day.

It gave him time to catch up with Mei and the other Unbound, to ask about what they'd learned from and about the Atlantians since they'd arrived, and, most importantly, to try to game out what the Atlantians might have learned about them. Therefore, Benson didn't feel too badly about leaning on Mei's hospitality. After all, it was the whole reason he'd been brought along on the expedition in the first place.

He dressed and braved an MRE from the stash they'd brought along from the shuttle. His empty stomach fought against the unappetizing mess for a time, but relented and accepted its fate soon enough.

"Back among the living?" Mei poked her head through the sheet that had been strung up to give Benson some privacy while he recovered. It had been cut up from the sail of their boat.

"Yes, with your help."

"You were fine by dinner yesterday. You're stalling."

"How did you know?"

Mei smacked him on the forehead. "I'm a mother, remember? Always know when boys are fibbing."

Benson smiled innocently. "But it was so relaxing."

"Out." Mei pointed at the village beyond. "Go play with the other kids."

"Yes, Mom."

Benson left the Unbound's shelter behind and strolled down the crater toward the building Chief Tuko had generously donated for the expedition's use. It was a surprisingly large structure, with spacious rooms and generous ceilings, the latter no doubt due to the fact the average Atlantian was a good twenty centimeters taller than their human guests. Benson's guess about the structures had been right; they were made from the same concrete-like material as the road system. In fact, the technology had started with the buildings and had only been expanded to the roads relatively recently, after the Ark had already started its journey some two hundred and thirty-five years earlier. Reinforced with mats of woven branches, the buildings could and had stood up against the strongest hurricanes the ocean threw at them. Necessity really was the mother of invention.

Benson spotted Sergeant Atwood standing watch outside the building's entrance. So Valmassoi was inside.

"Mr Benson," Atwood called out as he approached. "Good to see you moving around."

"I don't know, the rest was nice. I should get sick more often."

"So long as it doesn't involve throwing up on heads of state?"

Benson shrugged. "I only threw up near him."

Atwood shook her head. "Valmassoi's upstairs. I'm sure he's got some questions for you."

"Thanks." Benson moved around her and into the building.

Valmassoi had set up his quarters on the second floor, with most of the rest of expedition's personnel setting up cots and tents on the ground floor. The second story rooms not taken up by Valmassoi's apartment had been hastily appointed as conference rooms. Benson found Valmassoi and his advisors sitting in a circle, talking to Captain Mahama's giant floating head on a potable holo-com rig they'd schlepped in from the *Discovery*.

"Ah, Mr Benson," Valmassoi announced as soon as he was noticed on the other side of Mahama's ghostly cranium. "So glad to have you back in the fold. How are you feeling?"

"Much better, administrator."

"Well, maybe stay an arm's length away, just in case." The rib was met with polite laughter from the rest of the room, although

Mahama declined to join in.

"Food poisoning isn't usually contagious," Benson said. "I thought I'd check back in, and Atwood said you wanted to talk to me?"

"Yes. There's the matter of you needing to apologize to Chief Tuko for throwing up on him."

"*Near* him."

Valmassoi smirked. "Still, an apology is in order. I assume I don't have to order you?"

"No, of course not. I'll do it as soon as he's available."

"Excellent. I'll let his people know."

"His people? Can't I just walk up to him and say I'm sorry?"

Benson's question was met by another round of laughter, longer and heartier.

Valmassoi wiped a tear away from his cheek. "Ah, thank you. I needed that. This is why it's best to leave politics to the politicians."

Gladly, Benson thought, but did not vocalize. "So what are you all scheming about up here?"

"Preparations. Our hosts have called a… gathering of the other villages on their road network. It's quite impressive, actually. They use a system of mirrors to relay information from one village to another in real time. The other villages, some two dozen of them, are sending representatives for a formal meeting, where we will be introduced."

The hair on the back of Benson's neck stood at about forty-five degrees. "And we've agreed to this? Isn't that a pretty big security risk? We've only got four guns against several hundred villagers as it is."

"We've been in discussions with both Sergeant Atwood and Chief Tuko, and they have assured us that between their forces, security won't be an issue. It's not whole villages coming after all, just small delegations."

Benson nodded along, but a bad feeling continued to roil his stomach in a way that he was pretty sure didn't have anything to do with yulka beans.

"But we're all on pins and needles to hear your report, Mr Benson."

"My report?"

"On the Unbound, of course. You've been in their care for a day and a half, surely you gleaned something from the experience."

"I did spend the majority of that time running a fever and dry heaving, I'd have you remember. But yes, I did speak with Mei and a few others, and I think we're going to have very little damage control to do." Benson reflected on his impending apology. "At least on account of anything they've done."

"When did they get there?" Mahama's giant head asked. "Here, I mean."

"About six months ago. They scuttled their ship at night to avoid our satellites, like I thought."

"And they haven't said anything in that whole time?"

Benson shook his head. "Not about us or Shambhala, no. They spent most of that time just learning how to speak the native language with any level of competency. Mei's really got an ear for it. She's even jumped ahead of our translation software in some areas, but she's the outlier. They've hardly had the chance to talk about themselves until recently, much less us. You can all breathe easy. The Unbound made a good first impression for us."

"How can you be sure?" Valmassoi asked.

"They're still alive, aren't they? Without the benefit of rifles and armor."

"True..." Valmassoi tapped a stylus on his desk as he thought through what he'd just learned. "But that still doesn't answer why they came here in the first place."

Benson shrugged. "They wanted to get out from under our thumb."

"We let them start their own village!" Valmassoi said, hardly containing his exasperation.

"Only twenty kilometers away. They knew we were watching them closely."

Valmassoi huffed. "Not closely enough, it would appear."

"See, that's what I'm talking about. It's that paternalistic impulse that they found suffocating. You have to remember, these people grew up almost completely independent of us back on the Ark."

"As 'independent' as parasites can be of their host," someone muttered.

Benson held a hand out to the offender. "Anybody think *that* attitude helped?" He sighed heavily. "They wanted true freedom. That's what they were brought up to value above all else. Above comfort, above the little luxuries, above even knowing when they were getting their next meal. They couldn't get that living so close to us. And frankly, I think a lot of them still feel guilty about Shangri-La module and wanted to put as much distance between themselves and the rest of humanity as possible. I don't think they're in a hurry to bring up those memories. We should do our best not to remind them."

"That's your final recommendation, then? Ignore the problem?"

Benson folded his hands behind his back. "I don't think there *is* a problem, unless you make one. You brought me here to talk to the Unbound and report my findings. I've done that. What you do with those findings is, of course, entirely up to you."

Valmassoi looked around the room and took a quick census of the confused faces and indifferent shrugs before answering. "Thank you, Mr Benson. Now if you'll excuse us, we need to move on to the thorny issue of the sacrifice."

"Sacrifice? That sounds ominous."

Polite laughter made a lap around the room. "Not at all," Valmassoi said. "It's traditional at the beginning of one of these gatherings for each village to make an animal sacrifice to one of their gods or another."

"Like the offerings they used to bring the rover?" Benson asked.

"Quite so, except larger. Tuko has set aside a… dux'ah, I think they call the broom-heads. We need to secure our own animal for the ceremony."

"So the question is do we try to buy one off Tuko, or go capture one ourselves?"

"Just so."

Benson smirked. "I have a better idea."

Valmassoi managed not to roll his eyes. "We're breathless."

Benson ignored the sarcastic tone and turned to Mahama's hologram.

"Captain, can you spare a chicken?"

•••

Days later, a crowd of hundreds looked to the sky as the reentry capsule cut free of its parachutes and fired its retro rockets. Sergeant Atwood ordered her detail to clear the landing zone to avoid any injuries to the spectators as great billowing clouds of steam slowed the last few meters of the capsule's decent. A very clever system of piping sapped heat away from the ablative shield at the craft's bottom and used it to flash boil a couple of thousand liters of water, which was then directed out of four nozzles built into the capsule's base. There was a significant weight penalty inherent in the system, but it had the advantage of being infinitely reusable, so long as there was water to refill it.

Valmassoi leaned over and shouted into Benson's ear. Not to be rude, but just to be heard over the roar of the thrusters. "Mahama is going to want it back, you know."

"Why would she want a dead chicken?"

"Not the chicken, the reentry pod."

"No problem. We'll stick it on the shuttle and send it up the elevator when we get back."

The winds above the village's ring of trees caught the trio of orange and white parachutes and blew them out of sight as the capsule settled down onto its landing pads. Several brave onlookers cautiously moved toward the pod, but Korolev shouted a warning. The heat shield was still several hundred degrees from the friction of reentry, after all. They moved back and blended into the larger crowd of enthralled Atlantians.

"Correct me if I'm wrong," Valmassoi said. "But this seems like another of those shows of force you turn your nose up at."

"Not at all. This–" Benson held out his arms as the capsule gave a dying hiss, "–is all about style points. May I?"

Valmassoi laughed and invited Benson forward. "Be my guest."

Benson strode confidently up to the capsule and popped the latches on the outer door. Strapped to the floor inside a custom-fitted foam packing crate struggled the most wide-eyed and panic-stricken chicken in the long, anxious history of the species. To be fair, it had been through a lot over the last few hours.

Benson hunched over to fit through the small door to get inside. The frame around the hatch was still warm to the touch, but not painfully so. Once inside, it was just him and the wildly clucking chicken. He reached down and found the latches for the crate.

"OK, Nuggets, just relax." He tried to stroke the bird's head to calm it, and was promptly rewarded with a nasty bite.

"Ow! You little shit." Benson clamped down on the chicken's neck. "And I almost felt bad for you." He undid the latches and pulled the lid off the crate, expecting to grab its wings with his free hand.

Instead, freed of its restraints and driven over the edge of terror into blind fury, the chicken proceeded to reenact a historic illegal Mexican cock fight, despite itself being a hen.

"Jesus Christ!" Benson's arms windmilled through the air as the chicken's beak and claws made a beeline for his face.

"Everything OK in there?" Valmassoi's voice taunted from outside.

"Fine!" Benson shouted between the furious flapping of wings. "Just peachy."

Then, in an unmatched feat of strength and desperation, the chicken wrenched itself free of Benson's grasp and managed to awkwardly flap its way out of the open hatch into the open air. The chicken's first and final flight was as valiant as it was short. It came to rest less than a meter outside the capsule's door among a cloud of slowly descending downy feathers.

Benson emerged from the pod, bleeding from a dozen superficial wounds to his face and forearms and mad as hell.

"Nobody touch the damned thing!"

The circle of human and Atlantian bystanders took a collective step back, despite the majority of them not having the first clue what he'd said. Some because of the crazy-eyed, blood-covered human leaning out the door, and some out of cautious respect for the tiny alien creature that had inflicted his wounds. Undeterred, Benson took off his shirt and held it out as a makeshift net, then jumped down on the offending fowl like an avenging angel and quickly wrapped it up.

His pointy, squawking foe vanquished and wrapped up tightly in his shirt, Benson walked purposefully over and handed the writhing package to the grinning administrator.

"And how many 'style points' did that earn you?" Valmassoi asked innocently.

Benson held up a finger. "I don't care how you make it happen. I get to be the one that kills it."

Valmassoi held a hand against his chest. "I'm shocked. Is the famous Zero Champion always so vindictive toward his foes?"

"My foes never went well with honey mustard before."

"Well, you never know until you try."

Benson actually laughed. "What a tasteless joke, administrator."

"Careful, we're about to get stuck in a joke loop. I'll be sure you get the honor, Mr Benson. Now, if you'll excuse me, we have some preparations to make." Valmassoi held the chicken up over his head and made his way through the rapidly parting crowd toward the temple.

The ceremony started not long after. Chief Tuko, being the host, was the first to make an offering. He'd selected his own personal dux'ah mount to really drive home the importance of the occasion. Benson winced as the chief plunged his ceremonial spear into the unsuspecting creature's torso, just ahead of its legs. The immense dux'ah shrieked in surprise and terror at its master's betrayal, a sound Benson wouldn't soon forget. Mercifully, Tuko's aim was true. The beast staggered once, then collapsed.

Benson leaned over to whisper to Korolev standing guard. "Broom-heads don't have hearts. What the hell did he hit with that spear?"

Korolev shook his head gravely. "No idea. Sure would be a handy thing to know, though."

"I'll make sure to ask him."

A representative from each village stepped forward to sanctify the sacrifice with a short prayer before throwing a handful of reddish powder into the air. Then they cut out a choice piece of flesh for the coming feast. In short order, Tuko's offering was butchered and distributed among the crowd. In an order determined by a dizzying formula including how long each village had been on the road network, harvest sizes, personal favors among the elders, and who knew what else, the rest of the representatives took their turns at the sacrificial altar.

Not every offering went as smoothly as Tuko's, however. Even fitted with blinders to calm them, the dux'ahs' agitation grew with every dying shriek, until it took a great deal of wrangling to get them into place. And not all of those striking had Tuko's aim and skill with a spear, either. Several of the animals took multiple stabs and many minutes to succumb.

The penultimate sacrifice was muscled into position. It was a bruiser, and made it immediately apparent to everyone that it wanted nothing to do with the proceedings. While not as big as the broom-head Tuko had offered, this one was alert and tense as a coiled spring. It reeked of musk, and its skin flashed waves of rapidly shifting spirals. The pattern changed so fast, Benson had to glance away or risk getting vertigo.

<I don't like the look of this one,> he said into the security detail's private com line.

<Me either,> Atwood agreed. <Is it even domesticated?>

<Seems pretty damned wild to me,> Korolev added.

<Keep your weapons secured,> Atwood said. <We can't risk offending one of the factions.>

<I'd rather be offended than dead,> Benson said.

<Not our call.>

Benson took a very deliberate step backwards. The feral dux'ah strained against its restraints with a determination fueled by desperation. His earlier encounter with the chicken seemed comical in comparison.

The elder stepped up to finish the animal, but his first thrust missed its mark, sending the broom-head even deeper into its frenzy. With a mighty twist of its head, the beast yanked one of its handlers clean off his feet and sent him pinwheeling through the air before he collapsed into a heap on the ground.

The Atlantian's limbs were crumpled at impossible angles from the impact. Benson's first instinct was to run to the downed alien's aid, but to his amazement, the "injured" creature untangled his horribly bent limbs and shot right back to his feet. Benson wasn't the only one to notice.

"Resilient little bastards, aren't they?" Korolev said under his breath.

"No kidding." Benson watched in fascination as the Atlantian who'd just been thrown like a child's doll scampered back to his rope and helped get the beast under control as if nothing had happened.

A call for help went out and four more warriors from other villages, including one Benson was nearly certain was Kuul, stepped up and drove their spears into the broom-head. It took many strikes before the animal finally fell. After the prayers were said and the flesh was collected, it was the humans' turn to make their sacrifice.

"Showtime," Valmassoi handed the hooded chicken to Benson. "Make us proud."

"Thanks." Benson took the bird under an arm and grabbed the handle of his survival knife.

He squared his shoulders and strode up to the sacrificial altar. A chorus of laughter followed him. With the spectacle of the reentry capsule now a few hours old and the parade of broom-heads that had come before, the bird looked a little undersized for the occasion.

Kuul shouted something from the sidelines. "Do you need us to tie it down for you?"

"I'll manage," Benson shouted back as soon as his translator fed him the reply. This was met with another round of laughter, but Benson ignored them and set the bird down on the cool black stone. The chicken was calmer now than it had been in the capsule, doubtless due in part to the hood covering its eyes. Benson's previous bloodlust faded as he glanced down at the condemned and pulled the knife from its sheath. He held it up toward the sun, imitating what he'd seen the others do. Sunlight glinted off the polished metal as the crowd's laughter was replaced by a hush of reverence.

He'd never actually taken a life before, not personally. In Benson's days as chief constable, he'd captured people who had later been put to death. He'd even shot a man, once. But he'd been armed with a knife, and had had every intention of leaving it inside Benson's chest cavity.

Now, he held the knife. And even though it was just a chicken, Benson didn't feel any better about it.

"Sorry, buddy," he said under his breath. "But you were going to be Buffalo wings either way." With the eyes of the crowd on him, Benson tensed for the strike, but it never fell.

From the edge of the forest, an Atlantian came running down the hill, waving its arms and shouting wildly. Whatever it wanted, Benson's translator couldn't make out the words. An instant later, dozens upon dozens of blackened warriors came streaming out of the forest behind the newcomer. At the same moment, several warriors inside the crowd nearest to the quartet of Atwood's security detail lifted their spears and charged.

<Multiple contacts!> Benson shouted into their com line. <Pavel, behind you!>

Then, the real sacrifice began.

CHAPTER ELEVEN

Kexx moved carefully through the thick bramble of Cuut's Tentacle vines weaving through the trunks and branches of the halo trees. The vines themselves were harmless enough. Dried, beaten, and braided properly, their fibers made stout rope. Their seed pods, on the other hand...

Ze ducked gently under one of the large, purple pods. As long as one of Kexx's arms, it was deadly serious business at such short range, but the color of this one meant it hadn't dried out enough to pose an immediate danger. Behind zer, the startled sounds of sacrifices at the altar permeated the forest. The gathering's opening ceremony was in full swing. Soon, the succulent aroma of roasting dux'ah meat would waft through the village.

Kexx's stomach gurgled in anticipation of the evening's feast, but there was still work to be done. The signaler had reported noises around the tower before the ceremony had begun, so Tuko had sent Kexx to scout the forest for anyone who wasn't supposed to be there. The dangerous vines did an admirable job of keeping out stray uliks and the occasional nomadic tribe turned marauders. But their visitors had come from other villages on the road network, villages almost identical to Kexx's own. The forest wouldn't present much of a barrier to any of them.

Generations of smaller animals had laid down safe paths through the tangle of seed pods, if you knew where to look for the signs and kept your head low enough. Kexx kept mostly to these paths, but also had to keep a sharp eye out for traces of wanderers who didn't know the little tricks of the forest as well as ze did. Despite being just after midday, the canopy above blocked out most of the light from reaching the forest floor, and the intermittent beams and stripes of light that did reach only managed to break up outlines and confuse Kexx's eyes as they constantly tried to shift from day to night viewing.

The shifting light used to give zer a headache, but Kexx had spent enough time in the woods to grow out of it. Zer own skin shifted to match the contrasting patterns. A camouflaging trick zer mentor had ground into zer until it took almost no conscious effort at all. Kexx's tracking skills took over. With the clutter of leaf litter covering the ground, there was nothing as obvious as a footprint in the dirt. Instead, ze searched for tiny disturbances in the leaves, broken twigs, vines moved out of place. Ze started at the base of the signal tower and moved outward in a spiral, ignoring the path the signaler used to focus on the wild woods.

It was tedious, mentally draining work, but Kexx soon fell into a rhythm. There was actually quite a bit to see. The jurki bushes were flowering, soaking the air with their sweet fragrance and bringing out a swarm of hungry flies. They were too busy gathering the energy-dense nectar to bother stinging Kexx, for once. In another two days, it would be time to harvest the slightly wilted flowers to distill them into wine, perfumes, and a half-fullhand of other products unique to Kexx's village. The bushes preferred the salty air near the ocean. Other villages had tried to cultivate their own crops, but the end products always proved inferior, giving zer village valuable leverage in trade.

But for how much longer? The old assumptions and alliances that had built trade between the villages, the road network, and the signal towers were all about to be completely upended by the humans' arrival. Their tools were mindbending. The sort of things the humans took for granted, like their great bird, were simply beyond Kexx's comprehension. What could G'tel, or any of the villages, possibly offer them? And what industry would the humans not immediately come to dominate? Kuul and Tuko were worried about their guns, but Kexx was coming to think the real danger the humans posed was more subtle and wider reaching than something as blunt as a new weapon.

As ze followed the lazy spiral, Kexx's frustration grew. Ze

found a nest that had fallen out of the canopy during last night's high winds, a flattened spot in the leaf litter where a stray ulik had bedded down for the night, a pile of fresh excrement from the same. Lap after lap, ze saw life in the forest carrying on as usual, and no signs of intrusion whatsoever.

Ze was wasting zer time in a hunt for what felt more and more like the aural hallucinations of a distracted signaler with each lap, while all of the excitement was happening back at the ceremony. That was where zer eyes could be put to use. Maybe that had been the point of sending zer out here, to make sure the truth-digger wasn't nearby when anything actually important happened.

The thought lodged itself into Kexx's mind and stuck there like a thorn. It dug deeper with each lap until Kexx was so distracted ze walked right past the dried fungus stems strewn across the ground near the base of a tree trunk. It was another three steps before the strangeness of it clicked and ze spun back around. Ze leaned down and picked up one of the shriveled stems. It was grey with dark red dots. Kexx bit off the end experimentally and ground up a small piece between zer teeth. It was bitter and meaty, but ze didn't recognize the variety and spat it back out. Ze'd learned early the dangers of eating unfamiliar fungi.

There weren't any fungi in zer woods that were unknown to Kexx. This was an invader brought into the forest from the outside, and recently. So close to the ocean, the air was humid. Things here didn't desiccate, they rotted. They'd been brought into the woods and eaten, probably within the last day. But by whom, that was the question.

Kexx's tongue and gums started to tingle where ze'd chewed on the stem. So, it was a drug fungus. Most likely the remnants of an amorous trio sneaking off into the woods for a private tryst, the fungus playing the part of some kind of aphrodisiac. Probably a mixed group from two or more of the other villages. Gatherings offered one of the few opportunities each year for such intervillage dalliances, and while the practice wasn't openly acknowledged, it did keep the breeding pools fresh.

The only real danger was to the bearer. If it was discovered they carried a brood from another village, the consequences could be severe. No village could afford to have their bearers splitting their loyalties.

A careful reading of the leaves near where ze'd found the stems revealed the subtle depressions where they'd laid down, all but confirming zer theory. Kexx breathed a sigh of relief and rested zer spear across zer shoulders. Another mystery solved, it was time to get back to the ceremony before ze missed all of the action, not to mention the food.

Ze started back toward the center of the village, but something nagged at zer, fighting for attention. Kexx glanced down at zer feet, trying to think through whatever ze could be missing. Suddenly, ze ground to a full stop and stared at the ground around zer feet as the realization dawned.

If ze was right, then where were the tracks leading back to the village? Kexx knelt down, then got on all fours trying to spot any little disturbances in the leaves. The trio would be in the post-mating glow, in a haze of drugs, and in a hurry to get back to the village. Hardly the best frame of mind for the delicate work of concealing your movement. But no matter how hard Kexx looked, ze just couldn't make tracks appear.

Flustered, ze stood back up and pondered the situation. If they hadn't come from the village, there was one direction they *could* have come from. Kexx spun around, and immediately had to throw out zer theory about the amorous trio.

For one thing, there were more than three of them. A lot more. For another, their skin was coated in a thick layer of dried mud mixed with ash and leaves. And if that wasn't enough, the spears pointed at Kexx's throat sealed the deal.

Kexx took a long step back and spun the spear hanging on zer shoulders around, deftly knocking the nearest point away. Zer feet wanted to run, but the moment zer back was turned, the painted intruders would run zer through like a dux'ah tenderloin. Instead, Kexx brought zer spear up to a ready defensive posture and spoke low and slow.

"You obviously took great care to get here undetected. If I see one muscle twitch, I start screaming and bring the village down on you like the Seeds of Cuut."

Kexx caught a flicker of movement in zer peripheral vison. Ze was being flanked.

"Stop where you are, I'm not bluffing."

A ripple of light passed between members of the intruders through small, uncamouflaged patches of skin, flowing in the direction of a particular member in the back. Their leader. Whoever they were, they were highly trained and communicating in coded bursts. Kexx's hopes for surviving the encounter sank, but ze'd be damned if ze was going to let them step one foot closer to zer village.

The leader set down zer spear and walked forward with hands held out. Kexx's hands tightened on the spear shaft involuntarily, but allowed zer to approach. Softly, careful not to let zer voice carry, the leader spoke. "Truth-digger?" Kexx nodded. "And a good one. Your village would miss you if we had to kill you." Zer voice was heavily accented in a way Kexx couldn't place.

"Then turn around and leave," Kexx demanded, but the leader ignored zer.

"Lay down your spear and allow us to pass. You will not be harmed."

Kexx shook zer head in the human way, not even aware ze was doing it. "That's not going to happen."

"Then we will stake your feet and hands to a tree at the edge of the forest and open your belly for the uliks to feast on."

"How vivid. But I doubt you can do all that before I can scream and bring Kuul's warriors running."

"Kuul?"

"Your opposite. Most disagreeable, that one, and spoiling for a fight."

The ashen specter held zer arms out. "And what do you suppose my warriors are spoiling for? I am not fond of needless bloodshed, truth-digger, but I can't say the same for some of the spears pointed at you. Let us pass, or let us speed you to Xis's warm embrace. It's your choice, but make it quickly."

There was a finality in zer voice that Kexx felt compelled to obey. Then, a not-so-gentle prodding at Kexx's side reminded zer that ze was surrounded. Crestfallen, Kexx threw zer spear into the dirt and surrendered, sure that the killing blow would follow, but determined to put every bit of zer last breath into a warning cry at the first prick of a spearpoint.

But the blow never landed. True to zer word, the leader signaled zer troops onward. Silently, they flowed around Kexx like a slow river trickling around a rock, leaving no trace of their passing. And no warning of their arrival.

Kexx stood there for a long, tense moment, watching them advance on the village. They stretched out in all directions. First fullhands, then hundreds. They had completely infiltrated the forest. Kexx must have walked within arm-spans, hand-spans of some of them without spotting any of them.

Whoever they were, Kuul wouldn't stand a chance so long as they carried the element of surprise. The humans might fare better for a time, but only four of them carried the miraculous guns. Kexx couldn't imagine even their mighty technology saving the humans from being overwhelmed by what was coming.

Kexx looked down at the spear by zer feet, knowing full well that the outcome of the coming battle hinged on what ze did in the next few moments. A decision crystalized in zer mind.

"Fuck it."

Riding high on Mei's words of irreverence, Kexx got a toe under the spear and kicked it back up into zer grip, then heaved it for all ze was worth at the biggest seed pod in sight, hanging just over the heads of the advancing warriors. Kexx hit the ground and curled up to protect zer head.

The instant the obsidian point touched the husk of the seed pod, filaments inside the skin stretched taut over Varrs finally tore the fragile membranes that held the four sections together. In the blink of an eye, each section of husk coiled back like a spring, revealing fullhands of hard, teardrop-shaped seeds each the size of a clenched fist and flung them in all directions faster than could be thrown by any arm.

Caught out in the open completely unaware, nearby intruders were pummeled, but the first wave was only the beginning. Two of the seeds struck other pods by chance, which then erupted, throwing fullhands more seeds, striking still more pods. A chain reaction quickly spread through the vines and turned the woods into a boiling cauldron of projectiles, falling leaves, broken branches, and the screams of the wounded.

Even curled into a tight ball, Kexx was struck twice on the

back, leaving angry welts. The seeds were seldom deadly with anything but a lucky hit to the base of the neck at the right angle, but a victim could suffer deep bruises, have the wind knocked from their air sacks, or even receive a concussion severe enough to lose consciousness.

As soon as the hailstorm of seeds began to ebb, Kexx was back on zer feet, running full out for the safety of the village. Ze hurdled over still prone intruders, many of them writhing in pain and clutching blows to their arms, chests, and heads. Ze bent down just long enough to snatch up a dropped spear. Directly ahead, Kexx spotted the intruder's leader standing back up. With anger and battle lust surging through zer bloodways, Kexx shouted a war cry, leveled the spear in zer hands, and charged right for the leader's face.

At the last moment, Kexx's target turned and saw the attack coming. With practiced reflexes, the leader's own spear came down and deflected Kexx's spearhead away from zer face, causing the deathblow to miss low. But the parry wasn't entirely successful as the black glass tip pierced the leader's upper thigh, shredding muscle and sinew until it erupted out the back of zer leg. Ze fell back to the ground with a crest-shriveling cry. Ze would survive, but was out of the fight.

Without missing a step, Kexx let go of the spear shaft and continued running blindly through the forest even as the other warriors got up and returned to their senses. Spears whistled past Kexx as ze ran, each one threatening to bring zer down to be torn apart by the intruders now bent on revenge.

Most of the seed pods in the immediate area had been triggered by Kexx's trap, but not all. Kexx did zer best to dodge those that remained without giving up the speed which was keeping zer alive. With zer legs burning, Kexx broke through the tree line, momentarily blinded by the bright light of the early afternoon. Ze accelerated down the rim of the bowl even as zer pursuers emerged from the forest.

Waving zer arms, Kexx started shouting in G'tel, human, whatever would get enough attention to summon help. Preferably of the heavily armed and irate variety. With clear sightlines, the accuracy of zer pursuers' spears improved immensely. Kexx weaved back and forth as ze ran, trying to throw off their aim. A fresh stab of pain rang out as a speartip grazed zer leg, tearing a nasty gash in the skin but fortunately leaving the muscle untouched.

Ze quit zigzagging and ran flat out for the first ring of homes where ze could finally get behind some cover. Just as Kexx reached the first house, a spear struck the wall not half an arm-span to zer left. The glass point shattered against the rock-hard mudstone, sending a hail of shards in all directions and cutting Kexx just below zer left eye. A finger thickness higher and ze would've been blinded.

It's nothing, keep moving, Kexx told zerself. Ahead at the ceremony site, ze could barely make out Tuko and the other village elders standing near the visiting human delegation. For once, Kexx was relieved to see Kuul standing close by. Ze called out to them again, but even as Kexx shouted, a commotion broke out among the delegations. Warriors ze didn't recognize started attacking the humans. Mei's friend, Benson, dove at one of them and they began to wrestle. Without warning, a sharp sound like a giant tree snapping in the wind slammed into Kexx's ears.

Then, the thunder rolled in.

CHAPTER TWELVE

Benson took six steps before realizing he'd made the decision to start running. Korolev was already on the ground, pinned underneath one of the foreign warriors. The Atlantian had tried to run his friend through from behind with a spear, only to watch the point snap off against Korolev's riot armor. The big bruiser didn't miss a beat and knocked Korolev down before he could get his rifle up, then started choking him out with the spear shaft.

While completely unarmed, Benson wasn't a small man. He'd been an athlete for more than half of his life and had never let his conditioning slip, even after retiring from Zero. For the last three months, he'd been running American football drills right alongside the team he was training. So when he got up to full speed and tucked his shoulder for an open-field tackle, nothing short of one of Shambhala's prefab concrete buildings was going to remain unmoved.

Benson plowed into the alien straddling his friend like a runaway elevator car. The Atlantian's lack of a rigid skeleton was the only thing that kept his ribcage from shattering, and, quite possibly, from Benson dislocating his shoulder as well. They rolled together once, twice, before coming to rest.

The Atlantian won the roll and landed on top. He grabbed for Benson's throat with strange, rubbery hands and squeezed for all he was worth. But Benson had dealt with enough domestic disturbances in his time as a constable to know how to handle a choke hold. He had five, maybe ten seconds to react before blacking out; plenty of time to snake his hand up between his attacker's arms and jam a thumb in the alien's eye.

It's a constant throughout the universe that things really, really don't like getting poked in the eye. The Atlantian proved no different and released his death grip on Benson's neck to get away from the thumb. The Atlantian reached back and grabbed an obsidian dagger from somewhere in his skirts, then raised and pointed it at Benson's chest, ready to drive it through him and into the ground like a tent stake.

The bark of Korolev's rifle struck Benson's ears like a hammer, but not nearly as hard as the bullet struck his attacker's head. It popped like a party balloon filled with red velvet cake. The nearly headless body spasmed and slumped backward, spurting blood and gore as it folded into the dirt.

Then, the thunder of guns erupted.

Benson squirmed out from under the lifeless body as fast as he could and found a hand waiting to help him to his feet.

"We gotta move, chief!" Korolev shouted over the rat-tat-tat of automatic weapons fire.

"No shit!" Benson pointed at the flood of charcoal-colored warriors streaming down from the edge of the forest.

Korolev's eyes went wide as the full realization of their situation hit home. <We've got incoming!> he shouted into their private com line. <Down the hill to the west.>

<Holy fuck,> one of the others said.

<Secure the chatter,> Sergeant Atwood replied, calm and professional. <Conserve your ammo. Switch to two-round burst and check your targets. Hamilton, take up sniper position in one of the structures. DeSanto, form up on me. Korolev, grab Napoleon and get him to shelter.>

"Napoleon?" Benson whispered to Korolev.

"Valmassoi's call sign. It was randomly generated."

Sure it was, Benson thought before speaking into the com. <And Chief Tuko?>

<Not our problem,> Atwood said in between bursts from her rifle. <We don't even know who's attacking us.>

<Roger that.>

Atwood and her people made short work of the assassins

hidden among the ceremony's ranks. Bodies, both Atlantian and human, proved that it hadn't been without casualties, but there was no time to count the dead and wounded with the real fight charging down on them.

"I could use a hand, chief," Korolev said.

Benson, still flying high on adrenaline, wiped the blood and brain matter off his face and ran his hand over his pants. "Lead the way."

Valmassoi wasn't far away, but someone had gotten to him first. Benson spotted the administrator lying face down near the sacrificial altar as the shouting of warriors and the percussion of rifle fire echoed through the crater.

Benson pointed. "There! I think he's hurt."

<Sergeant, Napoleon is down. I repeat, Napoleon is down.>

The two of them ran the last few steps to where Valmassoi had fallen. Blood soaked through his tan shirt and stained it brown in a half dozen places.

"Oh, he's hurt all right." Benson leaned down and squeezed Valmassoi's neck. "I have a pulse, but it's faint."

"Can we chance moving him?"

Benson nodded toward the coming horde. "We can't chance *not* moving him."

Korolev bent over and rolled Valmassoi over, then gathered up his arms to pick him up. But Benson stopped him. "No, I'll carry him. I'm stronger than you and I need you to cover me with that cannon."

Benson grunted as he hefted Valmassoi's limp body onto his shoulders into an army man carry and stood.

Korolev shouldered his rifle and pointed it for the hill. "Where to, chief?"

Benson scanned his surroundings, looking for the most secure place to hole up, but nothing recommended itself. The Atlantian's buildings were robust, but they'd been built to withstand hurricanes, not invading armies. Most didn't even have doors.

But he knew one place that did.

"The reentry capsule. Let's go."

Korolev nodded and started for the pod at a jog. Benson followed, struggling to maintain his balance under the awkward load. Fortunately, the capsule hadn't been moved since landing east of the temple, carrying them away from the invaders and buying them precious time.

"Hurry, chief. They're gaining!"

"Some of us are running for two, constable," Benson huffed.

"Just be glad he's not Lindqvist," Korolev said, referring to the Mustangs' middle linebacker.

Benson shuddered at the thought. Suddenly, Valmassoi didn't feel all that heavy. The crater's incline was just starting to ramp up as they reached the capsule. Korolev swung the hatch open and jumped inside just as Benson's legs threatened to combust. He set Valmassoi down on the lip of the entrance as gently as he could, then grabbed the unconscious man's feet while Korolev pulled the administrator inside by his arms.

They set him down on the floor and Korolev checked for a pulse again.

"Still with us, barely."

"Put pressure on the worst wounds," Benson said.

"Here?" Korolev pointed to a nasty stab wound below Valmassoi's heart.

"Yes."

"I can't believe he's still alive after all this."

"I don't think they knew where to stab him." Benson looked back out the hatch to see the first wave of blackened invaders crash headlong into the hodgepodge of Atlantian warriors hastily assembled to oppose them. Short, paired bursts of fire from Atwood's security team tore mercilessly at the advancing hostiles, but weren't having the effect one would hope.

"Lock this hatch behind me," Benson grabbed Korolev's shoulder. "Shoot anything that tries to come through that isn't human. Valmassoi is your priority now."

"Where are you going, chief?"

"To help." Benson crawled out and slammed the hatch shut behind him, then waited just long enough to hear the locking bolts click into place. Satisfied Korolev was following instructions for once, Benson turned and ran back toward the sounds of battle, not at all confident that it was the smart thing to do.

<Benson,> Atwood shouted into their shared com. <I've lost

Korolev's feed. Do you have eyes on him?>

<He's fine, sergeant. He and, ah, Napoleon are locked up in the reentry capsule. The hull is just blocking his signal.>

<Smart thinking. What's Napoleon's status?>

<Alive, but seriously wounded. He needs a medical evac, pronto.>

<Understood.>

The line went silent as Benson reached the edge of the mêlée. Chaos reigned among the fighters exchanging spears, daggers, and gunfire, and the civilians trying desperately to get out of the way. The battle lines, such as they were, had shifted toward the boundary of the second ring of buildings. Kuul and his warriors had formed up into a defensive line to try to break the wave of painted invaders. DeSanto had joined Hamilton on an adjacent rooftop using his rifle to pick off targets of opportunity, while Atwood had waded right into the thick of things. The human delegation had moved out of sight.

Benson reached down and plucked a spear off the ground next to a fallen Atlantian. It had a big center point with two smaller tines jutting out at about thirty degrees. From the look of it, it was probably a fishing trident grabbed in desperation rather than a proper battle implement. The weapon was long for his arms and felt a little unwieldy, but it was better than nothing.

<Mr Benson, we have a problem,> Atwood said.

<You mean a *bigger* problem than being overrun by hostile savages?>

<I can't raise the shuttle.>

Benson stopped. They were already working near the limits of their plant's range just to communicate with the *Discovery*. Its communication equipment acted as a relay back up to the Ark and then back down to Shambhala. If they couldn't talk to the shuttle, they couldn't talk to *anybody*.

<That's a bigger problem,> he said.

<No shit,> Hamilton interjected as his rifle burped from the nearby rooftop.

<Can we signal the Ark with a flare or something?>

<Not for another seventeen minutes,> Atwood said. <We're in a satellite coverage gap.>

<Of course we are.> Benson's grip on the borrowed trident tightened. Another amazingly inconvenient coincidence. <I'm armed. Where do you want me?>

<Fall back to the temple and protect our civilians. Our rifles aren't doing the job like I thought they would.>

<Center mass won't cut it,> Benson said. <They don't have hearts to stop. But headshots work just fine.>

<Hear that, boys?>

<Yes, ma'am,> DeSanto and Hamilton replied in unison. Their guns opened up again as Benson ran for the relative safety of the temple. But before he reached the sanctuary, one of the black-clad invaders snuck through the line of defenders and jumped in front of his path. The alien wasted no time and thrust the tip of his spear for Benson's stomach. With a move borne more of desperate reflex than skill, Benson deflected the spear point with the shaft in his hands, then shoulder-checked the warrior as hard as he could.

But instead of flying back, the Atlantian sort of folded around Benson with the impact. He was used to sparring with other humans who all had a defined shape you could count on. These aliens, on the other hand, were so unnervingly flexible, he may as well have been fighting butterscotch pudding.

Benson fell back as fast as he could without tipping over himself, but the intruder pressed the attack, thrusting wildly with the spear as he advanced. Benson parried as quickly as he could, and even managed to trap his opponent's spear between two of his trident's prongs for a split-second before he pulled it free and reset for another thrust. Benson took a long step back, but, to his horror, something caught his trident and stopped him dead. He glanced back and realized the butt of its overly long shaft had caught in a small hollow.

Before he could free it, the intruder pounced. In a panic, Benson drew the head of his trident up, closed his eyes, and braced for the spear that was about to run him through. His body shuddered from the impact, but instead of being impaled, he was surprised to feel only a small sting just below his hip.

Benson peeled his eyes open and saw a small rip in his pants where the speartip had pierced, but nothing more. He looked up into the alien's oversized violet eyes, or more accurately, eye, the other one having been skewered like an oversized cocktail olive by the trident's large center spike, the last few centimeters of which protruded out the back of his attacker's head in a most grisly fashion. The alien's legs continued to walk forward while its hands tried in vain to grip a spear shaft that was no longer there. It would take a little longer for the rest of its peripheral nervous system to get the memo that the brain was stone dead. In the meantime, the corpse soldiered on, shuffling like a windup toy, held in place by Benson's trident. Benson had never killed anyone before. He looked at the alien's slack, dead face in dawning horror.

An extraordinarily confused sacrificial chicken chose that instant to wander past, stopping to scratch for grain near the alien's still-milling feet. For a mad moment, Benson broke out laughing as his brain rebelled at the absurdity of everything he was seeing. *No way* that *doesn't turn into a recurring nightmare*, he thought as the image found a nice comfortable spot to burrow into his subconscious.

Someone shouted from the temple behind him and snapped Benson back into the moment. It was one of the members of the expedition. He forgot the trident and ran for the door. Benson dove the last meter and rolled to a stop just inside the entrance.

A forest of hands, both human and Atlantian, reached down to help him back to his feet. It took a moment for Benson's eyes to adjust to the weaker torchlight inside the temple. He scanned the room for Mei or any of the other Unbound.

"Weapon," he said hurriedly. "I need a weapon."

His software produced a translation, and instantly a dozen hands waved a dozen obsidian knives in the air for him to choose from. Benson was on somewhat firmer ground when it came to knives. They'd been the weapon of choice for the desperate or disturbed during his law enforcement career aboard the Ark, and he still carried the scars to prove it. He'd taken the time to get trained up on them. He grabbed one of the offered blades and flipped it around in his palm to get a feel for its weight and balance. The handle was a little thick in his hand, but he'd manage.

<Sergeant Atwood, I'm in position inside the temple.> Benson adjusted his grip and moved to just inside the door to get a good look at the approach. <Sergeant?>

<Atwood's down,> Hamilton said from his perch. <We can't get a line on her without leaving the nest.>

<I'll get her. Cover me.>

<Negative,> DeSanto said. <We're almost black on ammo.>

<How's Kuul holding up?>

<Not well. We can buy you five more minutes, max.>

Benson rubbed the sweat from his forehead. <Understood. Give them hell.> He cut the line and glanced around at the mix of humanity and aliens holed up in the temple around him. Most of the faces from the expedition were sprinkled among the survivors. He had no illusions about what would happen to them if he didn't act. If Kuul's line broke and the village was overrun, the temple would offer no defense, and there was still another ten or twelve minutes before he could expect any kind of help from the Ark.

If they didn't move right now, everyone inside the temple would die.

Benson was tucking the knife into his waistband when he realized something was missing.

"Where's the Unbound?" he asked the closest human, one of Valmassoi's clique.

"I, ah…" Uncomprehending shock was etched into the woman's face. She looked around as if in a fog. "I think they went to their shelter."

Benson nodded, then cleared his throat and raised his arms. "Eyes on me!"

The humans inside broke off their nervous conversations and turned to face him, while many of the Atlantians did the same. The sudden silence and attention threw him off for a step.

"Good, good." He tried to regain his mental balance. "Here's the deal, we have maybe five minutes before our guys run out of bullets. We can't be here when that happens."

"Where's the administrator?" someone shouted from the back.

"He's alive," Benson said, hoping it was still true. "Valmassoi is locked inside the reentry capsule under guard."

"Well why don't we just join him, then?"

Benson shook his head. "Because even if we all fit, which we wouldn't, we'd suffocate in about ten minutes."

"But we don't even know who's attacking us!"

"Why does that matter?"

"Well, maybe they aren't interested in us. Maybe if we go talk to them…"

Benson held his arm out to the door. "Be my guest. Let us know how it goes."

"Well, I didn't… I mean, I'm hardly qualified–"

Benson cut the man off. "Any other volunteers? No? Good. So, as I was saying, we have to move out while the security detail can still cover our retreat. That means right now."

"We're going back to the shuttle?"

"No, we lost contact with the shuttle. We have to assume it's been lost."

The crowd's attitude shifted. Benson had seen it before, the moment when a group of anxious individuals turned ugly and a violent mob was born. Except he could really use a violent mob right about now. The only trouble with mobs was controlling them.

"Everyone, please, stay with me. In another ten minutes the satellite network will be back in visual range and the Ark will realize something's up. We just have to stay alive until that happens, so if no one has any better ideas, follow me."

Filled with fresh hope, the mob settled back down into a more orderly form and made their way outside behind Benson. They'd gone a hundred meters before he realized what a colossal idiot he'd been.

"Stupid, stupid, stupid," Benson admonished himself as he realized his mistake.

"Come again?" someone asked.

"Nevermind! Back to the temple, everybody."

"But you said–"

"Forget what I said and listen to what I'm saying. Temple, double time!" The crowd did an about face in spite of their confusion and jogged back toward the shelter. Benson opened a com line. <DeSanto. You still alive?>

   <Never better, sir.>

   <And Hamilton?>

   <I'm holding position for now, sir.>

   <Good. Fall back to the temple with the rest of us, the both of you.>

   <We can't defend that building for long enough, sir. You have to evacuate.>

   <Don't worry,> Benson said. <I have an idea.>

   <Oh, God,> Hamilton lamented.

   <What's that?>

   <I mean, oh, good.>

   <That's what I thought. Now move.> Both men acknowledged the order, despite the fact Benson didn't actually have the authority to give it. But with both Valmassoi and Atwood down, and their link to the Ark cut off, someone had to take charge. He waited anxiously outside the temple, knife in hand, while the rest of the expedition filed back inside. Further east, the gunfire fell silent as DeSanto and Hamilton abandoned their positions. Emboldened by their retreat, the shouts and taunts of the attackers only grew louder.

"Keep celebrating, assholes," Benson muttered. He stayed by the door and waited for what remained of the security detail to arrive and take over guard duty. He glanced down at the dagger and royally regretted not taking Korolev's rifle before he locked the two of them in the capsule, but it was too late now. He glanced at the clock his plant projected into the left side of his vision and watched several painfully long seconds tick away. It was only a short jog from where they'd taken up sniper positions and the temple. What the hell was taking them so long?

A short burp of rifle fire betrayed DeSanto and Hamilton's position just before they came around the corner of one of the buildings. Hamilton hung onto DeSanto's shoulder for dear life as he dragged a leg behind him.

"Give us a hand!" DeSanto shouted. "His ankle's broken."

Benson sprinted out past the corpse of the warrior he'd killed and took Hamilton's weight.

"What happened?" he asked.

"I jumped from the second-floor balcony and landed bad," the young man said through clenched teeth.

DeSanto walked backwards next to him, rifle at the ready waiting for Kuul's line to finally collapse. "We're down to whatever ammo's left in the guns. Whatever you're going to do, make it quick."

They reached the temple entrance. Benson looked over at the injured man hanging off his shoulder. "Can you fight if we get you a comfy chair, maybe an iced tea?"

That at least got a smile. "I can fight, sir. Just prop me up by the door."

"Done." Benson leaned him up against the inside of the concrete archway where he'd at least have some cover.

"Hurry," Hamilton said, wincing as he shifted his weight. Benson nodded and ran inside to the little dome covering the rover. It had a nuclear power pack measured in decades and a high-gain antenna that could reach out to Tau Ceti's Kuiper Belt.

And it was broadcasting everything it saw and heard.

"Hey!" Benson shouted into the binocular camera mast. "We're under attack! We've lost contact with the shuttle. Valmassoi's hurt and our security detail is about to collapse. Send help immediately. Acknowledge!"

Benson stared into the cold black glass of the rover's camera lenses, waiting with bated breath for a response, any response. A sudden eruption of rifle fire echoed through the temple's interior. Benson's head shot back over his shoulder to see Hamilton firing downrange on single-fire, conserving what little remained of his ammo.

He turned back to the rover and grabbed the camera mast in his thick hands. "This is serious!"

Nothing.

Benson looked around at the temple within a temple and saw the problem immediately. The new layer of concrete was blocking the signal, and a quick glance told him the entrance was too narrow to drag it out.

"Hamilton," he shouted. "You don't happen to have any grenades, do you?"

"Would've used them if I did."

"I was afraid of that." Benson slapped his palm against the dome to gauge its strength. His hand hurt.

"Anybody got a sledgehammer?" he shouted to anyone within earshot. By then, several curious Atlantians had pushed their way to the dome to see what Benson was up to. One of them carried a staff that identified them as one of the village elders. Their words were translated into Benson's head about a half sentence behind.

"What are you doing?"

Benson thought through what he wanted to say, then carefully enunciated the translation. They were running out of time and couldn't afford a misunderstanding.

"I need your help. We need to widen the door and get the..." He hit a snag when he couldn't find a translation for rover. What had they called it? "The emissary! We need to get the emissary out of this dome as quickly as possible."

The Atlantian's features and skin pattern changed. Benson still couldn't read them, but the silence said volumes. After several long heartbeats, they spoke again. "Are you suggesting we desecrate the emissary's inner sanctum, *human*?"

Benson didn't need the translation software to know the elder had rubbed some spicy mustard on that last word, but there wasn't time to placate their delicate sensibilities.

"If it will save my people, and your people, absolutely." He straightened. "We're about to be overrun and slaughtered. If I can get the emissary out, I can use it to talk to my..." No translation for "ship" either. They were apparently such good swimmers that the idea had never occurred to them. "Great bird, at the end of the line of light. They can send help and we might just all leave this temple alive."

The elder made a show of carefully weighing his words before turning to his people and barking orders. In moments, every Atlantian surrounded the dome and dug furiously at the ground.

"Well don't just stand there supervising," Benson shouted to the rest of the expedition as he fell to his knees and began to dig. "Help them."

They did so, and soon a hundred hands, both human and Atlantian, had dug out the bottom edge of the dome.

"Everybody get a good grip," Benson said. "We're going to flip it. Ready?"

The human half signaled ready, while the Atlantians did the same for their elder. Benson held up three fingers to the elder to signal a countdown.

Finally given a task to pour their fright into physical expression, the crowd of humans and Atlantians strained against the immense weight of the dome while Hamilton and DeSanto took potshots from the doorway.

"C'mon, put your legs into it!" Benson shouted while the elder yelled encouragement in their own language. Among the groans, a creak of masonry shifting sent Benson's hopes soaring.

"That's it! It's moving. Heave!"

Powered by fresh exhilaration, the crowd surged upwards as the dome began to pivot up.

"Push!"

Momentum was on their side, and the dome hinged upward, freeing the rover from its tomb. With one last great shove, the dome rolled back and became the largest soup bowl Benson had ever seen. He wasted no time as he jumped in front of the camera mast and waved his arms furiously enough that some of Atlantians thought he was trying to take flight.

"Wake up! We're under attack!"

This time, the rover sparked to life as the binocular camera mount whirred around, jolted from a deep sleep.

"I'm empty!" DeSanto shouted from the archway. "Somebody give me a spear or something."

Whoever was controlling the rover found their bearings and focused in on Benson. "What's the situation?" came the tinny voice.

"We're under attack from an unknown hostile Atlantian force. Valmassoi is secured, but severely wounded. Our security detail is at half strength and out of ammunition. We've lost contact with our shuttle. We need immediate evac or reinforcement."

"Uh…" the voice stammered. "I'm just an exolinguistic tech."

For just a moment, Benson had to hold back the impulse to strangle the camera mast. "So transfer the feed and get Captain Mahama on the line!"

"Stand by."

Benson threw up his arms as the sound of battle encroached. "Take your time!"

The seconds stretched out until Hamilton's rifle also fell silent.

"I'm black on ammo," Hamilton shouted. "What do we do, chief?"

"Block the door," Benson said. "We only need to buy a couple more minutes."

DeSanto and Hamilton moved inside and cast their empty rifles to the ground while a stone table and podium were hurriedly shuffled into position.

"How's it look out there?" Benson asked.

"Their line collapsed," DeSanto answered. "Tuko's warriors are still harassing the enemy on the edges, but they'll be on us in no time."

Benson acknowledged the grave news and looked up at the ceiling, hoping for a miracle. He should have gone with his first instinct. He should have led them all out of the temple and into the woods. Now they were trapped like rats and were about to die without even knowing who was killing them.

"Sir!" DeSanto yelled. "They're turning away from the temple."

"What? Why?"

"It's the Unbound! They're running down the crater to attack the enemy flank!"

Benson ran to the archway and peered through to see for himself. Charging down the face of the crater as fast as her legs could carry her, Mei led her people into the fray, screaming like a banshee and waving a meat cleaver as her raven hair blew in the wind.

Of course she is, Benson marveled as he pulled the dagger from his waistband. "Don't just stand there," he fumed. "Get this shit away from the door and help them!"

CHAPTER THIRTEEN

Kexx sprinted down the hillside toward the mass of invading warriors, brandishing nothing but a large grain splitter, screaming obscenities, and wondering exactly how ze'd ended up in such a ludicrous position in the first place.

The day had started out rather dull, after all. Now, surrounded by three fullhands of humans whipped into a frenzy and hurtling toward a much larger, and, it should be noted, better-armed hostile force, Kexx resolved never to complain about missing out on the excitement again. Provided ze survived the next little while, a possibility which shrank with the distance.

Ahead of zer, Mei ran downhill in her stiff, halting way. Ze was armed with a proper weapon, even if it was just a large butchering knife. The rest of zer people had grabbed whatever they could find: clubs, rocks, a shovel. One intrepid human ran into battle armed with a chair. You couldn't fault their enthusiasm.

Kexx had watched in horror as the tide of battle turned against the unprepared, fragile coalition of representatives from three fullhand tribes, plus the human contingent. They outnumbered the intruders, but the various tribes had never fought together before and broke up into smaller groups. Easy pickings for the more disciplined intruders. The only reason the battle lasted as long as it had was the brutal efficiency of the handful of humans with their infernal guns.

Ze'd been caught on the wrong side of the fight to join up with Kuul. Before long, the survivors were all retreating back to Xis's temple. Sensing defeat was imminent, Kexx's priority turned to the humans in the shelter at the far side of the village. There would still be time to lead them through the halo trees to safety. But when ze explained the situation, Mei would have none of it. They were going to fight for their new home, and there was no talking zer out of it.

No one could call Kexx a coward. Ze'd been in many fights, and had survived. But as the village's truth-digger, ze was able to decide the time and place when confrontations happened. Ze was the predator stalking prey. Ze waited until ze had the greatest advantage to spring the trap. Now, ze was in the mouth of the trap, outwitted by an enemy ze couldn't even identify.

Cuut sure loves zer tests, Kexx thought. Ahead of the charging mob, the intruders spotted them. In practiced unison, the black-smeared enemy turned their attention away from the siege of the temple to face the new threat, which was simultaneously the plan and the last thing Kexx actually wanted to happen.

We're going to get cut into jerky strips. Committed to zer fate, Kexx lifted the club high in the air and let zer skin flash its most intimidating war pattern as the intruders formed ranks and began to advance toward them and away from the temple.

But as the two forces converged, humans and G'tel began to pour from the mouth of the temple like sakor bugs swarming from their nest. For the slimmest of moments, the invaders were distracted by the sudden appearance of a new threat at their rear. It was also the moment Mei's enraged rabble crashed into their line.

The battle became a blur of blades, screams, and blood. Kexx vaguely registered the pain in zer side as a spear point bit home before ze caved in the intruder's face. All around zer, people were dying, mostly among Kexx's own friends, but their frenzy didn't abate. The humans, stiff and undersized, nonetheless proved themselves to be vicious, mindless killers. When they lost a weapon, they picked up a rock. When they lost the rock, they used their fists. When they could swing their arms no longer, they tried to trip their enemy and bite them with their teeth.

We really *need to stop underestimating these people,* Kexx thought. To the rear, the fighters from the temple gave as good as they got, thinning out the rapidly dissolving ranks and throwing the whole mêlée into chaotic, one-on-one fights. But it wouldn't be enough. The defenders were still outnumbered and would soon tire.

The ground trembled.

Kexx didn't notice it at first, thinking the vibrations were coming from the frenetic mass swirling around zer. But soon, the rumble and noise overwhelmed even the din of battle. To the west, the nose of the humans' great bird crested over the top of the halo trees and started gliding toward the battle.

The scene paused, like a diver drawing a deep breath before taking the plunge. Every face in the village stared up at the approaching silhouette with either hope or dread etched onto their faces.

In an instant, the fortunes of battle flipped. The intruders' spirits withered like yulka seeds left on the stalk. The defenders closed ranks and pressed their sudden advantage, pinching the enemy formation between them. With invigorated fighters on both sides and the long shadow of the great bird falling over them, the intruders broke and ran for the tree line.

A chorus of celebration erupted from the villagers as they shouted taunts at the intruders' retreating backs. But the great bird, a "shuttle" the humans called it, wasn't finished. It swooped down, skimming just arm-spans above the buildings on its way to the knot of intruders as they scrambled up the hill toward the relative safety of the woods. They tried to run from the approaching monster, but it was faster, buffeting them with the screaming, hurricane winds that blew from its massive triangular wings. Several unlucky souls found themselves caught in the powerful downdraft and were either flattened against the ground, or sent spinning off like a child's toy thrown in a tantrum.

Needless to say, they didn't get much sympathy from the survivors, who laughed and jeered as the invaders who had come so close to annihilating them only moments earlier were tossed about like so many fallen leaves. Their spirits broken and their ranks shattered, the blackened and bloodied warriors disappeared into the woods. Cheering erupted, loud enough to just be audible over the roar of the shuttle as it circled back around and settled over a flat space near the pond at the center of the village. It suddenly sprouted five thick, wheeled legs which swung down from compartments that had been hidden until only a moment before, then settled gently onto the ground amid a billowing cloud of dust. As the beast rested, its whine died away, and Kexx realized not all of the shouting around zer was out of celebration.

All around, the injured of both sides of the battle moaned and rocked with their pain. They were the lucky ones. Too many lay silent. Kexx recognized the faces of villagers. Friends. The elders would be busy with rituals of returning for days.

"Mei!" shouted a human ahead of zer. Kexx looked up to see Mei's friend, Benson, running out among the dead and wounded. Ze hadn't really appreciated Benson's size while ze was sick and lying down in Mei's shelter. Benson was big, twice the size of Mei and larger than most any of the other humans Kexx had seen save for one or two. While ze still wasn't as tall as the average G'tel, zer was certainly thicker.

"Mei!" ze shouted again, obviously desperate for a reply.

"Here, Benson-san," Mei called out from directly behind zer. Kexx stepped aside to let Benson pass as the human charged at the sound of Mei's voice. With a great sweep of zer arms, Benson scooped Mei up and hugged zer for a long moment, then set zer down again.

Benson pointed at Mei. "Don't you ever do something like that again," ze said sternly. Kexx had seen Mei take the same tone with zer own child. Were they kin? Kexx couldn't be sure. Ze didn't know what facial markers to look for. But how could they be when Benson was so much bigger than zer?

"You're welcome, stupid," Mei snapped back. Then they started arguing faster than Kexx's limited command of their language could keep up with. Definitely related.

"I am glad you're both safe," Kexx said, "But we have bigger problems now."

Benson's head snapped up and stared at Kexx with a blank, uncomprehending expression. Ze pointed a finger, er, thumb at Kexx.

"You taught him English?" Benson asked Mei.

"Ze *learned* English," Mei shot back.

"Why English?"

"To get them ready for *you*," Mei said, agitated.

English? It would have to wait.

"This is Kexx," Mei continued. "Ze is my friend."

Benson looked at Kexx with fresh eyes. "You're the village's truth... ah..."

"Truth-digger," Kexx finished for zer.

Benson smiled and held out zer hand. "Mei's friends are my friends."

Kexx took the human's stiff, knobby hand, like skin stretched taut over a bag of sticks, and shook it in the humans' greeting tradition. It was an unpleasant feeling, but ze supposed it was just one of those things ze'd have to get used to.

"We must help the wounded," Kexx said after the awkward handshake had thankfully concluded.

"Yes, of course. But first, I need some help with the shuttle. Can you fight?"

"I need rest."

"Me too. So we'll have an incentive to be quick."

"What is 'Insentiv'?"

"C'mon." Benson slapped Kexx on the shoulder, ignoring the question. "Grab a spear and follow me."

Benson ran off in the general direction of the shuttle. Kexx looked over at Mei in a haze.

"What just happened?"

"You were volunteered. Go with Benson-san."

Kexx realized zer feet were moving even before ze decided to obey, like ze had been compelled. Oh well, at least the humans were never boring. Ze jogged along behind Benson, not bothering to try to catch up on account of the nagging stab wound to zer leg. They blazed a path toward the shuttle, but then Benson turned sharply away as though ze'd changed zer mind. Instead, they headed for the smaller white cone that had delivered the human's sacrifice earlier that day. Benson skidded to a stop in front of it and started pounding on the door.

"Korolev!" ze shouted, another word Kexx didn't recognize.

"Korolev, it's Benson. Open up."

"Prove it!" came the muffled reply.

"Seriously, Pavel? How many Atlantians speak English?" Benson looked up, remembering Kexx standing there. "Sorry," ze said in a conversational tone.

Kexx waved off the apology.

"OK," the voice trapped inside the cone said. "I'm opening the hatch."

A sharp, scraping sound stabbed at Kexx's ears as the small door swung inward. Kexx peered into the shadows beyond and saw the unmoving figure of Valmassoi on the floor, covered in the bright red of human blood. Kexx had already seen more of it today than ze ever cared to. One of their warriors crouched next to the fallen leader scrambled to zer feet at the sight of Kexx's face and hurriedly thrust the point of a gun at the door, but Benson threw zerself in front of the deadly weapon before the warrior could act.

"Pavel, stand down!" Benson shouted, leaving Kexx to puzzle out exactly how someone could be expected to do that. "He's a friend."

The warrior dropped zer gun in obvious relief. "We're clear?"

"Yes," Benson answered. "They've been run off. Pavel, may I introduce Kex."

The red fungus again. It must be something about the way human mouths were shaped. "Hello," Kexx offered. "Nice to meet you."

Pavel stiffened and looked at Benson. "You just said they don't speak English."

Benson shrugged. "Actually, I asked *how many* of them speak English. Turns out the answer is 'one'. How's Valmassoi?"

"Holding on," the warrior said, visibly shaken. "Barely, he's just lost so much blood."

"He's not the only one," Benson said. "Stay with him and keep pressure on the wounds. I need to borrow your rifle."

Pavel handed it up to zer without hesitation. "Thought we were clear?"

"The village is. Just going to check on our ride."

"Roger that. Swapping permissions to your plant. OK, safety's off. You're ready to rock."

"You need a rock?" Kexx asked, trying to be helpful.

The two humans shared a look. "Not just now," Benson said. "Follow me."

They ran to the shuttle, still settling into the soft ground near the pond. The underside was the flat black of charcoal, but as smooth as skin. Kexx reached out to touch it. The pads in zer finger gripped it easily. It was hard, like mudstone, but it didn't have mudstone's taste. A lattice of perfectly straight lines revealed that it was made up of thousands, tens of thousands of tiles fitted together so tightly a leaf couldn't pass between them. It was simply astonishing craftsmanship.

Benson opened a small flap in the shuttle's skin and twisted something. With a click and a pop, a whole section of underbelly swung down to form a set of steps and reveal a doorway.

"Stay behind me and be ready," Benson said.

"What's inside?"

"No idea. Let's find out."

Kexx couldn't be completely sure, but ze strongly suspected Benson was enjoying zerself.

They walked up the stairs, and Kexx was blown away to discover that the shuttle was almost entirely hollow. Row after row of short, high-backed chairs covered the floor from one wall to the other. Suddenly, Benson waved a hand in Kexx's face and pointed toward the front of the shuttle. Two of the black-painted intruders lay motionless on the floor. There was no obvious signs of blood or struggle. If anything, they looked asleep.

Benson swayed and dropped zer gun. "I don't…" ze collapsed to zer knees. "Get out," ze said with a last breath before zer eyes rolled back in zer head. Kexx grabbed zer before ze fell backwards, limp as a day-old fish. Kexx tried to pick zer up, but Benson was even more solid than ze looked, which was saying something. It was then Kexx noticed zer own vision was starting to blur. Ze shot a glance at the figures sprawled out on the floor. They'd been knocked out. There was something wrong with the air in here. Kexx took one more deep breath, but zer vision only worsened. Ze needed to get Benson out, fast.

Kexx grabbed the human by the wrists and dragged zer

backwards through the path between the chairs. Ze made it several rows before the vertigo threatened to send zer crashing down as well. It felt exactly like being underwater for too long, except zer air sacks weren't screaming for breath. Desperate instinct took over and Kexx left Benson's unconscious body behind as ze dove for the door. Overcome with dizziness and on the cusp of passing out entirely, Kexx missed the handrail and fell down the steps, landing heavily on the ground outside. Ze took a gasping, ragged breath of the outside air. Instantly, zer vertigo cleared and vision sharpened.

Zer theory confirmed, Kexx took several deep breaths, exhaling fully between each, just as ze would before a deep dive, then ze ran back into the shuttle and dragged Benson a little further. It took three trips, but eventually ze managed to pull the human down the steps, hopefully without too much damage.

Mei came flying in from somewhere. "What happen?"

"We couldn't breathe in there." Kexx tipped zer head back at the shuttle.

Mei leaned down and held an ear over Benson's mouth. "Ze's still not breathing." Without another word, Mei placed her mouth over Benson's and breathed out until Kexx saw Benson's chest rise.

"What are you doing?"

"Shut up." Ze repeated the process twice more. Without warning, Benson started to convulse. Ze sucked down a long, echoing breath. One of zer hands shot out and grabbed Kexx's lower leg and squeezed painfully, as if to keep from falling off the world.

"What happened?" Benson finally managed to say while holding zer head.

"You passed out in the shuttle," Kexx said. "I pulled you out, and Mei... did something to your mouth."

Benson wiped some saliva off zer lips and looked up at Mei. "You should've asked if you wanted a kiss that bad."

Mei slapped zer on the chest. "You want me to tell Theresa you said that?"

Benson laughed. Mei laughed. Then, they all laughed together, even if Kexx wasn't exactly sure what about.

CHAPTER FOURTEEN

Theresa paced the main hallway of the Beehive like a nervous cat. An *angry* nervous cat. Something had happened at the first contact site. Something bad. Bad enough that her superiors were keeping a lid on the whole affair so tight they wouldn't even tell Shambhala's chief constable. Which was still her, to the best of her knowledge.

Even worse, her husband had been out of contact for hours. And while Mr Benson wasn't always the best about remembering to tell her where he was or when he was getting home, the stretching silence couldn't be attributed to his inconsiderate forgetfulness. The plant connection itself was down. She'd tried to raise him a dozen times over the last two hours, but each attempt was met with the same error message.

With Atwood and the rest of her detail on the expedition, protecting the Beehive had fallen to Theresa and her constables. She'd taken a shift herself almost as soon as the sudden blackout happened, figuring the assistant administrator and his staff would be first in line to learn of the expedition's fate. No matter the news, she needed to be there when it came.

He's a big boy, she told herself. Hell, the idiot managed to survive a stabbing, meteor strike, habitat decompression, and a fucking nuclear bomb going off in the room with him. How wrong can a greeting ceremony go, really? Theresa straightened her shoulders. Besides, it's not like I'm the little doting wife pacing around the house waiting for him.

She looked down at her feet and realized they *were* pacing.

Had been for the better part of an hour, in fact. Theresa willed her feet to stop moving and stood at attention by the door to the conference room.

"Idiot," she mumbled, not entirely sure if she was talking about her husband, or herself.

The door opened and expelled Merick into the hallway. "Ah, Mrs Benson. We're about to finish a debriefing with your husband, then we're taking a short recess before continuing. He's asked to speak with you."

"You could have told me he was OK!" she blurted.

"You're right. I'm sorry," Merick put up his hands. "It's been a tense conversation. Things have... not gone to plan."

"Why can't we connect over the plants?" Theresa asked. "I've been trying for over an hour."

"There's been some technical snafu in the plant network between here and there, probably in the shuttle's node. We're working on it, but for now we have a connection through the rover in the village. Why don't you head inside, they'll be done in a minute."

Theresa nodded and sent a quick plant burst to her junior constable in the atrium letting her know she would be taking a short break, then stepped past Merick and into the conference room where a larger-than-lifesize holographic projection of Benson stood in the center of the table.

Captain Mahama's image stood next to him, while the chairs around the table were filled with the usual gallery of politicians, business moguls, and affiliated sycophants. Benson noticed her enter and threw her a quick smirk. If anyone else noticed her enter, they didn't acknowledge it.

"One final point, Mr Benson," Mahama continued. "The exobiology department has asked me to inquire about the status of the chicken we sent down to you."

"It got away."

"It got away?" Mahama repeated.

"Yeah, the enemy attacked just as we were about to sacrifice it and it very smartly winged it out of the area."

"And you don't know the current location of the animal?"

"I've been dealing with other issues, sir."

"I see." Mahama inhaled. "The exobiology department would like you to locate the animal as soon as possible and destroy it, to avoid any possible contamination."

"Contamination?"

"Well, it's an invasive species."

"Invasive spe–" Benson took a deep breath. "It's one chicken. There are no roosters. Don't tell me I have to explain sexual reproduction to the exobiology department?"

Mahama sighed. "Just keep an eye out for it, will you?"

"I think that chicken has been through enough."

"Are we still talking about the chicken?"

A round of nervous laughter went through the room. Benson took it in his stride. "Is there anything else, captain?"

Mahama smiled and shook her head.

"Good, then if you all don't mind, please get the hell out and give me a moment alone with my wife."

The rest of the room turned to the door, noticing Theresa for the first time. Without another word, everyone stood up from their chairs and quietly filed out of the room, several of them nodding to Theresa as they passed. Captain Mahama signed off and her image faded into the air like a clearing fog, leaving only Theresa and her husband in the room.

"Hello, Esa," Benson said quietly.

Her relief at seeing him intact and safe was tempered by concern at how disheveled and exhausted he looked. His jacket was nowhere to be seen, while his normally pristine shirt was soaked through with sweat and covered in dirt, and, more ominously, blood. How much of it was his, she couldn't tell. She didn't let her competing emotions reach her face. It wasn't her way. Instead, she said simply, "Jesus, honey. You look like shit."

Benson gave a tired little chuckle. "I feel worse than I look, if you can believe it."

"But, your face."

"These are mostly from that fucking chicken. No wonder people used to eat those goddamned things."

Theresa pointed at his shirt. "Is that your blood?"

"No. Well, not most of it, anyway. Hell, it's not even all human."

"Ah, good. At least you didn't almost die, then. That's a plus."

"Oh, I did that," Benson said almost giddily. "Wasn't breathing for a good minute, but Mei gave me the kiss of life, so I'm all good."

Theresa cupped her face, feeling a headache coming on.

"Honey?"

"I'm fine," she said. "You want to rewind and help me unpack that last sentence?"

"Well, it's complicated. Basically, we were getting overrun by this force of hostiles, and we'd already lost our connection with the shuttle. So I convinced some folks to lift a giant rock dome with their bare hands so we could get the rover working again. The Ark took remote control of the shuttle, realized the crew had been lured out and killed by hostiles, who were still inside, so they shut the hatches and blew the fire suppressors, which scavenged all the O_2 from the passenger compartment and killed the intruders. But when it landed in the village, I didn't know that, so I went inside to clear it and passed the hell out, but the village cop named Kexx, great guy by the way, dragged me outside, where Mei knew enough to do some rescue breathing, which brought me back to life, and now I'm here talking to you. How was your day?"

"I hate you."

"It's an occupational hazard."

"You're the recreation director. People are supposed to be happy around you. It's literally your job."

"Yeah." Benson paused. "About that..."

Theresa's stomach did a little flip. She knew his expression too well. He was about to say something very stupid that was going to make her upset.

"Just spit it out."

"The council has temporarily reinstated me as a detective."

"And?" Theresa said, waiting for the other shoe to drop.

"And... In the interest of building ties with the Atlantians, I'm going to be sticking around here for a while to help Kexx figure out who attacked us."

"What, by yourself?"

"Well, not entirely. Mei and her people are staying here too.

The villagers have sort of adopted them."

"This is insane. I'm going to talk to Merick about this."

"It won't do any good."

"And why is that?"

"Because it wasn't Merick's idea."

Theresa's jaw set. She'd been ready to blame Merick, or Mahama, but it wasn't their fault. It was her husband driving the bus.

"No," Theresa said simply. "You're loading up on the shuttle and coming home."

"I can't do that, Esa."

"You're a detective, that makes me your boss, so you're bloody well going to do it," she said, her face flushing with anger.

"I'm not a part of the Shambhala force, so I'm not in your chain of command. I'm more like a private dick."

"That's half right," she snapped back.

"Sweetie, I know you're mad–"

"Noticed, did you?"

"–but we lost some good people today, on both sides. We have to find out who attacked us or else this whole thing blows up. I can help them do that. You know I can."

"I think it's someone else's turn to save the world."

"Oh, I agree, but I'm already here. Just a rotten run of luck. First, our recon drone was attacked by some birds, then we get attacked just as we're falling into a gap in our satellite coverage." Benson shook his head. "What are the odds?"

The set of his features told the story. What he didn't say, what he was actively trying *not* to say over an unsecured connection, sent an electric shock jumping down her spine from one vertebra to the next. Benson didn't believe in coincidences, and neither did she. Whoever attacked the expedition had help. Either from the Ark, or from somewhere within Shambhala.

A look of understanding passed between them. He knew his message had been received. Theresa shook her head, trying to seem jovial. "Why do these things only happen to you, baby?"

"No idea." He glanced out of frame. "They're loading up the wounded onto the shuttle. I gotta help."

"Go," Theresa said. "I'll hold down the fort."

"Love you, wife."

"I love you too, Zero Hero. Good hunting."

"Watch your six."

The connection cut and Benson's image evaporated. Theresa, conscious of the people in the hallway, took a moment to collect herself. She imagined a small jewelry box, into which she carefully folded her fear and her rage, and closed the lid tight. Her face passive, betraying nothing, she opened the door and stepped into the hallway.

"We're all finished," she heard herself say. "Thanks for giving us the time."

"Not at all," Merick replied. "But we really must get back to work."

"Of course," Theresa said, even managing a weak smile. As the delegates filtered back in, she quietly filtered out. <Gorski,> she said to her constable. <Can you cover the rest of my watch?>

<Ah, sure, chief. Where are you going?>

<For a walk,> Theresa said, then cut the link. She stepped briskly past the Beehive's outer doors into the late afternoon sunlight. Some evenings, she'd take in the sky, losing herself in the patterns of clouds and palette of colors until the sun finally set. But tonight, her mood was already dark.

A million feelings fought for supremacy in Theresa's gut. Relief that Bryan was alive. Anger that he was stupid and arrogant enough to stay behind. Guilt that she hadn't been there to help him. And jealousy that Mei had locked lips with her husband, even as she knew how foolish and selfish the emotion was.

It hadn't been easy the last few years, trying to step out from behind her husband's shadow. It grated on her nerves whenever people called him "chief" while she was in earshot. Not because he hadn't earned it, but so had she, goddammit, and she hadn't been fast-tracked for the job for being popular. Bryan, infuriatingly, never seemed to notice, or downplayed the problem. He'd grown into a more humble and private man than he'd been at the height of his Zero career. The adulation, no, *canonization* he'd experienced since thwarting the Kimura attack made him uncomfortable. And since he didn't want the attention and recognition, he couldn't understand why maybe she did.

He could be the most blind, clueless, insensitive...

And she loved him for it. Bryan started every relationship, every conversation, assuming the best about a person. He made them prove him wrong before he'd give up on that idealized version of them he held in his head. Despite everything, in spite of personally witnessing the deaths of twenty thousand people, the idiot somehow remained an optimist.

And Theresa had that beautiful idiot all to herself.

Theresa walked down the boulevard towards their home with purpose, her anger growing with each step. Someone had tried to kill Bryan, again. The last time that had happened, she'd been sidelined, out of the fight. Powerless. She cracked her neck. Not today. Bryan had given her a clue. Someone in Shambhala or on the Ark was in on the attack.

Part of the plan or not, someone had tried to kill her husband. No matter the reason, Theresa was going to open her little jewelry box and see to it that they fucking paid in full.

CHAPTER FIFTEEN

Benson watched from the roof of Chief Tuko's house as the shuttle lifted into the air. Soon, its engines transitioned from hover to level flight and it accelerated toward the horizon and the approaching night.

The chief, severely injured and unconscious, lay inside while the village healers attended to him. He'd lost an arm during the battle, which was of surprisingly little concern to anyone else. Apparently, the Atlantians could regenerate them in a few months. Tough bastards. The wounds to Tuko's head were far more serious. No one knew when, or even if, he would wake again. Rumors of a succession fight were already swirling. The expedition's medic had taken a look and done what she could, but the alien's unfamiliar anatomy and physiology meant she didn't dare administer any but the most rudimentary treatment. Better to leave him in the care of his own people's medicine, no matter how primitive it might be.

Benson's thoughts returned to the shuttle. All of the expedition's members were aboard, as well as several of the Unbound who had been seriously wounded during the battle. There had been some dissent about accepting help, but Mei straightened them out. Korolev had fought with him to stay, loyal to a fault, but Benson had managed to convince him that it was Theresa who would really need his help with what was coming. It had the advantage of being true, especially if Benson's suspicions were right. He did allow Korolev to leave one thing behind: a rifle and all of their spare magazines, almost five hundred rounds' worth. Benson ran a hand over the sleek polymer casing of the rifle scope. "If you're going to insist on going it alone, you should at least be the baddest motherfucker on the continent," Korolev had said.

In addition to the rifle and a set of riot armor, Benson kept his duffle with a few changes of clothes and basic toiletries, a couple of weeks of MREs, and a med kit. His only other equipment was an emergency mobile satellite link and a solar recharger so that his plant connection to the Ark wasn't lost as soon as the shuttle left. Still, it would only afford an hour or two of contact between recharges. He was going to be roughing it for the duration of the investigation.

On the east side of the village, the signal tower was busy using what little sunlight they still had to send frantic updates further down the loose network of villages that made up the Atlantians' civilization.

"You're quiet," Mei said, quietly.

"Sorry."

"You're never quiet. What's wrong?"

Benson took a deep breath as even the shuttle's red-orange jet exhaust became too faint to track against the mottled twilight. "You mean other than watching a bunch of people get killed and uncovering evidence of a conspiracy?"

"Other than that, yes."

"Or the fact I'm now thousands of kilometers from home, isolated and alone, and expected to go out into the wilderness to find the people who tried to kill us and ask them very politely what the big deal is?"

Mei bobbed her head as she considered his answer. "Yeah, that would do it."

"How's Sakiko?" Benson asked.

"Fine. Sleeping at a friend's house."

"An Atlantian friend?"

Mei nodded. She pointed to one of the single-story dwellings near the southern edge of the village. "Pu's family. They're good babysitters."

"And she doesn't mind being looked after by aliens?"

Mei shrugged. "Why should she?"

Benson smiled and shook his head. "Kids. It's amazing what they can do before adults teach them to 'know better.'"

"She's fearless," she said with a trace of worry.

"So was I, once."

"Not now?"

"Not even close."

"What changed?"

"You were there," Benson said. "I watched a lot of people get hurt and die."

"Like today."

Benson nodded.

"But you stayed anyway."

"Because I'm the only one who could help."

Mei snorted. "Not fearless, still arrogant."

Benson shrugged. "Nobody's perfect."

The sound of footsteps called their attention to the stairwell behind them. An Atlantian head popped up. Even after four days among them, Benson had trouble picking out individuals, but he was pretty sure it was Kexx. The alien started speaking English and removed all doubt.

"Trouble," he said simply.

"What's wrong?" Mei asked.

"One of our bearers hurt during the fight returns."

"Oh, well that's good, right?" Benson said.

Kexx looked startled, while Mei elbowed him in the ribs.

"Kexx means the bearer returns to Xis."

"Who's Xis?"

Mei rolled her eyes. "One of their gods. The bearer is dying."

"Oh, OK, that's not good…" Benson said carefully. "What's a bearer?"

"Ugh. Just follow us." Mei grabbed his forearm and pulled him to the stairs. "Forgive zer," she said as they passed Kexx on the way down.

With Kexx following close behind, Mei strode purposefully to the center of the village.

"Where are we going?" Benson half asked, half protested.

"Say nothing," Mei snapped. "Stand by the wall and watch."

"What wall?"

She shot Benson a withering look that he was sure had been deployed at her own child to great effect over the last couple of years, so he let it drop. Frankly, he was running low on energy anyway. The last few days had been a neverending sprint from one crisis to the next. A good night's sleep was soon going to move from a luxury to a biological imperative.

Mei stopped in front of a building in the innermost ring, directly opposite the temple on the other side of the pond. Unlike the temple, it was squat and unadorned, little more than a mound with a hole in one side. He'd passed by it several times over the last few days without a second glance, but now he was ushered through the door and down a steep staircase that curved to the left. The steps, built for Atlantian legs, were about ten centimeters too tall. As the scant light from outside faded, Benson misjudged them and nearly sent himself flying several times.

They'd gone down at least two floors before the stairs ended on a floor made of bedrock. Torches on the walls cast a warm light over the rough-hewn rock, the tool marks worn smooth by the feet of generations. Gently nudged from behind, Benson stepped through the high door into a huge, almost perfect hemisphere reaching back up to ground level. Benson realized with no small amount of awe that it wasn't a mound he'd entered, but the very top of the dome. The walls were coated in the same concrete that made up the Atlantians' roads and buildings. At first glance, it was identical to the interior of the temple, except instead of built up into the sky, it was carved out of the ground.

"Wow," he whispered to Mei. "What is this place?"

"Xis's temple."

"But I thought they worshiped Cuut?"

Kexx stepped in. "What Cuut destroys above, Xis creates below." The truth-digger pointed at the collection of figures hunched over a low table at the center of the dome. Still more Atlantians huddled against the far wall, eying him suspiciously. They were smaller than the other aliens he'd seen, less adorned. What were they doing down here in the dark?

"We must hurry," Kexx said.

One of the figures looked up from the table. The Atlantian's gently glowing skin flickered hesitantly before waving them over. A body lay face down on the low table. Atlantian blood trickled out of deep gashes in the poor soul's flesh and down the sides of the slab to pool at their feet. Even more unsettling than the blood was the huge, disfiguring lump on the body's back. Something had stretched the skin taught, like a balloon ready to burst.

"What's that?" Benson whispered to Mei. "A tumor, hematoma?"

Mei elbowed him in the ribs again.

"That's not actually an answer, you know."

"Quiet!" she whispered as loudly as she could.

Something stirred inside the mound of flesh and set Benson's skin crawling like an ant hill. He barely suppressed the reflex to recoil in horror. Before he'd even started to work out what he was seeing, one of the elders began chanting a low, pulsing melody that reached Benson's ears and the soles of his feet simultaneously. The rest of them joined in the chant, even Mei, while the writhing lump of flesh on the injured Atlantian's back churned in reply.

Benson looked on in growing alarm at the horror movie scene playing itself out in front of him. The leader of the chant produced an obsidian dagger and held it high. It was highly refined, sharing more with the ceremonial spears Benson had seen during the sacrifices than the simple tools of the other villagers. The glimmering black blade seemed to drink in what meager light fell on it.

Benson realized his hand had fallen down onto the grip of his rifle. He had a very bad feeling about what was coming next.

The chanting reached a crescendo as the elder lowered the knife onto the prostrate figure. But where Benson had expected a stabby, plunging affair that would bury it to the hilt, the elder instead took great care to gently slice through a layer of skin, then another. There was no sign the patient was aware of the cuts, or even alive. The glass blade was incredibly sharp, cutting cleanly and easily through the flesh until a great eruption of water surged from the incision like a wellspring.

The rest of the attendants rushed in and started grabbing strange lumps of flesh from inside the body. Miraculously, curiosity won out over disgust as Benson leaned in to get a better look at what they were pulling free of the body. More than a dozen had been pulled out already, with no signs of stopping, and they were moving.

In a moment of blinding revelation, Benson saw the ugly, twisted, translucent lumps for what they really were.

"Babies!" he shouted. "You're saving her babies!" Benson's knees felt like they would give out as the thrill of it hit him. He'd never seen a birth. Few humans had, actually. Until very recently, everyone born on the Ark had come out of a vat. Everyone except for the Unbound like Mei, who was staring at him like he'd grown a second head which was busy reciting Shakespeare in German.

"Sorry," he said, his hands held up. The procedure continued until almost three dozen tiny wriggling infants had been pulled free of what Benson could only assume was their deceased mother. The attendants took great care removing each one from a thin, transparent sack trapping them, then lined them up in front of the same elder that had made the incision.

Benson looked on with a new reverence for what he had been permitted to witness. The elder arranged the infants into two groups on the table. By gender? The chanting continued at a slower pace. If there were lyrics being sung, the translation software wasn't picking them up.

One group of infants was growing quite a bit larger than the other. Benson eyed the piles suspiciously as the elder gathered up the smaller group of four and handed them to a pair of Atlantians who embraced them tightly and stepped away, turning their backs on the others as they cooed over the infants in their arms.

"Mei." He let his hand rest on her shoulder as he whispered. "What's going on?"

Before she could turn to answer, the elder positioned one of the remaining infants and decapitated it with one deft stroke of his dagger. For a moment, Benson was paralyzed between disbelief and white hot rage. Most of his conscious mind simply refused to believe what his eyes reported. But then the elder grabbed another and positioned the tiny squirming infant for the killing stroke.

Without thinking about it, Benson's rifle shot up to his shoulder as he sighted through the holographic sight at the elder's forehead and clicked off the safety.

"Drop the knife, NOW!" he screamed in untranslated English. The Atlantian equivalent popped up in his vision a moment later and he repeated the command in their language with no less force. The shellshocked aliens froze in place, unsure what to do, but utterly certain of what the unhinged human with the assault rifle could do to them if they didn't obey.

It was Mei who moved first... by putting herself directly between the elder and the muzzle of Benson's gun.

"Mei, get out of the way."

"No."

"What the hell are you doing?" Benson half shouted, half pleaded.

"This is their way," she said firmly.

"But they're killing babies!"

"Go wait outside," Mei said in a voice that was not accustomed to being ignored.

"You can't tell me you're OK with this," Benson protested.

She ignored him and pointed for the stairs. "Go!"

Benson realized his hands were shaking. He felt faint. Whatever wave of adrenaline he'd been riding for the last few hours was about to come crashing down. The rifle suddenly felt very heavy.

"I ah... don't feel very well." He lowered the gun and fumbled to sling it back over his shoulder as he staggered back up the steps. He burst out of Xis's temple into the cooling night air, skin clammy and head spinning. His knees buckled, and Benson fell onto all fours and retched, again. He'd thrown up more in the last four days than he had since the week after the two-eighteen Zero championship title, but for entirely different reasons.

By the time he sat up again, Mei had sat down next to him.

"Eat strange seeds again?" she asked.

Benson wiped his mouth. "Talk to me. Make me OK with what I just saw."

Mei took a deep, centering breath. "I can't, because I'm not. But maybe I can make you understand."

"They're killing the rest of them down there right now, aren't they?"

Mei nodded gravely. "They don't have a choice."

"They don't have a choice not to lop the heads off their own children?" he snapped. "Seems like a pretty easy choice to me. It never even occurred to me as an option before."

"We don't have thirty children at a time," Mei said gently. "Could you and Theresa feed thirty hungry mouths? Teach thirty thirsty little brains?"

"We would try."

"And fail," Mei said matter of factly. She wasn't wrong, as difficult as it was for him to admit. "They kept four today. Usually they only keep two, and one of those dies anyway."

"From what?"

Mei shrugged. "No sickbay to go to here."

"Don't they have healers?" Benson asked. Mei gave him a pleading look.

"They... do their best."

Right, Benson thought. Treat fevers with bloodletting. Got a headache? Drill holes in the skull to let out evil spirits. That sort of thing.

Mei seemed to follow his line of thought. "We were not any better for a long time."

"Sorry, I'm just having some trouble with the idea of a ninety plus percent infant mortality rate. Picking and choosing which ones deserve to live."

"It's not different from the Ark," Mei said. "You left all of the unwanted back on Earth to die in Nibiru. Only the beautiful people got their tickets."

"That's not fair. That was about survival. This is very different from the Ark," Benson said defensively. "We don't kill babies if they don't turn out the way we like them."

"No, you kill them before they ever become babies. You make big batches of embryos, pick out the good ones, throw out the rest. No 'bad' babies ever get made at all."

"That's not the same thing."

"*Is* the same thing," she insisted "Only difference is time. Time you have because of technology. They have to make the same choice without it." She drew a lazy spiral in the dirt with her finger. "I'm not saying it's good or bad, they just do their best. It's just as much about survival for them as it was for you."

"*Us*, Mei. You're the product of those 'beautiful people' too."

Mei angrily grunted her response to the jab.

"These people," Benson said, changing the subject. "You respect them a great deal, don't you?" Mei nodded. "But you're a mother. How do you deal with seeing what we just saw?"

"You think of them like babies. That's not right. Think of them like..." Mei paused, searching for the right word.

"Like fish fry?" Benson offered.

Mei shrugged, conceding that she couldn't think of a better term. "They're not babies for another year. The ones that survive get a name then. Then they love them just like we do." She looked up at the stars and was quiet for a long moment. She loved looking at the stars. He did not.

"Why'd they keep more of them?" Benson asked, trying to get the conversation going again.

"Hmm?" Mei looked back down to him.

"You said they kept four this time instead of two. Why?"

She spread an arm across to where the battle had taken place. "Because they lost a lot today. Too many, can't feed them. Too few, can't work the fields or defend the village from raiders. Everything in balance."

Benson nodded. After spending the first three and a half decades of his life locked up inside a self-sufficient metal tube, he knew a thing or two about maintaining balance.

"Esa and I can't conceive."

The words hung in the air. Benson was as surprised by them as Mei was. He hadn't planned to say them, they just sort of rushed out. The silence between them stretched on uncomfortably. Under different circumstances, Benson would've called it a pregnant pause, but...

"How long?" Mei finally asked.

"Since the showdown with Kimura. The doc isn't sure if it was the radiation poisoning from the nuke or the chemo and nanites after, but my shit is busted."

"You mean you can't, ah–" Mei's eyes darted down to his

crotch, then back to his face.

Benson put up his hands in defense of his virility. "Oh, no, all the plumbing works, thank God, but there's no fish in the tanks. It could've been worse. They've already had to cut two tumors out of me."

"Can't the crew do something?"

"Eventually, maybe. But all our geneticists and techs are working overtime right now trying to get our food to grow on the surface instead of turning into sludge. My testicles are alarmingly low on their priority list at the moment."

Mei leaned in and hugged him tightly. "I'm sorry."

Benson fought back unexpected tears. "It's OK."

"It's not OK," she said. "You saved every family at the cost of having your own."

"The thought had occurred to me," Benson agreed. "Who were the two people who took the infants?"

"The parents," Mei said.

"The parents? But the mother–"

Mei shook her head. "Not mother, bearer. They carry the babies, but they're not parents."

It was Benson's turn to look at her funny. "How does that work, exactly?"

Mei paused for a long time, considering. Finally, she started again. "As far as I can tell, there are two genders, but not like men and women."

"Then what are they like?"

"It's complicated. They all go through both, one when they're younger, then the other when they become elders. They call it the transition."

That raised Benson's eyebrows. "They're both men and women at different times?"

"No. Well, sort of. It's like they go through puberty twice. What looks like old age, faded colors and smaller build, is just them transitioning to the other gender. The young and elders pair off, but to have children, they need a bearer. The bearers actually carry the children until they are ready to be born, but they aren't parents. They have eggs laid in them."

"That's... really gross," Benson said.

"It's not their fault, Benson-san. It's their nature. And bearers don't come along in every brood."

"Is that why this was the first time I've seen any of these 'bearers' after being here for four days?" Benson asked.

"Fewer of them are born. They are precious."

"So they're treated like a commodity," Benson said scornfully. "Hoarded like sex slaves."

Mei shook her head. "So quick to judge. Don't be in such a hurry. Learn, absorb, consider. Then decide."

The Atlantians returned to the surface. The two parents, whatever that meant, carried their quartet of newborns. Behind them, the limp, pale body of the bearer was carried by four others, held high in a position of reverence while the procession softly chanted. Kexx spotted the two of them sitting on the ground and peeled away from the rest.

"Benson-san," he said, a lingual artifact he'd almost certainly picked up from Mei.

"Just Benson is fine, Kexx. Look, I'm really sorry about the, um, misunderstanding down there."

Kexx waved him off, a very human gesture. He'd picked up a lot from his teacher. Did "he" really apply? Benson didn't know what to think.

"We'll talk about it later. Rest now. We wake with the light and go to work."

The old detective nestled in Benson's brain screamed to keep going. Not to let the trail get cold. To start working immediately while his memory was still fresh, the scene undisturbed, and the evidence untampered with.

His exhausted, early middle-aged body which had just been through combat for the first time in years, on the other hand, thought Kexx's suggestion held plenty of merit.

"That sounds lovely," Benson said.

The lanky alien nodded, then walked away, silent as a ghost. It was a useful skill in a partner, but Benson still couldn't help be a little unsettled by it. He glanced at Mei.

"I don't suppose you've got any whisky back at the shelter?"

"No," Mei puffed up with pride. "We have sake."

"That'll do."

CHAPTER SIXTEEN

Theresa stood at the edge of the landing strip and watched the blinking red and green lights grow against the night sky as the shuttle settled in for its final approach. Deputy Administrator Merick stood next to her, along with most of the rest of the council, business leaders, an emergency response team, and at least a couple of thousand curious onlookers.

"Word's gotten out," she said.

"Hard to keep something this big secret, I'm afraid," Merick said.

"Wish I had a couple more constables for crowd control."

"Probably unnecessary. I doubt our enemy has any sleeper agents hiding in *this* crowd."

"Our enemy?" Theresa repeated. "We don't know that our people were being targeted. It could have been a tribal dispute for all we know."

Merick shrugged off the point. "A semantic distinction at best. Don't forget, chief, we're out here to welcome home corpses."

Theresa had more to say, but let it go as the shuttle glided in to land on the improvised runway. Usually, the pilots would simply flip the engines over to their VTOL configuration and set down vertically on the pad. However, there were no qualified pilots aboard, the crew having been the first casualties of the battle. The shuttle was coming in on autopilot. Most of the shuttle's fuel reserve had been burned up in the unplanned maneuvers over the Atlantian village, giving the autopilot only one shot at a safe landing before the tanks went dry.

Even though she knew the shuttle was coming in at over two hundred kph, Theresa couldn't help but think it was just hanging in the night like a balloon. It was just so damned big, her mind had trouble believing it could fly at all.

Soon though, the rear wheels screeched against the tarmac and the shuttle leveled out. Theresa's hands shot up to protect her ears as the shuttle's thrust-reversers snapped into place and the engines ramped up to full power with a deafening roar, throwing out ringed cones of blue flame. In a shockingly short distance, the shuttle bled off almost all of its speed until it rolled to a stop near the end of the runway.

The large cargo-loading platform at the center of the fuselage dropped down, covered in bodies. Theresa recognized Korolev standing among the stretchers. He cupped his hands over his mouth and shouted loud enough to be heard over the dying engines. "Bring the defibrillator."

Theresa grabbed Dr Russell and headed for the platform. She skidded to a stop next to Korolev and the expedition's medic hunched over a body covered in shredded clothes and blood-soaked gauze and bandages. Theresa gasped when she finally recognized the face hiding under the dirt, dried blood, and tangled hair.

"Valmassoi," she said just as she was shoved out of the way by a medic.

"What's the story?" Russell asked Korolev.

"No pulse."

"How long?"

"A couple minutes ago. I don't understand, he's been stable the whole flight."

Russell nodded and retrieved a small white box from her kit. She pulled out the two contact patches, ripped off the protective plastic, and then slapped them into position on Valmassoi's chest and side. The box went through a short diagnostic to ensure that it wasn't about to shock a live person to death. A high pitch rose as its capacitor charged for the jolt until the "Ready" button turned green. In a calm synthetic voice, the defibrillator instructed everyone to step back, then delivered the shock.

Valmassoi's limp body went rigid for an instant, arching his back before going slack again. The process repeated twice more, increasing the voltage each time, but the result was unchanged.

"He's not responding. Bring the cart over," Russell ordered. One of Shambhala's few electric quad cars backed up to the platform and Theresa and Korolev loaded Valmassoi's stretcher onto the back. "I'll be back as soon as I can," Russell said. But even as the car pulled away toward the city's hospital, Theresa knew the gesture was merely a formality.

"He's going on the Clock," she said, still using Ark slang to mark a death. "Where's Atwood? We're going to need to debrief all of you as soon as possible."

"They didn't tell you?" Korolev shook his head, then pointed at one of the five sheets lying on the platform. Theresa knelt down and reached to pull the sheet back, but Korolev put his hand on her wrist. "I wouldn't. It's not pretty."

Theresa ignored him and yanked the sheet back, then immediately wished she hadn't. Atwood's head lay sideways, her throat shredded so that Theresa could see white spots of exposed spine. It looked like her neck had been torn apart by some wild animal. Korolev was right; it wasn't pretty.

Theresa covered her mouth as she replaced the sheet, then took a moment to collect herself. "What happened to her?"

"I was locked away when it happened, but I was told she got caught out in the open when the villager warriors' line collapsed. Her rifle didn't make her any friends among the invaders. Hamilton and DeSanto were on the roofs sniping the crap out of them, and the rest of us had fallen back into the temple. She was the only one they could get at and they swarmed her. Their spears and knives couldn't get through her riot gear, so they attacked the only exposed skin they could find." Korolev drew his thumb across his throat to illustrate the point.

"DeSanto and Hamilton?" Theresa asked, nodding toward the other sheets.

"No, they're alive. DeSanto should be good in a couple days, physically at least. But Hamilton broke his ankle jumping off a roof. He'll be out of commission for weeks."

Theresa nodded and glanced back down at Atwood's body. "We were in class together, you know. We were sort of friends.

Not real close. We fought over a boy once. Bryan always said she was one of the best Zero arrows he ever flew against."

"She was. Dislocated his shoulder once with a massive hit from above. I didn't see most of the attack, but everyone said she fought like an animal. She didn't abandon her position even after her rifle went dry. She killed a lot of them, made them pretty mad in the process."

Theresa stood up and straightened her shirt. "Who attacked us out there, Pavel?"

"I have no idea, ma'am."

"Well then we have our work cut out for us. C'mon, I need you to tell me everything you saw and everything Bryan told you."

Once news of Administrator Valmassoi's death became public, Shambhala went wild. Theresa and her constables spent most of the rest of the night running around the city asking protestors to disband. Sometimes, they had to ask pretty hard.

"It's 0340, Hallstead," Korolev said to one of the more pigheaded of the provocateurs. "And you're drunk."

"Says you," Yvonne Hallstead said without slurring. However, the effort of controlling her tongue overwhelmed what little spare operating capacity her inebriated brain had and caused her to sway like a gyroscope losing its spin.

Theresa grabbed her forearm to steady her, but Hallstead twisted her skinny arm away.

"Get'chur hands offa me," she said through a gaunt face and angular mouth. Theresa remembered this one. She was a computer tech and former crew member who'd been given the boot years earlier when she'd been caught fiddling with pharmacy records to get extra pain meds, which then ended up in the hands of "recreational users." A real winner. Theresa gave the rest of the hangers-on in her little protest circle a pained expression. Most of them had the good sense to look embarrassed for their choice of spokesperson.

Sensing the tide turning against her, Hallstead looked around accusingly. "Oh, I see. Just because I had a couple've beers, y'all think I'm spouting shit, huh? Well I didn't carve up Valmassery."

"Valmassoi," Korolev corrected.

"That's what I said. Anyway, I didn't do Valmasonry, those fan-headed fish-lizards done it."

"Who was buying your drinks tonight, Yvonne?" Theresa asked.

"What's that s-posed t' mean?"

"It's supposed to mean that I know you've run up a pretty big tab with Marinello's and they're not taking your credit at the moment. So I'm confused how you came to be so drunk outside their bar."

"My money's as good as anybody's."

"When you've got any, sure," Korolev quipped.

"I pays my bills!" she shouted. "And I don't like your tone, con-stable," Hallstead said, infinitely more proud of her wordplay than it justified.

The rest of the circle unraveled and evaporated into the streets. Theresa was exhausted and running very low on patience. "Here's the deal, Yvonne, you're drunk and disorderly. I can arrest you right now if I want to cause you trouble. But I don't, so I'm giving you the choice. You can sleep it off in your own bed, or in one of my cells. But you're going to choose right now."

Korolev moved in for his turn as good cop. "C'mon, Yvonne. Go have a lay down. I'm sure Juanita is worried sick."

"Yeah," Hallstead said slowly, unwinding a thought. "Yeah, you're right. Gotta work in the morning anyway."

"You have a new job?" Theresa asked.

"I'm an independent contractor, thank you very much, Mrs Patronizing." Without another word, she staggered off in the general direction of her house.

"Juanita isn't worried sick, is she?" Theresa asked.

"The only thing she's worried about is Yvonne catching her in bed with Raul Galveston. I'd almost feel bad for her if she wasn't such a dipshit." Korolev looked at Theresa's face. "Everything OK, chief? What are you thinking?"

"I'm thinking I'm exhausted. Aren't you tired? You haven't stopped since getting off the shuttle."

"I grabbed some rack time on the flight back."

"Right after being in combat, you mean?"

Korolev shrugged. "I'm trying not to think about it too much. It helps to keep busy."

Theresa bobbed her head, only half listening. "Doesn't any of this seem strange to you?"

"You mean standing on an alien world, harassing drunks at four in the morning? Or something else?"

Theresa smirked. "It's all relative, I suppose. I mean tonight."

"What part?"

"All of it. Our shuttle comes home days ahead of schedule to a crowd of thousands? 'Spontaneous' protests pop up all over town in the dead of night, led by the likes of Yvonne Hallstead?"

"Our leader was assassinated by aliens. That's going to get a rise out of anybody."

"Yeah, but *Hallstead*? She's not exactly a political activist, is she? She couldn't even pronounce Valmassoi's name."

"She was pretty drunk. You know how ideas get stuck in people's heads when they've been hitting the sauce."

"Sure, but who stuck it in there?" she asked.

Korolev put up a finger. "Just a second." He disappeared into the bar's back entrance, leaving Theresa alone with her thoughts. Maybe her conversation with Bryan had left her paranoid, jumping at shadows. But she couldn't help but feel like the whole thing, from the crowds at the landing strip to the protests, didn't feel too "spontaneous."

Korolev stepped back out from the alley. "Maya says Yvonne paid off her tab tonight. That's why they started serving her again."

"When?"

"Just after the shuttle landed."

Theresa's eyes rolled. "And she paid cash or some other untraceable barter, I bet."

Korolev nodded. "All cash."

"Of course."

"You think she stole it?"

Theresa shook her head. "No. Hallstead's history means she knows we're keeping a close eye on her, it wouldn't be worth the risk. I think an anonymous donor chose tonight to mint themselves a loyal patriot. Probably more than one of them."

"The person who hired on her services as a contractor?"

"That would make sense," Theresa said.

"Why, though?"

"That's the question, isn't it? C'mon, we both need to sleep."

"You go on ahead, chief. I'm going to walk Maya home."

Theresa cocked an eyebrow. "Are you now?"

"It's not like that. She's a little shook up from the protests and wants an escort back to her house is all."

Theresa smiled and put a hand on his cheek. "Pavel, you're adorable. A little thick, but adorable. Just make sure once you're done 'escorting' her that you actually get some sleep tonight, OK?"

"OK…" Korolev said uncertainly. "Goodnight, chief."

"Goodnight." She watched him return to the back entrance, then turned and walked down the wide radial street toward the Beehive. There was end-of-shift paperwork to submit. Funny, she thought, the only paper she'd ever seen was in the museum, but the name still stuck. Even out here, trillions of miles from the world of their birth, humans were still creatures of habit.

She'd picked up a few of her own habits over the years. Theresa had been a constable for most of her adult life before taking over as chief so her husband could go play ball with kids of all ages. It was a pretty good arrangement, actually. Coaching suited his temperament better, since shouting at the top of one's lungs wasn't only tolerated, but expected. Bryan had many fine qualities, but Zen-like calm was not among them. Besides, she'd been angling for the job since before they'd started dating. It was one of the reasons they'd started dating, if she was going to be honest with herself.

After more than a decade in law enforcement, Theresa felt like she had good habits. First among them was knowing the only way to let out the pus was to keep picking at the scab. Tomorrow, once she'd had a chance to sober up, she was going to have a chat with dear Yvonne Hallstead and see if she could find out who her new benefactor was.

Second among her habits was knowing how to keep her inquiries quiet until she had enough evidence. But that required people who understood the need for discretion. On a whim,

Theresa turned away from the path to the Beehive and headed down one of the concentric roads, to the high-rent housing district.

All of the homes and buildings in Shambhala had been preprogramed and printed in only the last three years and change, so everything had a certain uniformity that was difficult to shake off. Some occupants did their best to stand out with clever landscaping in their postage-stamp "lawns," but the vegetation in this part of Gaia was about as varied and inspiring as the utilitarian, straight-angled homes themselves. The Ark's geneticists were far too busy trying to get their grain crops to take root to worry about thawing out any Old Earth topiaries.

But not here on the "Golden Mile." Here the custom homes of former crewmembers and business moguls sat. The families that had built the exclusive residential towers, restaurants, and luxury goods during the Ark's long journey. And they weren't about to live in the prefabbed hovels of the plebs. Architectural inspiration taken from Rome to Taipei adorned the homes with columns, tile roofs, bay windows, anything to announce the conspicuous consumption that everyone liked to pretend had been left behind on Earth centuries before. The largest of them belonged to the Alexander family. Which was only proper, as they had built the rest of them as well.

Theresa found the house she was looking for. It was the smallest and least adorned on the block, barely up to the standards of the neighborhood, but allowed in almost as a charity. She'd been here once a little over a year ago when, miraculously, she and her husband had been invited to the housewarming party. The walk home that evening had been… muddled. Confident she wasn't about to wake a council member unexpectedly, she rang the doorbell and waited.

After that didn't work, she rang it again, then respectfully pounded on the door.

"I know you're in there," she said into the com unit in the door frame. "I can see your locator on my plant."

The door opened slowly, reproachfully. In the dim streetlight, former First Officer Chao Feng glared at her.

"Are you aware what time it is, constable?"

"Painfully aware," Theresa said. "May I come in for a minute?"

Feng scoffed theatrically. "If this is some sort of booty call, you'll need to grow a cock pretty quick." He pointed at her chest. "And ditch the tits."

Theresa grabbed her breasts in mock affront. "What? Everyone loves boobs."

"Not in this house, honey." Feng paused. "Although my son is almost ten and is starting to ask some really awkward questions. Maybe you could–"

"Nope. Pass. That's all on you."

Defeated, Feng opened the door wider and invited her inside. "Can I get you anything? Tea?"

"I'm fine, thanks. So, Jian isn't taking after his old man in the dating department?"

"If his database searches are any indication, it would appear not."

Feng collapsed onto his antique couch sideways. A *leather* couch, Theresa couldn't help but notice. Even in the dark, the interior of the house betrayed its opulence. It wasn't quite as overt as the first officer's quarters Theresa and Benson had raided for stolen art, but Feng wasn't exactly suffering in exile either.

"Mrs Benson, I have to be to work in a few hours, and I expect it's going to be a *very* hectic few days. So, without wanting to sound rude, but not really caring if I do, what the hell do you want?"

Theresa sat up straight and folded her hands in her lap. "Your help, if you can believe it."

Feng's relationship to the house of Benson had a strained history. During much of the Edmond Laraby investigation three years earlier, Feng had been a prime suspect. *The* suspect, actually, and her husband had hounded him tirelessly. Ultimately, Feng had been innocent of the murder, but he'd tried to use his power and influence to derail the investigation instead of coming clean about the intimate nature of his relationship with the late Mr Laraby. Feng and Theresa's husband had badly misjudged one another, and it almost came at the price of the entire human race. It wasn't an easy thing to forget.

Feng smoothed out a wrinkle on his velour, monogramed

robe. "I can't, but I'm listening all the same."

"Bryan's in trouble."

Feng snorted. "You can say that again. If he had any sense, he'd have come home with the shuttle."

"I think he wanted to, but he's got his nose on a scent, and you know how singleminded he can be."

"Better than most," Feng said bitterly before motioning for her to continue.

"Bryan noticed some... fortuitous happenstances leading up to and during the attack."

Feng sat up at this. "Fortuitous for whom?"

"For the people doing the attacking."

"Such as?"

Theresa paused, considering just how much she wanted to share. At the moment, all she had were suspicious coincidences. If they were going to be more than that, she'd need information that important people would've taken great care to keep hidden from official channels. That meant cozying up to and ultimately trusting someone who sometimes worked outside of "official" channels. Feng was about as honest as that sort came.

Screw it, she thought. *Gotta trust someone*. "On their walk into the village, a flight of birds came out of nowhere and disabled Atwood's recon drone, which let a group of the village's warriors get the drop on them and almost started a shooting incident right then."

"Maybe they were territorial birds."

"Maybe, but we've been here for three years, and Pathfinder's drones have been flying around for almost four. Have any of them been attacked before?"

Feng pursed his lips. "One of the crawlers was trampled in a broom-head stampede, but we haven't lost any of the fliers to wildlife as far as I can remember. Still, it's a mostly unexplored continent. Maybe we just haven't run into this particular species before."

"That's possible," Theresa admitted, "But it's only the first example."

"Continue," Feng said, slipping into the tone he used to employ on the Ark's bridge when listening to a report. That was probably good, it meant he was taking the conversation seriously enough to fall into old patterns. Creatures of habit.

"When the attack came three days later, it was perfectly timed with the local satellite coverage gap caused by those two platforms we lost last year."

Feng sucked air through his teeth. "I hadn't heard that part. That *is* pretty convenient."

"It gets worse." Theresa leaned forward and propped her elbows on her knees. "The only other way to get a signal into orbit was the shuttle's transmitter, and it picked that moment to shit the bed? Er, so to speak."

Feng smirked. "You don't need to censor yourself here, Theresa. Unless I'm very mistaken, you didn't intend this to be an official visit."

"Not exactly, no."

"Well then fuck it. However, your husband was still able to get a signal to the Ark, yes?"

Theresa nodded. "But only because he convinced the villagers to help him wreck the temple they'd built for our rover and use its transmitter instead. I don't think whoever was planning this anticipated that possibility. The Ark crew used the rover to piggyback a signal to the shuttle and remote pilot it. If that hadn't happened, everyone, and I do mean everyone, would've been dead by the time the coverage gap passed. Our first indication anything was wrong would've been orbital pictures of the village after it had been sacked."

Feng was sitting upright by then, his fingers steepled as he contemplated what he'd heard. "That all sounds very suspicious. One issue I have. If the shuttle's transmitter was sabotaged, it would've had to be one of the flight crew that did it. It's buried pretty deep inside the avionics bay, not the sort of place you could explain how to find to a native who has only recently cracked the mystery of the wheel."

"True enough," Theresa said.

"But the whole flight crew was killed, yes? Why would one of the crew members agree to be in on the conspiracy if their reward was a spear point?"

Theresa shrugged her shoulders. "Maybe they weren't

told about the spear point. Or maybe the natives got overly enthusiastic. I don't know, I don't even have a working theory yet. I'm just at the point where I see a lot of weird shit that doesn't add up and feel the need to shake it until it falls into place."

"Sounds like a terrible compulsion to live with."

"No doubt, but a useful one in my line of work."

"Too true." Feng seemed to switch gears. "Why me? Where do I 'fall into place?'"

"I need a back-channel guy. Official channels have a habit of getting stonewalled as soon as uncomfortable questions start getting asked about important people. I'm sure you wouldn't know anything about that—"

"Cheeky."

"—but it's true. I need a go-between that understands the dealings of both the front and back of house. That's you, Feng. You're the very definition of a go-between. You've been holding the unstable alliance of the Ark crew and Shambhala's provisional government together almost singlehandedly for three years already."

"I'm flattered you noticed."

"It's my *job* to notice."

Feng put up a hand. "I understand. But, the thought occurs. Why trust me? Your husband is out in the bush with no backup. If I held a grudge over our previous... unpleasantness, now would be a wonderful opportunity to act on it."

"A few reasons." Theresa started counting off with her fingers. "One. You've had plenty of opportunities over the years. Two, you've been very good about keeping up appearances, inviting us to the housewarming, for example."

"Thank you for the candelabras, by the way," Feng said. "I don't remember if I sent you a note."

"You didn't. Three, you didn't act out of malice the last time. Don't get me wrong, you acted stupidly, but you did so to protect your family. I understand that now, maybe better than I did back then."

"Marriage will do that to you."

Theresa held up a final finger. "Four, unless I'm very much

mistaken, I think it would amuse you greatly to put my husband in the uncomfortable position of owing you a *very* big favor."

Feng sank back into the white leather of the couch. "Oh dear girl, would it surprise you to hear that thought hadn't occurred to me until just now?" He inhaled sharply through his nose and smiled. "Yes, I would find that very amusing. When do we start?"

"Tomorrow," Theresa said. "Well, today, I suppose, considering the time. But after I've slept in either case."

"Fair enough." Feng stood up and walked her to the door. "Where do you want me to start?"

"Start with the satellite gap. See if you can find a list of database queries for when the gap would fall over Atlantis."

"A lot of people coordinating the expedition would have perfectly legitimate reasons for that kind of search."

"True, but while you do that, I'm going to run a search on correspondence to and from the flight crew, then crossreference them manually."

"Keeping your final list off the grid to avoid setting off any alarms." Feng nodded approvingly. "Smart."

"I'm not just a set of tits, Feng."

"Perhaps *more* than just a set of tits would be more accurate. They are definitely among your assets."

Theresa rolled her eyes. "Men. There's a repressed little boy hiding inside all of you."

"I've had more than one repressed little boy inside of me," Feng countered.

Theresa slapped him on the arm. "Too much information, Feng." She let her tone become quieter, more serious. "Can I ask you something personal?" He nodded acquiescence. "I've never seen you out with anyone. It's been a while now since... Since your wife passed on, and you seem so lonely."

Feng shrugged. "I still scratch the itch when needed, but to be honest..." Feng glanced over his shoulder and up the stairs to where Jian slept in his own little bedroom. "My standards are quite a bit higher than they used to be."

"I understand."

"No," Feng shook his head. "You won't until you have your own family. I may have some personal history preventing me from liking Bryan very much, but even I can see you've got a good man in him. Take advantage of it while there's time."

Theresa found herself holding back sudden tears. She'd tried to take advantage. They both had. After a year of trying, Bryan had finally gone to Dr Russell and learned the awful truth; that his fight with Kimura had cost more than either of them could've imagined.

The revelation had hit her pretty hard, but if she was honest, it appeared to have been even more devastating for Bryan. He'd never said as much openly, but Theresa suspected that Bryan felt like something less than a whole man since learning he couldn't give her a child. She wondered idly how much those feelings of guilt and emasculation had weighed on his decision to stay behind in Atlantis.

Always something to prove, her man.

"Believe me, I'd love to. Goodnight, Mr Feng."

"Ciao," he said, and closed the door.

As she walked away, Theresa realized she wasn't sure if he'd meant the salutation, or his name.

CHAPTER SEVENTEEN

As ze did every morning, Kexx rose before the light of dawn. It was a habit passed down from master to apprentice and a point of pride among truth-diggers. Most of the rest of the village was still asleep, waiting for the light of morning to warm their stiff limbs before venturing out in the day.

Waking so early had not come naturally to Kexx in zer youth. In the end, it took five days of zer mentor, Fullo, waking zer with a bucket of cold water so ze knew what "real cold feels like" to finally drive the point home.

There were still days that Kexx awoke bolt upright, clutching zer chest, expecting to be soaking wet. Today was not one of them, somewhat surprisingly. Ze stood and performed zer waking prayers to Cuut and Xis, anointed zerself with the prescribed oils (which also conveniently protected the skin against sunburn) and then donned zer few bits of jewelry and cloth. Zer thoughts flickered to Mei and the other humans, who insisted on covering their bodies with cloth to an absurd degree. Except when they swam in the lake, where a whole different set of rules seemed to apply.

Kexx laughed. They were a strange people, with a lot of strange ideas, but ze had grown fond of them in the short time since Mei's refugees had landed on their shores. And now ze was tasked with working with one to solve a mystery and hopefully avert a war.

At first light, messages from the other villages would flood the signal tower, all of them demanding answers for the attack and satisfaction for their dead. A wave started to build as soon as the announcement went out last night. It would build higher the longer it took Kexx and Benson to find out who was responsible. And if they couldn't, Kexx had no illusions about where that wave would come crashing down instead.

It was a short walk from Kexx's home to the humans' shelter, but ze jogged anyway, partly to loosen up stiff muscles, partly to warm up in the cool air of predawn. The stab wound in Kexx's thigh burned as ze ran, but considering what so many others had suffered, Cuut had shown zer considerable favor.

Kexx walked into the humans' shelter, although "shelter" probably didn't apply anymore. They'd been busy expanding the modest structure for months, adding awnings and lean-tos as the need arose. There were even a couple of outbuildings they used for storage and strange racks they used to farm some of their own small crops they'd brought over on their boat to supplement their rations from the village's supplies. They were very fond of one fungus in particular, something Mei called shitake. They used it in nearly everything and had at least a fullhand of different ways to prepare it, exactly none of which had been to Kexx's liking so far.

The humans, by and large, seemed to handle the morning chill with less hassle than Kexx's people. Several of them were already wide awake and busy preparing their large morning meal. That was something else about the humans: they ate a *lot*. Kexx had watched tiny Mei put down enough food in one sitting to keep zer own belly full for the entire day. And they did it three or four times every day. How they managed not to puff out like a startled hala fish, ze had no idea.

One of them looked up from chopping tubers and nodded a greeting as Kexx passed. Ze'd spent enough time in the shelter to be a common sight.

"Benson?" Kexx asked the young human. Some of them had started to learn G'tel, especially the children. But none of them had yet risen to Mei's proficiency, so it was best to keep things simple. The youth got up and took Kexx's hand without hesitation and tugged zer toward the back of the shelter.

Lying in a hammock sagging near the floor and dangling an

arm, Benson snored in blissful oblivion. Zer comfort ended when the young human yanked off zer blanket and poked Benson in the back. Benson jerked awake like a startled dux'ah, tumbled out of the hammock and landed hard on the ground in a pile. The younger human found this immensely entertaining and laughed freely.

Clutching zer head with one hand, Benson grabbed the youth's ankle and growled.

"Coffee. Now," ze said.

The youth shook zer head. "No coffee."

Benson moaned. "Tea, then."

Still giggling, the smaller human headed back for the food prep area. Kexx looked down and offered Benson a hand up.

"I'm fine down here just now, thanks."

"Benson. We must begin our work."

Benson sat up slowly, then crossed zer legs and cradled zer head in zer hands. "After my tea."

"Are you ill?"

"I'm hung over is what I am."

Kexx grimaced. "Hung over what?"

"Don't you people get hangovers?" Kexx shrugged uncomprehendingly. "How lucky for you. Yes, I'm ill."

"Our work cannot wait."

"It will wait until I've drank my tea," Benson said irritably. "Then I'm all yours." The youth returned with a steaming hot cup of water with dried leaves floating in it. Benson held out his hand without looking up and gripped the offered cup. Ze held the cup under zer... nose, Mei had called it, and inhaled. "Ah, oolong. That'll do the trick." Ze swirled the cup around as the water within slowly stained black, then took a long drink.

Kexx waited patiently for zer new companion to finish zer tea. Benson threw zer head back and drained what was left from the cup, then spat the dregs back into the cup.

"Mmm, good stuff." Benson picked a leaf off of zer tongue and flicked it away. "Wish they had filters, though. Care for a cup?"

"No, it hurts my stomach," Kexx said. "Benson, I think we should speak my language while we work."

"Agreed," Benson answered in G'tel after a slight pause.

"Where to first, Kemosabe?"

Kexx stumbled over the last word. "I don't know what that means."

"Sorry. It's from... actually, I have no idea where it's from. It just means friend from another land, I think."

Benson rose on shaky legs. Kexx held down a hand to steady zer. Benson took it. "Your hand's freezing," ze said. "You should warm up by the fire."

"I'm fine. I think we should start in the forest where I first ran into the intruders."

Benson shook zer head. "That can wait. The prisoners have been cooling their, whatever the back of your feet are called, for long enough now. We can start sweating them for info."

"What prisoners?"

Benson looked at zer confused. "The dozen invaders we captured yesterday, remember? Blacked-out skin, disagreeable attitude?"

"The intruders are all dead, Benson."

Benson stared at zer for a long, uncomfortable moment.

"You killed them," ze said finally with a bite in zer voice not even Kexx could miss. It wasn't a question. It was an accusation.

"They were allowed to kill themselves, Benson, as is their right as defeated warriors."

Benson threw up zer arms in frustration. "Great!" ze shouted in human. "I'm working with a samurai squid." Ze took a deep breath. "I'm sorry. That was rude," ze said, switching back to G'tel.

Kexx didn't know what "samurai squid" meant, but assumed it wasn't intended to be complimentary. "I'm surprised, Benson. You had no reservations about killing yesterday."

"That was combat. Our lives were in danger."

"Our lives are still in danger, Ki-mo-sa-bee." Kexx sounded out the new word to try it on for size. "The gathering happened in our village. The other villages will stain the ground for the deaths of their emissaries. Either with the blood of those responsible..."

"Or the blood of your village," Benson finished for zer quietly. Kexx nodded.

"We could have found out a lot quicker if there was someone

left to ask," Benson protested. "Can we at least have a look at the bodies?"

"They are probably being prepared by the elders by now."

"Prepared for what?"

"Their pyres, of course," Kexx said as if explaining it to a child. Which, ze supposed, ze was. Benson had only been here for a halfhand of days. The fact ze could speak the language so effectively made it difficult to remember that ze was still a newcomer.

"Where? Show me where."

"What do you expect to find?"

"No way to know until we get there. Hurry."

Kexx shrugged. "Follow me."

With Benson trailing, Kexx reached the small building near the edge of the village where the bodies of the returning were prepared to meet Xis once more. Business for the two elders inside was rather more robust than usual. Outside, two lines of the returning had been carefully laid out on the ground. One line had already gone through the rites, while the others waited patiently for their turn on the table. *Very* patiently.

The lines had no regard for who was who. Kexx recognized two of zer friends lying next to two of the invaders who'd killed them, their skin still cloaked in black. Death had united them all. Benson knelt down to inspect one of the returning that awaited preparation. "I recognize this one." Ze pointed to the significant hole running through the body's left eye. "I think it's the one I killed outside the temple."

"With a fishing trident."

"How did you know that?"

"Words spread."

"Yeah, well, it was the only thing I could find. Can we get some light out here?"

Kexx grabbed the body's feet and nodded at the door. "Let's take zer inside."

They ambled with the awkward load through the doorway and into the small preparation room.

"Truth-digger," Chak looked up from zer work, surprised and annoyed by the interruption. "You can't be here now."

"You know I can, Chak. We have to inspect this body before you perform the rites."

"We?" Chak looked past Kexx and saw Benson standing at the other end of the body, holding its arms, and promptly turned bright blue with incandescent rage. Chak pointed an accusing finger at the human. "What is that *defiler* doing here?"

"Defiler?" Benson asked. "That's a little strong, don't you think?"

Chak's finger hadn't budged. "You shattered the Emissary's Sanctuary!"

"'Sanctuary?'" Kexx asked mockingly. "You mean that shoddy dome we built four days ago?"

"And saved your life in the process, if I remember right," Benson shot back at Chak. Kexx would have preferred to handle it zerself. Benson had proven to be... less than diplomatic since zer arrival in the village.

"And as if that wasn't bad enough, ze threatened an elder in Xis's womb during a birthing ceremony. Namely me!"

That one carried a little more weight.

"Yeah, you've got me there," Benson said more quietly. "It was a misunderstanding. I'm sorry. Won't happen again."

"Ze has no right to be in here. I demand ze leaves immediately."

"Humans were killed in the attack too, Chak. They are back in their village being prepared for their own returns even now."

"As if Xis would have them!"

Kexx was known throughout the village for zer calm temper and respectful nature, but Chak was testing even zer patience. Zer skin grew darker, its patterns hardening into jagged edges.

"That was ugly, elder, and does not become someone of your position. The humans fought with us. You are alive to prepare our dead because of them, and they have just as much cause to dig for the truth as we do. You will *not* deny them the opportunity."

"I can and will. You know the rites, Kexx. I have to finish preparing the returning before sunrise. The sky already glows with morning."

"Then we will be quick, and we will help you finish."

Chak pointed at Kexx. "*You* will help me finish." The finger then stabbed back at Benson. "*Ze* will wait outside."

Kexx bowed and let a soft glow return to zer skin in a conciliatory gesture. "As you wish, elder."

Without another word, Chak set down zer anointing cloth and stormed out of the room with a huff.

"Quickly," Kexx said. "Get zer up on the table."

Benson obliged, then tipped zer head toward the door. "Kind of a hard ass, that one."

"Ass" was new to Kexx's vocabulary, but the meaning seemed obvious enough in context. "In fairness, you *have* been somewhat disruptive since your arrival, Benson."

"I get that a lot."

"I don't doubt it." Kexx motioned at the body lying on the table in the torch light. "We're here now. What are we doing?"

Benson walked around the body once, stopping here and there to inspect the fingers, a wound, the returning's black coating. Abruptly, ze stopped and stood straight up.

"Well, I have no idea what I'm looking at. I need you to tell me what you see, Kexx."

"A body?"

"Go deeper. Explain everything you see. Walk me through this like I'm a child."

Kexx laughed. "I think I can do that."

"Yes, yes. Laugh it up. But we're on the clock."

"Clock?"

Benson grimaced. "Time. We're low on time."

Kexx nodded. Time, humans were obsessed with it, always checking it, labeling it, and cutting it up as if they could take a knife to something they couldn't even hold in their hands. Kexx had trouble with the whole concept. Cuut already defined the year, Varr's passings broke up the year, and Xis's spin punctuated the days. What further divisions were necessary?

Still, Cuut really would rise soon, so ze took to the task, looking over every detail of the corpse and explaining what ze saw to zer new apprentice. "Height and size are on the large side, but normal for a warrior from any of the villages or nomads."

"Nomads?"

Kexx nodded. "There are tribes in the west and south that never settled in villages. They wander the plains, hunting wild herds."

"Are they violent?"

Kexx flickered. "Usually not, but in times of drought they have been known to raid our fields and steal from our herds."

"But nothing of the size of yesterday?"

"It's not just the size, it's the coordination and goals. They steal food to survive, they don't come into our villages to make war. Besides, I actually spoke to their commander in the forest. Ze spoke much too well to be a nomad."

"You actually spoke to him?"

"Zer," Kexx corrected. It was a strange affectation. Mei had shared it in the beginning and took many days to break zerself of the habit.

"Sorry, zer," Benson said. "Could you tell where they were from?"

"No, I didn't recognize the accent."

Ze returned to the body and rubbed off some of the black coating the invader had used to cover zer skinglow, tasting it on zer fingers. It was smoky and bitter.

"Charcoal pigment, mixed with plant sap as a binder."

"Do you recognize the plant?" Benson asked.

Kexx rubbed the pigment on zer tongue to try and refine the flavor, but shook zer head and spat it out. "No, I don't. Very bitter, I doubt it's edible." Kexx moved down the rest of the body. There was very little to see. The invader wore no necklaces or bracelets that could give away any clues to zer village of origin, probably by design. Ze reached the end of the table and inspected the returning's feet.

"Ah, that settles it."

Benson perked up. "Settles what?"

Kexx picked up the foot and bent the leg forward so Benson could get a good look at the bottom of the returning's toes. Oddly, the human covered zer mouth and shut zer eyes. Ze almost looked sick.

"What's wrong?"

"Sorry," Benson said. "It's just when a human leg bends like that, something went very badly."

"What, like this?" Kexx rotated the knee joint around its full range until Benson turned away.

"Hilarious. Do you mind?"

"Sorry." Kexx gripped the lower leg and squeezed hard, pulling on the tendons and splaying open the foot's four toes. "If you look closely, you can see a pattern of wear and calluses on the skin."

"I'll take your word for it. What does it mean?"

"That our intruder here spent a lot of time walking on bare rock." Kexx lifted zer own foot to illustrate the similar pattern. "It's common among those who spend time on the road system or walking around on mudstone floors."

"And the nomads don't use your roads as trails?"

Kexx shook zer head. "No, they think the roads are unnatural, cursed."

Benson stroked zer chin. "So villagers, then. That narrows it down to, what, two dozen different places?"

"Minus one. We can be sure they weren't from our village, after all."

"Not a huge help, in the end. Is there anything else you can tell me about the body?"

Kexx stood back and tried to take in the entire scene, searching out anything ze might have missed from being too close, but failed.

"No. They went to some effort to frustrate any truth-diggers."

Benson leaned against the wall and crossed zer arms. "We should line everyone from the other villages up and ask them if they recognize any of the invaders' bodies."

"It's already been done," Kexx said. "Without result."

"You think someone is lying?"

"I try not to dwell on what I can't know," Kexx said with a forced serenity.

The human seemed sympathetic. "So, where do we go next?"

Kexx took zer own spot leaning against the wall and considered their options. "I think once the light comes up, we go to the spot in the forest where I found them. From there, we can pick up their trail and see how far we can follow it."

Benson crossed his arms and smiled. "Outstanding. Do we have time for breakfast?"

CHAPTER EIGHTEEN

The trail ended less than a kilometer outside the village's halo trees. Or, more precisely, scattered like leaves thrown into a strong wind, branching off in a hundred seemingly random directions. Benson stood back and watched quietly as his Atlantian partner tried in vain to follow each new trail, tasting the air and ground with his outstretched fingers. But with each dead end and double-back, it became apparent even to Benson's untrained eye that Kexx's body language grew frustrated.

"I don't understand," Kexx said. "If this was their escape route, it would make sense. But these are the tracks they used to come *in*. It's like broken pottery shards all jumped up off the floor and made a pot."

"That's an impressive level of coordination," Benson said. "For all of them to arrive from different places at the same spot at the same time, that's no easy feat. Have you seen anything like this before?"

Kexx sat down heavily among the rows of yulka stalks before answering. "Among hunting parties converging on prey, but not on this scale."

Benson sat next to him and crossed his legs. "What about the warriors who hid among our guests and attacked us from inside the village? Someone must have noticed them sneak in."

"I already thought of that. They were there the whole time. They came in with the rest of the envoys. No one recognized them, but everyone just assumed they were from one of the other villages."

Benson laughed an angry little laugh. It was exactly what he'd warned Valmassoi about. Too many bodies and no way to run backgrounds on anybody. It wasn't like the Atlantians had an extensive ID database to work with. It was a nightmare scenario from a security and crowd control standpoint, yet they'd walked straight into it, whistling in the wind without a care in the world.

He'd opposed the presence of Atwood's people initially because he believed an armed escort, especially one with firepower beyond even the understanding of their hosts, sent entirely the wrong message for what was supposed to be a diplomatic expedition. But now he had to admit the truth; not only had Atwood's detachment been the only thing that prevented the entire village from being sacked, but not even their crushing technological superiority had been enough to prevent a complete massacre.

They'd all been overconfident. The image of Atwood's ravaged throat would remain a potent reminder for him personally. She'd been tough, a competitor. She was smart and aggressive and knew how to use her small size to its greatest advantage. If Madison Atwood could be brought down, anyone could.

Benson absently stroked the top of his rifle, knowing full well that it held the power to take dozens of lives with the ammunition he had, but that it was a price the enemy they faced was only too eager to pay. If even a handful of warriors remained standing when his gun ran dry, nothing would save him.

He knew exactly where their assumptions had gone wrong. Every living human, except for the handful of infants who had been born on Gaia in the last three years, had lived their entire lives locked away in a fish bowl, fixated on the ultimate goal of preserving the last thin strand of humanity from oblivion. Eleven generations had lived in a permanent state of crisis. Every life was precious. Every child a miracle.

It was exactly that shared belief that had made Kimura's attempted genocide and the loss of two fifths of the Ark's population so unconscionable. Most of the survivors had never really dealt with the tragedy, not really. Instead, they made planetfall on Gaia, got off the Ark, and busied themselves with the work of building a new world, never looking back to think of the old one. There were exceptions, like the Returners who wanted nothing more than to go back to their comparatively leisurely lives in Avalon, lives that simply didn't exist anymore no matter how much they yearned for them. But the majority of them hadn't had any real ties to anyone in Shangri-La module. For most everyone else, the catastrophe was simply too big to risk thinking about in all but the most abstract, superficial terms.

For the Atlantians, life was not nearly so precious. Benson's mind returned to the birthing ceremony and the culling of the... unworthy. As a people, they'd been groomed literally from birth to accept staggering casualties when necessary.

"Benson?"

Benson looked up to see Kexx staring at him. "Yes, sorry. I was just wool-gather... I was just thinking."

"About?"

"How many trails have you found already?"

"Over two fullhands. They branch off and lead–"

"West, right? Towards all the other villages."

Kexx made a non-committal gesture. "Roughly. We can't be sure without tracking them individually."

"But that's obviously what we're supposed to think, right?"

"Possibly."

"OK, and if that's true, why not frame just one other village? A village you have a feud with, for example? We chase down the false trail, your enemy gets the blame, you get away clean. So why wouldn't you? Unless..."

"Unless the enemy wants suspicions to fall on every village equally. It would keep us busy longer if we had to eliminate each possibility. And it would keep them pointing fingers at each other, sowing mistrust."

"Maybe." Benson let the idea twirl around in his head for a few seconds. Something about it was nagging at him. "Or maybe they didn't know enough about the villages to pull off the frame. You're sure it couldn't have been nomads?"

Kexx was adamant. "No, their feet were worn wrong to be plains walkers, and the one I spoke to sounded too refined."

"And where is the leader, anyway? You said you put a spear through their leg."

"I did. The other warriors must've carried zer off."

"Without a blood trail? Without digging tracks in the dirt from dragging them on a litter?"

Kexx's skin patterns only fluttered in the alien's approximation of a shrug.

Benson rubbed his chin. "What *did* they sound like?"

"What do you mean?"

"I mean, where from, would you guess?"

"I don't know. Each village has a slight accent, and I hadn't met every village until this gathering. But the leader's accent was *very* different. Almost as bad as, well, yours. Which brings me to a question of my own, Benson..."

"Yes?"

"I wanted to ask how you and the rest of your people learned our language so fast. Mei picked it up faster than any child I've ever seen, but it still took zer Varrs."

"That's because I didn't really learn it. Our rover has been listening to you since you found it. Some very smart people onboard..." Benson stopped himself before talking about the Ark. He didn't know how much Kexx already knew, nor, frankly, how much he could absorb all at once. "Smart people back at our village translated it. Then the translation was, ah... you probably don't have a word for 'downloaded' do you?" Kexx shook his, *zer*, head. "Right. The translation is put into a, a tool in our brains where we can know it without having to learn it."

Kexx's face was skeptical, to say the least. "I'm not sure I understand how that works."

Benson shrugged. "I'm not sure I do, to be honest. We call them 'plants,' but not like plants we eat. See?"

"No."

"Right." Benson glowered while he tried to come up with a better way to explain himself. "These plants communicate and store information. You have a way to write down information, numbers, words, yes?" Kexx nodded. "And you have the signaling tower that can move information around very quickly without speaking, yes?"

"But our signal towers use light."

Benson perked up. "Yes, exactly. Our plants use a type of light too, except you can't see it." The look on Kexx's face told Benson that the concept of "light you can't see" was fighting for the label of oxymoron. "I know that probably doesn't make much sense."

"I'm trying," Kexx admitted. "So, these... plants that aren't plants use invisible light to think for you?"

"No." Benson put up his hands. "Not at all. Well, kind of. They just... they store extra memories for us. But we still do all the thinking."

"We are the sum of our memories, Benson. If your memories are not entirely your own, then you are not entirely yourself."

Benson raised a finger to object, but realized he couldn't. It wasn't a question he'd ever really wrestled with. His plant had been there from the beginning. It had always been a part of him. And being out here, cut off from the real-time updates and database searches he'd taken for granted his entire life, there was no arguing with the Atlantian that he wasn't entirely himself without it. The question was, did the plant make him less than he would have been without it, or more?

It was a question best left to philosophers and poets, neither of which Benson had ever made much time for.

"If what you're saying is true," Kexx continued, "then why didn't Mei pick up our language as quickly as you did?"

"Because Mei and the rest of the humans living with you don't have plants."

"Why not?"

"Because they didn't believe in them. They left to be independent from us."

"But they were of your village."

Benson wasn't sure what Kexx meant by that. "We're not a village, Kexx. We're a race. We have disagreements, sometimes serious disagreements. I'm sure you have disagreements with the G'tel in other villages."

"They are not G'tel."

"They're not? Then what are they?"

"They are of their village."

"OK, yes, but what do you call your people then? All of the people in all of the villages?"

"I don't understand."

Benson furrowed his brow. He'd known the Atlantians were tribal, but this was at a level he'd never expected. How to explain the concept of a species? "No matter where we live, anyone like me calls themselves a human. What do your people call themselves?"

"G'tel. Other villages are not like us."

"But... You all worship Xis and Cuut, right?"

"And Varr, of course. They are the gods of all creatures. It is only natural that all worship them."

"Even humans?"

"Er..."

"What if I told you we worshiped different gods from Xis, Cuut, and Varr? That we've never heard of them before we came here. That we have different gods, even different gods among humans. Or that many of us worship no gods at all?"

He could see the line of questioning was beginning to fluster the Atlantian. Benson switched tracks. "People from other villages. They are more like you than say, uliks, yes?"

"...yes."

"And uliks live in packs, just like you live in villages, but they're all still uliks, right?"

Kexx contemplated the apparently new concept silently for a long moment, then decided to return to the topic of Benson's plant. "What happens when the tool breaks? Will you be able to talk to me?"

"That's very unlikely." Benson said. "Plants are very stable, even self-repairing up to a point."

"But if it did?"

Benson bobbed his head in surrender. "Then, no, I couldn't access your language. I'm not really speaking it now. I think what I want to say in my language, and the plant tells me the translation. I sound it out, but the words don't have any meaning to me yet."

"So Mei's way is better, because she is actually learning and remembering the words."

Benson shrugged. "I'll get there eventually too. When I was young, it took me a few years to learn Mandarin well enough to not need the plant anymore. It'll sink in eventually. But in the meantime, we can still talk, so both ways have their advantages."

"Mandarin?"

"Sorry. It's a different human language from English, which is what I speak."

The patterns on Kexx's face and arms stopped and reversed abruptly, a physical manifestation of his mind coming to a halt and trying to back up. "Humans have more than one language?"

"Oh, yes." Benson nodded. "There was a time we had hundreds, even thousands of spoken languages. We still have six or seven, but English is the dominant language. Mandarin used to be just as popular, but most of the people who spoke it, well, they…"

"They, what?"

"Died," Benson said flatly, hoping he wouldn't have to explain the circumstances of their deaths. "Hasn't Mei told you any of this?"

"No, ze hasn't. What's the point of having so many? Language is supposed to make communicating clear and simple."

"It wasn't planned." Benson thought for a moment how to keep a million years of human migration and linguistic development simple. "Humans used to be scattered all over, sometimes separated by great mountain ranges or oceans for very long periods. Each small group's language changed until two different groups weren't speaking the same one anymore."

"On your world, you mean," Kexx said. It wasn't a question. Benson froze, unsure what to say. "Don't be surprised, Benson. I am far from stupid, and Mei has already taught us much. You are unlike anything anyone has ever seen. Besides, I watched your stars appear in the sky. We all did. Then, we watched you travel down to our world on a beam of light."

Benson glanced up at the faint glinting of the elevator tether, still visible in the morning light. "So we didn't sneak in the back door, then?"

"Your arrival was hard to miss."

"I can see that now."

Kexx took a deep breath. "Benson, there is one other thing I need to ask you."

Benson braced himself, fairly sure he knew the twist the

conversation was about to take. "Sure, go ahead."

"About the incident in the temple last night…"

"Yes, I know. It was inappropriate and I'm very–"

"No," Kexx stopped him. "I don't want an apology, I want to understand why. Mei trusts you, I trust Mei. So I trust that you didn't suddenly lose your mind and decide to point your gun at our elder. You had a reason. What was it?"

"That's a… complicated question, Kexx. But it comes down to the fact I didn't understand the differences between us. Humans have one child at a time, sometimes two, but very rarely any more than that, and it takes many, many years to raise them into adults. For the last two hundred years, there have been so few of us left that every child is precious. Deliberately harming a child, well, there is no greater crime among our people. It's an abomination."

Kexx nodded along, encouraging Benson to continue.

"So when I saw your elder killing the babies, I… I thought something horrible was happening."

"Because you saw them as you would see human babies," Kexx said.

"Yes."

"Even though they were not of your kind."

"Yes."

"And you wanted to protect them."

Tears welled up in Benson's eyes. "Yes."

Kexx put a hand on Benson's shoulder. "Then there is nothing to apologize for, Benson. You fought to protect our people in both our temples yesterday. I see now why Mei trusts you so completely. You are unafraid of doing what's right, even if you're not always right about what that is." Then, the truth-digger stood back up. "Come, we've chased our shadows long enough out here."

"Yes," Benson rubbed his eyes clear. "Of course. Where to next?"

Kexx shrugged and fluttered his markings. "I'm open to suggestions."

"Maybe back to the village and see what's come in on the signal towers?"

"Could do."

"It might help to be up high anyway, get a better perspective on everything. Too bad I don't have any remote cameras to put on one of your birds, make my own little jerryrigged drone."

"One of our birds?" Kexx said. "What do you mean?"

"You know, trained birds, like the ones Kuul sent after our aerial drone when we were walking in."

Kexx stepped in front of Benson and glared down at him. "Why didn't you mention this before?"

Benson, unsettled by the sudden intensity coming from the normally calm alien, put up his hands defensively. "Because I assumed you knew. I figured they were hunting birds."

"*We* don't use trained birds to hunt," Kexx said evenly.

"You don't?" Benson asked, before the full implications finally caught up with him. "Oh. *You* don't."

Kexx nodded. "Now you see. Take me there. Now."

CHAPTER NINETEEN

Theresa glanced at the plant clock in the periphery of her field of vision. 1547. The demonstrations had been going on for four hours already and showed no signs of letting up anytime soon. She tried to blink away the exhaustion eating away at her sleep-deprived focus, but it was a lost cause. An entire pot of English breakfast tea hadn't made a dent yet.

In contrast to the sporadic, booze-fueled disturbances from the night before, the group picketing outside the Beehive was both larger and more organized. Theresa guesstimated it had grown to almost a thousand people over the last hour broken into splinter groups of Valmassoi's supporters, isolationists, and Returners taking advantage of the opportunity for free publicity. It would probably swell again once the day shift let out. Valmassoi's death had sparked far more passion, and revealed far deeper political divisions than she'd ever guessed existed in the population.

There had been some trouble early when a handful of demonstrators tired of throwing slogans and started throwing rocks. However, a judicious application of stun-sticks to the offenders and a firm explanation of protesting decorum put a swift end to the budding violence for the time being.

Theresa had already tagged the leaders' IDs into her plant for later review, and a locator analysis would be able to identify everyone else. She had no doubt that the majority of them were here of their own accord, at the gentle nudging of their friends, or on the advice of the talking bobble-heads that passed for journalists on this rock, all of which were on hand at the "Rally

for Justice" to cover what was undoubtedly the biggest story to
come down the wire since Landing.

Ostensibly, this was all to protest the assassination of
Administrator Valmassoi by parties yet unknown. A noble
enough cause, Theresa thought, but suspicious in the face of the
fact she couldn't remember Valmassoi being nearly so popular
prior to his untimely death. She tried to come up with a list of
people who would've taken a bullet for the late Administrator
(outside of his security detail, naturally) and couldn't use up all
the fingers on one hand. Still, for all his faults, he'd had all the
appearance of cruising towards victory in next year's elections.
His death threw that calculation into chaos, forcing a special
election to fill the vacancy and bringing old rivalries and new
grievances boiling back up to the surface.

Korolev, animated by some unholy magic, stood on the
opposite side of the platform, arms crossed over the assault
rifle hanging menacingly on his chest from a sling. He'd been
holding it in a relaxed ready position, but Theresa had said his
aggressive stance was antagonizing the crowd. Somehow, this
new arrangement wasn't any better.

<Korolev, do you ever not look like an action figure?>

<When I'm removed from my factory packaging, ma'am.>

Unwanted images flooded Theresa's mind. She tried to block
them with limited success.

<TMI, Pavel. At least pretend I'm your superior officer from
time to time.>

<Yes, ma'am.>

<How much sleep did you get last night?>

<I spent four hours in bed, ma'am.>

Theresa smirked at the cleverly worded response. Four hours,
the bare minimum required by regulation between shifts. And
while she was sure they were all spent in bed, she was equally
sure based on the coy, blushing look she'd caught from the
young bartender Korolev had walked home that they weren't all
spent in a restful slumber.

<Right. Doesn't any of this seem a little, I don't know,
overblown to you?>

Korolev sent a mental shrug. <I don't know what *this* is

supposed to look like, ma'am. But I do know we had to disperse crowds bigger than this after Zero matches back home.>

<People *cared* about Zero, Pavel. That's my point. Something's off.>

<They're rallying around a common enemy.>

<You mean the Atlantians.>

<They did attack us. It's ugly, but it's hardly the first time in history.>

Theresa looked over the crowd, forcing herself to really look at the hastily constructed protest signs for the first time. They were of a kind with the sort of placards people used to make for Zero rivalry matches, but without any of the good-natured comradery that went along with it. There were crudely drawn cartoons of cuttlefish and frequent references to calamari, all of which left Theresa feeling more than a little queasy.

<I thought we left this bullshit behind on Earth,> she said.

<We did, among ourselves,> Korolev said. <This is something new.>

<No,> Theresa shook her head. <It isn't.>

Theresa spent another three hours at her post before the crowds finally thinned out enough for her to stand down and hand off her watch to another constable. What she saw once she opened her front door did nothing to improve her mood. Reclining in perfect comfort on her couch, wrapped up in her Afghan, sipping her sweet tea, Chao Feng smiled radiantly.

"What the hell are you doing in my house, Feng?"

"I let myself in. I hope you don't mind."

"I do mind, actually. I've been on my feet all day, I've gotten very little sleep, and all I want to do is get out of this sweaty uniform, take a hot shower, and then lie on that couch and watch something mindless until I fall asleep. And how did you 'let yourself in,' anyway?"

Feng stretched like a cat, the first of which to exist in more than two centuries had just been decanted a few months earlier and was now acting as a surrogate pet for everyone still living in Avalon module.

"Captain Mahama may have neglected to repeal a few of my

command permissions from my time as first officer."

"Which are of course completely illegal for a private citizen to have, so of course you'll be reminding her to disable them as soon as possible," Theresa said.

"Oh, naturally. First thing tomorrow."

"Uh huh. I'm going to go take a shower. If you're not off my couch by the time I finish, you're getting the stun-stick."

"For a nonviolent B&E suspect? You wouldn't."

"I've already used it today. That always seems to raise my appetite for police brutality a few notches."

"Fine, but you may change your tune once you hear what I have to say." Feng sat up and set his glass on her coffee table.

"Coaster," Theresa chided. Feng obliged. "All right then, let's hear it."

"Last night, you asked me to get a list of queries on the satellite gap."

"You have it?"

"I do, it's printed out on flimsies on your kitchen table. Never went over the network or through my plant, so you can do your cross check without raising any red flags. But, I've gone one better."

Theresa cocked her head curiously. "Go on."

"Those disabled satellites? They weren't disabled. They were commandeered."

"What?" Theresa nearly shouted.

Feng nodded. "I couldn't believe it either, but it's true."

"How? How could that happen?"

"Embarrassingly easily," he said. "We're still trying to reconstruct exactly what happened, but it looks like someone broke into the sats' OS and triggered a series of fake hardware error messages over the course of a few weeks, leading up to a cascading failure that looked to the handlers on the Ark like a complete system crash. We tried a hard restart and reboot, but when that failed, we wrote the sats off."

"Why didn't anyone try to repair them?"

"Because we're phasing out the original Pathfinder sat network anyway. They're all over two hundred years old, remember. They've been in storage the majority of that time, but even in space, components deteriorate over time. It wasn't worth repairing them when we already had their replacements in the manufacturing queue."

Theresa waved her hand. "OK, fine, but two sats going down in the same way at the same time? Didn't that raise any eyebrows?"

"Might have, except the hacks took place three months apart and mirrored two other actual sat failures that we saw previously. We just assumed it was a repeat."

"OK," Theresa said. "How'd they get such deep access to the OS and other software?"

"That's the embarrassing part," Feng said sheepishly. "They weren't encrypted or firewalled. All the hackers needed to do was fake their network address to look like an authorized user and they were in."

"They weren't even password protected? Are you fucking kidding me?"

Feng shrugged. "The people who built and programed them didn't think to put a jail on the Ark, remember? Besides, why would someone want to steal a GPS satellite? What good would it do?"

"Well that's the question, isn't it?" She rubbed the raw spot on her shoulder where her rifle sling had dug in. "Any fingerprints?"

Feng shook his head. "Our techs are still looking into it, but whoever it was seemed to cover their tracks very effectively. People outside of the crew don't seem to understand just how juryrigged the Ark's OS is at this point. It's a two century-old quilt of updates, patches, and workarounds. A digital archeologist would probably have a field day uncovering all of the firewall holes and backdoors in the code. It's like the ship. We couldn't ever afford to shut anything down or risk a crash, so we just fixed problems on the fly."

"I still can't believe there wasn't *some* security, especially after what happened with Kimura. The crew should have hardened everything."

"Those were chaotic times, I don't have to tell you. All of that takes time and manpower. We landed a few weeks later, everyone was swamped with setting up Shambhala and it fell off the priority list. It's being fixed now, believe me. There won't be a repeat."

"Thank goodness for small favors. So, you have the sats back now? They won't be able to exploit the gap anymore?"

Feng sighed. "About that. Our ping triggered some buried command and the sats emptied their station-keeping thrusters into decaying orbits and burned up in the atmosphere."

"How thorough," she said bitterly.

"Quite, but at least they're not under control of whoever hijacked them anymore. What do you suppose they were up to?"

"No idea, but whatever it is, I'm sure I don't like it. Any other hardware that just happened to go missing in the last year or so?"

Feng frowned. "What do you mean?"

"I don't know. Drones, rovers, suborbital relay balloons. Those sats were multi-functional GPS and com platforms, they could have set up their own shadow network with ground assets for all we know."

"God, I should've thought of that," Feng admitted. "I'll run an inventory search and make a list of everything else that's gone offline in the last year."

"Go back to Landing, just to be sure." Theresa plopped down in what was normally Benson's chair and put her feet up. "I don't like the smell of this. It's beginning to feel just like the Laraby case." Remembering who was sitting on her couch, she quickly amended to, "Edmond's case. Sorry, Chao."

Feng waved her off. "It's fine. Besides, I played no small part in that. To be honest, I'm still surprised you're trusting me with this now."

"Devil you know, I suppose."

"Touché."

Theresa glanced up to see a surprisingly warm smile cross Feng's face. He hadn't had it easy these last few years, she knew. While you wouldn't know it from looking around his house, Feng's personal fortunes were much reduced. He still grieved for his late wife, and felt the shame of deceiving her for so long. And while his position as the gofer between the Ark and the provisional Shambhala civilian government gave him considerable influence, he was basically an outsider, not fully trusted by either.

It was his fault, but that didn't prevent Theresa from sympathizing. She was about to say something comforting when a call came in on her plant. She growled and checked the ID: Acting Administrator Merick.

"Well this should be good," she said just above a whisper and connected the call.

<Chief Constable Benson?> he asked.

<Yes, go ahead.>

<Chief, your presence is required in council chambers.>

<I just came from there, sir.>

<Yes, I'm sorry about that, but council has just concluded an emergency session and needs to speak with you about a... sensitive issue.>

<Can I shower first?>

<Clock's ticking, chief.>

<Naturally.>

<Is Mr Feng there with you?>

Theresa and Feng's eyes met across the room. <Yes,> she said, trying to keep the sudden alarm bells going off in her head from reaching her plant voice.

<Good, ask him to join you. It concerns him as well.>

<Understood. See you in ten.>

The connection dropped. She stood and motioned for Feng to do the same. "C'mon, we're wanted at the Beehive."

"What for?"

She shrugged. "Only one way to find out."

"They know we've been speaking," Feng said once they were a few blocks away from her house.

"They know we've been in the same room together a couple times. That's all. And at this point, we don't know who 'they' even are."

"What should we do?"

"Keep working the angles and try to stay out in public. The more visible we are, the riskier it'll be for someone to take a shot at one of us."

"Metaphorically speaking, of course," Feng hastened to add.

"I'm not so sure," Theresa said weightily. "I'll try to make sure one of my boys keeps an eye on your son until this blows over."

Feng straightened his shoulders. "I appreciate that."

"Don't mention it."

They reached the Beehive steps a couple of minutes later. The demonstrations were still going on, but had lost steam around dinner time. Korolev, who Theresa could have sworn had been relieved at the same time she was, noticed their approach and opened a link.

<What's up, chief?>

<Just a little visit with the council, Pavel. Stay put, but keep your eyes open.>

<Roger that.> He signed off.

They reached the council chamber. Feng stepped ahead to hold the door for her. Inside, all the usual suspects were seated around the table, with Merick in the large chair so recently occupied by the late Valmassoi.

"Ah, chief constable," Merick stood to greet them. "And Mr Feng. Thank you for coming on such short notice. Please be seated."

Theresa and Feng took two open chairs as far apart as they could, with Feng sitting in his usual spot just outside the circle.

"I'm here," Theresa said a little impatiently. "What's the problem?"

"Chief constable, I hardly need to tell you the gravity of today's shocking events…" Merick said, transitioning smoothly into the cadence of a politician giving a campaign speech. Which, she figured, he very well could be. The special election would either confirm his interim appointment or choose a new administrator altogether. He had a mighty narrow window to solidify his position with the public. A desperate politician was an unpredictable one.

"…and after careful deliberations, this council has decided that it's in the best interests of Shambhala's citizens to expand our defensive capabilities. Pursuant to that goal, you have been tasked with recruiting and training a reserve force of no fewer than one hundred new deputy constables to supplement your existing officers, should they become necessary."

"A hundred?" Theresa said, not even trying to mask her surprise.

"Is that going to be a problem?"

"It's unnecessary," she replied. "That's twice as many officers as I have now. Equipping them alone would wreck my budget, to say nothing of the man hours we'd eat up training them."

"Funding will not be an issue," Merick said. "Just send us an updated budget reflecting your expected requirements and–"

"I'm sorry," Theresa interrupted, "But did the crime rate suddenly triple without my noticing?"

"Not at all," Merick said. "Your officers have upheld law and order admirably. This reserve is intended more for, external threats."

Theresa crossed her arms. "You mean the Atlantians."

Merick didn't bother with an evasion. "That would be the immediate threat, yes."

"They're on the other side of an ocean and don't know how to build boats. Not exactly what I'd call an *immediate* threat."

"Oh, climb down from your high horse, constable," Gregory Alexander said, joining the conversation.

"I'm sitting down, Mr Alexander."

"They attacked our peace delegation and killed half a dozen of our people."

"They did no such thing," Theresa reminded him sternly. "The Atlantians lost people too, quite a few more than we did from what I hear. They were victims just as much as we were."

"Of other Atlantians," Merick pointed out calmly.

"Yeah, well, we haven't been great about that ourselves recently."

"Kimura's attack was the work of a madman and a handful of brainwashed disciples. This was larger than that," Alexander broke in.

"We don't know what *this* is," Theresa countered. "My husband is busy figuring it out as we speak."

Merick raised his hand. "And he will be given every opportunity and assistance in doing so. And once he does know who is responsible, this reserve force will be ready to round the perpetrators up and bring them to justice."

"You want me to ready an invasion." Theresa said, dumbfounded.

"Well it's not like we have an extradition treaty with them," Alexander said to a round of laughter.

"My constables are keepers of the peace, acting administrator," Theresa said, placing just the tiniest emphasis on "acting." "What you're talking about is the beginnings of an army."

"It's just a precaution, chief," Merick said reassuringly. "With any luck, they won't be necessary."

"Where am I supposed to find the people? We're not exactly dealing with high unemployment around here."

"Look outside," Alexander said, motioning to the demonstrators still milling about on the street. "I'm sure you'll find some patriots willing to donate their time."

Theresa could scarcely think of people less qualified, yet more enthusiastic to sign up to fight the savage natives than the idiots she'd just spent the entire day babysitting. The thought of it turned her stomach. She had half a mind to explain the fact.

"We'll manage," she said instead.

"Excellent," Merick announced. "Mr Feng, will you coordinate with Captain Mahama and the Ark's manufacturing department to make sure Chief Benson has everything she needs?"

"Of course, administrator. She has my full support," Feng said. Theresa hoped no one was wise to his double meaning.

"Then this session is adjourned." Merick stamped a handleless hammer on the table and rose to leave. "Chief constable, a word in private?"

Projecting calm annoyance, Theresa stood and followed Merick into the hallway. They walked a short way deeper into the atrium, away from prying ears.

"Chief," Merick said just above a whisper. "I just wanted to tell you personally that I didn't bring this motion to the table, nor did I vote for it. But support was… quite strong among the rest of the members."

"They're panicking," Theresa said accusingly.

"They're responding to public pressure," Merick corrected. "That's their job in a democracy, remember?"

"They're supposed to lead the people, not succumb to their ugliest impulses."

"Just go along with this for now. It will let the council tell people we're taking steps to protect them. Things will calm down in a few days."

Not if whoever's whipping up the crazies keeps stirring the pot, Theresa thought.

"Anyway," Merick continued, "I can see you're uncomfortable with this assignment, I can't say I blame you. But with Sergeant Atwood's death, you're the most logical choice for it. Just think of it as doing what you can from here to help Bryan."

"Oh, Bryan doesn't need any help finding trouble. I shudder to think what he'd do with a hundred-person army backing him up."

Merick snorted. "Me too." Then he put a hand on her shoulder. Theresa managed not to flinch. "Let's just hope we don't have to find out. Goodnight, constable."

Theresa nodded. "Administrator."

She ran into Feng again near the front door. "What was that about?" he asked quietly.

"Pandering."

"What are you going to do now?"

"Right now? I'm deputizing you."

Feng paused, shocked. "Me?"

"You. Welcome to the Tactical Reserve, Constable Feng."

"Are you mad?"

"Livid." They were outside now. Korolev was finally coming down from his watch. Theresa grabbed him by an elbow and whispered. "Pavel, I have some new training for your football buddies to do. Set it up."

"Okaaay," he said, confused. "For how many?"

"All of them."

CHAPTER TWENTY

Kexx pawed at the broken pieces of the crashed drone, running zer fingers over their glassy-smooth surfaces, trying to pick up tastes and smells as well as the texture of the object. It was, strange. Most of the pieces had no taste at all. Even rocks had distinct tastes. The obsidian of spear points was the only other material Kexx knew that had no taste at all. But these parts were light and flexible where obsidian was hard and brittle.

Other parts had a bitter taste reminiscent of certain types of river stones, and were impossibly strong and stiff for their weight. Benson called them "metal," another human concept to add to zer growing list. The strange little spinning wings on the corners seemed much too small to keep such a large bird in the air, but Benson said they made up for their small size by spinning very fast. One of them had snapped off at the root. Here, there was a faint trace of blood, probably from striking an animal in midair, but the blood had dried, making it almost impossible to tell what it had come from.

Kexx raised zer head. "This isn't helpful. I need to see a body."

"I'm sure I saw one of them go down in the crops," Benson said. "I'll look around."

Kexx waved ze off. "Just shout if you find something. And watch for uliks."

With zer partner trampling through rows of yulka stalks like a lost dux'ah calf, Kexx pushed the racket aside and held zer hands outstretched, fingers splayed into crosses to catch the most wind, and tasted the air. Slowly, deliberately, ze swept through each row, carefully sampling the mix of flavors caught on the breeze.

The winds ran parallel with the rows, making them natural wind channels. If ze was lucky, the crop rows would isolate any scent of decay and drastically narrow the search.

Of course, the trick would only work so long as the carrion was downwind from zer. And with the smoke of the funeral pyres of the previous evening's returned in the air, the task wouldn't be a simple one.

Kexx marched down the rows with purpose, confident in what ze was looking for, but afraid of it all the same. A childhood memory grabbed hold of zer, an image of zerself near the beach with zer parents. The tide had pulled out. Kexx and zer older sibling, Zuke, ran down the warm sand, chasing after jubins left behind in the shallow pools. In their exuberance, Zuke missed the signs of the sucking sands and both of zer feet caught in the pull. Ze struggled and struggled, but to Zuke and Kexx's horror, ze just sank deeper with each pull of zer legs.

Zuke was eventually pulled free, but it took a fullhand strong backs to do it. Kexx remembered the look on zer sibling's face as ze sunk deeper into the sand, the panicked chaos playing across zer skin.

Kexx felt that way now. Sinking deeper into something terrible, with only a half-crazy, naïve human to depend on to pull zer out again. It was not an encouraging thought.

On the tip of one finger, Kexx caught the faintest whiff of death among the aroma of ripening grain. Ze stopped and turned both of zer arms in the direction of the telltale scent. It was weak, but present. Ze moved over a row, then another as the smell strengthened, waiting for it to weaken again.

Kexx zeroed in on the row where the sickly-sweet aroma reached its apex, then ran down the row, ignoring the yulka stalks lashing at zer arms and legs. The smell of decay grew, accumulating on zer fingers until it drowned out the scent of dirt and pollen and beans.

Ze skidded to a stop in front of a yulka stalk kinked over near its base. Something had knocked it down. Carefully, Kexx lifted the plant and gently set it aside.

What ze found crumpled underneath sent a shimmer through zer skin.

"Benson, come here!" ze shouted, then sat and tried to calm zerself.

Benson came charging up, huffing like an ocean gale.

"You found it?" the human said between labored breaths. Kexx nodded. "What is it?"

"Trouble," ze said simply. "It's an injri."

"An injury?" Benson asked.

"*Injri*," Kexx corrected. "They are trained as hunting birds."

"Trained by whom?"

"The Dwellers."

"Ah, naturally. That settles it, then…" Benson paused. "Who the fuck are the Dwellers?"

"You don't know?"

Benson crossed zer arms, a gesture Kexx had come to recognize as annoyance or defiance when Mei did it.

"Indulge the ignorant human. How do you know this animal was trained and not wild?"

Kexx gave zerself a little shake. "They dwell in Xis's womb, deep below ground in caves. The injri live in the mouths of these caves, normally only coming out at night to hunt. But trained birds will come out in the light. These attacked your drone in daylight, yes?" Benson nodded. "That is how I know."

Benson absorbed the explanation. "And the Dwellers? What's their deal?"

"Later," Kexx said tersely as ze gathered up the injri corpse and slung it over zer shoulder. "Now, we must return to the village."

The chill throughout the temple had nothing to do with the temperature. The Emissary's Sanctuary still lay on its roof like the largest bowl ever made, but everyone's eyes were firmly fixed on the dead injri Kexx had slapped down onto the ceremonial table only a moment before, its stink of decay slowly filling the temple like a fog. You could hear a seed hit the floor.

Kexx glanced around at the hastily called assembly. Their faces and skin were muted, listless, as if they still hadn't brought themselves to accept that the events of the last day were real. On the far side of the room, Benson leaned against the wall, arms crossed and eyes set. Mei paced near him. Whether out of anxiety or anger, Kexx couldn't say.

Kuul was the first to find zer words again. "Our vengeance must be swift as the wind and merciless as a starving ulik pack."

"Against the Dwellers?" Chak spat. "With what? The smattering of warriors who they haven't already maimed or killed?"

"This threatens the entire village," Kuul snapped. "We *all* go."

The silence in the temple returned as Chak was stunned pale and speechless. "Send field tenders, mud stoners, children, and bearers into the Dwellers' caves? Is your head cold?" Chak demanded.

"Well, obviously not the bearers..." Kuul added.

Chak's skin flared blue. "If Tuko was here, ze would never–"

"Tuko isn't here, elder Chak," Kuul interrupted. *So, it had started.* Kexx thought. Kuul was making zer move to take control of the village. That couldn't be allowed.

"Tuko sleeps, it is true," Kexx said evenly. "But our chief has not yet returned to Xis, and it would be inappropriate to speak in zer stead."

"Someone must act," Kuul said. "We go, unless you prefer to cower here and wait for them to finish us off? Have you forgotten what happened to our roadbuilders?"

"That is years past, Kuul," Kexx said. "We've had many seasons of good trade with them since."

"Many seasons of extortion, you mean. Our traders are harassed and intimidated into accepting far less than what is fair. Those who don't bow to their unreasonable demands never make it back over the Black Bridge."

Chak was having none of the younger warrior's bluster. "So we march into their dens? Their mazes?"

"They would not expect an answer on their own lands so quickly."

"Because only a chief with a brain of ice would give that command! I should hold a torch to your head until you start thinking straight again."

Kuul's muscles tensed and bulged threateningly. "You are welcome to try, elder Chak."

Chak stuck a finger out at the young warrior's face. "Was that a threat?! I've served this village since before you were born. I sorted your brood, child, and I'm starting to wonder if my head was cold when I spared you the knife."

Kuul shrugged ze off arrogantly. "Maybe. We all have to live with our mistakes. But if the burden is too much to bear, just say the word and I will return you to Xis, because that was the only chance you ever had to kill me."

Kexx forced a calm pattern onto zer skin and slid between the two of them. Anyone who looked closely would know it was forced, patronizing even, but ze didn't care. They were wasting time.

"Elders, please. Our adversaries lie beyond our fields, not inside these walls."

"You're so sure of that, truth-digger?" Kuul pointed at the humans on the far side of the room. "Nothing but death has followed their arrival."

"Standing right here," Benson called out.

"I wasn't talking to you, deadskin," Kuul said, zer voice drenched in scorn. "But since you interrupted, you should know I have half a mind to throw you all back into the sea."

Benson rested a hand provocatively on the top of zer gun. "You are welcome to try, Kuul," ze said, throwing Kuul's own words back in zer face. "Unless you're only fit to fight an elder twice your age."

Kuul stared in blank-faced shock as if Benson had reached out and physically slapped zer. Chak's face, meanwhile, seemed torn between amusement and humiliation, with neither winning full control. "Not helping, Benson," Kexx chided as ze put zer hands on Kuul's shoulders in case ze needed to be held back once zer senses returned. It proved necessary.

"Did you hear what that dux'ah shit said to me?" Kuul exploded, suddenly pressing against Kexx's chest with all of zer considerable strength.

"Yes, I did. And I also heard what you said to Chak, and what Chak said to you, and it's time all of you started acting like elders instead of bickering children!"

Miraculously, Kuul calmed, and all three of them had the good sense to look embarrassed. At least that's what Kexx assumed Benson's face looked like. Ze suspected it was an unfamiliar state for the human to be in.

"That's better. Now, we're not emptying the village to march three days on the road and three days off just to die on Dweller spears."

"We're not?" Kuul said, zer eyes narrowing and zer skin jagged.

"No," Kexx held zer ground, "We're not. Not without knowing who ordered the attack and why."

Kuul pointed at the injri corpse on the low table. "We know they did it. *You* brought us the proof, truth-digger. Your job is done."

"With respect, it is not. We do not know which of the Dwellers ordered it, if it was their deep chief, one of the smaller lords, or some other faction."

Kuul spat on the floor, a most disrespectful act inside the temple. "What does it matter? Dwellers are all the same."

"Which is exactly what they say of us. Isn't that remarkable?" Kexx let zer words sink down through the thick mud of Kuul's mind before continuing. Kuul had many admirable traits. Ze was fearless in the face of danger and fanatical about protecting those ze counted among zer own. But no one would accuse zer of being a deep thinker. Kexx had learned how to use that lack of imagination to zer advantage. "Your warriors fought so bravely yesterday, Kuul, and sacrificed much. They deserve to unleash their vengeance on the *right* people. Let me do my job, then we will know for certain you are doing yours."

"How long are we to wait?" Kuul demanded.

Kexx thought carefully about the question. Too short a time and ze wouldn't have enough time for travel and to complete zer work. Too long and Kuul's impatience for violence would boil over.

There was a third way, ze realized.

"You won't have to wait at all, because you're coming with us."

"I'm what?"

"We'll be treading deeply into the Dwellers' territory. We'll need an escort."

"Yes," Chak spoke up. "I think that's a wonderful idea."

"What, by myself?"

"No, of course not," Kexx reassured the warrior. "Bring two of your strongest with you. Our travels will give the rest time to heal." Kuul blanched at this, a fresh objection trying to bubble its way to the surface. "Is that a problem? You were willing only a moment ago to lead the whole village into open conflict. Is this any more dangerous?"

And with that, Kexx knew ze'd won the round. Kuul's mind was a straightforward affair. It picked a single trail and sprinted headlong down the path with impressive speed. Ze never saw Kexx's trap coming until it had already sprung. Still, ze would be a dangerous and unstable ally. Kuul would bear close observation during the journey.

"Three isn't a big escort," Benson observed quietly. "We could use a few more."

"I agree," Kexx said. "We'll go to the envoys from the other villages and ask for volunteers."

Benson smiled. "I like it. They have as much reason to find the truth as we do."

"OK," Mei said suddenly. "Then I volunteer."

"What?" Benson said, switching to human and leaning over Mei. "No. Absolutely not."

Mei put zer hands on zer hips. "Why not? I lost people too. They don't count?"

Benson stumbled a response, and Kexx knew Mei had won the argument.

"Fine," Benson said, "But you're staying glued to my side, understand?"

"I protected you last time, remember?" Mei said.

Their little side conference over, Benson switched back to G'tel so everyone could understand. "I apologize for interrupting. Please continue."

"I think we're about finished," Kexx said. "I will talk to the other villages and assemble the party. We leave in the morning. Agreed?"

Looking around at the constellation of shifting skin patterns, Kexx knew many held objections, but they remained unspoken.

CHAPTER TWENTY-ONE

Another fitful night passed. Benson snapped awake twice from the same old nightmare: sucked out of the hole in the side of Avalon module's hull, spinning free and untethered through space as the Ark shrank to a point, besieged by the disembodied voices of all the people he'd left to asphyxiate in Shangri-La module. A stillborn infant floating face down in the growth tank. That component was more recent, but the novelty had worn off pretty quickly before he'd grown just as tired of it.

Benson missed drinking. The nice thing about a good blackout was it was dreamless. He still partook from time to time, like the previous night. But his nearly four decade-old body didn't snap back like it had when he was a young, elite athlete. That and Esa had come to expect her husband to be more than an incoherent pile of flesh snoring on the couch come the early hours of the morning.

Esa. He missed her terribly. In many ways, she'd stepped into his life and taken over many of booze's duties. She comforted him, calmed his jagged nerves, helped him go back to sleep. The warmth of her body lying next to him late at night, her slow, even breathing, the curve of her waist and the swelling of her hips. It was a kind of inebriation worth sobering up for.

It seemed no time at all had passed between when he fell back asleep after the last nightmare and Mei tried to flip him out of his hammock. Fortunately, momentum, or rather the complete lack of it, was on his side and she only managed to get him halfway out.

"Get up, lazy." She planted her feet to try again.

"Good morning to you, too, crabby."

"My daughter's been up for an hour already."

"She's three. Wait until she's a teenager, then tell me if she's so damned perky."

"Sun's already up. We're leaving soon. Get up."

With a groan, Benson swung his legs over the side and executed the sophisticated balancing act necessary to successfully exhume oneself from a hammock. The tamped clay of the floor was still cool on the soles of his feet. He wished he'd thought to pack his slippers.

"I still don't like you going, Mei," Benson said as he slipped a leg into his trousers.

"And I still don't care. Somebody has to represent my people. And watch your ass."

"Let's hope that's not necessary."

"It's *always* necessary."

Was that a fleeting smirk on her face, Benson wondered. He finished dressing, then gathered up his bag of supplies. It was quite a bit lighter than he would have preferred for an excursion that was to last a week at minimum, but it would have to do.

Outside the Unbound's shelter, the village bustled with preparations for their own expedition. Two large bonfires burned brightly in the crisp air as villagers huddled around them, rubbing warmth into their stiff muscles. Atlantians weren't exactly coldblooded, but they suffered in the early hours.

Next to the fires, two broom-heads... dux'ah contentedly ran their mouthparts through piles of seeds and pollen while their handlers loaded their backs with provisions. The signal tower was already busy capturing and redirecting the orange light of the dawn to the other villages on the network, updating them with what they'd learned and informing them of Kexx's plan to confront the Dwellers. Benson wasn't thrilled about the danger for leaks, but he'd been outvoted.

Kexx stood off to the side of the bustle, quietly watching things come together. Benson still wasn't very good at picking out individual Atlantian faces, relying more on their size and ornamentation than anything. But he'd spent more time around

Kexx than any of them. The truth-digger carried himself, zerself, in a certain detached way. Always observing, always one step removed. Never quite fully a part of the group.

Benson recognized the loneliness. As a Zero Hero, then later as the savior of mankind, he'd gotten used to being held above the rest. But standing on a pedestal was still standing apart.

"Truth-digger," Benson greeted him.

"Detective," Kexx answered.

"How long before we can move out?"

Kexx looked glance over zer shoulder at the dawn. "Later than I would like, but we should be walking the road by midmorning."

"You know we're probably going to be ambushed out there, right?"

Kexx shrugged. "It's hard to set an ambush when your prey expects it." Ze pointed at the rifle hanging on Benson's shoulder. "And when it has such sharp teeth."

"Don't rely on me to save us," Benson objected. "All they need to do is send more warriors than I have bullets, and we're dead."

"Fortunate, then, that we're the only ones who know that."

"And if they're stubborn enough to figure it out the hard way?"

Kexx's skin fluttered. "How fast can you run?"

Benson sighed. "Not as fast as I used to."

Kexx rubbed absently at a fresh, angry looking scar on zer thigh. "I know the feeling."

It was closer to midday by the time the caravan pulled out of the village's northern gate and pointed down the laser-straight road toward the horizon. Benson's eyes actually had trouble looking down it. Maybe not his eyes so much as his sense of depth. He'd spent the first thirty-five years of his life inside an artificial habitat only two kilometers long and two kilometers in diameter. Avalon and its twin module Shangri-La were, without a doubt, the largest enclosed spaces ever built by mankind, but they were still miniscule compared to an actual planet. He'd had enough trouble upon landing dealing with an infinite sky, especially after his incident in the EVA pod, but somehow the straight line of the road reaching all the way out to horizon helped define the distance, fixing it in his mind. The longest street back in Shambhala was less than three kilometers, and he'd watched it being built incrementally over the span of three years.

This Atlantian road, by contrast, was many dozens of kilometers long. Some part of his stunted visual cortex told him it was impossible. Benson actually felt a pang of vertigo when he looked down it for too long. Instead, he spent quite a bit of time looking at his shuffling feet.

Aside from Benson, Mei, Kexx, Kuul and zer two bodyguards, the caravan was made up of one surviving warrior from each of the other twenty-three villages for a total of twenty-nine. It took a little more than an hour to walk clear of the swaying crops and out into true wilderness. There was no defined border. The rows of yulka simply grew more disorganized until they couldn't be differentiated from chaos. Undergrowth and stands of trees sprang up, although not into anything thick enough to be considered a forest. Birdsong, the buzzing of insects and the chirps of animals hiding in the underbrush filled the air.

A particularly nasty-looking customer with four dragonfly-like wings and a pair of pincers that could have been stolen from a fiddler crab landed on Benson's forearm.

"Ah, hi," Benson said to the chitinous interloper. He raised his arm and presented it to the Atlantians. "Is this thing venomous?"

"To us? No," Kuul called out. "To you? Who knows?"

"Thanks for the help." For a scary moment, Benson debated whether swatting or shooting it would be more prudent. He settled on gently brushing it off in the hope it would continue about its day elsewhere. It buzzed around his head once in protest, then moved on.

For the first couple of hours, almost no one spoke. No boasting of their accomplishments during the fight, no tales of past hunts. But then, why would they? Aside from Kuul and zer two companions, none of them knew one another. And it was among this group of strangers that they were all marching into danger.

No wonder everyone preferred the company of their own thoughts. Still, some team-building was in order. This wasn't any different from a crop of fresh recruits. Maybe tonight around the fire he could get a chorus going or something. Something to get them all laughing.

Several times, Benson caught Kuul eying him, trying to get his measure. It made Benson's skin crawl. There was another situation that justified planning ahead for. Benson slowed his pace a little and dropped back to where Kexx and Mei were chatting.

"Hey," Benson said in a low voice, speaking English so as not to be overheard. "I don't care for the way Kuul is looking at me."

Kexx very deliberately did not look in the warrior's direction. "Yes, I've noticed. Ze isn't very subtle."

"Are we going to have a problem with zer?"

"There will always be problems with Kuul," Kexx whispered back. "The only questions are how big, and how soon?"

"What's the problem, do you think?"

"Kuul is not happy with me. Ze thinks I tried to embarrass zer yesterday by continuing our investigation."

"Didn't you?"

"Not intentionally," Kexx said. "But... it was a consequence."

Benson smirked. "What's that got to do with me?"

"It's not you, Benson, it's your gun. Kuul fears it, envies it. Ze knows that as long as you have it, ze cannot move against me."

"Ze's welcome to try and take it, but it won't be any use to zer."

Kexx scrunched zer face. "A weapon that powerful would be of great use to Kuul."

"Sure, if Kuul could fire it. But it only works for me."

"It knows you?" Kexx asked, glancing down at the rifle.

"I guess that's the simplest way to explain it."

"More human magic." Ze paused, considering. "That is good, but still, if you are killed, Kuul and his spears will be the strongest group."

"What should we do, then?"

"Make friends and keep our eyes open," Kexx said simply.

"I was thinking the same thing." Benson became aware of a growing number of Atlantian eyes glancing back at their conversation. "We should probably stop talking before everyone thinks we're conspiring back here."

"Aren't we?" Kexx flashed a strange, lopsided attempt at a smile, showing zer beak-like teeth.

"Jeez, that's creepy, Kexx."

"I did it wrong?"

"Not... exactly. Anyway, I'll keep my eyes peeled."

"That sounds most unpleasant."

"It just means I'll keep them open."

"I would hope so. How else will you see where you're going?"

"Nevermind."

They marched on through the afternoon along the long, flat, featureless road with only the occasional milestone to break up the monotony. The further from the village they walked, the more the environment encroached. Vine-like runners from wild plants reached out and tried to find purchase. The crisp edges of the cement blended with windblown sand, fallen leaves, and dirt. Here and there, cracks meandered across the pavement, giving small, ambitious plants a place to set up shop.

"How old is this road?" Benson asked in Atlantian, just a little bit louder than he needed to.

"Five years," Kexx replied.

"Seems older."

"It is our newest."

"Really? Doesn't seem to get a lot of care."

"That's because it doesn't go anywhere."

"OK," Benson said. "Then why are we walking on it?"

Kexx chuckled. "It would be more accurate to say it goes halfway to somewhere. Whenever we add a new road, the villages on each end commit to building half of it, starting at their own gates and meeting in the middle."

"Sounds sensible."

Kexx snorted. "You would think. But even that led to arguments. The smaller villages would say the larger should build more because they had greater resources, while the larger villages would say the smaller ones would reap greater benefits from trade and demand the same. It seems we can always find something to fight about."

Benson nodded along. "That's politics for you. So, what happened to this road?"

"Years ago, we reached out to the Dwellers, tried to mend our troubled history. After a long time, we reached an agreement to build a road and connect with them, bring our trade with them out from the shadows. We built our road, expecting to meet them in the middle as we'd always done."

"But they never showed up," Benson said.

"No. At first, we thought their inexperience building roads had caused their half to stall. We sent envoys and mud-stoners to offer assistance and training."

"And they didn't come home again," Benson said, anticipating the rest of the story.

"Their heads did. As for the rest of them, I couldn't say."

"Charming." Benson pulled his rifle in just a little closer and wondered not for the last time just what the hell he'd been thinking when he agreed to this crazy-ass mission. It wasn't like he had anything to prove at this point. But then, his mind inexplicably drifted back to a conversation he'd had just over three years ago as he lay on a bed in Avalon's sickbay, half deaf and a quarter burned from his final confrontation with David Kimura, the fanatic who'd killed twenty thousand people and came a hair's breadth from killing the rest.

Kimura's accomplice among the crew, Avelina da Silva, had asked him as she was taken into custody, "And who will stand up for the Atlantians?"

The words still echoed in his mind. At the time, he'd said he would stand for them, and he'd meant it. Benson had given his word, even if it was to a genocidal maniac. He'd come out here to look after Mei and her people, to see that they were all right, for the chance to meet genuine aliens, and if he was being honest, to be present at a moment that had few equals in human history.

But, after the attack on the village, he'd decided to stay because an all-too-familiar feeling in the pit of his stomach told him something was wrong. This wasn't just inter-tribal conflict. The timing of the satellite gap and the attack, the downing of the drone, the shuttle transmitter going dark, it was too convenient. And now he could add another point to the timeline. It was a six-day march from the village to the Dwellers' territory. The attack happened only four days after the first contact expedition had touched down. Even if they traveled fast overland, they would've barely made it in time. But to move over a hundred armed troops across open country unseen by anyone, that wasn't something one could do fast.

More likely, they knew of the expedition and had begun to head for Kexx's village even before the shuttle touched down. Maybe as soon as planning for the expedition began several days before. That meant someone, either in Shambhala or on the Ark, was in contact with the Dwellers and interfering in Atlantian affairs.

And that Benson wasn't going to stand for.

The caravan came to a small bridge crossing over a shallow washout, no more than a couple of meters at its deepest point. Only a tiny trickle of water flowed down the center of the dried-out riverbed toward the ocean several kilometers to the east. Rounded stones and sun-bleached branches hinted that the trickle turned into a raging current during the wet season.

One stone in particular caught Benson's eye. Not for its size or shape, both of which were utterly unremarkable, but for its color and the way it caught the light. Benson stepped off the road and tottered down into the small gully, upsetting a small burrowing creature in the process which was only too eager to express its displeasure through chirps and kicking sand.

"What do you see?" Mei called down to him.

"Just a second," Benson said as he reached down to grab the rock. It was round and pitted, worn smooth by water, then sand. It was heavy for a small rock.

And it was yellow.

"Oh, shit," Benson said under his breath.

Mei appeared at his side and leaned in to get a better look at the precious nugget sitting in his palm.

"Oh," Mei said. "Shit."

"Kexx!" they called up to the road in unison.

Kexx walked gracefully down the steep riverbank and joined the growing huddle.

"What is it, Benson?"

Benson held the nugget of gold up to the truth-digger and handed it to zer. "Do you recognize this?"

Kexx hefted it in zer hand once, then ran the tips of zer fingers over it. "Of course. It's jie."

"And it's just *lying around*?" Benson said incredulously.

Kexx shrugged. "Why wouldn't it be? There's no reason to collect it. It doesn't take an edge and it's too soft to hold its shape."

Benson and Mei looked at each other with disbelief. Gaia orbited an older, metal-poor star. The system wasn't supposed to have much in the way of heavy metals, especially not nuggets of gold just lying around in dry riverbeds.

"I seem to be missing something," Kexx said. "Is this rock important to your people?"

Benson cleared his throat. "That's an understatement."

"How important?"

"Important enough to kill for," Mei answered.

"Oh." Kexx looked down at the nugget in zer palm. "Shit."

CHAPTER TWENTY-TWO

Theresa forced herself to blink. Her eyes were dry, tired, and probably bloodshot. It felt like she'd been staring at the tablet for her entire adult life, filling out and updating arrest reports. Flying in the face of Acting Administrator Merick's predictions, the protests had not abated. Indeed, they'd grown and morphed from peaceful picketing into acts of civil disobedience, vandalism, and even a pair of assaults during the night.

Shambhala, it seemed, was spoiling for a fight. Or at least an angry, vocal minority of it was. One of her third-shift constables had been called in on a domestic and caught Yvonne Hallstead roughing up her girlfriend for not showing enough enthusiasm for violent reprisals against the Atlantians. Whether or not that was the ultimate outcome, Hallstead would be sitting out the final round in the town jail.

Theresa quite liked finally having a purpose-built jail for the town's drunks and hotheads to cool their heels in. It was handy for those middle-ground situations where the extremes of community service or execution weren't entirely appropriate punishments. It only had eight cells, which for a population of twenty-five thousand and growing struck Theresa as optimistic bordering on naive, but it was still a big step up from just throwing them in an emptied-out equipment locker as they'd done back home on the Ark.

Home. Theresa put down her tablet and mulled the word over in her mind as she looked around the house she and her husband had built. Well, the house a multi-axis concrete extruder and finishing crew had built, but they'd picked the layout and furnishings. It felt like a home in a way the Ark never had.

And now it was all in danger. The city was simmering just below a boil while her stupid, glory-seeking husband was gallivanting around the Atlantian outback, one misstep away from death by tooth or spear. Theresa swore, if something big and nasty didn't kill him out there, she would be waiting by his return shuttle with a baseball bat. Nothing lethal, maybe just a shattered femur to keep him from wandering off like a rebellious teenager for a few months. He could still coach his football team on crutches. She'd even help nurse the idiot back to health to show him how much she loved him.

The incoming call icon blinked at the edge of Theresa's vision. An avatar of her husband's face materialized.

"Speak of the devil and he will appear," she said, parroting her sanctimonious aunt, one of a very few Roman Catholics left who managed to believe Revelations hadn't already played out back on Earth two centuries ago, and that she wasn't living some cursed existence outside of God's protection. Theresa envied Buddhists; their faith made room for existence after Armageddon without the need for complicated theological gymnastics. She connected the call and projected it onto the nearest wall.

"You're late," Theresa said in an even tone, conveying her frustration more effectively than yelling ever could.

"I'm sorry, Esa. We've been a little busy out here."

"And I've been getting my nails done?" Theresa held up her tablet and shook it. "While you're out enjoying the scenery, this whole place is trying to fly apart. The Returners are threatening riots, the isolationists are running around screaming 'I told you so,' and everyone else is itching for revenge."

"I'm sorry, Esa. I was debriefing with the council for the last hour already. I don't know how much charge I've got left."

"Well I'm flattered you got around to me, eventually."

Her husband adjusted his grip on the handheld and brought his face closer to the camera. "Look, I didn't want to talk to those assholes any longer than I needed to, OK? But I'm here now, and I want to make the most of it."

Theresa recognized the sultry undercurrent in Benson's voice.

PATRICK S TOMLINSON   213

She'd heard it enough times after a couple of bottles of sake or apple wine back when they'd been dating in secret, sneaking off between shifts for a taboo interlude.

"Seriously?" was all she could muster today.

"C'mon, honey," he purred. "It's sooo lonely out here."

"You're surrounded by Atlantians."

"Yeah, whose sex organs I don't understand or even recognize. I might be getting fluids on me whenever I shake hands." Benson shuddered.

Theresa sighed. "That's really setting the mood, baby."

"Please? It's important," he pleaded. There was something about his expression. In all the years they'd been together, Bryan Benson had never been one to beg for sex. It wasn't necessary and he knew it. Partly because Theresa wasn't the withholding kind, and partly because his ego had been fed by years of female Zero fans catering to his every carnal whim. It was irritating, to say the least.

But now his face had an earnestness to it totally out of proportion to the situation. Maybe he was just really desperate, but Theresa knew her husband. If he said it was important, it was. She decided to play along.

"OK, you want a show big boy?" She ran her thumbs under the shoulder straps of her top.

"Yes please," he said eagerly.

"I hope none of your new friends are watching."

"I doubt they would know what they were seeing if they were."

"Honey?" Theresa said.

"Yes?"

"We really have to work on your sexy time talk." Theresa stood up and threw her top at the camera mounted to the wall.

"Um, why exactly are we watching this?" Korolev's baby-smooth cheeks started to flush crimson.

"What you're looking for is at the very end," Theresa said, advancing the video quickly enough to go through the more private bits in a blur. The projection on the wall shifted back to Benson's face.

"That was wonderful, baby," Benson's recording said. "When I get back, I'm going to give you those new gold earrings you've been talking about."

Theresa paused the video with a swipe of her hand.

"Notice anything?"

"Are you saying there's some sort of hidden message here?" Feng asked.

Theresa nodded. "Bryan knows these messages are probably being monitored. So he hid it where only I would see it."

"OK, what are we looking for, then?" Korolev asked.

"Do you see anything missing from my face?"

Korolev studied her for a moment. "A mouth. A nose. Two nostrils. Two eyes. Two ears." He shrugged. "Looks intact to me."

Theresa signed. "You're bucking for detective, Pavel. Anything else? Anything about my ears?" She stuck two fingers behind them and wiggled her lobes. "Anything missing?"

Korolev leaned forward, taking in her ears in detail. Theresa was about to give up when she saw the dawning realization across her constable's face. "You don't have any piercing holes!"

"Correct."

"So what earrings was he talking about?"

"That's the question," Theresa confirmed.

"You don't wear clip-ons?" Feng asked.

"Exactly what kind of girl do you take me for?"

"Sorry. But you never got ear piercings? Never?"

"I don't like needles."

"So," Korolev continued. "We can assume the chief was trying to hide a message. And since you don't wear earrings, we can ignore that part of the message. What's left?"

"New gold," Theresa said.

Feng's face changed from playful banter to deadly serious. "You aren't suggesting what I think you're suggesting."

"Why not?" Theresa asked. "Bryan suspects a conspiracy. We've already uncovered some evidence for it. He's not going to speak openly because he knows all of his communications are being monitored."

"Are we saying the chief found gold?" Korolev asked. "Just lying around? That's not possible. We already did spectrographic studies of the surface for precious metals and came up empty. Didn't we?"

Theresa turned to Feng. "That's an excellent question."

Feng grimaced. "We did. However..."

"However?" Korolev said.

"However. Anyone with enough network access and coding expertise to hack and repurpose two of our satellite constellation without our noticing is the sort of person who could also manipulate the spectrographic data coming from those same satellites, or replace it entirely."

Theresa blew out through pursed lips, just below a whistle. "Well, there's a motive."

"Over gold?" Korolev asked. "I mean, I know it was a big deal back on Earth, but here, now?"

"Think deeper, Pavel," Theresa said. "Gold is pretty far down the periodic table. Gold means a whole bunch of precious and semiprecious elements must be lying around that we weren't expecting to find here. Silver, palladium, cadmium."

"Iridium, osmium." Feng counted off elements on his fingers. "Tungsten, platinum. They should all be present if gold is, at least to some degree."

"Well that's good news, isn't it?" Korolev asked. "We need all of them to manufacture tech, and if we can get them here now instead of mining asteroids in another five years or whatever, that's a bonus."

"You would think so. But then, why hide their existence?" Theresa asked.

"Because you're the sort of person who likes to keep good news to yourself until you can take maximum advantage of it," Feng said. "Because if word gets out before you're in place to stake claims and start mining immediately, the news will just trigger a gold rush."

"Anything else you'd like to share with the class, Constable Feng?" Theresa said.

The former first officer nodded. "I looked into our assets on the ground like you suggested. Rovers, aerial drones, looking for units that had dropped off the grid and may have been coopted in the same way our two sats were."

"And?"

"And, two Pathfinder fliers and a rover have all the telltales of being hijacked."

Theresa listed intently as the other shoe hit the floor. "So, not only did whoever this is have eyes in the sky, but they have voices on the ground."

"I can't be sure of that," Feng said. "It's solid conjecture, but that's all it is at the moment."

"What will you need to be sure?"

"Without tripping off a million alarms a minimally competent hacker would've set up?" Feng asked. "Go to the source data. Any queries I send up through the beanstalk are going to be logged and recorded."

"Laser com?" Korolev asked. "We used them between the Ark and her EVA pods for decades. You could sneak in that way."

Feng shook his head. "They were designed for vacuum. Even if we had a laser powerful enough down here, which we don't, we never adapted the receivers to compensate for atmospheric disturbances. We just use the data trunks built into the beanstalk."

"We use radio every day."

"Which can be intercepted and decoded. If I'm going to do this without giving away the game," Feng pointed up to the sky. "I have to go back up to the can."

"When was the last time you were up there?"

"About three months ago."

Theresa rubbed absently at her chin. "That's about normal, right? And you can make some excuse about going up to advise the crew about the current situation and unrest."

"Sure, but it's still a four-day trip up the beanstalk."

"No way you could commandeer a shuttle?" Korolev asked. "They can get there in under a day."

Feng shook his head. "Not without one hell of a cover story, and even then, an unscheduled shuttle flight is going to raise all kinds of suspicions. Especially after we just burned up a bunch of fuel for the first contact expedition."

He was right, of course. The shuttles ran on algae-derived biofuel which took time to grow and process. Theresa sighed. "Do you think you can pin our guy from the Ark?"

"A solid maybe. It'll all depend on how clever they were covering their tracks. But I know I can shut down, or even take over their hijacked assets before they know it's happening and have a chance to suicide them."

"Nothing for it then. You'd better be on the next lift up."

Feng glanced at his wristwatch, an ostentatious anachronism passed down his line for ten generations. Now awaiting his son's eighteenth birthday before changing caretakers once again. "Next lift is in three hours. I need to arrange a sitter and pack."

"Hold on," Theresa said, then disappeared into the bedroom to grab something. She returned and pressed a small metal cylinder into Feng's palm.

"Pack this," she said.

"A stun-stick?" Feng asked, frankly stunned.

"Never know when it might come in handy."

"But, I'm not cleared for one of these."

"I deputized you, remember?" Theresa said. "I've already linked it to your plant. It's a simple point-and-click interface."

"I remember," Feng said sourly. He spun it around in his palm once like a slightly oversized stylus, then slipped it into a pants pocket. "Thank you."

"Thank me by finding these jackasses so I can arrest them."

Feng nodded, then hugged Theresa firmly before heading for the door.

Korolev watched the door close behind him. "Wouldn't have called that a couple years ago."

Theresa shrugged. "Feng was never a bad guy. Selfish and shortsighted, sure, but he wouldn't be the only person to put that behind them after Shangri-La."

"Amen."

Theresa walked to the door and grabbed her jacket. "C'mon, Pavel. We have 'football' practice to coach."

CHAPTER TWENTY-THREE

It was almost nightfall of the second day before they reached the end of the road. Halfway to the Dwellers' canyon, but with no road, the other half would be twice as hard. Kexx signaled for the caravan to stop.

"What's wrong?" Kuul asked.

"Nothing," Kexx said, pushing aside the feeling of mud crawlers doing laps around zer stomach. The end of the road was more than just symbolic, it also marked the nominal end of the village's territory and Tuko's authority, assuming ze was still alive. Here, there was true wilderness. It was no one's territory, not even the Dwellers, not really. Nomads, raiders, and wild predators ruled these grasslands. It wasn't a place for civilized people of any race.

"Nothing," Kexx repeated zerself. "We make camp here for the night."

"Already?" Kuul looked at the sun creeping toward the western horizon. "We can march another two stones before dark."

"There are no stones out here," Kexx said.

Kuul chuckled. "Afraid of the night, truth-digger?"

"How many nights have you spent beyond the trees, Kuul? Alone, with the day's heat seeping from your bones with no fire to replace it, only a spear between you and whatever lurks in the shadows? Of course I'm afraid. Only the cold-headed wouldn't be."

Kuul's skin flickered irritation, but ze let it drop. "What would you have us do?"

"Put up camp while we still have the light. Clear the brush as far out as you can so we can put palm to spear if anything steps out from the dark with ill intentions."

"Does anything step out from the dark with good intentions?"

Kexx laughed. "No. Not generally."

"And the deadskins?" Kuul managed not to spit out the last word, but it took effort. It wasn't the first time Kexx had heard the slur, referring to how the pale, monotone skin of Mei's people resembled a freshly returned G'tel corpse. "What will they be doing while we set up camp?"

"Our *human* friends–" Kexx emphasized. "–will be collecting firewood."

"Ah. A task equal to their talents," Kuul said. It was not a compliment. Collecting firewood for camp was the sort of work reserved for children or the very old, but Kexx didn't know what else to do with Benson and Mei at the moment.

"Let's hope one of them doesn't get a splinter," Kuul said. "What a tragedy that would be."

"It would be unfortunate if anything happened to *any* member of our group. We are already too few."

"We would have been many more if my plan had been followed."

"Yes, an army of farmers and fishers just large enough to draw out the Dweller warriors and small enough to be crushed like baitworms." Kexx shook zer head. "That's not a plan, Kuul. Except for a noble, but futile death."

"You spend too much time with the deadskins. You've even picked up their mannerisms. That's why you overestimate them. Without their gones, what are they?"

"Guns, Kuul. And if you hadn't been pinned on your back by invaders, you would have seen what the humans did without their guns outside the temple. It was memorable."

"You should pick your friends more carefully, truth-digger. If Tuko doesn't wake–"

"Then I will mourn zer," Kexx cut off the budding tirade. "Do you wish to say anything else?"

Kuul's skinned darkened like dux'ah meat cooking on a fire. "Not to you, no."

"Good, then please get camp established and assign the early watch."

The warrior stalked off and barked orders to zer followers. Kuul was a perfectly good ally to have, provided you could keep zer pointed toward a fight. Otherwise, ze would make one for zerself.

Kexx scanned for Benson. It didn't take long. The human's tan skin, dark hair, and dark clothing stood out against the grassland as if it were trying to be seen. The humans were clearly very skilled at many things. Camouflage did not number among them.

"Benson." Kexx motioned zer over.

"Everything all right?" the human asked. "I saw you and Kuul talking. It sounded heated."

"Kuul was just reminding me of zer disapproval. We're stopping here for the night to set up camp. I need you and Mei to gather up as much firewood as you can."

Benson glanced around the grassland plain. "Um. I don't see a whole lot of trees out here."

"Forgive me. We pick the straight grass, then tie it into tight bundles with gut to keep them from burning too fast."

Benson's eyes narrowed. "We'll need a *lot* of grass."

"And you have the rest of the day to pick it. Start where we're digging the fire circle and work outwards."

Benson put up zer hands, palms outward. Kexx recognized the gesture as a sign of surrender/acquiescence. "OK, I get it. Low man on the totem pole."

"The *what* pole?"

"Totem pole." Benson held a hand high over zer head. "Great big stack of faces of gods and spirits and so forth. First American tribes used to carve them out of the trunk of a whole tree. We've got a small one back in the museum."

"These were human tribes?"

"Yeah," Benson said. "You would probably have had a lot in common with some of them. They were experts at living off the land and staying in balance with nature too."

Kexx nodded. "They sound very wise. I should like to see this 'totem pole.' Someday."

"Bet on it," Benson said. "I should get to work."

The caravan laid out camp quickly. By the time the sun had ducked below the horizon, the tents were erected and the fire circle had been dug. Benson and Mei, with some help from members of the other villages, picked a clearing large enough that an adult couldn't cover the distance in less than three great strides. By the time the last splash of red-orange faded from the night sky, the first grass bundles were burning brightly. They'd been fortunate; the grass this far from the sea was parched and lit easily. As it burned, the strips of dux'ah gut that held the ends together dried and tightened, pulling the bundle together until it was nearly as dense as actual wood, slowing the burn and letting the fire last well into the night.

Kuul's warriors sat closest to the fire, roasting the flesh of some unfortunate creature whose curiosity had drawn it within range of one of their spears. It had been an excellent throw, Kexx had to admit. The rest of the caravan sat in a semicircle just a little further away. Benson and Mei sat just a little further back still, sharing their own food and talking quietly in one of their languages.

Kexx didn't try to eavesdrop. Instead, ze sat down with the warriors from Jumar and Icho, villages west of G'tel and Pukal, and traded some of zer dux'ah jerky for a generous portion of candied bitterroot and a pair of still-wriggling popper bugs. Bitterroot was a foreign delicacy near the coasts, where it refused to take in the salty water. Jumar did a brisk trade in it, as their crop's flavor was intense enough to burn the mouth. Some said one could make river water safe to drink just by sucking it up through the hollow in the root's center. Kexx snapped off a piece as long as a finger and put it on zer tongue. It was sweet at first, owing to the sticky coating of nectar it was rolled in as a preservative, but in moments the heat and sharpness of the dried sap hit zer mouth like a liquid dagger, stabbing at zer tongue and cheeks as it flowed into every crevice. Kexx's face scrunched up even as zer skin sent out and involuntary warning pattern. The older of the warriors laughed.

"It's not so bad," Kexx said, trying to recover. "Would make a weak tea."

The one from Jumar laughed even louder as ze cut off strips of jerky and started chewing diligently.

"What are your names?"

"Surea," ze said with a mild accent through a mouthful of meat. "And this is Eklo." Surea slapped the younger warrior on the back. Surea had seen many summers. Ze was starting to show the telltale signs of transitioning to elder. The softening of zer muscles, fading color at the edges of zer crests. It would probably be zer last year as a warrior, assuming they survived this trip. Eklo, by contrast, was very young with vibrant crests, smooth skin, and no scars to tell the stories of past battles. Ze was quiet, nervous.

All but two of the warriors Icho had sent to the gathering had been killed in the attack back in G'tel, and the more experienced one was needed to escort their chief back to their village. That left young Eklo as Icho's contribution to the caravan by default. Surea seemed to have adopted the youth.

"Is this your first time in the wilds, Eklo?"

"Yes, elder."

Kexx chuckled. "There are a few years yet before I transition to elder, young warrior. Stick close to Surea, ze looks like ze knows the tricks."

"Most of them, anyway," Surea added with a smirk.

"Do you two need anything? Blankets? Water?"

"We're well-provisioned, truth-digger Kexx. We're fine for now. Thank you for the jerky."

Kexx thanked them for the treats, tucked the popper bugs away for later, then walked off to the edge of the perimeter. Ze would take the first watch. Kuul had volunteered zer pair of guards for the duty, and surely they would perform it, keeping themselves warm and limber by the fire waiting for the first sign of trouble. But Kexx didn't want to wait to be found by trouble.

Ze knew about nighttime on the plains. It was quiet. Peaceful. Deceptive. Only out here, removed from the crackling and snapping of the burning bundles, facing away from the fire that would foul zer eyes to the dark, could ze spot trouble before it could surprise the camp. It wasn't that the warriors didn't want to do the job properly, they just didn't think in those terms.

Warriors were all drawn to fire. Battle was something done during the day, when everyone was hot and flexible, and the sun cast its light down to illuminate the battlefield. Warriors didn't hide in shadows, and they were usually half deaf from the shouts and screams of war. All but the very best of them, the legends, simply reacted to situations as they arose. They didn't spend much thought trying to anticipate them.

Truth-diggers, on the other hand, spent their lives trying to work backward to reconstruct how things had happened. It wasn't a stretch then to flip it and guess how things were going to happen. Ze had to remain alert. Kexx slipped into the shadows just beyond the clearing and blended into zer surroundings, patient, quiet, and eternally vigilant.

Kexx shot up with a jolt and tried to grab the hand clasping zer shoulder, but zer cool body was tight and slow and it pulled away before ze could get a finger on it. Instead, ze rolled forward and planted zer feet into the sandy soil, then spun around, coming face to face with.

"Benson," Kexx said breathlessly.

"Yes, it's me, Kexx." The human stood erect, one hand held out, palm down urging calm, while the other gripped the handle of zer gun. Light poured out of a cylinder on the side of the weapon. "I'm sorry, buddy. You fell asleep."

"I did not," Kexx bristled. "I was… checking my eyelids for mites."

Benson smirked. "Sure, we'll go with that."

"Why do you hold your gun, detective?"

Benson pointed north. "You were overdue coming back from your watch, so I came out to find you. I thought I heard something moving around in the brush just now."

Kexx froze. "Put your light out, and don't move," ze said quietly. Benson obeyed without comment. Kexx stuck the point of zer spear into the ground, then held out zer hands, tasting the air, looking for any hint of sweat, musk, urine, any signs of something nasty hiding in the dark. Ze listened for the rustling of grass being brushed aside, felt through the pads in zer feet for the rhythm of footsteps, extending zer senses as far out into the dark as ze could, but the search came up empty. All ze heard was the ocean breeze playing through the stands of grass.

"I'm sorry, Benson, but you must have heard the wind. There's nothing out–"

The impact took Kexx clean off zer feet. A moment later, the ground struck zer as well, but ze'd braced for it at least. Searing pain shot through Kexx's shoulder as a hundred teeth thin as bone needles sank into the flesh. Kexx shrieked in pain and surprise, then shoved hard against the animal with zer free arm and one of zer feet, but to no effect. Whatever it was, it outweighed Kexx by double or more.

Ze managed to get a hand on the creature's face, felt around for its eye socket, and dug in with a finger. For a moment, the beast released its grip, but then it redoubled the attack and clamped down until Kexx heard something in zer shoulder give out with a sickening pop.

A light flashed on in an instant, bathing both Kexx and zer attacker in a pure white glow, bright enough to nearly blind them both. Kexx saw the outline of the monster trying to eat zer and gasped. It was an ulik, but far bigger and more solidly built than any of the half-starved, mottled packs ze was used to seeing scavenging near the village.

And it was warm. Much too warm.

Zer spear was out of reach. Shock and pain were quickly giving way to panic. A hand reached out from the light and grabbed the freakish ulik by the nape of the neck. A human hand.

"Hold still, you ugly motherfucker!" Benson shouted in human as ze pressed the point of zer gun against the creature's face. Thunder clapped and lightning flashed three times, deafening Kexx even as the ulik's head exploded in a shower of bone fragments, blood, and brains. The corpse was still convulsing as Benson rolled it off Kexx's chest and offered zer a hand up.

"Thank you," Kexx said.

"What?" Benson shouted back, cupping a hand over zer ear. Kexx could barely hear the reply over the ringing in zer ears.

"THANK YOU," Ze shouted back.

Benson nodded, then pointed at Kexx's shoulder. "ARE YOU HURT?"

Kexx felt at zer shoulder joint, felt it dipping out of place. Ze'd felt it like that once before after falling out of a tree as a youth. Kexx gripped zer forearm with zer good hand, and with a decisive jerk, shoved the shoulder back into its proper place. Zer knees almost gave out from the surge of pain, but it worked.

"I'll be fine," ze shouted, the ringing in zer ears abating the slightest amount.

"Don't be too sure," Benson yelled back, sweeping zer gun's light across the grassland. Dozens of eyes shone amber back at them.

Kexx reached for zer spear with zer good hand as Benson shouldered zer gun.

As one, they turned back toward the camp and shouted, "Kuul!"

CHAPTER TWENTY-FOUR

For the second time in four days, Benson found himself fighting for his life. The pacing of the occurrences seemed to be quickening, but he didn't have time to worry about that right now. A huge pack, really a herd, of alien predators stared him down through the holographic sight on top of his rifle. They weren't invincible, as evidenced by the very dead one missing the top of its head. But if the rest of the group was riled by the fate of their comrade, it didn't show.

Benson had hoped the light and noise of the rifle would startle the creatures and drive them off. Instead, they charged in a wave. Fortunately, the rifle's internal threat assessment VI was keen enough to peg toothy charging alien monsters as hostile and prioritize them by distance. The rifle jumped back into his shoulder as he pulled the trigger, a short burst centered on the nearest target, then moving to the next, and the next. The animals fell, eventually, those he didn't kill outright keening into the night with their injuries.

But the rest of them didn't break and run. Instead they halted the attack, held their ground, and studied him. Alarms built into his amygdala through millions of years of ancestors working their way up the food chain all went off at once, threatening to turn him around and send Benson bolting off into the night like a startled rabbit.

His rational mind knew that was the worst thing he could do. The one that had attacked Kexx had moved like a sprinter. The pack would be on top of him before he'd finished turning around. Just barely above the ringing in his ears, Benson could make out shouting coming from the camp as the warriors stirred from their slumber to face the sudden threat.

"What do we do?" Benson asked Kexx without bothering to translate it from English.

"Hold firm, don't take your eyes off them. If one moves, hit it, or they'll all move."

"What are they?"

"I don't know."

It was not a reassuring answer. Names could be frightening, but something with no name was somehow worse still. What stared back at them didn't even move like a pack of wild animals, but a single, coherent unit. There was far too much calculation and intention looking back across the grass for Benson's peace of mind.

"Let's call them calebs," Benson said.

"Why?"

"Because I knew a Caleb. Ugly as sin and a dirty fighter."

"Calebs it is," Kexx agreed.

The shouting behind them grew closer as Kuul organized zer warriors and approached the new threat. In the minds of the calebs, the calculation shifted. As one, they charged.

"Fuck me," Benson cursed. "Get behind me!" He started firing again. Benson watched his round counter drain down with each burst, twenty-eight, twenty-five, twenty-two. The calebs kept coming as if they sprang up out of the ground. A pile of corpses began to mount in front of where Benson stood, forcing the attacking animals to scramble over the top of their fallen brethren and giving Benson an extra, crucial moment to get a proper bead on them.

Abruptly, the attack shifted. The charging beasts broke off into two columns heading in opposite directions. Benson tracked one of them and put it down, but the rest moved too fast through the grass, coming in to flank Benson, Kexx, and the warriors running up from camp. Spears, claws, daggers, and teeth collided in the dark.

The wedge of light from Benson's rifle cut through the dark, jumping around wildly as he swept it from one target to the next. Wherever he turned the muzzle, calebs and warriors were already on top of each other. He couldn't risk hitting his allies. He wasn't that good of a shot. He'd have to get right up in their faces, just as he had with the beast that attacked Kexx.

"Find Mei," Benson shouted over his shoulder to the truth-digger. "Protect her."

The Atlantian nodded and ran into the fray toward the camp gripping zer spear, even as blood seeped from dozens of punctures in zer shoulder.

"Tough fucker," Benson mumbled. He spotted a straggler just outside of the fur ball, sighted on it, and squeezed the trigger with a jerk. The shot pulled right, striking the creature in its shoulder, but missing the head. It noticed him and turned into the attack.

Benson pulled the trigger again, but instead of the bark of a gunshot, he was met with only a small *click*, barely audible above the ringing in his ears. He pulled the trigger again in a panic with no results at all. His eye flickered over to the round counter even as the beast picked up speed.

Zero flashed red at him.

"Dammit!" Benson's feet backpedaled as he fumbled for the magazine release, cursing himself for not spending more time practicing with the new equipment. The empty magazine clattered against the hardpack dirt. Benson slammed a fresh magazine home and almost had time to rack the charging handle before the charging caleb crashed into him.

Almost, but not quite.

In an instant, Benson found himself wheeling through the air, grass below him one moment, stars the next. The rifle wrenched free of his grip and spun away. He fell back to earth like a pile of bricks. His head still spinning, Benson managed to get a foot underneath himself and kicked up onto all fours. The beast that hit him had overshot. It looked back, pinpointed its prey, then dug its claws into the clay and spun back around. Benson saw the light from his rifle a couple of meters away and frantically scrambled to reach it, but a heavy paw landed between his shoulder blades and shoved his face into the dirt.

The beast's thick black claws flexed, trying to pierce the

strange wiggling creature it had trapped underfoot, but the back plate on Benson's riot gear held fast. He tried to roll out from under the caleb, but it was too heavy, and he remained pinned as it snorted hot, sticky breath onto the back of his neck. He screamed, more out of frustration than fear, dug his fingers into the clay, and dragged both himself and the monster on top of him, inch by agonizing inch, toward the butt of his rifle. Teeth tried to tear into his shoulder, just as they did to Kexx. Were they trying to immobilize their prey? It didn't matter now.

Benson's hope soared as he managed to get a single fingertip on his gun, then another. But just quickly as it had come, his elation was snatched away as another foot stepped on his wrist. An Atlantian foot, followed by an Atlantian hand wrapping its tentacle fingers around the handle of his rifle.

"Kuul!" Benson shouted up at the warrior. "What are you doing?"

Kuul ignored him and picked up the gun, then dropped zer spear and turned, content to leave Benson to his fate. "You son of a bitch!" Benson shouted at zer retreating back.

But the moment Kuul moved away, the beast on Benson's back shifted its attentions. It already recognized the danger anyone holding the rifle represented. With a surge of pressure, the caleb lunged off of Benson's back.

"Behind you!" Benson shouted in untranslated English, but Kuul heard him and turned anyway, just in time to see the beast's claws reaching out. Kuul snapped the rifle up, leveled it at the Caleb's head and pulled the trigger, flinching in anticipation of the bang. Ze'd obviously been studying Benson carefully.

But the bang never came. The shifting light and patterns of Kuul's skin had just long enough to register zer confused surprise before the animal reached zer. Fortunately, zer warrior reflexes moved Kuul far enough out of the beast's line of attack that ze wasn't taken straight to the ground, but it lashed a paw out as it passed, leaving three deep gashes in Kuul's abdomen that began seeping blood immediately. In a flash, the creature wheeled around with disturbing speed and was on top of Kuul once more, slashing viciously as the warrior tried to parry blows with the rifle.

Benson scrambled back onto his feet and took up Kuul's abandoned spear in his hands. Summoning a growling shout, he leveled the point at the caleb and sprang forward; his powerful legs pumped like pistons, building up as much speed as he could over the short distance. Benson aimed the bouncing spear right for the dead center of the beast's forehead.

A small depression in the dirt threw off Benson's gait on the last step and sent the spear plunging into the caleb's shoulder with a sickening tearing sound, followed by an equally sickening squeal of pain. Benson jerked back on the shaft to ready another stab, but the spear point wouldn't budge. Instead, Benson reached over and grabbed his rifle from Kuul's uncomprehending hands, racked the charging lever, then shoved it into the beast's face and blew it messily in half with a three-round burst, throwing bits of bone and brain tissue in every direction.

Without missing a beat, Benson spun around and trained the muzzle of his gun on Kuul's left eye. For the briefest of instants, his finger tightened, taking the slack out of the trigger. The gun seemed to beg for the release that would send a tiny electric charge into the base of the caseless round sitting inside its chamber. It would be so easy. Just another few grams of pressure and a persistent and growing threat would be eliminated. It wouldn't even burn up a calorie.

Cutting through the adrenaline, Benson's rational mind asserted itself. The red faded from his vision. Murder was not why he'd decided to stay. He shook his head and eased off the trigger. "Don't touch my shit!" he shouted at Kuul, then turned back to the fight.

Five of the longest minutes of Benson's life later, the last of the calebs tucked tail and ran off into the night. Funny how that particular mannerism transcended lightyears. It had been a hard fight, and not without cost. Two of the caravan's warriors, including one of Kuul's handpicked guards, had returned to Xis. Four more had suffered serious injuries, including one missing arm, and everyone else had suffered scrapes, bruises, and lacerations.

In that regard, Benson had gotten off light. Despite rolling around in the dirt with a caleb doing its best to open him up like a can of beans, his body armor had taken the majority of the abuse, including long furrows carved into the high-impact plastic panels on his back and shoulders. That left him with only a few small cuts and abrasions to tend to. For the last two days, he'd been whining endlessly about the way the ill-fitting gear's straps dug into his clavicles, how he felt like a roast cooking inside it, and how much its weight slowed him down. Now, there was a real chance someone would have to cut it off him before he'd part with it.

He broke into his small med kit for bandages and antiseptic salve. Couldn't be too careful about infections. God only knew what kind of microorganisms were lurking around in the ground out here. Aside from the bandaids and cream, the fight had cost almost two full magazines' worth of bullets, which were not a resource he'd wanted to part with.

Mei sat next to him, quietly munching on a ration bar she'd snatched. Unlike the rest of the caravan, her porcelain skin was dusty and streaked with sweat, but otherwise unblemished.

"There's not a scratch on you." Benson said. "How'd you manage that?"

"Unbound, remember? Good at hiding."

"No argument there." They went back to eating and dressing wounds in amicable silence. The adrenaline spike had worn off and Benson knew he was going to crash hard in another handful of minutes. Three of the others returned to the fire with the dux'ah that had panicked and run off during the fight, half the caravan's supplies with it. Finally, a little luck.

Benson felt Mei's small body tense at the approach of footsteps. He looked up to see Kuul bearing down on where they sat. Benson's eye flickered over to where his rifle sat, loaded and ready. He considered reaching for it, but Kuul's hands were empty. Benson decided to let the encounter play out and hope for the best.

"Deadskin," Kuul said as ze came to a stop, towering over where Benson sat.

Benson nodded. "Cuttlefish."

"That is not my name," Kuul said.

"And 'deadskin' isn't mine."

Kuul's skin flashed irritation, but ze quickly suppressed it. "Benson."

Benson got up and smiled politely. "Kuul. I'm sorry about your warrior."

"Ze fought bravely and earned zer place with Xis."

"Indeed ze did." Benson pointed at the three parallel tears in the warrior's abdomen. "Are you all right?"

"I can fight," ze replied. "But, I do not understand why." Kuul looked down at the rifle. Benson tensed for a split second, believing the warrior was going to make another play for it. But instead of avarice, Benson was almost certain he recognized shame in the alien's features. "I took your gon, left you to die."

"I haven't forgotten."

"Then you saved my life."

"I did."

"Why?" The question was direct. It wasn't pleading, or searching for absolution. It just wanted a direct answer to something that didn't make sense.

"We've both lost enough people. I'm here to find out who's responsible so we can have justice. That's my mission. You're a powerful warrior. My mission has a better chance of success with your help."

"That's it?" Kuul asked.

"That, and I'm not a murderer."

"You are, I watched you murder today."

Benson almost took offense, but there was confusion in Kuul's response. Instead, he ran the word "murder" through his plant's translation software. Sure enough, the Atlantian language didn't have a concept of murder distinct from the simple act of killing. They were the same word. It explained quite a bit.

"Only to protect myself, and everyone else. I don't kill without a good reason."

"I think I understand," Kuul said.

"Good, now understand this. I don't want to hurt you or anyone else here. We're a team, with the same goal. But I swear to Cuut, if you try to pull some shit like that again, Kuul, I'll shoot you in the knee and your ass can crawl back to the village. Are we clear?"

Kuul's jaw tightened at the threat and his skin fluttered, but ze remained calm, like a soldier receiving a dressing down from a superior. "Clear as still water."

"Good. I respect your strength and dedication, Kuul. If we survive this, maybe we can be friends."

"Perhaps." Kuul wandered back to sit with zer surviving guard, some of the color dimmed from zer flesh. Mei snorted. "You have a way with people," she said in her accented English.

Benson shrugged. "It's a gift."

"Would you really shoot zer?"

"Ze makes another play for my gun? Count on it. But I'd just as soon win zer over, or at least make zer stop seeing us as potential enemies."

"That'll be easier now that Dluz returned." Benson tilted his head at the name. "The dead guard. Kuul feels vulnerable."

"It does seem to have taken some wind out of zer sails, hasn't it?"

Mei nodded agreement. Kexx appeared and sat down next to them by the fire. "Detective," ze said in Atlantian.

"How's your shoulder?" Benson waved a hand over the half-moon of tiny puncture wounds in the truth-digger's flesh. They already looked inflamed and angry.

"It will be very sore by tomorrow. I fear it will weep."

"Weep?" Benson asked.

"Ze means infected," Mei translated.

"Oh, here," Benson handed his tube of salve over to Kexx. "Rub this into them."

Kexx took the tube and touched the head of it with a fingertip. Ze recoiled and flashed blue. "It tastes rancid."

"You don't have to eat it."

Mei sighed and took the tube. "Ze needs zer hands to rub it on, stupid."

"Oh, right," Benson said.

Mei shook her head as she started to apply the salve to Kexx's wounds.

"What is it?" Kexx asked.

"You're not going to have a word for it," Benson said. "We call it an *antiseptic*. It kills all of the, um... tiny bugs that cause infections."

"Tiny bugs?"

"Bacteria," Mei said, not bothering to dumb it down for the Atlantian. "Animals so small, your eyes can't see them."

Kexx looked unconvinced. Benson had to admit, if he'd lived in an age before microscopes, he'd have probably thought it sounded like a load of bullshit too.

"Ann-tee-sep-tick," Kexx experimented with the new word. "Back-tear-e-ah."

Kexx winced as Mei moved around and rubbed the salve into a particularly deep wound on zer back. Once she'd finished, Kexx seemed to relax. "You seem to have made an impression on Kuul."

"Sure looks that way. What kind of impression is harder to guess."

"We'll know soon enough. I have news to share."

"Let's hear it," Benson said.

"The calebs that attacked us were not wild."

Benson leaned forward. "What makes you say that?"

"Several reasons." Kexx began to count off points on zer fingers. "One, they were far too organized, even for an old pack. Two, wild uliks tend to avoid tough fights. They prefer to attack weak, old, or injured animals, and only then once they have a clear advantage in numbers. Even then, they will retreat once they've lost more than a couple members. Their packs rely on numbers for strength, they can't afford to lose more than a few members. This pack continued to fight until they were almost completely wiped out."

Benson nodded along. The limited footage of uliks in the wild Pathfinder's rovers and drones had captured reminded him of wolves, or maybe hyenas from Earth. "OK, I follow you so far. Anything else?"

"Yes, something I noticed while I was trapped under the one that attacked first. They were warm. Much too warm for this late at night."

Ze was right about that. The temperature swing from day to night around here felt like thirty degrees. Benson could see his breath if he turned away from the fire. "Someone was keeping them near a fire," he said. "But the land is flat as a table out here.

We'd see another fire from many stones away."

"Not necessarily. There are ravines and valleys some stones ahead where a fire could be hidden. Or they kept the calebs under blankets, or underground," Kexx continued. "These animals were... I hesitate to call them domesticated, but they were certainly trained and held."

"You think it's the Dwellers?"

"Not the Dwellers proper. We're still too far from their caves for the calebs to reach us in time and still be so hot. But an outpost or a scouting party? Perhaps."

"Sounds like a lead to me," Benson said.

"Indeed."

"So, what do we do?"

"Right now? We sleep and recover." Kexx worked zer stiff shoulder. "But at first light, I track them back to their camp and we ask them some very uncomfortable questions."

Benson smiled. "I'd be delighted to."

CHAPTER TWENTY-FIVE

Theresa's feet fell quietly on the marble tilework of the museum's main exhibition hall, yet they still echoed. It was another two hours before the hall opened to the public. It was quiet as a tomb, which it was, in a way. The building, the largest in Shambhala, larger even than the Beehive, held the mortal remains of Earth, Luna, and scraps of Mars. The artifacts, books, and art were keepsakes of a civilization now more than two centuries dead.

The new museum had over three times the floor space of its predecessor on board the Ark, which meant three times as much display space for pieces that had been patiently waiting in the vault to see the light of day. Looking around, Theresa felt the weight of millennia as if it was a physical presence. The building itself was virtually brand new, only completed eighteen months ago, and opened to the public six months after that. Yet the place felt, even *smelled* old, as if the age of the artifacts it housed had already seeped into the walls and columns.

It made Theresa uneasy. She'd never felt any particular connection to Earth. She'd never known it, no one had. Everyone dealt with that separation differently. Some threw themselves wholeheartedly into genealogical studies, digging through the lives of ancestors long dead as if it would help define who they were today. Others studied Earth history, binged on old TV shows and movies, or embraced the culture and traditions of their ethnic group or their dominant nationality. Theresa secretly harbored a suspicion that anyone actually from Earth would openly laugh at their efforts, but whatever made them happy was fine with her so long as she didn't have to break up fights or get thrown up on. Saint Patrick's Day was not her favorite holiday.

For her husband, it was his strange love of nature documentaries about plants and animals that were now long extinct, many never to exist again. She'd lost count of how many nights she'd fallen asleep on the couch with her head resting on Bryan's shoulder while he watched some dead guy named Attenborough drone on about penguins and how shitty living in the Antarctic was.

Theresa lived in the now. She was distantly aware through her mother that she was of Mediterranean ancestry, primarily Portuguese and Sicilian with a smattering of basically everything else on three continents to go with it. But the knowledge didn't tell her anything about herself. Maybe some things were better left in the past.

One person who most decidedly did not share that opinion was the museum's curator Devorah Feynman, whom Theresa was there to see. If only she could find the woman.

"Devorah?" she called out into the stillness, but there was no answer. The grimacing face of a red suit of samurai armor, bristling with teeth and a horsehair mustache, seemed to leer at her as she passed. It had given her the creeps as a kid. Now, with the museum darkened and empty of life, it positively made her skin crawl.

"Devorah?" she called again with a renewed urgency.

"Keep your voice down, young lady," came a raspy voice from directly behind her. Theresa nearly jumped out of her shoes.

"Jesus Christ, Devorah!" She whirled around to face the curator. "You scared the shit out of me!"

"Sorry, dear. An old lady has to entertain herself somehow."

"It's dead quiet in here. How did you sneak up on me?"

"I'm actually a ghost." Devorah held up her hands and wiggled her knobby fingers. "Whooooooh."

"You're not the first person to say that," Theresa said.

"Really?"

"No. Some of your former interns believe you're undead."

"Zombie, or vampire?" Devorah asked.

"Debate rages. But they all agree that you don't sleep."

"I sleep, just not as much as a hormone-drenched teenager."

"But you're always here. Day and night."

"I take naps."

"At work?" Theresa said with mild surprise.

"What the hell do you think an office is for?"

"Ah, I assumed working."

"No work has ever gotten done in an office. Offices are for people who slow down the actual workers with meetings and performance reviews and training seminars. I use mine for cat naps. I figure it boosts productivity around here by twenty percent. People assume I'm doing paperwork, I get the three hours of sleep I need a day, everyone's happy."

Theresa's eyes went wide. "Three hours? How are you conscious?"

"Tea," Devorah said. "Sleep's overrated. Benjamin Franklin slept three hours a day, and he had enough time left over to be an inventor, businessman, founder of America, ambassador, and bed half of the women he encountered."

"Who?" Theresa asked, embarrassed.

Devorah tisked and shook her head. "I must speak with your old teachers."

"Oh no, don't blame them for how I turned out. They did their best."

"Well, I suppose you could've been worse. You could've gone into politics."

Theresa chuffed. "Seems like half my job is politics these days."

Devorah shrugged and changed the subject. "I noticed you looking at this piece." She gestured to the red armor with a hand.

"Oh, I just remembered seeing it as a kid."

"That's not surprising. It was down in the vault for many years. But we've been trying to display more Asian artifacts since..." She trailed off uncomfortably.

"Since Shangri-La," Theresa finished for her. The attack that had wiped out two fifths of humanity, the attack her husband had tried but failed to stop, and indeed barely survived himself, had come within seconds of snuffing out Devorah as well. By unguided self-selection, Shangri-La module had been primarily home to descendants of populations from Earth's eastern hemisphere. Only five thousand people from Shangri-La had survived, and only because they'd been in the stadium watching the Zero Championship.

Devorah cleared her throat. "Yes. Since then. This piece was the personal armor of Yamagata Masakage."

"It's tiny," Theresa observed. "I don't think I would fit in it."

"It's a little loose on me."

"You've *worn* it?"

"Purely for research purposes, I assure you," Devorah said with a twinkle in her eye.

"Still, I assume it was cut for a man, yes?"

"He lived in Japan during the sixteenth century. People were much smaller back then."

"Who was he?"

"A famous samurai. He took over for his brother after he committed seppuku in service of their lord."

"Seppuku?"

Devorah stuck out her thumb and drew it across her stomach, making a ripping sound as she did.

"He gutted himself? Why on Earth would he do that?"

Devorah shrugged. "No idea. You'd have to ask him. Seems like a mighty silly thing to me."

Theresa stuck her chin at the lacquered breastplate. "And him? Did he fare better than his brother?"

"Depends on how you look at it. He was shot off his horse in battle. As deaths go, I'm sure a samurai would be thrilled with it." Devorah reached out and very gently touched the spot of the armor that would cover the heart. "Just between you and me, I'm pretty sure this is a reproduction, probably a movie costume, no matter what the provenance docs say. It was 'rediscovered' at an awfully convenient time."

"Then why keep it?"

"I don't know. I've just… always liked it. And if it's a repro, it's a simply brilliant example of the craft. Maybe that's an art form that deserves recognition, too."

"Is that a trace of sentimentality I hear in the 'Machine of the Museum'?"

Devorah smirked. "Is that what they're calling me out there? I thought I was a zombie, not a cyborg."

"Debate rages," Theresa smiled warmly. "It wouldn't hurt to

make an appearance outside now and then."

"I know. I just... there's so much I have to do yet. This place is a mess."

"It's immaculate," Theresa objected.

"Well sure, it's *clean*, but that just hides the chaos downstairs, not to mention everything we still have to bring down the beanstalk. There's just so little time."

Theresa almost objected. Against all the odds, mankind had made it. The city was growing. The future stretched out before them with endless possibilities. But then she realized whose time the prickly old woman was talking about. She glanced down and saw tears threatening to form at the corners of Devorah's eyes. How old was she now? Seventy? Seventy-one? In all likelihood, she still had another ten, maybe fifteen years of life left ahead of her, and everyone was too scared of her to seriously try to force her to retire one second before she was ready. But then Devorah had always seen things on a longer timescale than the average person.

Not knowing what to say, Theresa reached down and embraced her tightly. She held the withered woman for several seconds, consoling her.

"Ack, enough." Devorah pushed back and brushed away tears with her wrist. "You didn't come here before breakfast for a pity party. Which begs the question: what are you here for, constable?"

The moment had passed, and Devorah had fallen back into her comfortable role as curator. "I have a few questions," Theresa said.

"About the administrator's assassination?" Devorah asked. "Don't know what good I can be to you there. I was a few thousand kilometers away from where it happened."

"Not the assassination, at least not directly," Theresa said. "I'm curious about gold. Silver, precious metals."

"They're shiny and people like them, especially women."

Theresa ignored her reflexive sarcasm. "Have any pieces made of gold or other rare metals gone missing from the museum's collection since we landed?"

Devorah bristled. "Things don't go missing on my watch. Besides, you would've been the first to know. Well, the second after me. Actually, the third after me and whoever stole them."

"Has anyone shown an unusual amount of interest in them? Asking a lot of questions? I'm only asking because I've already done a review of search queries on the net and found nothing unusual."

"Not that I can... Well, then again."

"Yeah?"

Devorah rubbed her chin as if trying to remember something. "A couple years ago, while we were still under construction, some business types came in here and tried to lean on me to strip the gold leaf off of the frames of our classical paintings and replace it with paint in exchange for a 'generous donation.'"

"What did you tell them?"

"What do you think I told them? I said you can't add to the museum by subtracting from it." Devorah shook her head in disgust.

"What did they want it for?"

Devorah shrugged. "They were not forthcoming about their intentions for it, only that they wanted any gold that wasn't 'an intrinsic part of the artifact,' as if the goddamned frame isn't part of the painting. I swear, the shortsighted arrogance of some people. They'd burn the Library of Alexandria to get through a single chilly night in comfort."

Theresa was carefully recording the conversation with her plant, adding notes and follow-up questions as she went. "What came of it, in the end?"

"They didn't lay off, I can tell you that. At first, it was donations, then bigger donations. When the carrot didn't work, they started threatening to mess with my funding. It even made it to a couple of closed-door council sessions, but they went nowhere. Then one day, they just quit. Never heard another peep out of them."

"Why'd they lay off?"

"Your guess is as good as mine. But, they were *very* insistent. I'd say they found another source."

"You may be right about that," Theresa said. "Last question, Devorah. Who were these 'business types'?"

"They were stooges, mostly, and I don't know who all they represented. Except Alexander. His fingerprints were all over it, that slimy bastard."

"But didn't his company design and build this place?"

"Not because of an abundance of options, constable," Devorah said. "I never liked that entitled, corner-cutting jerk. Wrestling with him for two years to make sure this place was actually built right and didn't start leaking during the first hurricane season only reinforced my opinions of his business ethics."

Theresa smirked at the feeling of tugging at threads and watching the tapestry unravel. It was a surprisingly addictive sensation. "Thank you, Devorah. That's all I have for now. And if you could keep this confidential, I would greatly appreciate it."

"I assumed that already. Nothing else would bring you here."

"I'm sorry. It's just that I've been so busy lately."

Devorah reached out and lightly touched Theresa's wrist. "Can I show you something?"

"OK," Theresa said hesitantly, but Devorah's grip had already tightened as she pulled her forward through the halls until they'd reached the central atrium. Devorah brought up the lights. Sitting among the museum's permanent exhibits, nestled in a place of honor between Ramses the Great's sarcophagus and Neil Armstrong's boots, sat a brand new display case. Through the thick glass, with red velvet shaped around its lines, sat a very special handgun. Once used by a madman to plunge all of humanity into war, and then, centuries later, used by a completely different madman to save it. That lunatic was Theresa's husband, and she was standing next to the woman who'd broken all the rules and risked everything she'd achieved to smuggle it into his hands.

"It's a beautiful presentation," Theresa said at last, not knowing what else to say.

"Thank you."

"I'm amazed they let you put it on display."

"Are you kidding? It's an icon. The whole city has been demanding to see it. But you're the first. Well, the second. Well…"

"Yes, yes. The usual caveats apply." Theresa smiled down at the curator. "I'm honored. Thrilled."

"You don't sound thrilled." Devorah touched her arm. "I know he's out there again. Right in the teeth of it."

Theresa nodded, fighting down a rising tide of dread. "With another gun in his hand. He doesn't like them, you know. Hates the idea of them, actually. He's a competitor, not a killer. He'll work himself into the ground, train like mad, skip sleeping, whatever he has to do to beat you. But that's all he wants to do. I swear the man is incapable of the sort of hate it takes to want to kill anything."

Devorah squeezed her arm. "He's proven himself as a marksman, sure enough."

Theresa laughed humorlessly. "That's just it, he didn't. Everyone knows about the 'Shot Heard Round the Ark,' but it's all crew propaganda. When he faced down Kimura, he couldn't stop him from pushing the button. He just ended up shooting wildly until the gun was empty. It was pure, unadulterated, dumb fucking luck that one of the bullets hit the casing on that bomb. It wasn't part of the plan, the idea never even occurred to him. He wasn't a hero, he was just lucky."

Devorah tisked. "Of course he is. He put himself in danger and did whatever he could to help. That's what heroes do. That's what defines the word. The lucky ones just live long enough that people know their names."

"Better lucky than good? Is that what you're saying?"

"The enemy can prepare for good," Devorah said. "Nobody can prepare for lucky."

"Let's hope you're right."

"I usually am," Devorah said.

Theresa was spinning up a cutting retort when her plant alerted her to an incoming call. It was from Feng, and it was marked "Emergency."

"Excuse me one moment," she said to Devorah and opened the call. <Chao, what's up? Aren't you still in the elevator car?>

<And this is where I'm staying, apparently. My permission to board the Ark has been revoked.>

<What? They can't do that. You're a deputy constable. I'm going to conference in Mahama and–>

<That's the problem, chief,> Feng cut her off. <Captain Mahama is dead.>

CHAPTER TWENTY-SIX

The sun returned much too quickly for Kexx's taste, not that ze had expected it to take zer opinion into consideration. Ze'd spent what remained of the night huddled close to the fire where the cold kept its distance. Ze was overtired and zer shoulder was still sore from being bitten, but at least ze was warm-headed and loose.

Most of the rest of the caravan had taken the same precaution, either cramming in close to the fire or sleeping beneath the dux'ah for warmth. The large creatures released their own heat slowly through the long nights, greeting the morning none the worse for wear on all but the coldest days. The humans, for their part, alternated between standing watch for the calebs to return and sleeping in their "tent," an ingenious little shelter that they could set up or take down in moments which fit inside an impossibly small bag when not in use. Kexx had asked Mei what sort of leather it had been sewn from. Whatever this "plastic" beast was, it must have been a very odd creature indeed.

By now, the caravan was well practiced at striking camp and moving out, although there were fewer hands this morning. They'd prepared Dluz and... Celiapak? Kexx struggled with the exotic name. Ze'd been from Yptari, a village almost as far from G'tel as it was possible to be. Kexx hadn't gotten around to talking to zer yet. It was a missed opportunity, one ze wouldn't have a chance to rectify. Kexx resolved to get to know everyone in the caravan by the time the sun set.

They prepared the dead to return as best they could, absent

the guidance of an experienced elder, well before that dawn as tradition demanded. Their bodies were wrapped in sleeping blankets and placed under a low tree for retrieval when the caravan returned.

Assuming it returned.

Kexx banished the doubt from zer mind. It did no good for a truth-digger to dwell on what could not be known. There was a trail to follow, and it grew colder with each wasted moment. Some of the more adventurous members of the caravan were cutting up and cooking strips of caleb meat for breakfast, while leaving others aside to smoke and cure into jerky. Kexx had eaten ulik meat before and found it tough and gamey. Ze doubted the calebs would prove more flavorful, but ze needed the flesh to help zer own flesh recover, and anything they found out here was that much more food left in their pouches.

Ze looked around the camp with a great deal of satisfaction. They'd not only survived the night's surprise attack, but drawn together in the aftermath. The different villages mixed and blended around the fire for the first time since they'd stepped onto the trail. They'd even started to mingle with Mei and Benson, if a little awkwardly.

Kuul's position had not come out of the evening untarnished. News of zer attempted betrayal against Benson in the heat of the battle had spread through the caravan like wildfire. Kexx did nothing to help the rumor spread. Then again, ze hadn't needed to. Trying to kill an ally during battle was bad enough. But being so below their notice that they didn't bother trying to return the favor? *That* was humiliating. Robbed of half of zer attendants, Kuul sulked just outside of the fray, gingerly cleaning the wounds on zer abdomen. They looked angry... in-fac-ted; Kexx rolled the human word through zer mind. Zer own injuries hurt, but they did not weep, just as Benson had promised.

Kexx glanced over at Benson trying to share a joke with the one from Jumar. The human finished and held out zer hands, but the warrior just stared at zer uncomprehendingly. "Had to be there," Kexx heard Benson say. Kexx buried a giggle at zer new friend's expense. Such power and wisdom at their fingertips, yet the humans seemed to be perpetually lost, like infants treading water, waiting for someone to direct them toward land. It was probably the only thing preventing the rest of the caravan from openly worshiping them at this point. Ze couldn't quite decide if that was a good or a bad thing.

As ze watched, Benson excused zerself from the conversation and started speaking into the small black box ze called a "fone," more human magic that let zer communicate instantly with zer own village... on the other side of the ocean. Benson had tried to compare it to the signal network, careful to praise Kexx's own people for their ingenuity, but Kexx couldn't help but feel a little patronized. Ze'd seen Benson talk on it every day since they'd left the village, but this time was different. The human grew louder and more animated the longer the conversation went on. Kexx didn't need to recognize all of the human's body language to know ze was agitated. Mei joined zer and put a hand on Benson's shoulder.

Benson put away the fone. Kexx only caught a few human words of the hurried conversation, but it sounded like someone important had died. Ze got up and walked briskly over to where the humans stood.

"What's wrong, Benson?" Kexx asked, speaking human because the topic seemed sensitive. Benson's head twisted around in surprise as if ze hadn't heard Kexx walking up.

"Nothing," ze said hurriedly, then slumped. "Everything, actually. One of our... chiefs died of a heart attack."

"I am sorry," Kexx said genuinely. "Have you caught the hart responsible?"

"What?" Benson's face was blank. "Er, no, Kexx. A heart isn't a person, it's an organ." Ze patted a hand on zer chest. "It pumps blood around our bodies. Hers, I mean zers, quit working suddenly. We call that a heart attack."

"I see," Kexx said, pretending to understand and hoping it would all become clearer. "Do your... harts stop working often?"

"Not anymore," Benson said. "And not in someone who was only fifty-three."

"Fifty-three, what?"

"Sorry, fifty-three years old. Actually, our years are, were, longer than yours. So she was..." Benson went silent for a moment, "Seventy-six by your measure."

Kexx gasped before ze could catch it. Ze hoped to live a full, satisfying life of fifty, maybe sixty years. Seventy-six was ancient, verging on legendary. To hear the human speak of it as though it was a young age to return to Xis was jarring. What would one do with that much time?

"So, zer death was not normal? Is that what you're saying?"

"It's goddamned suspicious is what it is," Benson said. "And awful convenient. Lots of convenient things happening lately." The last, ze shouted straight up into the air, as if chastising the gods themselves.

Kexx took the human's anger and frustration in stride. "Is there anything you can do about it right now?"

Benson's fists balled up. "Not a damned thing."

"Has our task here changed?"

Benson sighed and relaxed a bit at the question. "No, I suppose not."

"Then we should focus on our jobs until that changes, yes?"

"Yes." Benson breathed deeply. "You're right, Kexx. Thank you."

Kexx nodded. "Come. We have a long day ahead of us."

It turned out to be a very long day indeed. Tracking the retreating calebs was not difficult. Wild uliks tended to wander through the landscape and stuck to the hard-packed mud when they could, disguising their tracks to make it more difficult for other, larger predators to shadow them and steal their kills. But these beasts had no such instinct. They simply ran straight as a spear shaft back wherever they'd come from. The only problem was that they'd run very fast. There was a tremendous amount of ground to cover, despite the fact they'd only had a short head start.

There were four survivors, and Kexx could tell from the halting, asymmetrical gait and slight drag in the tracks that one of them had an injured front left leg. That was good and bad. If they accidentally cornered the animals while they rested, ze'd rather not have to face them down at full strength. On the other hand, injured animals could be unpredictable and dangerous. Kexx glanced over at the gun slung over Benson's shoulder and felt the strange mix of reassurance and dread that came with understanding the power it represented.

With the human fighting along zer side, their power was almost unmatched. But what happened if Kexx ever found zerself facing down their length instead of standing behind them? How many humans with guns would it take to subdue the entire village network? A few fullhands? Certainly not more than a hundred, an easy fit inside a single one of their great birds. A vision of humans and their terrible weapons sweeping from one village to the next like a plague of luka flies danced through Kexx's mind.

Ze pushed the nightmare aside. The humans had done nothing to make Kexx believe their intentions were hostile, and had gone out of their way to assure zer otherwise, for now at least. But Benson's worries about their discovery of "gold" and zer suspicions over the death of their chief Mahama left Kexx with the impression the humans were not nearly so unified in their motives and intentions as they first appeared. Was it possible that creatures of such wisdom were still just as fractured and contentious as zer own people? Was that a good or a bad thing? Kexx didn't know.

The caleb tracks changed abruptly, shortening their gait and dropping from a run to a canter, then down again a few strides later to a brisk walk. Kexx held up a hand, signaling a stop.

Kuul appeared at zer side and whispered. "What is it, truth-digger?"

"They slowed to a walk just here," Kexx said. "I believe their shelter is very close."

Kuul's skin flushed a warning and the other warriors set up a circle around the caravan.

Benson stepped up to join them. "What's going on?"

"Trouble," Kexx said. "We draw near their lair."

"Better ready your gon," Kuul said begrudgingly.

Benson unslung the gun and brought it to zer shoulder. "You don't have to tell me twice."

"Everyone else, stay put and protect the dux'ah while the three of us scout it out," Kexx said to the rest of the caravan. The unlikely trio advanced, weapons held ready, as Kexx followed

the tracks the short distance to where they ended in a hole in
the ground.

"Not down there?" Benson asked.

"Yes, down there," Kexx answered as ze held a hand over the
entrance, tasting the air. "They're down there now, I can smell
them."

"How far?" Kuul asked.

"Some distance, but not far."

"Can we enter without being seen?" Kuul asked.

"Seen, maybe. But heard?" Kexx glanced over at Benson
tellingly. "Or smelled?"

"What's that look for?" the human said.

"You have a… distinct aroma," Kexx said delicately.

"You smell like Varr-old dux'ah shit," Kuul added helpfully,
exaggeratedly wiping zer hands on zer loincloth.

"Yeah, well you two don't exactly smell like apple blossoms
yourselves," Benson said. Kexx didn't know what an apple
blossom smelled like, but zer meaning was clear.

"No, but your smell is totally foreign here. I'd be surprised if
the calebs haven't already caught the scent."

"So what do we do?" Benson asked.

"Go inside."

"Into an unfamiliar cave?"

"Yes."

"In the dark?"

"Yeees."

"When they know we're coming."

Kexx grew annoyed. "Do you see another solution, Benson?"

"I don't suppose you have any napalm."

"What is na-palm?"

Benson sighed. "Then no, not really."

"We're giving them time to prepare for us," Kuul said sharply.

"Ze's right, we have to go now," Kexx said. "Kuul and I will go
in first. We handle the darkness better. Benson, you will follow
with your gun and your light to make sure nothing attacks us
from behind."

"Fair enough."

"And keep that light pointed backward," Kuul added with a

hint of menace. "Or it will ruin our eyes for the dark."

"I understand," Benson said. "If I have to shoot in there, the walls will trap the sound. It will be incredibly loud. If I say cover your ears, do it immediately, or it might be the last thing you hear for days."

Kexx nodded understanding, while Kuul's skin flickered the same. Kuul had spent enough time around the humans by now to recognize some of their simpler mannerisms, but zer warrior's pride and sense of purity prevented zer from using them. Without another word, both Kexx and Kuul's skin glow dimmed as their dark contrasting stripes expanded to cover almost the entire surface of their skin. They would be almost invisible against the unlit walls of the cave. The human, on the other hand...

Benson had repeatedly proven ze could handle zerself, despite zer body's deficiencies when it came to camouflage. Kexx just hoped Cuut was in a mood for accommodating fools today.

After a brief inspection with the light on Benson's gun, they started the climb down into the cave. It was a short climb, no more than four or five arm spans. Kexx and Kuul reached the bottom quickly. The human, however, found it more difficult.

"Your pet is no climber," Kuul observed.

"Their hands are different from ours. You would have trouble too."

"Ze'd have less trouble if ze'd take those ridiculous garments off zer feet."

Kexx couldn't help but agree. "Shuus," Mei called them. But as to their purpose, Kexx could only guess.

"It gives our eyes more time to adjust to the dark," Kexx said, ever the optimist.

"And more time for our quarry to set traps and ambushes."

Kexx couldn't help but agree to that, either.

"How are your wounds?" ze pointed at the angry claw marks along Kuul's abdomen. "They have begun to weep."

"I can endure, truth-digger."

"Of course, you're a warrior. But the humans have an oil, an-tee-sep-tic," Kexx sounded out the foreign word. "I used it on my shoulder last night. It works very well."

Kuul chuffed. "You sound like a traveling merchant with your pouch of miraculous herbs. If there's anything better than boiled-off urine for cuts, I've never seen it. And I've had a lot of cuts."

Kexx considered pressing the issue, but let it sit. Kuul was set in zer paths and unlikely to change quickly. Behind them, Benson's foot slipped, spilling zer unceremoniously onto the floor of the cave from about an arm span up.

The human clambered to zer feet. "I'm good."

"Hardly," Kuul taunted. "Just keep anything from biting our backs, deadskin."

"Will do, cuttlefish." Benson's light came on with a click, flooding the rear of the cave with harsh light. Not a cave, as it turned out, but a tunnel. It reached back until the light faded back into complete darkness.

Kexx looked at zer feet and noticed the rocks strewn about the floor, just about enough of them to cover the hole in the ceiling. Ze ran a hand over the cool stone wall and muttered a curse. It was rough, and free of the hanging teeth of the caves ze'd explored before.

"The Dwellers *dug* this?" Kexx said incredulously. "It's enormous. It must go on for stones."

"I don't think so," Benson said. "It looks like a lava tube. The ceiling probably just collapsed recently."

"Lava?" Kexx asked.

"You know, liquid rock?"

"Like mudstone?"

"No, really hot rocks, glowing hot. Comes out of volcanoes?"

"Volcanoes?"

"Er... fire mountains?"

Both Kexx and Kuul looked at the human like ze was running on a cold head. "Nevermind," Benson said, breaking the silence. "What I mean is it's probably natural."

"It certainly smells enough like a Dweller cave," Kuul said.

"You've been in one?" Kexx asked.

"Well, no. But you hear things from traders."

"Let's move on," Kexx said. "Quietly."

"Which direction?" Benson asked.

"That way," Kexx pointed down the tunnel. "Stay close."

"That won't be a problem."

For a hundred spans or more, they walked on in silence. Benson kept zer light pointed behind them as ordered, but enough of it bled back up the tunnel to cast everything in a faint, unnatural glow. Patches of fungus clinging to the walls, excited by the light, glowed back in response hoping to be eaten so their spores would spread.

Kexx's skin glowed, reflexively changing to match the color and luminosity of the fungus patches as ze passed. Kuul, having never spent the time wandering the forests and the night to learn the skill, remained dark. In all ways, Kuul was an unsubtle creature. Ze'd never needed nor wanted to remain hidden from a potential foe. It wasn't a warrior's way.

They stalked onwards, carefully placing their feet to muffle the sounds of their footsteps. They really needn't have bothered, considering the racket Benson made behind them, shuffling zer shoes through the thin layer of silt and pebbles.

"Ze makes as much noise as a dux'ah herd," Kuul whispered in annoyance.

"At least we won't have to wait long before they find us," Kexx said, always looking for the bright spot in any situation.

"I'm sorry, all right?" Benson shot back at them in a loud whisper. "But I'd like to see you two try walking backwards in a dark tunnel quietly."

Without breaking stride, both Kexx and Kuul turned around, reversed their knees, and continued walking without any apparent additional effort.

"All right, all right, nice trick," the human admitted. "Now do it with knee caps."

The bickering came to an abrupt close as a low, rumbling growl echoed through the cavern, filling the space and making the point of origin difficult to pin down.

"What was that?" Benson asked.

"Our prey," Kuul said as ze lunged forward, spear held high in attack. "I see it! To the right, four fullhand armspans."

Kexx caught sight of it as well and followed after Kuul. A solitary caleb, out in the open, its left front paw mangled and held above the ground. Something was wrong with the scene. It was injured, it should be hiding, or protected by its pack mates.

Unless... it was bait.

Kexx grabbed Kuul's shoulder and tried to reel zer back. "Kuul, wait. It's an–"

Before ze could say "ambush," a shrill whistle cut through the tunnel, so loud Kexx winced from the assault on zer ears. Above them, three large shapes detached from the ceiling and fell to the ground like shadows.

"Ears!" Benson's cone of light swept upwards, tracking one of the calebs as it fell to the ground. Kexx slapped zer hands over zer ears just in time for the thunder and lightning to roll in. The entire cavern flashed in time with the pulses jumping from Benson's gun as tiny spear after tiny spear struck the beast, shredding muscle and sinew as they burrowed.

Drawing on reflexes honed by years of practice, Kuul spotted the caleb falling on zer head in time to plant the haft of zer spear into the silt and brace. With a stomach-churning shriek, the spear point pierced the creature's belly as its weight and momentum carried it sliding down the shaft until the black glass point blossomed from its spine like a morbid flower, severing one of its nerve tracks and paralyzing its right side.

Panicked and furious, the beast thrashed about on three legs, trying and failing to compensate for its dead hind limb. Zer spear lost, Kuul quickly transitioned to zer knife, crawled on top of the crippled creature, and thrust the tip into the spot just behind the caleb's shoulder blades where the nerve tracks crossed, instantly ending its struggles, if not its life.

That left only one monster to contend with.

Kuul and Benson closed in on the beast, circling it and cutting off its available lines of retreat. Perhaps focused on Kexx's spear, perhaps noticing Kuul's abdominal wounds, the caleb turned on the warrior and tensed for a charge.

"Ears!" A pair of flashes from Benson's gun ensured that it never had the chance. With a greater sense of self-preservation than its fellows had shown, the injured caleb retreated down the tunnel with impressive speed, considering its limp.

"Well, that was easy," Benson said just below a shout.

"It's not over yet," Kexx replied. "Detective, shine your light along the walls, please."

The human obliged, tracing a circle of white light down the rough tunnel surface. It passed over a lumpy outcropping, much smoother than the coarse rock surrounding it.

"There!" Kexx pointed. "Hold your light there." Benson obliged as Kexx and Kuul moved to flank the outcropping. "You may as well come down," Kexx announced. "There's no chance of escape."

The lump remained immobile.

"Well, talking didn't work." Kuul reached down and picked up a fist-sized stone from the floor, then heaved it at the lump with an expert flick of zer arm, striking the person clinging to the wall squarely in the back of the head.

The figure shouted out in pain as it peeled off the wall, but managed to land on its feet. Benson's light, and therefore gun, trained on it in an instant.

Kexx continued as the person stood and shielded zer eyes from the harsh light with a forearm. "I don't know if you were watching just now, but my friend's weapon is... well, awe-inspiring. If I were you, I would stop moving and start talking."

The stranger's skin went white as ze started shouting a string of words Kexx didn't recognize in the least. Kexx glanced over at Kuul. "Did you catch any of that?"

Kuul shrugged. "Not a word."

"I did," Benson said, nearly embarrassed.

"You did?" Kuul repeated. "Is ze speaking *human*?"

Benson shook zer head. "No, no human language, but my plant is still feeding me a translation."

"It's not any tongue I know," Kexx said. "How is it possible your head tool knows it?"

"I have no idea," Benson said. "It shouldn't be possible. Unless..."

"Unless?"

"Unless someone has been listening in on their tribe as long as we've been listening in on yours and they forgot to lock out the dialect in the translator upload."

"What's an upload?"

Benson waved a hand. "Way too long to explain that one."

"That can wait," Kuul said, losing patience. "What is ze saying?"

"Ah, hang on." Benson leaned in and listened to the stranger, who hadn't stopped jabbering the entire time.

"They say they're the brood sibling of the under chief, and we wouldn't dare kill them for fear of... er, something about Cuut's garden? Does that make sense?"

"Perfect sense." With a wet-sounding jerk, Kuul yanked the shaft of zer spear free of the paralyzed caleb, then strode forward and stabbed the babbling stranger right through the knee. The stranger's voice switched from shouting to screaming as ze grabbed zer leg and collapsed.

"What'd you do that for?" Benson demanded.

"Ze's right, I wouldn't dare kill the under chief's brood sibling. Ze's far more useful as a hostage."

Unsubtle indeed. Kexx sighed and looked back at the hole in the ceiling.

"We're going to need rope."

CHAPTER TWENTY-SEVEN

It took half an hour to properly bind the squirmy fucker. Benson was pretty good at fixing restraints after a career in law enforcement (not to mention certain… erotic proclivities enjoyed by both he and his wife), but tying decent knots onto someone whose joints were more like guidelines to be ignored at their convenience was a difficult task indeed.

In the end, Kuul simply knocked the stranger in the head with a rock hard enough to leave zer dazed and limp. Benson certainly didn't agree with such rough treatment of prisoners, but neither could he argue with results.

They hauled their semi-conscious prisoner up through the hole in the ceiling by rope, while Benson puzzled over jurisdictional boundaries. Wherever his might lie, he was certain he was far, far outside of them.

"When in Rome," Benson muttered to himself.

"Where?" Kexx asked, reminding him just how good the Atlantian's ears were.

"Rome," he answered. "It was a great city, long ago. The saying just means 'do as the locals do.'"

"Wise advice for guests, maybe not as much for invaders."

"Which are we?" Benson asked.

"Somewhere in between, I expect."

Benson looked around the caravan. "Invaders usually bring more people."

"The successful ones, certainly."

Kuul and two other warriors busied themselves lashing their

prisoner to the back of one of their dux'ah. From the looks of it, ze wasn't going to be taking any bathroom breaks for a while.

Benson pointed at the trussed-up animal trainer. "Whoever this under chief is, they aren't going to be happy about that."

"I expect not. But I'm not terribly happy about the people we lost in the caleb attack. I'm quite angry about it, actually. The under chief will hear my grievance."

"About that," Benson started. "How exactly are we going to get this audience? They've already tried to kill us twice. Why do you think we'll be able to walk right into their territory and make demands?"

"I won't be making demands, I will be airing accusations."

"And that's better?"

"It's protected," Kexx said. "Once accusations have been leveled, my work as a truth-digger cannot be interrupted. Uncovering the truth is a sacred duty, not even the Dwellers would interrupt it."

Benson smiled. If only his own people had been so accommodating to the requirements of his job. "All right, then what?"

"Once the truth is known, the elders of each village confer and settle on appropriate punishments or compensation."

"And if the elders of different villages disagree on what's appropriate?"

Kexx was silent for a second. "Then the warriors sharpen their spears. But we will be back in our beds long before then."

"Still, there's so few of us here. You're putting a lot of faith in procedure. What's to stop them from slaughtering all of us and sending our heads back up the road?"

"I know you mean no offense, Benson, but this is just how things are done here."

"Times change, Kexx. We were attacked by the calebs, after all. That sounds like 'interference' to me."

Kexx's skin fluttered involuntarily. "They may not have known there was a truth-digger in the caravan."

"I doubt that. Someone among my people is feeding them information. I'm surer of it now than ever."

"They could plausibly claim that they didn't know before.

That will be difficult now. Besides, stories of your gun and the presence of our hostage will give them pause."

Benson didn't like where his new friend's thoughts were going. "Don't count on me to fight a war for you, Kexx. I only have so many bullets, and I'm not a warrior."

"Nonsense. You are brave. I've seen you kill."

"That's not how humans define bravery," Benson said, knowing it wasn't entirely true but wanting to believe it anyway. "You've seen me kill animals, not people."

"You killed a warrior back in the village, with a lowly fishing trident."

Benson's memory flashed back to the Atlantian from the fight that started all of this, zer head impaled on the center spine of a trident, the body still trying to march forward, not yet aware it had already been killed. The image turned his stomach even now. He'd never killed before that moment. He'd tried to, once, but Kimura's suit had protected him from Benson's bullets, just not from his own bomb.

"That was self-defense, and it was more of an accident than anything. Ze charged straight into it. I just held the shaft."

Kexx considered this for a while before responding. "You are an interesting pile of contradictions, Benson."

Benson laughed genuinely. "I've been called worse."

"We must move on. There's still a day's hard march ahead of us."

"Ugh," Benson said. The march seemed endless. He already had blisters on his heels where his shoes had been rubbing for three days. He was dirty and exhausted. Out of morbid curiosity, Benson checked his plant and was startled to find that since leaving the village, they'd gained almost fifteen hundred meters in elevation. That explained why he was so damned exhausted. He decided to remove his chestplate for a while and let himself breathe. They were out in the open now. If there was trouble, he'd have time to slap it back on.

The caravan headed further into hostile territory, tension building with each uneasy step. Kexx was certainly confident in zer belief that they would pass through without further harassment. The rest of the Atlantians, however...

They walked in silence for an hour, another, a cloud of dust rising into the still, hot air behind them, alerting anyone who cared to look to their presence for kilometers around, yet they remained alone on the trail.

For a time, their prisoner ranted and raved at zer rough treatment. But after three hours, zer throat went dry and hoarse. Ze asked for water, but no one was in a big hurry to quench zer thirst and invite renewed auditory assault.

The blessed quiet gave Benson a little time to think. He'd seen other veins of what looked like metal inside the lava tube. Not gold, but then again nearly any metal would be worth its weight here. Iron, aluminum, lead, magnesium, nickel, they would all be of immense importance. And in concentrations high enough for old-fashioned pick-and-shovel mining instead of the parts-per-thousand chemical stripping processes and asteroid mining they'd been planning for. It would shave years off their projections, accelerating the growth and development curve of the entire colony by a generation, maybe more.

And make someone very rich in the process. The only things that stood in their way were the rightful land owners, and of course any humans in positions of authority burdened with a conscious. People like Captain Mahama, for example.

Benson's mind recoiled at the thought, but it was hard to escape the logic, the coincidences. First, Administrator Valmassoi is mortally wounded in an ambush that was almost certainly organized with outside help, then Captain Mahama dies of a heart attack in the same week, of all the preposterous things that could happen to her.

The heads of both the colony and the crew, dead inside of a few days of each other. This conspiracy was starting to look more like a coup.

And Esa was standing smack dab in the center of it. She was sharper than he'd ever been at deduction; her mind must have already gone down these tracks. But if she pushed too hard too fast, she'd be painting a target on her back. These people obviously didn't care about the popularity or status of their victims.

Benson's sweat turned to ice at the thought. Here he was,

marching through the grasslands thousands of kilometers from home looking for the killer, while his wife was probably no more than a stone's throw away. Like a fool, he'd taken himself out of the real game. Now he was mired on the sidelines while the casualties mounted. He had to figure out a way to help her without giving it all away.

Kexx sauntered up alongside Benson and offered him a pull from zer waterskin. The thought of drinking from an unidentified bladder was less than appealing to him, but he had a better sense of diplomacy than to refuse the gesture. The water was warm, foul tasting, and probably held more than a few tiny surprises that his immune nanites would have to contend with, but he slurped it down anyway.

"Thank you," he said.

"Not at all." Kexx pointed at the lines of dust-stained sweat trailing down Benson's forehead, cheeks, and neck. "You look like you need it more than I."

"We humans do like to sweat."

"You never seem to tire," Kexx said admiringly. "Your legs move like broken branches, but it seems you can do it forever."

"We walk, we run, it was one of the things humans were best at, actually. We weren't the fastest animals on Earth, not by a long shot. But our ancestors could run further and for longer than anything else alive."

"Your world must have been large, then, if you could wander so far."

Benson shrugged. "I never saw it, except in video."

"Ve-de-o?" the Atlantian asked.

"Er, moving paintings, very detailed and lifelike. We watch them to learn and to entertain. Earth was actually just a tiny bit smaller than your world. With bigger oceans and less land."

"Did humans share their world well with each other?"

"That's a very long story. For much of our history, no, to say the least. We were a lot like your people, focused on our small differences, ignoring our enormous similarities. There was a long time where we believed one group of people or another was something other than human, too. But we got better toward the end, and during our time on the Ark, we learned to live together peacefully. Well, most of us did."

"Then why did you decide to leave it, Benson?"

"We didn't. Decide to leave, I mean. Our world was going to be destroyed by a..." He thought for a moment. Kexx got hung up badly enough with radio waves and bacteria. An invisible star collapsed down to an infinitely dense point with enough gravity to bend light was probably going to be beyond zer capacities. Frankly, it was beyond Benson's capacities.

"It was destroyed," he said instead.

"Your *whole* world?"

Benson nodded. "Every pebble and raindrop. Everything we didn't bring with us is gone forever."

"Only the gods could do such a thing."

Benson felt the same chill drip down his spine as the first time Captain Mahama had confirmed Kimura's insane claim that the black hole Nibiru had been pitched at Earth deliberately. They may not be gods, but their power was such that it was a semantic distinction, at best.

"Maybe so," Benson said.

"Why did you choose to come here and live with us?"

"Again, we didn't choose it, Kexx. This was the only world close enough for us to reach. And we didn't think anyone was living here. Hell, we didn't think anyone *could* live here."

"I don't understand," Kexx said. "If you thought our world wasn't livable, why come at all?"

"No, that's not it. We knew your world had life on it. We could, um, see what kind of air it had and know plants lived here. But we also knew about your, what do you call them, Cuut's Seeds?" Kexx nodded. "We call them asteroids or comets, and your planet is surrounded by ten times as many of them as ours was. On our world, an asteroid as big as a mountain would hit us every few tens of... I don't suppose you have a word for million?"

Kexx shook his head. "No."

Benson struggled for an example until one presented itself. "If you counted every yulka bean in a harvest, it would be millions."

Kexx's eyes widened as he tried to process the concept. "Why would you ever need numbers so large?"

Benson couldn't help but chuckle, thinking of the tens of *trillions* of kilometers the Ark had traveled to get here. "Trust me, someday soon, your people will need numbers much bigger than even that. Anyway, every few tens of millions of years, a huge asteroid would hit Earth and wipe out all life much bigger than this." Benson held his hands approximately mouse-length apart. "Every time it happened, it took life a very long time to regroup. And here, we assumed an asteroid that big was hitting your world ten times as often. Our, er, wise men didn't think that something as smart as humans could have grown up quickly enough between the strikes."

Kexx nodded along, absorbing the lesson. "You didn't know about our caves," he reasoned.

Benson shook his head. "No, we didn't."

Kexx adjusted his legs and sat up a little straighter before continuing. "The number of times Cuut's Seeds have razed the surface and sent us into the safety of Xis's womb has been lost to memory, but it surely numbers in the hundreds. Sometimes it's only a year before Cuut relents and the clouds give way to sunlight again. Sometimes, it's much longer. Once, a thousand years ago, an entire generation passed below ground, dwindling as the food ran out until there were only so many left as the cave fungus could feed."

"How many was that?" Benson asked. Kexx held up both his hands and splayed his eight fingers. A *fullhand*, as the Atlantians counted. "Eight? Your entire civilization is based on only eight people?"

"So the legend goes."

Benson blanched. He remembered reading once about a great population bottleneck in human prehistory. But even that cataclysm had only reduced their numbers to a few thousand, not *single digits*. Suddenly, the Atlantians' huge litters of young didn't seem like such a bad evolutionary tactic. It could all just be an overblown legend, of course, but Benson knew just enough about anthropology not to dismiss native mythology out of hand. There were usually more than a few kernels of truth hidden in them.

Kexx continued. "It is said we once had many fingers, like the dux'ah or the ulik, but after the Shrinking, Cuut changed our hands, one finger to represent each of the chosen, so that we would never forget the lesson."

"Which was?"

"Do more with less."

Benson considered what he'd just heard, and what it told him about the Atlantians. As alien as they had seemed when he'd landed little more than a week before, it was hard to avoid the parallels. Disasters beyond their control or comprehension had decimated both of them, reduced their societies to a shell of their former selves and driven them into exile from the world they knew, forced to live for years on the barest essentials, leaving lasting scars on their collective psyches.

All things considered, Benson figured exile on board the Ark had probably been more comfortable.

"When was the last time your people were forced below ground?" Benson asked.

"Cuut has been lenient since the Shrinking. Seeds have still fallen, but they've been small, their clouds lasting Varrs, not years. It's why we've had the time to build our villages and roads. Still, many believe we have forgotten Cuut's lessons, that our expansion taunts zer, and that we are overdue for another reckoning."

Benson could only chuckle at that. "Well, they weren't exactly wrong. You would have gotten hit last year if we hadn't caught it in time. Big sucker, too."

Kexx's face went pale in a way that not even Benson could miss. "I… I don't understand. What do you mean?"

"I mean we've been mapping all the, er, seeds around your world since before we arrived and tracking the ones big enough to be dangerous. One was on course to strike, so we shot it with a…" How did you explain a laser to someone with stone-age tech? "A spear made of light and knocked it out of the way. As long as we're here, you're never going to have to worry about Cuut's Seeds again."

"That's not possible," Kexx said flatly. "You would have to be gods yourselves to interfere with Cuut's will."

Benson realized he had walked out onto the thin ice of

religious orthodoxy. Of all the Atlantians he'd spoken with, Kexx was easily the most rational and levelheaded, doubtless a byproduct of zer years as the one person in zer village tasked with seeing past everyone's bullshit. But apparently even ze had zer limits.

Benson proceeded cautiously. "That may be true. But the seeds, the asteroids, are just rock and ice. Some are tiny, no bigger than a bean, some are as big as cities. But they're still just rocks. They don't have a will. They just roam around out there, zipping through space until they hit something. But if you hit them hard enough, they move."

Kexx, still pale as a sheet, shook his head. "That would be like hitting a spear in flight with another spear."

Benson smirked. "Oh, it's *much* harder than that. You can't even imagine how fast things move around up there, but we do it all the time. On the way here, our ship had to hit dust no bigger than pebbles dozens, even hundreds of times a day." Benson had a sudden, chilling flashback to tumbling through space after a bit of stellar dust the size of a grain of rice, just below the Ark's radar threshold, nearly vaporized his EVA pod. He'd almost died that day. It was not one of his fonder memories.

He shook himself back into the moment. "Anyway, if we can hit pebbles, hitting a mountain is child's play."

"Varr," Kexx said quietly, reverently.

"I've heard you say that before. What does it mean?"

Kexx collected himself silently. "Varr is… was Cuut's mate. Ze was exiled after the Shrinking for betraying Cuut and siding with Xis to try and shield us from Cuut's judgment."

Benson listened intently. A trinity of gods. It made sense, considering the Atlantian's apparent three-gender arrangement. Certainly more sense than the contortions the prelaunch Catholics had to go through to explain their Trinity.

"Varr fought with Cuut for zer children for three years without rest, causing the ground to shake and the sky to burn, until the fight ended in a draw. Unable to beat Cuut or change zer mind, yet also unable to bring zerself to kill zer lover, Varr accepted defeat, but promised to return once Cuut's loneliness was too great. Now, ze visits eleven times each year, hoping Cuut will finally listen to reason."

Moon, Benson realized, *Varr was the name of their moon.* "And stop sending seeds to destroy the world and drive your people underground," Benson finished for zer.

"How did you know that?"

"I've read a lot of stories. You pick up on the patterns."

Kexx nodded, some light and color returning to zer face. "When this becomes common knowledge, there will be many who believe your people are emissaries of Varr zerself. Many already believe this."

"Are you one of them?"

"Are you of Varr?" Kexx asked, zer cautious, deliberate mind crashing headlong into a long-repressed childhood faith.

A buried memory from one of Theresa and Bryan's first dates at the classic movie theater in Avalon module put a smile on his face. He couldn't remember the film's title, but a line jumped out regardless. *Ray, when someone asks you if you're a god, you say YES!*

"No, Kexx, we're not gods. I know it sounds like it sometimes, but we haven't done anything your people couldn't do with enough time."

"But much less time if we ally with you?"

Man, ze doesn't beat around the bush, Benson thought. "I don't think I'm the one to make that kind of offer, Kexx. I just want to find out who's responsible for what happened to our people. *Both* of them."

The conversation was interrupted by a flashing icon in Benson's field of vision. The small solar array draped over his shoulder had finished recharging his satellite uplink. He had an hour window to update Shambhala on the day's discoveries and to talk to his wife, maybe warn her off. He intended to use every second.

"If you'll excuse me, Kexx, I have to talk to my people back in our city."

Kexx nodded respectfully, then picked up zer pace and fell into formation at the head of the caravan to give Benson some privacy. He pulled the sat uplink out of his pack and unplugged it from the solar charger, then synched it up with his plant. Familiar icons appeared in his field of vision, including yet another software update notification demanding to be seen.

[Important Implant Software Update, Fixes Memory Leak Error #34788001. Install Now?]

Benson sighed his annoyance. Whoever was writing code for the updates and patches had the most secure job in all of human society. <Approximate time to download and install?> he asked his plant OS.

[Less Than One Minute.]

Fine, whatever, he thought. If he didn't do it now, it would just keep popping up before every link, wasting even more time.

<Download approved,> he said internally.

The flashing icon disappeared, replaced by a green download status bar. It filled up in less than five seconds. A small file, then. Good.

[Install Now?] it asked.

<Yes,> Benson said. <Quickly,> he added, knowing full well it wouldn't make anything happen faster, but feeling satisfied for having said it anyway. The cursor in his mind's eye turned into a small spinning circle.

[Installation Complete]

No sooner than the message appeared, Benson's vision blurred as his plant displays turned to static and noise. A sharp pain struck his chest, like being impaled. Benson's hand shot up to his heart, certain it would find the shaft of a spear sticking out of it, but it grabbed only the damp cloth of his sweat-soaked shirt.

"Mei!" Benson shouted in sudden, all-engulfing panic.

"Me...." His breath left him as his vison faded to black.

The last thing Bryan Benson felt was a sensation of falling.

CHAPTER TWENTY-EIGHT

Theresa and Korolev sat in her office and stared at each other in stunned silence. The news of Captain Mahama's death hadn't been made public yet, but it wouldn't be long before it leaked out somehow. News was even better than helium at escaping whatever tried to contain it. Reluctantly, and under pressure from the acting administrator, Theresa had ordered twenty of her newly recruited reserve officers to mobilize in preparation for whatever civil upheaval accompanied the news.

Korolev broke the awkward quiet. "They've only been drilling for three days, chief."

"I know, Pavel."

"And they haven't done any crowd control training."

"I know, Pavel."

"And just mustering them is going to let people know something is up."

"I *know*, Pavel!" Theresa snapped at her subordinate, surprising both him and herself. She took a deep, calming breath. "I'm sorry. I didn't mean to shout. But I already said all of these things to Administrator Merick, and he still wants them activated. And we follow orders around here until and unless we have a very compelling reason not to."

Korolev shrank a bit, like a scolded puppy. Or what Theresa guessed a scolded puppy looked like. "I understand, ma'am. And I wasn't suggesting we disobey. I'm just…"

"Worried," Theresa finished for him. "Well, so am I. You'd be stupid not to be, and it's good that you're recognizing these things. But you're trying to do a job one level above your pay grade, at least for now. What I need from you right now is to know that you're going to take these stupid orders and do your best to unfuck them on the ground. Can you do that?"

"You know I will, ma'am."

"OK, so how are you going to do it?"

Korolev rubbed his chin as he contemplated the question. Finally, he answered. "Pair them up, then link them with one of our existing constables as three-man units, and make it clear that the constable is in charge."

"And what do you do with the hotheads?" Theresa asked. "You're talking about football players, after all. Some of them are more than a little testosterone-soaked."

"Assign them to female constables," Korolev said without hesitating. "They might want to show off for each other, but they'll think twice about looking like goons in front of a lady."

Theresa smirked. "I don't know if that's always been my experience, but I'm going to let you write the roster assignments. Deal?" Korolev nodded enthusiastically. "I thought you'd like that."

Korolev nodded his thanks, but didn't move. Instead, he shuffled uncomfortably in his seat. "Is there something else, Pavel?"

"Yeah, maybe. I guess."

"Out with it, then."

"It's just that... The captain dying doesn't make any sense, does it?"

"The universe is under no constraints to make sense to us," Theresa replied. "Still, no, it doesn't."

"People her age don't die of heart attacks."

"It's rare, I'll grant you, but the stress of command can wear on a person, and she'd been in the chair for longer than anyone in decades. That, and she was alone in her quarters when it happened, with the door locked. Like, physically locked, which was why the medics couldn't get to her in time to resuscitate. So unless we're talking about ghosts..."

"But so soon after Valmassoi? That doesn't strike you as odd?"

"Valmassoi died of spear poisoning, Pavel. They're hardly related."

"Did he, though?"

"You were there. Are you telling me you're not sure how he died?"

"No, well, maybe. Look, Valmassoi was hurt bad, really messed up. But we got his vitals stabilized on the flight back. He was holding on right up until final approach when his heart just stopped. No warning, no change in his vitals, it just quit. Like someone flipped a switch. I didn't think much about it at the time, but now..."

"Now it sounds exactly like what happened to the captain," Theresa said.

Korolev shrugged. "It's an odd coincidence."

"It's a *convenient* coincidence," Theresa said, echoing what her husband had said when she broke the news to him over the link. "For someone, at least. OK, Pavel, I'm on board with the possibility, but how does someone stop a heart at will without touching the person?"

Korolev held up his stun-stick. "We induce seizures without touching people. How hard would it be to do the same thing to a heart?"

"What, through our plants?" Theresa said in disbelief. But the suggestion was anything but crazy. The plant was integrated with the brain before someone even left the tank. It was wired into the visual and auditory senses, monitored brain activity, body chemistry, vital signs, and in the case of their stun-sticks could even interrupt normal brain function through an electrical pulse. What if someone found a back door, or exploited a bit of code to redirect that pulse to a different part of the brain and shut off the signals that reminded the heart to keep beating?

Theresa whistled low. "Hold that thought." She punched in Dr Russell's contact info on her plant and made the call.

<This is Dr Russell.>

<Jeanine? It's Theresa. I need to speak with you, privately. Can you swing by the station house after your shift?>

<Theresa, hi. Um, look, if this is about Bryan's... condition, I'm afraid we still don't have–>

<No,> Theresa cut her off. <It's not about that at all. I just need to bounce something off you, see if it's feasible.>

<OK,> Russell said uncertainly. <I'm off at 1800. Will you still be around?>

<Meet me at my house. I'll make dinner.>

<All right. It's a date. See you then.>

Theresa cut the call and turned back to Korolev. "I'm going to have dinner with Dr Russell. We'll see what she thinks. No offense, Pavel, but I really hope you're wrong."

"Tell me about it," Korolev said.

"Still, I don't think they'd risk using it openly."

"What makes you say that?"

"Well it's not like you could hide a dozen sudden heart attack deaths in healthy people, could you?" Theresa rubbed her cheek. "No, if that's what's happening here, they're using it as a last resort. They organized the raid on the Atlantian village somehow, hoping he'd be killed during the battle. That was the plan."

"And when I saved him, they didn't have any choice but to zap him."

"Exactly, and he'd been so badly wounded that no one would question the cause of death. Then they get Mahama locked alone in her own room. Boom, no evidence of foul play, no suspects, no suspicion. But if one of us dies of a heart attack in the middle of trying to make an arrest for building a heart attack machine, that would be a little harder to cover up."

"Not that we'd be around to enjoy watching their trial."

"True, but–" Theresa jumped as something struck her office window hard enough to shatter it. Korolev was on his feet and moving for the door with his stun-stick in hand before she had time to blink. A spiderweb of cracks in the window prevented her from seeing what was happening outside, so she stood to follow, but Korolev closed the door and put his back to it.

"We'd better grab our riot gear, chief."

<This is an unlawful protest,> Theresa shouted through her plant directly into the minds of the crowd, yet still barely audible over the surging noise. <You are hereby ordered to disperse. Return to your homes.>

Word of Captain Mahama's death leaked even faster than Theresa feared it would. Administrator Merick had issued a statement on the steps of the Beehive to address the rumors and eulogize their fallen leader in a transparent bid to boost his visibility and standing with the voting public. After a respectful mourning period of no more than thirty seconds, the good people of Shambhala had taken to the streets in force. Theresa's constables barely had time to equip and meet them before the wave reached the Beehive. Their line was shaky and anxious, but holding.

The usual group of rabble rousers that had been agitating in the wake of Valmassoi's assassination had grown and been joined by other groups. People protesting for greater independence from the Ark and its crew saw the captain's death as a perfect opportunity to apply pressure, while the Returners fighting to overturn Mahama's policy preventing people from moving back up the beanstalk did the same. Naturally, all three groups were just as busy shouting at and shoving each other as they were in supporting their own causes. It was a powder keg just waiting for the right spark.

But at least they were too engaged in fighting among themselves to unify against Theresa and her constables.

<I repeat, this is an illegal assembly, and–>

"Bullshit!" someone shouted from the other side of her wall of clear acrylic shields. "We have the right to free assembly!"

Theresa scanned the rabble rouser. Trevor Cambias, twenty-six, machinist, no priors. She wasn't sure which faction he was protesting with, but he seemed closest to the isolationists. She tagged him and threw his info into her growing database of protestors. "You have the right to *peaceful* assembly, Mr Cambias." Theresa shot back with her own voice. "Which doesn't include throwing rocks through my fucking window! Which is why it's time to disperse."

"Or what?" Cambias challenged.

Theresa brandished her stun-stick. "Or I start cutting strings and dragging people into cells."

"You wouldn't dare," someone else shouted, not at all sounding like they believed it.

Oh, honey, you'd be shocked at what I'd dare, Theresa managed not to say. She had to walk a very fine line between showing resolve and authority and antagonizing the crowd into violence. The protest was much larger, and angrier, than before. Theresa guessed it was closing in on twenty-five hundred, maybe as much as three thousand people. If push came to shove, there was no way her few dozen constables could keep it contained. There could be fights, broken bones, maybe even bloodshed.

"Maybe I would, maybe I wouldn't. Who knows? Personally, I'd rather not have to find out. Now c'mon folks, we've let you come out here for days already, but it's getting out of hand. Vandalism is not acceptable. Violence is not acceptable. So we have to pack it in for the day. Come back tomorrow and we'll try again. But for right now it's bar time, ladies and gentlemen. You don't have to go home, but you can't stay here."

The less committed parts of the crowd laughed and worked their way toward the edges, where they peeled away. Slowly, and with a little more coaxing, the ominous crowd evaporated until it reached a more manageable size. Soon enough, all that remained were the three cores of true believers who still hadn't figured out how to put aside their differences long enough to present a united front against Theresa's constables. She was only too happy to exploit the fracture lines as she ordered the arrest of half a dozen of the most vocal and troublesome protestors, two of which broke into fisticuffs and had to be stunned.

By the time it was all over, they were actually offering to testify against each other. Theresa shook her head as they were put on one of the electric carts and driven off toward the jail. The crowd well and truly dispersed, Theresa let out a long sigh she hadn't realized she'd been holding in. *Humans,* she thought. *Even after all this, we're still so busy fighting among ourselves, it's a miracle we get anything done at all.*

"That was dicey, chief," Korolev said. "Well played."

"It'll get worse before it gets better."

"We tagged the leaders. We should be able to come up with enough excuses to hold them for a couple of days. That should calm things down."

"They aren't the leaders, Pavel." Theresa pointed to the cart receding down the road. "They're the patsies someone's spun up to create chaos and keep everyone distracted, including us.

A crowd that big doesn't assemble itself out of thin air. Someone leaked the captain's death to people they knew would cause a ruckus. And if she really was murdered, you can bet they were in contact with the people who did it, if they weren't one and the same. This whole thing is coordinated. I'll bet my house on it."

"So what do we do?"

"Everyone we arrested, comb their internet traffic, plant conversations, text messages, everything. See if we can spot the leaks."

"You really think whoever this was will be that sloppy?"

Theresa shook her head. "Not really, but you never know. We might get lucky. And I think it's time to tell Feng to break cover and go full throttle into an official investigation on the Ark."

"I thought they denied him entry."

"It wasn't him specifically. The crew froze all traffic in and out when they found Mahama dead. They lifted the freeze a few hours later. So he's in place."

"But we sent him up there under cover so he wouldn't spook anybody."

"I know, but my gut tells me this is building to a crescendo, and quickly. We're running out of time. Maybe Feng's investigation will make someone panic and flush them out of hiding."

"A lot of 'ifs' and 'maybes' in there, chief."

"Yeah, but the glorious thing about being us is our prey has to be perfect. We only need to get lucky once."

"Some of us would like to get lucky more than once," Korolev said, blushing at his own joke.

"Ugh, Pavel. I know a half-dozen girls who would let you cook them breakfast tomorrow if you would just ask them out."

"Really?" Korolev's eyes narrowed. "What're their names?"

"Oh no, you little chicken shit. Want to be a detective, work it out for yourself."

"Judas," Korolev said. "Oh, there was one other thing, I was going to mention it earlier."

"Yeah? What is it, Pavel?"

"Hallstead made bail."

Theresa jerked away from the crowds to look at her constable. "What? How? Her account was empty."

Krolev shrugged. "It filled back up today."

"From who?" Theresa said. "Where did the money come from?"

"She's just in for a domestic, chief," he said apologetically. "Our warrant doesn't extend to her financial records."

Theresa grit her teeth. Korolev was right, of course. But that didn't stop her from resenting the asinine restrictions placed on her investigative authority.

"Stall her."

"Chief?"

"Drag your feet releasing her"

Korolev nodded. "Now that you mention it, I think I may have misfiled her paperwork. Could take another day to straighten out."

"Good man... I mean, that was very careless of you, constable."

"Sorry, ma'am." Korolev smirked.

"Have we gone through her house yet?"

"Only the initial sweep when we picked her up. Why?"

Theresa rubbed her neck. "Not sure, actually. I just want a peek."

"We'll need to expand our warrant to include a search of the home. Magistrate might not like that."

"No we don't. Just knock on the door and ask... what was her fucking girfriend's name? Julia? Ask her for permission to serach."

"Juanita," Korolev corrected. "And that won't work."

"Why not?"

"She moved in with Raul as soon as Yvonne got locked up. The house is empty."

Theresa laughed. "Smart girl."

"Chief Benson," Administrator Merick said from behind them. Theresa turned around to face him.

"Administrator."

Merick surveyed the nearly empty steps and plaza. "That was good work handling the demonstrators, chief." His tone was subdued, at odds with someone giving praise. Theresa was immediately suspicious.

"Thank you, sir."

"I need to speak with you in private, if that's all right."

"Sure. Pavel, take over for a few minutes."

"No problem, ma'am."

"See you back at the station house. Lead the way, administrator."

They walked together past the Beehive's giant double doors, padded across the quarried marble, and into the small maze of hallways and office doors. The silence between them only heightened the tension.

Merick reached his office and held the door for her. "Please, chief, sit."

Theresa placed herself into the offered chair, a sumptuous leather antique that nagged at her memory, though she couldn't make the connection.

"Thank you for coming," Merick said.

"Let's just get down to it, administrator, please? What's this about?"

Merick took a deep, centering breath. "This is… difficult. It's about your husband."

The bottom fell out of Theresa's stomach. Her heart raced and her head started spinning.

"What's happened?" she managed to ask.

"We're not sure. We received a partial burst from his sat link. The connection was very short, only a few seconds. The stream never stabilized enough for video, but we can only assume he was under attack and calling for help."

Theresa fixated on the tense of the verb. "Was?"

Merick folded his hands. "The only usable data we got from the transmission was a few seconds of audio and his plant's medical feed. His heartrate became erratic and then… I'm so sorry, Chief Benson, but your husband was killed."

Theresa sat in silence for an eternal moment, stunned beyond words for perhaps the first time in her life. The colors in the room seemed to drain from her vision. She felt like her feet were sinking into the floor.

"Chief? Did you hear me?" Merick asked. "I said that your husband has been killed in action."

"Yes. I heard you, administrator," a cold, dark part of her soul managed to reply.

"I'm sorry. I really am. Your husband was a hero to our people, he will be sorely missed. But rest assured, the people who killed him will–"

"Who?" Theresa snapped. "*Who* killed him?"

"We don't know, but we're going to find out, I promise you that. We have GPS data from your husband's last known position. We're already coordinating with surveillance assets on the Ark to get a good look at the area. I'm ordering our new reserve force mobilized and deployed. We can have them there inside six hours. Of course, we don't expect you to–"

"No!" Theresa shouted loud enough to startle herself nearly as much as Merick. She took a moment to compose herself before continuing. "No. I'm going."

"Are you sure?" Merick was incredulous. "Chief. I don't mean any offense to your sense of duty, but given the circumstances, no one would blame you for taking a leave of absence to… recover from this."

"Over my dead body," she said. The tears came then, but she clamped down on them. There would be time for that later. "But I'll need a lot more than six hours. We've only been drilling with the new recruits for a few days. They need more time."

Merick held out his hands. "I do not mean to patronize you, chief, but you must understand that the longer we wait, the smaller the chance that we discover what happened."

"I understand that. But if you send in a hundred men before they're ready, there'll be a lot more than one life lost."

"I think a hundred people with guns can handle a rabble of primitives."

"My husband had a gun."

The seconds stretched out uncomfortably as Merick inspected her. There wasn't a better word for it. He considered her expression, her posture, like he was trying to take the full measure of her. Theresa had been examined by men many times before, but there wasn't anything sexual in the administrator's gaze. She could almost feel his eyes trying to tap into her thoughts. Finally, he reached a conclusion.

"How much time do you need?"

"Two days to get them qualed on the range." Theresa's voice

was clipped and flat as she forced her anguish and rising panic off to one side. "Then we hit them like a meteor shower."

"Two days it is, then. Make sure you're ready."

"Oh, I will be," Theresa said, no longer caring how much of her emotions leaked through. She excused herself and left the room, then walked singlemindedly back to the station house. She held her composure through the street, past curious onlookers who cleared her path, past the little shops and the pubs on the main street, even through the door of her station where a dozen sweaty, dusty constables were busy stripping out of their gear. They paused to look at her, and she could see in their faces her coworkers knew something was wrong.

Korolev stood up. "What's the matter, chief? What did Merick say?"

"Pavel," she grabbed his elbow and dragged him into her office. "Shut the door."

He did so. "What's wrong?"

"I want a list of people, coders, computer techs, anyone who might have the quals to program our heart attack machine, and I want it yesterday."

"OK, we can do that. What *else* is wrong?"

"It's..." Theresa's knees finally gave out as her desperation, sorrow, and rage came pouring forth. Without thinking, she grabbed up her chair and threw it through her doorway to shatter against the wall of the hallway.

"Chief!" Korolev grabbed her shoulders, as much to comfort her as to contain her. "Theresa," he said more softly once he'd gotten her under some measure of restraint. "What's happened?"

"It's Bryan," she said through ragged, sobbing gasps. "The fucking bastards got Bryan!"

CHAPTER TWENTY-NINE

Kexx looked back to the commotion and saw Benson lying on the ground in a pile. From the right, Mei jumped down off the back of the dux'ah ze'd been riding and ran to Benson's side. Whatever had happened, one glance at Mei's face told Kexx it was serious.

The caravan came to a stop as Kexx pushed past the semicircle of onlookers. "What's wrong with zer?" ze asked as Mei knelt down and put an ear to Benson's unmoving chest.

"No breath," ze answered in a clipped voice. "Zer heart's not beating."

"Zer what?" Kexx asked.

"Heart!" Mei pounded a fist on zer chest in obvious consternation. "Moves blood!"

"Like your chief?"

"Yes. Watch zer," Mei commanded as ze ran back to the dux'ah and ripped Benson's pack off the harness. Ze ran back over to where Kexx stood over Benson's body, fumbling with the flap until ze gave up and slashed it open with zer knife, spilling the contents onto the dirt. Ze reached for a smaller bag with a white circle surrounding two crossed red lines and opened it.

"Take off zer shirt," Mei barked. Kexx didn't argue, but the shirt did. Ze tried to tug, pull, even tear at it in an effort to get it off Benson's chest, but it wouldn't cooperate. Nor would Benson's elbow and shoulder joints, which had such little range of motion it seemed a miracle the humans could use them at all.

Mei grunted and just sliced the shirt from stomach to neck

with a knife, then threw it open to expose the uniformly colored flesh beneath. There was a single patch of dark color on one corner of zer chest in an unmoving pattern. Kexx reached out to touch the dark image, but Mei swatted zer hand away.

"Stay back!" It wasn't a request. Ze produced two patches of what looked like plastic leather, tore off a perfectly transparent layer of skin from the bottom of each, then slapped them onto each side of Benson's chest.

"What are you doing?" Kexx asked.

"Shocking zer heart. Don't touch zer." Mei looked up at the rest of the caravan. "None of you touch zer!" Everyone took a respectful step back, even Kuul, who had appeared at the edge of the circle. Mei grabbed a small box and ran a pair of curled threads to each of the patches, then pressed a large red circle at the center of the box.

A strange, lifeless voice sprang from the box, making several members of the crowd jump back. One of the warriors drew a spear on it, but Kexx shoved it out of the way and smacked the offender.

–Diagnosing,– the box said in flat, emotionless human. Kexx didn't recognize the word. –No Heartbeat Detected. Shock Recommended. Push Button To Charge.– Mei pushed the button again. A pure whine high-pitched enough to make Kexx wince leapt from the box, climbing in tone until it disappeared entirely.

–Delivering Shock. Stand Clear.–

Benson's motionless body jumped to life, arching zer back in a way that didn't look natural even for a human before falling back to the ground.

–No Heartbeat Detected. Shock Recom– Mei jammed zer finger into the button before the box could finish. The cycle repeated itself again, and again Benson's body fell back to the ground, inert.

Tears began to roll down Mei's cheeks as ze pushed the button for a third time. "Wake up!" ze shouted, but ze did not respond. Mei sobbed openly as the cycle repeated without change. "Don't leave me here alone!" Ze screamed, rage and fear mixing and fighting for control of zer voice. Kexx moved to put a comforting hand on zer shoulder, but Mei shrugged zer off angrily, then slapped Benson's face, hard. "You're strong! Fight, Zero Hero!"

Mei stabbed zer finger like a dagger into the button again as if ze meant to run it through. The whine built again, then fired. Benson's back arched once more, then fell. Mei screamed without words.

–Heartbeat Detected,– said the box. Mei threw it down and grabbed Benson's neck. Kexx wasn't sure why, but whatever ze found, a manic smile bloomed across the human's face.

"That's it," Mei said. "Come back, Benson-san. Follow my voice."

Benson lifted an arm weakly. Zer eyes fluttered. Then, as if waking up from a nightmare, Benson sat bolt upright and screamed, ripped the plastic patches off of zer chest, scrambled to zer feet, then ran out of the circle shouting human obscenities at the top of zer airsacks.

Kexx leaned over to Mei. "Is this normal?"

Mei shrugged. "No idea."

"What the fuck just happened?" Benson demanded, eyes wild, fists balled, and looking for trouble. The rest of the caravan gave zer a wide berth.

"I don't know," Mei said. "Your heart stopped. I shocked you." Ze pointed at the small white box lying discarded on the ground. Benson stole a glance at it and lowered zer guard a fraction.

"How long was I out?" ze asked.

"Two minutes," Mei answered. "Maybe less."

"Ugh," Benson clutched at zer chest. "What did you do? It feels like a lift car fell on me."

Mei's eyes rolled. "You're welcome." Ze turned to look up at Kexx. "Ze'll be fine."

Benson looked back at them both with a shocked expression. "What did you just say to Kexx?"

"I said you'll be fine," Mei repeated more slowly in their language.

"No, say it again in Atlantian," Benson replied, still in human.

Mei did so, and Benson shook zer head uncomprehendingly. "It didn't pick that up." Benson slapped the side of zer head. "I can't bring up my interface."

"What's ze talking about?" Kexx asked Mei, but ze only shrugged.

"My plant," Benson shouted. "My... head tool. It's not working!"

It was some time before Benson calmed down enough, and slowed down enough, that Kexx could make sense of zer words again. But once ze did, Benson's plea was unequivocal.

"We have to turn around and go back to the village right now."

Kexx took the demand in stride. "Why, Benson? We are only a day away from the Dweller village."

"Which is exactly why we have to leave, the sooner the better. I can't protect you like this."

"Without your head tool?" Kexx asked. "Both myself and Mei can translate for you when necessary. I can make the others understand your, um, disability."

"No, you don't get it, Kexx. It's not just about the translator. It's my..." Benson leaned in and pitch zer voice low. "It's my gun. It recognizes me by my head tool. Without it, I can't use it. It's just a big club. No gun, no defense."

Kexx frowned. "You are a good man, Benson, but sometimes I'm not sure you think very hard about your words. We have over two fullhand strong backs here who have already sharpened their spears in battle. We are not defenseless."

"But I can't–"

"Right," Kexx cut zer off. "You can't rely on your gun. You have to rely on us for protection now, and it scares you because you don't believe we are up to the task."

"You told me you're not up to it if the Dwellers don't cooperate!"

"And you told me that you can't win a war for us by yourself. So other than fewer dead Dwellers, how has the end result changed? Either we lose when our last spear is broken, or we lose when your last bullet is spent. In both cases, we're still dead."

Benson swallowed, hard. "I guess I hadn't thought about it in such... stark terms. I'm sorry if I've offended you."

"It's OK, Benson. We remain friends. And friends must trust each other. I must know, are you still committed to this task?"

Benson straightened zer back. "Yes, completely."

"Then we will see it through. We will get you a spear."

"No, keep the spear. I'll carry my rifle."

Kexx paused. "But you said it was no better than a club."

"It isn't, but you and I are the only ones who know that."

"And me," Mei called out from where she was stitching up Benson's shirt.

"And Mei," Benson corrected zerself. "I'd like to keep it that way so as not to worry the rest of the caravan. And if any of the Dwellers have heard rumors about it, I'd rather they *do* worry."

"A wise deception," Kexx agreed. "All right, I will keep your secret. What else? What will you tell your people?"

"Nothing," Benson said.

"I... don't understand."

Benson pointed a finger toward the sky. "Someone up there just tried to fry my heart. I don't know how exactly, but that's not really important. They probably used the exact same method to kill the captain."

"Then why did your leader return while you live on?"

"I don't know that either. Maybe help didn't get to her as quickly as Mei got to me. Maybe her age worked against her to a greater degree. In any case, they're trying to get rid of the people causing them trouble. I was obviously causing them trouble. And with my plant broken, they'll think I'm really dead, sorry, that I've returned..."

"And you are free to keep causing them trouble," Kexx finished for zer.

Benson opened zer hands and held them out, palms up, and smiled broadly. "Just so."

"You are a very clever man, Benson."

"Me? No, I'm dumb. But I make up for it by being very stubborn."

Kexx chuffed. Kuul had asked what the humans would be without their guns. Kexx saw the answer in Benson sitting in the dirt, battered, betrayed, defenseless.

Yet still unbending. Like a halo tree in a spiralstorm.

Ze felt zer affection for the strange creature grow further. The sun was past its apex. The day grew long, and they had made virtually no progress down the trail.

Kexx held out a hand to the human. "Can you walk?"

Benson took the hand and stood, albeit on a shaky foundation. "I can fake it." Benson's expression changed without warning. "Kexx, what are they doing?"

Kexx glanced back over zer shoulder. Half the members of the caravan had formed two parallel lines, sitting legs folded beneath them, hands held behind their backs and heads bent forward.

"They are awaiting your blessings, Benson."

"Sorry. My what?"

"Your blessings." Kexx took a moment to listen to their murmured prayers. "They think you have been resurrected by Varr, and they–"

Benson held up zer hands. "Oh no. Nononono."

"What's wrong?"

"Mei!" Benson called the smaller human over.

"What's wrong?" Mei asked.

"They want to worship me," Benson said. "Tell them I wasn't resurrected. Tell them you brought me back with a… a trick."

"That's not a good idea, Benson," ze answered.

"I agree," Kexx said.

"I am not going to be twisted into some Messiah figure," Benson protested. "That's not what we're here for."

"Refusing them blessings would be, ah…" Kexx struggled for the right word.

"Disrespectful," Mei contributed. "Sacrilegious. Rude."

"Yes, those."

Benson's arms dropped to zer sides. "I won't do it."

"You have to," Mei said.

"We're not gods, Mei. Or touched by gods. Or sent by gods."

"No, we're *running* from gods," Mei snapped back. "Gods chased us away from Earth. We're here now. Then where? If we're ever going to stop running, we need them." Ze pointed at the members of the caravan sitting in rows, exchanging nervous glances with each other. "And they need us."

Benson shook zer head. "I won't lie to them."

"You lied about the gun working," Mei accused.

"It's not the same," Benson said, suddenly on unsure footing.

"How's it different?"

"Well..." Kexx and Mei both waited patiently for zer answer. "It just is," Benson said finally without much conviction.

"If I may say it, Benson, this isn't about you lying. They already believe what they're going to. This is about respecting our beliefs."

"'Our?' Don't tell me you're looking for my blessings too, Kexx."

Kexx shook zer head. "Not just now. I'll let you know."

Benson let out a defeated sigh. "What do I have to do?"

"Just touch them gently on their first row of crests with three fingers of your left hand and say, 'Atumi Varr.'" Benson repeated the words three times more until Kexx was satisfied with zer pronunciation.

Kexx watched as Benson nervously made zer way down the receiving line, repeating the words without understanding their meaning in the least. The human's discomfort with the duty was obvious, but ze proceeded anyway, giving each person zer focus and attention before moving to the next.

Despite being bound and lashed to the back of a dux'ah, their prisoner, hostage, whatever ze was, felt compelled to start shouting. Kexx could only make out a handful of the words spewing forth, but "blasphemy," and "perversion" featured prominently. Benson paused and looked up at the disturbance. Kexx was about to move to silence the stranger, but Kuul beat zer to it. Ze ran up the back of the dux'ah in two strides and smacked zer smartly across the mouth.

Silence returned. Kuul locked eyes with Benson and motioned for zer to continue with the blessings. Benson nodded zer thanks and moved on to the next head.

Remarkable, Kexx thought. *We might actually pull together just in time to get slaughtered.*

CHAPTER THIRTY

Benson and Mei walked together most of the rest of the day, her spot on the dux'ah occupied as it was by their increasingly unpleasant captive. Not that Benson really blamed zer for being in a cross mood, even if ze had tried to kill him. The dux'ahs were entering musk and smelled, like, well, dux'ahs in musk. It was an odor of an intensity and unpleasantness outside Benson's experience, and he'd spent his teen years working in an aeroponics farm fed with waste water. He wouldn't want to be tied to one in the hot sun either.

In fairness, ze hadn't been the only person to try to kill him in the last twenty-four hours.

Someone did *kill you, old man*, Benson thought. *And that kid pulled your feet out of the fire. Again. After you told her not to come.* He shivered at the thought, his chest and ribs still sore from the intense convulsions that had accompanied the defibrillator's attempts to restart his heart. He glanced over at Mei. It was past time to stop thinking of her as a kid. Maybe she'd never really been one to begin with. Maybe she'd never been given the chance.

"Thank you," Benson said quietly, tapping his chest.

Mei didn't look over to answer. "Thank me by getting me back to Sakiko."

"I'm trying. I'll just need to think of something."

"We're doomed," she said flatly.

"Well aren't you just a little fucking wellspring of encouragement."

"I don't need to lie to you. You're a big boy. You can take it."

Benson chuckled. "Your English is much improved."

Mei shrugged. "I've been practicing."

"Still, a smidgeon of faith would be nice. We've gotten out of worse."

"Have we?" Mei asked.

"Well I doubt the Dwellers have a nuke."

It was Mei's turn to giggle. "Thank Xis for small favors."

"Xis? You're not going native on us, are you Mei?"

She shrugged. "They have a simple faith. You can learn it in a week, but it runs deep. They know how to take time for things."

Benson pondered that. For eleven generations, mankind had just been sitting on its collective hands on board the Ark, waiting for their turn to come up. But since landing, there had barely been time to breathe. The city was ever growing, and that meant work. Endless work. Benson's entire job was to make sure everyone enjoyed their prescribed amount of recreational time, whether they liked it or not.

He had to admit, there was a certain attraction to a culture that hadn't yet developed a concept of time broken down into units any smaller than morning, evening, and night. It certainly streamlined schedule keeping.

"Will they make us leave, Benson?"

"Getting a little ahead of yourself, aren't you? I thought we were doomed."

"I mean my people in the village. Will they be able to stay?"

Benson smiled at her. "You really like living with them, don't you?"

Mei nodded. "Yes. They have been kind and welcoming. Life is uncomplicated. They laugh easily, even if I don't get all the jokes yet."

"The cat's already out of the bag. I can't speak for everyone, but I doubt anybody on our end will be in a hurry to round you up and deport you back to Shambhala. Besides, we're going to need a connection between our people and theirs. The Unbound may have finally found their proper place."

"Our place?"

"Well, you've always existed in the inbetween spaces, yeah? Here's something you're built for."

Mei swelled at the possibility. "Something worth dying for."

"Indeed, but if it's all the same to you, I'm going to try very hard to keep us alive anyway."

"I know you will."

Benson noticed the resigned, accepting tone in Mei's voice, but didn't comment on it. The whole mission was insane to the point where he couldn't remember why he'd agreed to it in the first place. Maybe it had been anger at the people they'd lost. What they'd done to Atwood was barbaric. In the moment, he'd wanted to hurt whoever had killed her. But he wanted to believe he wasn't out here for revenge. Maybe it was the way an unsolved crime itched at his brain. Maybe it was pride and a selfish desire to relive the glory days. Maybe it was a little bit of all of them.

Now he walked through a hot grassland in a bloodstained shirt, reeking of sweat and caked in dust, unarmed, without his plant. He was marching into the heart of enemy territory with only a thin hope of staying alive against the same people who tried to massacre an entire village a few days earlier.

Tactically, it wasn't a great position to be in.

All he wanted to do was call his wife and let her know he was alive, for the moment at least. But if he did, they'd both be at risk. Whoever had tried to fry him would know he was still on the board, and she would know someone had tried to kill him. Benson knew his wife well enough to know that she would not react well to that. She would go straight after them like a missile, drawing a target on her own back in the process. He couldn't have that, so he had to keep her in the dark. The logic was airtight. That didn't make him any happier about it.

Theresa had tried to tell him. Tried to warn him off. Tried to get him to just step onto the shuttle for home and let someone else deal with it for once. With the benefit of hindsight, she'd probably been right.

She usually was. Damn her.

Benson tried to shake the thought, refocus on the facts of this case, come up with a plan to pull their butts from the fire. But he couldn't. He kept coming back to one idea. If he died out here, he would leave nothing behind. No family, no legacy. They'd probably pour some gaudy bronze statue of him as the man who saved the Ark and stick it in the museum where it would collect dust for centuries. But Theresa was still young and beautiful. She would mourn, but ultimately move on with her life and find a nice young man who wasn't shooting blanks. Not that he'd deny her that, but he still couldn't shake the thought of someone else giving her the family he couldn't.

There was only one chance of avoiding that future, and it was to survive the next few days.

"We're doomed," Benson announced to the universe, trying to pull it into his little pity party.

"Shush." Mei pointed to the head of the caravan. "We've stopped. Something's up."

She was right. Kexx and Kuul had stopped at the head of the line while everyone else ground to a halt to avoid bumping into the person ahead of them. Benson pulled his head out of his own ass and pushed through the crowd toward Kexx.

"Hey, Kexx. Why've we–"

"Stopped" never made it out of Benson's mouth. Instead, his lungs filled with a sudden inrush of air as he realized the ground simply... ended. What he'd thought was the crest of a small hill was instead the very top of an immense canyon. The ground fell away at a ninety-degree angle. A thousand layers of multicolored limestone cut into top-heavy towers, needle-thin chimneys and sweeping arches filled the canyon floor in three, no, four distinct levels.

"Holy shit," he said, taking a big step back from the edge. He'd known from the terrain maps loaded in his plant that there was an enormous canyon coming up, but without access to them, and with his mind otherwise occupied by a little thing like clinically dying, he'd forgotten. He'd even read how wide and deep it was in meters. But the abstract numbers paled in comparison to the dizzying reality spreading out before him. The canyon itself was so deep and so wide that Benson's brain simply refused to believe what his eyes were telling it, screwing up his depth perception and causing a sudden bout of vertigo.

His breath quickened, and he felt a chill despite the heat. "So, end of the road, huh?"

Kexx and Kuul glanced at him quizzically. Kexx translated Benson's words for Kuul, then turned to look at him. "What do you mean, Benson?"

"Well we've run out of ground, haven't we?" Benson glanced over the edge and immediately regretted it. It didn't make sense. He'd spent the first three plus decades of his life inside Avalon module, and it was "deeper" than this. Then again, there was no top of it to fall off. If you stepped off from the hub, the worst that would happen is you'd float off waving your arms ineffectually while people on the lifts pointed and laughed at you until someone threw you a tether.

The stakes here are a little higher, Benson thought, then chuckled nervously to himself at the unintentional pun.

Kexx put a steadying hand on his shoulder, then pointed at more than a dozen black specks at the base of the far canyon wall. "The entrances to the Dwellers' caves are there. That's where our trail leads."

"But," Benson pointed down the rock face, "there's a bit of a drop off!"

Kexx gazed back at him, face blank as if ze didn't understand the objection. Then, Benson remembered the lava tube. The ease with which the Atlantians had stuck to the rock, almost like geckos. Kexx didn't understand, because the cliff was no obstacle to zer.

"You've got to be fucking kidding me."

After some frantic explaining and ad-hoc translating, Benson and Mei managed to get across to their new friends just how ill equipped they were for making a thousand meter near-vertical free rock climb. They spent the waning hours of light scouting out a more manageable line of descent. About a kilometer and a half west, they found an outcropping that, while hardly inviting, was something less than straight down and offered several small plateaus along the way that would give them a chance to rest before the next leg.

Predictably, the old nightmares about freefalling through space woke Benson several times, and his thin bedroll didn't make falling back asleep any easier. He greeted the morning with an annoyed grunt.

"You awake?" Mei asked from the other side of their small tent. Benson grumbled his affirmation. "Good, just in time to fall to our deaths," she said.

"It won't come to that," Benson said. "It's just like when we climbed up the outside of Avalon module, remember?"

"We had a ladder," Mei answered.

"True, but I was in a spacesuit held together with duct tape. How is this worse?"

Mei pointed downwards. "Ground's waiting for us at the bottom."

"It'll be quicker than flying off into deep space and waiting for the oxygen to run out." Benson paused and rubbed his neck. "That wasn't very reassuring, was it?"

"Not really, no."

"Sorry. We'll be OK, Mei. Just take it slow and steady. You're light and have little hands, you'll be fine. Worry about me instead. I'm old and fat." Mei cracked a smile at that, which was all Benson had hoped for. "C'mon, we should get moving."

They tied the dux'ah off on long leashes to the sturdiest shrubs they could find, although Benson was sure they'd rip free with one good jerk. After some deliberation among the caravan, and no small amount of haggling on the part of Kexx, it was agreed that the three largest of the remaining warriors would alternate carrying Mei on their backs as they climbed down. Benson, too large by half to be carried, was tied off with ropes to two others who agreed to stay just above him as they made their way down the cliff.

Benson spent half an hour tying and adjusting a makeshift harness around his chest and running down to loops through his crotch and legs. He tried to imitate the safety harnesses he'd use once or twice back on the Ark, but the Atlantian ropes were stiff and unforgiving.

"The sun rises, my friend," Kexx chided.

"Just a min... I mean, I'm almost done." Benson fidgeted and fussed over the trim for another couple of minutes, but eventually even he had to admit he was just putting off the inevitable. He succumbed and handed one end of the rope to Kexx, who'd volunteered to be one of Benson's anchors. Then, much to his shock, Kuul stepped forward and held out a hand to take the other end. The warrior snatched it up while muttering a string of Atlantian that Benson couldn't hope to follow.

"What'd ze say?" he asked Kexx.

"Ze said if you slip because of your stupid shoes and kill us all, ze'll cut off your feet before you can hit the ground."

"Fair enough." Benson arranged himself at the edge of the cliff. He looked back at his twin anchors. "OK, once we're moving down the face of the cliff, don't let any slack build up. It'll be bad enough if I slip, but if there's any slack it'll snap tight and pluck you both off. Got that, Kexx?"

Kexx nodded and translated the instructions to Kuul, who acknowledged them with a flutter of zer skin patterns. Benson still couldn't read them for shit, but he did notice that their skin was unusually still, even pale. Despite their bravado, they were rattled. Scared, even, but Benson had his own anxiety to contend with. He looked back over his shoulder at the stunning view of the canyon. Layers of subtle purple, orange, and red weaved through the rock as though painted by a giant brush. It was beautiful. And terrifying. Benson swallowed hard and resolved not to look at anything but his foot and handholds until they reached the canyon floor.

The first step was the longest. Benson climbed meticulously down the outer face of the cliff, never moving more than one hand or one foot to the next hold at a time. The dew of the early morning hadn't yet burned off completely. Benson found himself frequently drying his fingers on his pants, but it wasn't long before sweat added itself to the dew, making for a slick mixture. Kexx and Kuul followed him from above, each careful to keep in line with his descent and the ropes taut, taking some of his weight off of his muscles.

A small yelp drew his attention. Above, Benson saw one of the largest Atlantians starting down the wall with Mei clinging to zer back like the strangest parent/child pairing in history.

"You OK up there, Mei?" he shouted.

"I'm fine," she called down. "Just climb."

Spurred on by the rising sun, a gust of wind kicked up through the canyon, blowing dust and sand into Benson's face. But at least it was burning off the dew. Short, bristly scrub brush clung tenaciously to the face of the seventy-degree canyon wall. Benson wished he had half of their grip. He worked his way down, slow and steady, right until he ran out of rock. Invisible from above, an overhang ran for hundreds of meters in either direction. From his vantage point, there was no way to know how deep the overhang was.

"Ah, I've got a problem down here," he shouted up to Kexx.

"What's wrong, Benson?" Kexx called down, voice strained.

"There's an overhang."

"So?"

"So? So I'm not a gecko."

"What's a–"

"I mean I can't stick to the ceiling, Kexx!"

Kexx grunted, then spoke at Kuul, zer words coming out rapid and clipped. After a short argument, Kexx looked back down at Benson. "Let go of the rock. We will lower you down."

"Are you nuts?"

"What are–"

"Oh for God's sake. You'll have to hold my whole weight, and I don't even know if the rope is long enough to reach the next holds."

"Then what do you want to do, Benson?"

Climb back up, walk all the way back to the village, find and eat that damned chicken while I wait for the shuttle, take an hour long shower, fuck my wife's brains out, then take another shower, he thought.

"You're sure you can take the weight?" Benson asked.

"For a short time, yes," Kexx said.

"How sure?"

"You're stalling."

"Damn right I am," Benson mumbled. He took a deep, cleansing breath and tried to get his surging heartrate under control. He moved down as far as he could, taking out what little slack there was in the ropes.

"OK. Are you ready?" Benson shouted.

"We are, Benson."

Wish I was, he thought. "Mei, if this doesn't work, tell Theresa I love her."

"Tell her yourself," Mei shouted back irritated, clutching her Atlantian climber for dear life.

Benson shook his head, then closed his eyes tight. His blood pounded in his ears. His palms were sweating so much that even if he didn't let go, he would probably slip off anyway. All he had to do was... let go. "Here goes nothing," he said to no one in particular. Summoning all of his courage, Benson relaxed his fingertips.

For a brief moment, he floated in the air, weightless and free as though he were playing Zero back onboard the Ark. But then the ropes reached the end of their limited elasticity and Kexx and Kuul absorbed the full weight of their load for the first time. They grunted under the sudden strain, and the makeshift harness dug into Benson's groin hard enough that he was pretty sure whatever chances he'd had of fathering a child had been cut in half.

Kexx and Kuul did their best to match each other's pace, but it was impossible. Kuul shouted out something angry.

"What did ze say?" Benson asked.

"Ze said you should start skipping meals."

"It's mostly muscle!"

"Can you reach the rock face yet?" Kexx said hurriedly.

Benson looked ahead. The wall was only a meter and a half away, but still out of reach. "Not yet. Lower me down more." The pair of Atlantians obliged haltingly, jerking Benson with one rope and then the other, their progress painstakingly slow.

"Can you go any faster?" Benson asked.

"We can cut the ropes and you will go a *lot* faster," Kexx bit back.

"Sorry."

"Quiet."

Benson shut his mouth as they lowered him down another meter. Another. Then, they stopped. He looked up to see if they'd hit a snag, but it was worse than that. Kexx and Kuul had reached the edge of the undercut. There was no more rope to play out. He looked down through his dangling feet to gauge the remaining drop. His ankles were not encouraged by what he saw. He reached out a hand to get a hold on the cliff face, but he was still a half meter shy.

There was only one way out. He'd have to swing for it and pray one of the Atlantians didn't slip.

"Hang tight," Benson called to Kexx. "I'm going to swing for the cliff." Benson pumped his legs like a child on a playground swing. He shifted forward, building momentum with each pump, adding precious centimeters to each swing of his pendulum. Kuul grunted loudly.

"Hurry!" Kexx shouted through gritted teeth as zer strange, boneless hands melted into the craggy rock, desperate to maintain grip.

Benson reached out his hand and growled, trying to grow it another few millimeters by willpower alone. His fingertip lightly brushed against the rock. The rope harness dug into his groin so hard he began to feel pins and needles in his feet and calves, while the rope began to fray from the repeated swinging where it rubbed against the lip of the overhang. A few more and either the ropes would snap, or Kexx and Kuul would finally tire. If either of them fell, the other would be left carrying the full weight of all three of them. There was no way even Kuul could hold on under such strain.

"Fuck this," Benson said and spun around to put the soles of his feet toward the rock. As soon as his shoes made contact, he pushed off with a snap of his football-hardened legs, sending him far away from the cliff.

The sudden jerk finally proved too much for Kexx's grip. Ze broke loose from the rock just as Benson's swing reached its apogee, sending zer sliding down the face of the cliff and scrambling for a fresh hold. The sudden slack on one side of Benson's body threw off his line as he started to pendulum back toward the rock. There was no time to adjust his aim. Benson shouted a curse as the rock came rushing for his face. His eyes darted around, looking for handholds. He spotted one, maybe another. They would have to do. His hands shot out and fumbled at them even as the unforgiving rock knocked the wind out of his lungs. Struggling for breath, Benson got two fingers, three, into one of the craggy holds. A foot found another, slipped, then planted more firmly. Benson's other hand got a solid grip on a knobby protrusion.

He braced himself for Kexx's body to tumble down behind him, the lifeline streaming until it suddenly went taunt and yanked Benson, then Kuul, off the cliff and sent them all tumbling down to the rocks below.

Benson closed his eyes and awaited the inevitable.

CHAPTER THIRTY-ONE

Theresa walked behind the line of recruits lying prone on the ground, one hundred and eighty degrees away from the muzzles of the P-120 personal defense weapons they were about to fire for the first time. They'd set up a firing range out beyond the shuttle runway pointing toward the ocean where the only victims of stray bullets would be fish. Not that her location made her feel the least bit safer with a dozen high-powered rifles in the hands of utter neophytes.

In truth, she wasn't significantly better. The caseless propellant the rifles burned was chemically complex and expensive to produce. They weren't in the habit of wasting them, even on practice. Theresa had put less than a hundred live rounds down range, which perversely made her one of the dozen most experienced shooters in the colony. Now she was tasked with training a hundred more. It was like the blind leading the blind through a fireworks factory holding a torch.

Not that she really cared at the moment. Bryan was dead. She'd skipped straight to the anger step of the grieving process and intended to stay there.

"Keep both eyes open. Don't focus on the reticule. Focus on the target beyond," she said, trying to inject the weight of experience she didn't actually have into her voice. "Imagine the target has gravity, and it's pulling the reticule toward it. When they line up, squeeze the trigger slowly and evenly until the gun fires. You may commence–"

BANG!

Theresa shot a withering look at the impatient trainee. "–firing."

The rest of the line clicked off the physical safeties on their rifles, took careful aim, and promptly hit absolutely nothing. In the bay, several fish fell prey to weapons they'd never had the opportunity to evolve defenses against. It was going to be a long afternoon. A call alert popped up in her vision, a red flashing border marking the call as urgent. It was from Feng.

She sent a message to Korolev on the far side of the line. <Hey, Pavel, take over for a minute.>

The constable nodded, then stepped to the middle of the line and took over range safety officer duties with a thumbs up. Theresa faded away from the noise and concussion of the rifles until she could hear herself think again. She connected the call.

<What's up, Feng?>

<What did you give me for my housewarming?>

<What?> Theresa bristled at the ridiculous question. <Did you forget? You marked the call urgent.>

<Just tell me what you gave me,> Feng demanded.

<For fuck's sake, it was a candelabra set. I'm teaching football monkeys to shoot guns here, Chao. Get to the point.>

<I'm sorry. I just needed to be sure it was you. I'm up here in Command with the IT nerds going through the network with a fine-toothed comb. We've already tagged over two dozen bots, viruses, trawlers, dazzlers, ghosters… It's a fucking mess up here, Theresa. I had to know who I was talking to.>

Theresa felt a spasm of fear. They'd known someone had been messing around in the Ark's peripherals, but to be that deep inside the core network? That meant crew members were in on the crime. In on Mahama's murder. She fought back the panic. Whoever they were, no matter how deep they'd burrowed, they were operating in the shadows and wouldn't do well once the light started shining. She had to be that light.

<Talk to me,> she said.

<Well, I've only been here for a few hours, and I had to fight like mad to get into Command. Even threatened one lieutenant with my stun-stick. But we've already confirmed a few things. First, somebody buried the real results of the Atlantis geologic survey, just like you thought.>

<What's really there?>

<Everything,> Feng said. <It's a damned gold mine, literally. The geologist up here is still scratching her head over it, but it looks like Atlantis was the impact point for a really big asteroid, maybe a hundred million years ago. Enough to cause a bunch of volcanic activity that squirted lava up from the mantle through fresh cracks in the tectonics. Resurfaced the whole damned continent with fresh upwelling from the core. There's deposits of all sorts of important shit all over the place.>

Theresa's head bobbed along with the confirmation of their theory. Motive, check. <That's good, Chao.>

<That's just the start.>

<I'm all ears.>

<Well, you asked me to look up anyone with coder training and access to the plant source files...>

<And?>

<And, I found someone. Yvonne Hallstead. Dismissed from the crew seven years ago for inserting a virus into an administrative program to hide her prescription drug abuse.>

Theresa gasped. <Are you shitting me?>

<Ah, no. Why?>

<Because she was in lockup for domestic abuse until this morning when she mysteriously posted bail with money she wasn't supposed to have. I *just* had her here.>

<Well you're not going to like this next part, then.>

Theresa's lips tightened. <Out with it.>

<She's been doing consulting work for Alexander & Associates doing app development. Someone on the crew even gave her a security clearance that let her back into the plant source codes.>

<Sounds like I need to have another talk with Ms Hallstead.>

<You'll need to hurry.>

<What do you mean?>

<I mean Acting Captain Hitoshi has decided to acquiesce to at least some of the Returners' demands and open up limited immigration between the Ark and Shambhala, and Ms Hallstead is slated to be part of the first group up the beanstalk.>

<What? Is he fucking crazy?> Theresa was shouting even through her plant.

<To that, I couldn't say. But the first lift car is departing within the hour. There was no public announcement.>

<I gotta go. Good work, Chao. Keep digging. And watch your ass, huh?>

<Hmph. No one else does these days.>

Theresa smiled. <Honey, I would if it did anything for you.>

<Alas, it wouldn't. Good hunting, chief. Nail the bitch.> The link dropped.

Count on it, Theresa thought viciously. "Pavel, shut it down. We have work to do."

They let the electric cart coast to a stop two blocks away from Hallstead's apartment. Korolev adjusted his riot helmet, crinkling the aluminum foil lining its inside.

"I can't believe you talked me into a mad hatter helmet," he moaned. "It's hot as balls in here."

"It's either that or let her give you a heart attack."

"Thought you said they wouldn't use it out in the open."

"They won't if they're thinking clearly. But backed into a corner? Who knows?" Theresa leaned back to the third man in the cart, Lindqvist, as he went over his rifle one more time. The gun was probably overkill. The linebacker took up the whole rear bench seat by himself as it was.

"You ready with that thing?"

"I think so, ma'am."

"You think, or you know?"

"I mean, yes ma'am."

"Good. There's no room for error here. We don't know what we're going to find in there. She may be armed, she's certainly dangerous. But I'd really, really like to take her alive. So hold your fire with that cannon unless absolutely necessary."

"Roger that."

Lindqvist had volunteered, despite the fact that the need to stay linked to his gun through his plant meant his helmet couldn't be lined with foil. Theresa had explained the risk, but it hadn't deterred him in the least.

Theresa consulted her tablet and queried Hallstead's plant location. She was in her living room. She dug a little further into the house's systems and found a video was streaming to the wall display. "OK, she's watching TV. Pavel, with me. Lindqvist, go around back and make sure she doesn't try to escape when we ring the bell."

The big man nodded and hustled down the alley. Korolev got out his stun-stick and walked quietly and purposefully at Theresa's side up to the front door of the small, utilitarian house. It was a standard four room, single-story unit distinguishable from hundreds of others only by the numbers on its door frame. The house was clean, but Hallstead had made no attempts to decorate or otherwise individualize the exterior, to the point that its very plainness made it stand out.

Theresa and Korolev took positions on either side of the doorway. She didn't want to risk requesting a warrant for the raid. Anyone who could hack the central network and rewrite plant source code could easily set up bots to alert them to something like a warrant and bolt before they ever arrived. Instead, they were here under the guise of a "welfare check," hoping that Hallstead was careless enough to either leave evidence laying around, or tried to run, anything incriminating. But if the inside of her house was as orderly as the outside, and she managed to keep her cool, there wasn't much Theresa would be able to do.

Well, nothing that would hold up in court and not get her fired. Not that she was in a mood to care.

Korolev nodded that he was ready to go. But even as Theresa punched her emergency override code into the door's keypad, something felt wrong. She hit the "Enter" key and the lock clicked. Korolev swung the door open immediately and swept into the entry hallway. Theresa was half a step behind him, both of their stun-sticks held in the ready position. The first thing she noticed was a sharp, almost metallic smell she didn't recognize.

"What's that smell?" she whispered.

"Not sure. Cleaning solvent?"

"Ms Hallstead," Theresa called. "We've had a report of strange sounds coming from your house. We're here to check on you." There was no answer. They turned the corner into the sparse living room. A faux leather couch took up most of the rear wall, the impression of an ass worn into its cushion on the left side.

A cheap throw rug, scuffed acrylic coffee table, and a vase with plastic flowers filled out the rest of the room. Ass print aside, it looked like a demo unit. On the wall display, two women in strappy leather outfits pleasured each other with rather heavily modified power tools.

Korolev sniffed. "Our girl is a kinky one."

"She's supposed to be sitting right there." Theresa pointed at the couch, waving her handheld.

"Check the bathroom?" Korolev asked.

The truth hit Theresa like a punch to the gut. Hallstead had a lift car to catch in less than thirty minutes. Who would be sitting on their couch watching porn thirty minutes before moving out of their house forever? "She hacked her plant locator. She was never here."

"To the beanstalk?" Korolev asked.

"To the beanstalk, fast."

They recalled Lindqvist and ran back to the cart. Korolev hopped behind the wheel and threw it into gear. "Head for the dock?"

"Yes," Theresa crawled into the passenger seat. "No, wait." She punched through a few screens on her handheld. "The ferry is already casting off."

"Shit," Korolev spat.

"No, that's good. If Hallstead is on it, she's got nowhere to run."

"Unless she wants to swim a kilometer back to shore."

"Exactly. Take us to the quadcopters. We might still beat the ferry to the anchor station."

The cart's suspension sagged under the fresh weight of Lindqvist. They took off for the airfield with a whine of electric motors. They were in luck. One of the small scout helicopters was still sitting on the flight line. Theresa jumped out of the cart even before Korolev had brought it to a full stop and ran for the cockpit. "C'mon Pavel. Lindqvist, take the cart and wait for us at the dock."

The large man acknowledged the order and moved to the driver's seat while she and Korolev strapped themselves into the copter's harnesses. Neither of them were certified pilots, but fortunately, they didn't need to be. Theresa simply punched in their destination and the autopilot system spun up the four rotors mounted to the corners and dusted off.

They made the short flight out to the anchoring rig in silence, passing over the ferry as it slowly made its way from the natural harbor out into the open ocean a kilometer out. The planetside end of the Ark's space elevator was mounted to an enormous floating platform with several sets of powerful thruster pods. Most of the time, they simply kept it stationary within the gentle outflow of current coming from the mouth of the river. But in the event a powerful enough hurricane threatened to damage the rig, they could move it many tens of kilometers out of the predicted path.

The quadcopter pitched backward slightly as it slowed for its final approach to the small landing pad on the far corner of the platform. The ten meter-wide, wafer-thin elevator tether reached straight and true to the heavens until it passed beyond the atmosphere, where it appeared to shrink to a one-dimensional line glowing white. In addition to providing a track for the lift cars plying up and down its length, it also served double duty, powering the cars via a photovoltaic coating only a few molecules thick, turning the entire tether into a solar array several tens of thousands of kilometers long.

"OK, what's the plan?" Korolev asked as the quadrotor settled onto its skids.

Theresa unbuckled herself and threw open the cabin door. "We go to the loading dock and check everyone coming off the ferry until we catch her."

"And if she resists?"

"Oh, please tell me we're that lucky," Theresa said with venom in her voice.

"Hey, chief," Korolev grabbed her at the elbow, gently but firmly. "Remember our job here."

She yanked her arm free. "You think I've forgotten?"

"I just want to see this done by the book so it sticks. I know how you feel right now, I want to crush skulls too, but I know you'd feel infinitely worse if this gets botched up and somebody walks on a technicality."

"She killed Bryan, Pavel. I'm sure of it. You really think I'm going to let anyone walk away from this?" Her voice was flat, emotionless. It wasn't a threat. It was a statement of fact. For a split second, Korolev faltered under her stare.

"I'd rather it not come to that. I don't want my first act as chief to be arresting my grieving ex-boss on murder charges."

Theresa forced herself to unclench. Her fists had balled up so tight, her nails left tiny crescents in the skin of her palms. She was obviously just one small step away from a psychotic break. She took a deep breath, expelling as much of her anger and fear as she could fit into the exhale.

"You're right. By the book."

"OK. Let's go."

"Pavel?" Theresa grabbed his arm. He stopped and looked at her. "You're going to make an amazing chief."

"Not too soon, I hope."

"Oh no, not just yet. Let's move."

They sprinted across the platform, past the enormous, five-story tall lift car waiting in its cradle. Panting, they reached the landing dock just as the ferry's ramp came down.

"Can I help you, constables?" asked the dock attendant standing by the gate waiting to check everyone in.

"What's your name?" Theresa asked, genuinely unsure of the answer because of the foil inside her helmet blocking her link to the personnel database back at headquarters.

"Aliaabaadi," she answered, her face trying and failing to hide her anxiety and confusion at the sudden appearance of the law.

"Well, Ms Aliaabaadi, we just need to speak to one of your passengers as they get off."

"Oh, OK. What's their name?"

"Hallstead. Yvonne Hallstead."

The gate attendant punched the name into her tablet even as the passengers started to queue up to disembark.

"I'm sorry, but I don't see that name in the passenger manifest."

But Theresa wasn't listening. She was too busy scanning the faces in the crowd, recognition software in her plant comparing each to Hallstead's profile that she'd saved to internal memory before putting on her helmet.

It pinged a match. Near the back, a hoodie covering the top of her head. Seventy-eight percent match.

"Thank you." Theresa pushed past the attendant. "We'll take it from here. Pavel, toward the back. In the gray hoodie."

"I see her."

"Go left. If she tries to run and gets past me, stop her."

Korolev acknowledged the order and stepped out of view behind a support pillar, lying in wait like an ambush predator. He'd gotten somewhat better at not standing out over the last few years.

Keep cool, girl. You can't arrest her. You've got no warrant. You just want to have a friendly little chat with the woman who killed your husband. By the book. Theresa pushed gently through the crowd as they passed by to be processed and released to the lift car. They mostly ignored her or regarded her with curious or annoyed glances. All of them, except for Hallstead. The moment she spotted her pushing backward through the line and recognized her uniform, she locked eyes with Theresa and frowned.

For her part, Theresa smirked and made her way toward her with greater speed. "Ms Hallstead!" she called, waving a hand. She took a big step back and griped the strap on her backpack tighter. Then Hallstead's eyes went a little unfocused the way people often did when they were sorting through their plant OS. Her left eye winced almost imperceptibly, a common tic when a command was executed.

Theresa knew exactly which command Hallstead had tried to execute. Her eye twitched again, again. When Theresa continued to walk toward her, she stepped back into a bulkhead and went pale. And now she knew exactly what to say.

"Why, Ms Hallstead. I'm surprised to see you here. You almost gave me a *heart attack.*" Theresa piled the emphasis on the last two words so her meaning was unmistakable. Hallstead's pointy brown eyes went wide.

"How? How did you…"

Theresa tapped the side of her helmet. "Mad-hatter, motherfucker. And now, you and I are going to have a little talk."

Hallstead's disbelief quickly slid into terror. "But, you can't–"

Theresa cranked up the pressure. She needed her to break. To say or do something incriminating. "See, you really fucked up. I didn't even come down here with a warrant to arrest you. Didn't want to risk alerting any agents you have trolling the network. If you'd have kept your cool, you could've breezed right past me and waltzed right onto that lift car and four days later, you'd be suckling up to your master's teat on the Ark, eating fresh pond fish in whatever penthouse they set you up in for killing Administrator Valmassoi, Captain Mahama... My. Husband. You were so, so close..."

"But, I didn't. They–"

"They *what*, Yvonne?"

Literally backed into a corner, Hallstead's terror snapped into panicked action. With surprising speed and power, the small woman shoved Theresa off balance, sending her toppling backward. Her arms pinwheeled trying to keep her on her feet, but Hallstead was already on top of her.

Stupid, sloppy, Theresa thought as the scrawny programmer pressed her attack. But while her desperation gave her a certain animal viciousness, she lacked finesse and discipline. Theresa had been training and rolling with alpha constables for as long as she could remember. She was used to sparring with people twice Hallstead's size and possessing an order of magnitude more competence. One of her whirling arms gripped her left wrist, and in the blink of an eye, Theresa rotated her mass around their mutual balance point and redirected Hallstead's momentum in a more productive direction. Productive for Theresa's purposes, that is. Hallstead flew face first into the bulkhead with the wet thump of a ripe melon wrapped in a towel.

To her credit, or maybe just owing to adrenaline, Hallstead shook off the hit and scrambled back up to her feet, but not before Theresa had leveled her stun-stick at her forehead. She pressed the stud on the silver pen-sized stick and waited for Hallstead's limbs to go into convulsions.

Nothing happened.

Now it was Theresa's turn to be surprised. She pressed it again with an identical lack of results.

Hallstead didn't wait around for her to figure out why her stick wasn't working. Instead, she jumped to her feet, grabbed the backpack she'd dropped, and ran up the exit ramp.

Oh no you don't. Theresa gave chase, but Hallstead grabbed the other passengers as she ran and shoved them into her path, slowing her down. She reached the top of the ramp first and broke into a flat run across the platform, headed for the lift car.

"Pavel!" Theresa shouted, springing the trap. The younger constable stepped out from his cover, cutting off Hallstead's line of flight. The programmer skidded to a stop, the soles of her shoes screeching against the grated metal deck plates. Hallstead tried her little cardiac arrest trick at the same time Korolev tried to hit her with the stun-stick. Neither worked, much to the surprise of both of them. Now Theresa knew it wasn't something wrong with her stick.

"She's blocked the sticks somehow, Pavel."

Korolev grunted and ran straight at Hallstead, but a sudden electric whine and a rush of movement stopped him as a small quadcopter drone swooped down in from of his face and shocked him with a miniature electric prod.

"Ow!" Korolev shouted as his forearm shot up to swat away the mechanical interloper, but it deftly dodged the strike, then hit him again. It was an artificial hawk, Theresa realized, one of a small fleet that kept the anchor platform and other important installations clear of the local bird analogues. Hallstead must have hacked it and convinced the stupid thing that Korolev was a bird in need of scaring off. The little shit was certainly full of surprises.

"It's over, Yvonne," Theresa shouted. "You're under arrest on two counts of assaulting a constable and one count of being a little bitch."

"Little bitch, am I?" Hallstead unshouldered her backpack and held it at arm's length.

"Aah! Drop it!"

"Gladly." She dropped the bag to her feet and gave it a contemptuous little kick. It came to rest about a meter away. Theresa took a long step toward it. "I wouldn't do that if I were you."

Theresa paused. "Why's that?"

"Because it's my little insurance policy. It's a bomb. A very powerful bomb. Which I can trigger with a thought."

Theresa's breath froze in her throat. "How powerful?"

"Well, I'm no demolitions expert, but it should be enough to wipe the deck clean, maybe even cut the ribbon, if I packed enough shrapnel. Your foil hat won't save you from this one. What do you say, chief? Want to risk it?"

By then, the rest of the passengers were falling over each other to get back down the gangplank to the ferry. Theresa, however, didn't dare move a muscle. What Hallstead was talking about wasn't just the death of everyone on the rig. With the tether cut, Shambhala would be cut off from the Ark's power and food supplies. She wasn't threatening Theresa with death. Hallstead was threatening the entire colony with starvation.

"That's what I thought." Hallstead casually strode over to the pack and heaved it back onto her shoulder. "I'll just hold onto this for safekeeping, as long as there are no objections? No? Good. Now, here's what's going to happen, chief. You and your friend here are going to stand perfectly still, doing nothing more ambitious than breathing, while I walk up to the lift car and–"

It was at that moment that Korolev interrupted what was developing into a very promising speech.

With his left arm numbed by the repeated prods of the faux-hawk, Korolev charged at Hallstead's gloating form and dropped a shoulder into the small of her back, just below the dangling backpack. The scrawny coder's head and arms snapped backwards even as Korolev's momentum shot her torso forwards with a shock, driving both of them toward the platform's safety railing.

Theresa realized Korolev's plan and hurried to join in. She sprinted at Hallstead and threw all of her weight into a fist aimed squarely at her solar plexus. It connected. Hallstead's body whiplashed forward, doubling over on itself as she struggled to recapture the wind Theresa had just knocked clean out of her, which brought her forehead into contact with Theresa's.

Together, Korolev and Theresa grabbed Hallstead by the shirt, hoisted her limp body into the air, and pitched her and her bomb over the railings with a heave. Doing her best impersonation of a Wilhelm scream, Hallstead belly-flopped into the water ten meters below.

"Did you think to waterproof that bomb, asshole?" Korolev shouted down to the woman now struggling to tread water.

"By the book, huh?" Theresa said conversationally. "I don't remember reading that in the book."

"It probably got cut in the rewrites," Korolev answered.

"Still, they should put it back in. Maybe they can add it to the movie."

"We should be so lucky."

Below them, Hallstead was busy shedding her backpack before the weight dragged her down to the bottom.

"Should we fish her out?" Korolev asked.

"In a minute. She looks like she could use the exercise."

"Taking over Bryan's job as athletic director now, too?"

"Someone has to," Theresa said, her voice sharp as the jagged end of a broken bottle.

CHAPTER THIRTY-TWO

Kexx's arms burned under Benson's constant weight tugging at the rope tied around zer waist. The humans were short, but so, so heavy for their size. Zer shoulder, still punctured by fullhands of tiny teeth marks from the caleb attack, strained migtily from the load.

Then, Benson started swinging on the ropes.

Next to zer, Kuul grunted mightily with the exertion of staying stuck to the rockface.

"Hurry!" Kexx shouted down to Benson in human.

In answer, Benson cursed and pumped zer legs, hard, swinging for the rockface beyond the overhang. The tension finally proved too much for Kexx's grip. One of zer fingers peeled free of the thinseam ze'd clung to, then another. Before Kexx even had time to scream, ze was slidding down the rock, frantically clawing at the rock trying to regain purchase, but finding only fresh scrapes instead.

Then, zer feet left the rock behind and floated free in the air. With one last, desperate lunge, Kexx thrust zer hands at the rock. Zer right hand found nothing. But, right at the edge of the overhang, zer left hand caught a knobbly hold jutting out into the air. Zer fingers clamped down around it, contouring to match it precisely and gain the maximum grip.

Zer momentum carried Kexx over the edge and into open air. With a painful jerk that threatened to rip zer arm clean out of zer shoulder, Kexx came to a stop. Zer shoulder, the muscles in zer forearm, and zer hand all wailed in pain, but zer grip held as ze dangled by one hand over the drop.

It was only then that ze realized the rope connecting zer to Benson had gone slack. Kexx looked down, expecting to see a frayed rope and zer friend freefalling through the air. But instead, Benson looked back up at zer, clinging to the rock beneath the overhang, laughing.

"Not funny, Benson!" Kexx shouted as ze found another hold for zer other hand.

"Sorry, Kexx. I'm just relieved you're OK."

"We have a long climb yet before we can say that."

Miraculously, they reached the bottom of the cliff without further incident. Kexx, Kuul, and Benson walked at the head of the convoy across the flat basin. Although it had been carved by a great river now dry, the valley floor was far from featureless. Immense stones protruded from the ground, worn around their bases by windblown sand until their tops bulged. It was like walking through a forest of stone trees. Nor were they alone.

"We're being shadowed," Kexx said casually to Benson in zer language.

"I know. I've seen three of them. Are they preparing an ambush do you think?"

"They wouldn't dare."

"You keep saying that..."

Kexx ignored the comment and focused on trying to spot the scouts. Ze'd seen at least seven of them, devilishly well camouflaged with body paint mixed from the surrounding rock and sand. For every one Kexx had spotted, ze expected there were another four or five hiding among the stones. Which was rather large for a scouting party. Kexx picked up the pace.

Ahead, the stone trees thinned out, then disappeared entirely. In their place, a line of enormous statues carved from black rock dominated the edge of a chasm that held the remnants of the river that had carved the valley. Each stood four times taller than an adult G'tel, and had been carved into exaggerated representations of great Dwellers of their past, mostly warriors, so their memories could continue to defend the city even after their return. They were impressive, imposing monuments, meant to intimidate anyone who dared to enter Dweller territory with ill intent. But still, none of them were as impressive as the Black Bridge.

A single, unbroken piece of the same dark stone as the statues arched across the chasm to connect both sides of the valley. It was as long as thirty G'tel, and so old that no one could remember who had carved it, or how they'd dropped it into place. Centuries, perhaps millennia of feet had worn a shiny path along the centerline of the bridge, while heat ripples rose from its surface into the air. Kexx had heard it described by traders returning to the village, but had expected it was just another exaggeration. For once, they'd undersold it.

"That's a big slab of rock," Benson said.

"You have a gift for understatement," Kexx said. Looking back over their party, Kexx could see the resolve wavering on many faces. Ze hardly blamed them. This was the definitive, no-turning-back moment. But, it had to be done. Swallowing zer own trepidations, Kexx stepped boldly forward and put a foot on the black stone ramp. It was warm on the sole of zer foot, almost uncomfortably so. Ze walked resolutely forward, daring the rest to follow with zer silence.

Kuul went next, then Benson, Mei. Soon, the entire caravan was walking single file across the Black Bridge, the first in living memory to do so who weren't traders. Behind them, the scouts who had shadowed them through the rocks emerged from their hiding places. Three fullhands of them, no, five fullhands. It was a none-too-subtle warning. *Act up inside our city, and there will be no escape.*

Ahead, the far wall of the canyon came into view.

The Dweller city entrance had been carved into stunning reliefs over the centuries. Temples to Xis, Varr, and even a small shrine for offerings to Cuut had been chiseled out of the soft rock layers. Multiple small caves and hollows had been dug out and expanded into homes and marketplaces. Shouts went out up and down the wall. Curious faces turned to take in the strangers. The shouting grew, and was quickly followed by footsteps as everyone ran to get a closer look. Children screamed at the sight of Benson and Mei. Adults shielded their eyes, cursing the humans as demons or deadskins, much to Kuul's amusement.

"See, it's not just me," ze said.

"Not now, Kuul. Stay alert."

"That won't be a problem."

A few of the bolder adolescents broke from the ranks of their parents and elders to run up and lay a hand on the humans, then run back either screaming or laughing. Mei took the abuse in stride, but it was making Benson very nervous.

"Can you please tell them to stop that?" ze asked.

"I can ask," Kexx said. "Whether they'll listen is another matter."

Benson grumbled, but said no more. The largest and most adorned entrance, and the one Kexx could only assume led to the bulk of the city below ground, lay just ahead, guarded by a line of warriors who looked to be more than a match for anyone Kuul had under zer command. Here and there, Kexx noticed fleeting flashes of recognition on some of the warrior's faces.

"I believe some of these guards were part of the attack on my village," ze whispered to Benson.

"I'm sure of it," Benson said. "See how they're all pretending not to notice my gun? They recognize it. They've either seen one before, or they've heard the story. Only one place that could've come from."

Kexx nodded. "Let me do the talking."

"Fine with me." Benson pointed at his head. "Can't understand a thing they're saying anyway."

Kexx made eye contact with Kuul. "Stay sharp. And don't let our guest out of your sight."

"Count on it."

Kexx squeezed the warrior's forearm approvingly. Their faces shared a rippling pattern of friendship Kexx had never expected to display for Kuul, nor expected to see displayed in return. Without further ceremony, Kexx turned to the entrance and strode forward until ze was finally ordered to stop. Revealing zerself, the senior guard stepped forward.

"What is your business here, Cuut spawn?"

Zer accent was harsh, guttural, and exactly like the warrior ze'd encountered in the forest days earlier. Coming from a Dweller, Cuut spawn was not a compliment, but Kexx let the transgression pass without notice. "My name is Kexx. I am a truth-digger representing many villages. And it is with regret that I come to lay accusation before your chief."

"You dare to come here to our sanctum, among our temples, and–"

"Forgive me," Kexx cut off the brewing diatribe. "But we have traveled many days and lost lives to bring our claims before your chief. So unless you are ze, I have no further need of you." Before the stunned guard could reply, Kexx pushed past zer toward the entrance and was immediately met by a fullhand of leveled spear points.

Kexx's eyes narrowed. Zer speech took on the angry tones of the Dwellers. "Have you fallen so far that you would interrupt a truth-digger in zer duties? Is so much evil hidden here that the light must be blocked?"

"Xis's warmth sustains us here, Cuut spawn. Not light," answered the guard.

"Since when does Xis fear the truth?"

The guard's crests flared and darkened, but Kexx held zer ground.

"Xis fears nothing," the guard said through strained teeth.

"Good, then you can lead us to your chief."

"No." The guard made a cutting motion with zer hand. "Just you, truth-digger."

"And my friend here." Kexx pointed at Benson.

"Absolutely not!" the guard bellowed.

"Ze is a truth-digger among zer people, just as I am. Ze has accusation to lay, just as I do. Under Xis's law, ze must be allowed to pass."

"But ze is not of Xis's womb!"

"Probably not," Kexx agreed. "In fact, I have no idea whose womb they come from. But humans were among the dead, so ze comes."

The guard thrust a finger at Benson's gun. "Fine, but *that* stays here."

"Why?" Kexx asked innocently.

"Because it is too powerful."

"So, you've seen a gun before."

The guard was about to answer when ze realized ze'd been backed into a trap. "Rumors have reached us," ze said instead.

"What's the matter," Benson asked.

"They don't want you to bring your gun."

"But you can bring your spear?"

"It is traditional that a truth-digger be allowed to carry a weapon for self-defense."

"Then why can't I bring my gun?"

"They're scared of it."

Benson smiled. "Good. Tell them it's not my fault they don't make better weapons."

Kexx smirked and relayed the message, which was about as well received as ze'd expected the insult to be, but left without any options and on the verge of self-incrimination, the guard relented.

"You two, follow me. The rest stay here. And we'll take your prisoner now."

Kuul gripped zer spear tighter. "No. You won't."

"Ze means it," Kexx said. "I wouldn't want to be the first to test zer word. Or the second, for that matter. Our... guest ambushed us with caleb, er, with very large uliks. We have an accusation to lay against zer as well. Ze remains with us until the truth is known."

The guard leaned in, close enough to Kexx's face that ze could smell the rotting bits of fungus stuck between zer teeth. "You make a lot of demands for someone so far from help, Cuut spawn."

Kexx leaned in just fractionally closer. "I ask only for the courtesies I am due, the same courtesies I would extend if our situations were reversed. Now, is it your intention to delay us all day?"

The guard's face twisted up, and for a moment Kexx tensed up in preparation for a violent outburst. But instead, ze spun around on zer toes and stalked off down to the entrance to the caves. "Try to keep up, truth-digger. I wouldn't want to delay you."

Kexx grabbed Benson's shoulder. "Stay close to me. Move as I move. And keep your eyes open for trouble."

"You do remember that I can't actually fire this thing, yes?" Benson lifted zer gun apologetically.

"Then try to look mean."

"I don't look mean now?"

"Not really. Too pale."

"First time I've heard that."

They took off after their reluctant guide into the mouth of the caverns. The light of day quickly faded into the dim light cast off from the shine worms, fungal mats, and the body glow of the Dwellers themselves. It took a while for Kexx's eyes to adjust from the bright of day to the dark of the cave. Benson had even more trouble.

"Kexx, can you do that glowing thing on your back so I can follow? I can't see my hand in front of my face."

Kexx obliged, expanding three parallel spots of light across zer shoulders so that zer human friend could gauge zer distance and orientation. "Does that help?"

"A bit. Thanks."

Above them, Kexx could see that the Dwellers had carved positively enormous caverns into the side of the cliff. The natural caves had been expanded manyfold in every direction. What everyone had assumed were underground cities actually extended far upwards as well, maybe all the way to the top of the cliffs. Even now, the drumbeat of hammer and chisel echoed through the space as Dweller rock workers toiled to expand their city. The scale of it all was simply staggering.

Overhead, Kexx heard the odd clicking of an injri flock hanging from the ceiling. Ze looked up just in time to receive fresh fertilizer on zer forehead.

"Are those injri?" Benson asked.

"Yes."

"And did one just–"

"Yes."

Benson chuckled. "Sorry."

Kexx wiped the guano off with the back of zer hand, then smeared it on Benson's shirt.

"Ugh, gross!"

"Sorry."

Their guide led them ever deeper, down into Xis's womb. It wasn't long before the cold started to bite into Kexx's skin. It wasn't unbearable, but it would start to effect zer mind before long, slowing zer thoughts, muddling zer perception.

"Benson. I am… cooling. Watch me closely. If I look confused, or lost, remind me what we're doing, where we are. Will you do this for me?"

"Of course."

"Thank you, my friend."

"Kexx?"

"Yes?"

"I still can't see a fucking thing."

Kexx laughed easily. Their guide did not approve. "What are you saying to zer?"

"I'm sorry. My friend speaks only zer own language. We were joking about the cold down here."

"Quiet," ze barked. It was only then that Kexx realized just how quiet the caves had become. Kexx's eyes had adjusted fully by then, revealing enormous patches, fields really, of a fullhand of different types of fungus being cultivated and tended by many fullhands of Dwellers. The ceiling here was low, and even more varieties of fungus clung to it. The sharp smell of urine grew with each step deeper into the fields until Kexx balled up zer hands to avoid tasting it on zer fingers. The tenders did not speak aloud. Instead, they used incredibly intricate patterns of skin glow to relay not only emotion and simple commands, but entire complex thoughts, whole sentences, entire conversations.

Kexx immediately understood why. Surrounded by a low rock roof stretching off in every direction, the echoes of a hundred shouted discussions would quickly break down into echoing chaos. They passed through another identical level. Another. Another still. The amount of food being grown down here in the damp, cold darkness rivaled the fields surrounding Kexx's village. Probably exceeded it in terms of edible mass being grown.

"This must seem very strange to you, Benson," Kexx whispered.

"Actually, you'd be surprised. Mei would feel right at home."

"Well, it's very strange to me."

"I said quiet!" their guide shouted, sending an echo through the fields and drawing the attention of every farmer within earshot. "Mind your mushrooms," ze commanded them. They returned to their work.

Everything changed on the next level. The roughly hewn walls, ceiling, and floors gave way to intricately carved patterning underfoot that mimicked tilework. Columns of rock formed into arms with their fingers arched to connect with their neighbors kept the crushing weight of the stone above at bay.

And it was warm. Heat radiated up from the floor through Kexx's toes. Something was fighting against the cold, and winning. Fires? Kexx couldn't see how. There was nowhere for the smoke to go, and no obvious mechanism delivering fresh air this far down. Yet ze could feel the warmth from the soles of zer feet moving up through zer bloodways. The warmth soon suffused the air, revitalizing zer body and mind.

A ramp, carved into the impression of a flowing river, the crests of the waves shining with the polish of centuries, led down into a new chamber at a steep angle. On either side, a forest of perfectly clear, white crystals each as thick as a tree trunk reached out from the floor at all angles as if they'd been grown specifically for the purpose. A warm, orange glow leaked out from the entrance. It was the glow of torches, although not nearly bright enough to account for the heat.

"Wait here," their guide instructed. Kexx complied, having no desire to wander off into the maze of tunnels. The guide entered the chamber and a brief, loud conversation followed. Many voices all speaking the same dialect their prisoner had shouted at Kexx in the tunnel.

The conversation died down as their guide reemerged. "You may enter. But do not forget where you are, Cuut spawn. I suggest you make your accusation brief."

Once inside, Kexx was struck by just how closely the sanctum mimicked the temple to Xis back in zer village. Perhaps theirs was the mimic, for this room felt much, much older. Soot stains streaked the curving wall from each torch mount up to a small central chimney which let the smoke escape to who knew where.

The room wasn't the only unsettlingly familiar thing present.

Even in the flickering torchlight, Kexx immediately recognized the warrior sitting to the left, staring at Kexx open-mouthed, as if one of zer long-returned ancestors had just walked through the door. Wrappings around the warrior's leg where Kexx's spear had skewered it just days earlier confirmed zer identity. This was the Dweller who had led the ambush. Ze wasn't alone. A trio of advisors sat sprinkled around the room, while bearers filled in the rest of the circle. Probably the chief's private harem.

"Surprised to see me again so soon?" Kexx asked.

"I don't know you," ze said flatly, eyes darting around to zer circle of bearers.

"We weren't properly introduced. But I can see your leg remembers my spear. My name is Kexx. What is your name, Chief of the Dwellers?"

An angry chorus of voices rose up from the circle, the skin of the assembled advisors and bearers a swirl of patterns and light. Only one of them, a small bearer two seats down from the warrior kept zer calm. Ze even smiled faintly.

The diminutive bearer held up a hand and the room settled. "I'm sure the truth-digger meant no insult. Our ways are doubtless very peculiar to zer. Isn't that right, Kexx, was it?"

"Yes…" Kexx confirmed, unsettled by the change of direction. Something was wrong. The others in the circle were showing a lowly harem bearer enormous deference. Had zer mind gotten that cold already?

"I'm sorry, bearer. What is your name?"

"Ryj is the name given to me by my parents, but you may address me as under chief."

CHAPTER THIRTY-THREE

Benson stood back near to the entrance of the circular chamber. It looked remarkably like the twin temples back in Kexx's village, minus the dome for their rover or the sacrificial altar in the basement one. Instead, the low chairs favored by the Atlantians circled the room. Kexx stood in the very center and exchanged heated words with several of the others, including one particularly nasty-looking character with an even nastier-looking leg wound.

However, it was one of the smaller ones, a bearer, Benson was almost certain of it, who seemed to be giving Kexx the most trouble. Benson couldn't understand more than the very occasional word of the conversation, but he could see Kexx suppressing frustration, even anger, as ze talked to the smaller Atlantian. Whoever ze was, whenever ze spoke, everyone else shut the hell up and listened. Zer body was unadorned by the sorts of jewelry and colorful dress Benson had come to associate with chiefs during the gathering back in the village. But then, this was zer house. Maybe ze just didn't feel like dressing up for the barbarians from the plains. Maybe it was a deliberate insult. Maybes were all Benson was going to have until he could speak with Kexx again. Damn the idiots who'd tried to kill him for burning out his plant. He could be eavesdropping even now if only his translation software was active.

Instead, he tried to focus on other things, like their body language, which he barely understood, or their skin glow patterns, which he didn't understand at all. He tried to keep his ears open for any slippage that might show contamination from Shambhala or the Ark, English or Mandarin words where they didn't belong, but heard none. He'd kept his eyes open as best he could on the trip down, scanning for human artifacts, an intact or even wrecked rover or drone, but the corridors and chambers were dimly lit and seemingly endless. They could've hidden the contents of the entire museum down here without Benson seeing anything.

The conversation paused as Kexx swept zer hand in Benson's direction. He recognized his name spoken, then all of the assembled Atlantians turned to look at him, their shining alien eyes made all the more discomforting by the flickering torches. Benson couldn't help but think of the night the calebs attacked their camp. The glowing eyes just tripped something deep down in his brainstem. Something very old that remembered eyes in the dark, reflecting firelight.

Kexx motioned for him to join zer in the center of the room. Benson made a small show of adjusting the rifle slung over his shoulder and straightening his mended shirt, then joined the truth-digger.

"It's time for you to lay your accusation."

"But I can't speak the language."

"Speak yours, clearly and with confidence. I will translate for their... ahem, chief."

Benson noticed the odd pause. "Something wrong with the chief?"

"We will talk later. Now, lay your accusation. They are waiting." Kexx took a large step back, leaving Benson to face down the eyes of the room alone. He cleared his throat and decided the beginning was the best place to start.

"Um, hi." Benson waved his hand, feeling like a kid talking in front of class for the first time as his did so. Kexx translated something that sounded a little longer, and a little more dignified. "I accuse... members of this village of attacking the village of G'tel while my, er, tribe was trying to establish peaceful, friendly relations." Kexx spoke behind him, firm and even, allowing Benson's emotions to carry through on their own. "And that during that attack, several of my tribe were murdered, I mean, killed without provocation or cause. Including one of our bravest warriors, Atwood, and our, um, chief, Valmassoi." Benson took a deep breath and looked right at their chief. "Oh, and some jerk who says ze's your cousin or something set these big ass dog-looking things on us while we were walking here that damned near ate my face and I'm still a little sore about it."

Kexx struggled through to the end of that one, then fell silent and stepped up to Benson's side. The chief leaned back and let the voices of zer advisors rise and fill the chamber, washing over zer. Zer eyes closed. Benson thought ze looked old and exhausted. After several minutes of listening to zer advisors bicker, or perhaps just gathering zer own thoughts, the chief leaned forward again as the chamber went silent in anticipation.

Benson listened passively, still not understanding a damned thing, still wishing his plant was functional, which was perhaps only the second time in his whole life he'd really appreciated having it. Suddenly, the chief stopped speaking and everyone rose, then started sweeping for the door.

"Ah, Kexx?"

"We are to follow."

"OK, I got that, but to where?"

"I gather we are returning to the surface to consult with someone they call, um, I don't know your word for it. One who sees over the horizon?"

"What, like an oracle?"

"Oar-a-coal," Kexx sounded, trying to expand zer grasp of English even now.

"Close enough."

They swept back up the ramp and into the labyrinth of excavated corridors, natural tunnels, and mushroom fields. Benson was relieved he was being led back out again. Even if his rifle had been functional, the thought of having to fight his way out gave him chills. Just finding his way would have been damned near impossible. Coupled with the dark, the echoing walls, cutbacks, dead ends, blind spots, and a nearly infinite number of ambush points and you had a recipe for a defender's wet dream, and an invader's tomb.

Still, Benson couldn't help but appreciate the place. It was, after all, an Atlantian version of the Ark, only stationary. They'd lived down here in the dark and chill for generations at a time, eating only what they could grow on bare rock and their own waste. The fields of mushrooms, the chill, and the smell of ammonia was the Unbound's tiny hideaway in the bowels of the Ark writ large. Mei really would feel at home down here.

This time, there didn't seem to be any prohibition against talking aloud. Indeed, it appeared likely that the under chief's advisors never shut up. Benson decided to take advantage of it.

"So, what's the deal with the chief?"

"Ze is a bearer," Kexx said simply, as if that was an explanation in and of itself.

"Yeah, I knew that. But you seemed, I don't know, upset by zer."

"Ze is a *bearer*," Kexx repeated. "It isn't zer place to lead. It's not the way of things."

Benson's eyes widened at the admission. "Ze seems to be doing fine down here."

"That's not the point."

"Then what *is* the point, Kexx?"

"I don't expect you to understand. Bearers are precious and rare. They grow up separate, protected. They are too important to risk in hunts, or battles, or working the fields. They understand these things because we educate them, but they don't *experience* them. That's why they shouldn't lead. Chiefs prove themselves by doing. The Dwellers disrespect their bearers by making them work, even fight."

Benson couldn't help but smirk. "Don't let Mei hear you talk like that."

"Why would Mei care? Ze is not a bearer."

"*She* bore a child."

"Yes... but, your people are different."

"Trust me, we aren't. Everything you just said was said about human women a few centuries ago. Hell, a handful of idiots *still* say it. Not that anyone listens anymore."

Kexx considered this in silence for a moment. "What changed?"

"People changed, Kexx. They stopped 'protecting' women and just let them go out and live their lives how they saw fit. Women became some of our greatest leaders, warriors, everything."

"So they changed to meet the new challenges?"

"No, Kexx. That's my point. Women didn't change. They had

always been capable of being leaders, warriors. In fact, they had
been throughout history. But those examples were forgotten or
hidden on purpose. What finally changed wasn't women, but
men. We finally recognized what women had always been."

"But our bearers are smaller, weaker. They have to be
protected if there is to be a next generation."

"Have you seen how much smaller Mei is than me? Did that
stop her from fighting in your village?" Benson shook his head.
"Kexx, I don't know how to explain this, and maybe it's not
fair to say at all, but your race is going to have to mature really
quickly. You're going to have to stop thinking one of your genders
is fundamentally different. You're going to have to stop looking
at other villages like they're a different kind of people, even the
Dwellers. And you're going to have to realize that humans aren't
just a different tribe. You're all going to have to unify and find
your common goals. You're already doing that with your road
network, but it's going to have to be all of you, the Dwellers,
the nomads, the raiders, everybody."

"That is easy to say." Kexx shrugged. "Hard to do."

"It has to start somewhere."

"Or your humans will divide us, is that what you're trying to
warn me about?"

Benson didn't want to be so direct, but essentially yes, that
is exactly what he was trying to warn zer about. For all the evil
Kimura and da Silva had wrought, they hadn't exactly been
wrong about human nature. Here they were, less than three
years on a new planet, and Benson was already neck deep into
what he was increasingly convinced was a conspiracy among
the powerful to swoop in and steal resources from the natives,
consequences be damned.

As if they'd learned nothing from the colonization of the
Americas, Australia, the African slave trade, and a thousand
other sins of the past threatening to blossom again in the present.

"I don't want to see that happen. I'd rather our people become
allies. We can do more through cooperation than conflict."

Kexx looked at him for a long time before answering. "You
really do mean that. Don't you? I've watched how you handled
Kuul. Ze was looking for any excuse to kill you when you first

arrived. Now… But what do we have to offer you as allies?"

"We can learn from each other."

"Really?" Kexx said, exasperated. "You walk among the stars themselves. What could we possibly teach you?"

"We're not as invulnerable as we look. We're one asteroid, one power failure away from starving. We're growing almost all of our food up there." Benson pointed at the ceiling, toward the Ark up in the sky. "If we lose that, we die. Your crops, your livestock, we need them. You can teach us how to live down here. And in return, we can teach you how to live out there." Benson let his arm wave to encompass the sky on the other side of the hundreds of meters of rock.

"We will never be one people, but we can be siblings, er, brood mates. We will argue, we will fight, we may even hate each other now and then. But what we do now, here, can mark the start of a family coming together. And we'd better come together pretty quick, because whatever killed Earth is still out there gunning for us. We won't be able to stay hidden forever, and when that day comes, all of us here on this planet better be ready to either run, or stand and fight."

"And you believe we will be stronger together?"

"Damned right we will."

Kexx smiled. "You have big ideas, Kemosabe."

Benson snorted. "Yeah, I guess I do. It would sure shock the hell out of my primary school teachers."

"How do you think I'm doing with the Dwellers?" Kexx's voice carried a hint of worry and self-doubt.

"Well, we're still alive, so that's good."

"You didn't expect to be?"

"I wouldn't have bet heavily on it, no."

"Why not? If you're wrong, you'd never have to pay up."

Benson laughed again. One of the advisors shot him a withering look, which Benson was only too happy to shoot right back. Ze and Kexx had a small exchange before ze looked away.

"What was that about?" Benson asked.

"Ze doesn't think this is a time for laughing."

"Those are usually the best times," Benson said. "Did the chief say anything else about this oracle?"

"Ze was... vague. But I get the sense even ze is wary."

"And we have to go back to the surface to speak to zer?"

"Yes. Ze apparently prefers the daylight."

A knot suddenly tied itself in Benson's stomach. He had a strong suspicion who, or more specifically, what the oracle would turn out to be. And if he was right, they would need to be ready to run, and run fast.

"Don't let your legs get cold," Benson said. They reemerged from the caverns into the valley minutes later. Kuul, Mei, and the rest of the caravan hung back from the entrance, spears in hand, but not pointed at anyone in particular. Their captive sat at the center of the group, now gagged, which was a nice change of pace from the last two days. But as soon as they emerged, ze sprang to zer feet and started trying to yell through the cloth in zer mouth while zer skin patterns flickered and flowed like a torrent.

The under chief stepped up to the edge of the caravan's circle and motioned everyone out of the way. Much to Benson's surprise, they complied, even Kuul. The little bearer chief had gravitas, that much was sure. Ze and Devorah would probably get along swimmingly. Ze inspected zer brood mate like a buyer inspecting livestock for quality, touching zer arm and running a finger over the fabric of the gag in zer mouth, then inspected the dressing on zer leg wound. Benson was glad their prisoner had been well treated, mostly. Less for the chief to blame on them.

Seemingly satisfied with zer condition, the chief spoke some hushed words to their captive, then started back along the track ze'd been on. Benson motioned to Mei and Kuul for everyone to follow, including their prisoner. If what he thought was about to happen actually happened, they would need to stay close together.

They walked along a short path of fresh stones to a small outbuilding that looked nothing like the grand architecture carved into the cliffs to their right. The ill-fitting stones were stacked and mortared at odd angles, as if they had been hastily assembled from backfill.

"Hardly seems a fitting home for an oar-a-coal," Kexx said in a low voice.

"I think ze just moved in recently," Benson said flatly. "Kexx, I have a bad feeling about this."

"Don't offend our hosts, Benson. We have been treated with respect this far."

"We'll see how long that lasts."

The procession halted, and the chief motioned two of zer advisors into the shelter. Benson realized he was holding his breath. He touched Mei's shoulder. "Be ready to move."

"You'll be right behind me," she said humorlessly. Apparently, they'd had the same thought. The advisors reemerged from the darkened interior of the hut holding the ends of a makeshift stretcher. Benson couldn't see through the Atlantian at the head of the stretcher, but gasps from members of the crowd all but confirmed his suspicions.

Then, the stretcher turned sideways and removed all doubt. Lying there, about a meter across, was a quadcopter drone. Its photovoltaic skin caught the bright, early afternoon sun and drank it in.

"Ah, Benson," Kexx said. "Isn't that a–"

"Yep."

"And won't it–"

"Probably."

"So you should be–"

"Hiding." Benson backed away slowly, trying to put the taller Kexx between himself and the drone. The sound of rotors spinning up signaled the drone was about to launch. Damn, but they charged quickly.

The under chief began to chant, zer advisors joining in at the chorus. A voice fed through a tinny speaker answered with its part of the chant. Prerecorded, if Benson was any judge. Whoever was controlling the drone, they'd been playing the oracle game for quite a while now. That confirmed Benson's suspicion of how the Dwellers' dialect had ended up in his translation software. Somebody had forgotten to block it off from the linguistic database updates. It was the little fuckups that got most perps caught in the end.

The chant reached a crescendo, and as one, the Atlantians fell to their knees in prayer. All of them, including Kexx.

With his hiding spot lying on the ground, Benson stood there feeling very, very naked. The hovering drone spotted him instantly and swiveled in the air to point its main visible spectrum camera at him.

"Uh." He waved a hand dumbly. "Hi."

Kexx looked back over zer shoulder at him. "Oh, shit."

"What are you doing?" Mei hissed from the ground. "That's the part where you get down."

"Sorry, I forgot my hymn book," Benson bit back.

The synthesized voice started shouting angrily. The only part Benson caught was his name, but its meaning was clear by the way several dozen spears leapt up and pointed at him.

Kexx put up zer hands and started to object, but it was Kuul who really got their attention. Ze grabbed their prisoner by the crests and hauled zer to zer feet. Several guards turned their spears to face the new threat, but stopped dead in their tracks as Kuul calmly, coolly placed the tip of zer obsidian dagger into a hollow between the prisoner's neck and shoulder.

Everyone froze as Kuul spoke, slowly and evenly. Benson didn't have to know the language to know what ze was saying; they were all walking out of there, together, and if anyone so much as twitched in a way ze didn't like, the chief's cousin was going to do zer best impersonation of a pin cushion. That Kuul's voice was even and emotionless, and zer skin placid only helped to punctuate zer resolve to see the threat through.

As one, the members of the caravan retreated carefully from the little hut. The chief and zer retinue of advisors and guards, as well as the drone, shadowed them with every step. Twice Kuul had to stop and order them further back, repeating zer threat and even drawing a small stream of blood from their captive.

"One of these times, I'd like to be wrong," Benson said. "Just to break up the boredom."

"This is boredom?" Kexx asked. "What do we do?"

"Me? I'm going to let Kuul keep backing us up until we aren't surrounded anymore."

"And then?"

"And then I'm going to run straight for that fucking bridge like a scalded cat."

"A good plan," Kexx said. "You can tell me what a cat is on the other side."

Benson dug his sat link out of his pocket and looked at it

nervously. His cover was blown anyway. Whoever had tried to kill him knew he was still alive now, so there was no point to his radio silence. Of course, he had no way to know if whoever he connected with was working with them or not. He looked back up at the semicircle of spears, war clubs and daggers a few meters away, waiting for their chance to carve him up like a lake perch. He needed to worry about surviving the next few minutes, and to do that, he needed his rifle. He'd sort the rest out later.

Benson manually punched in a connection to the Command deck on the Ark and waited.

"This is Command, Ensign Harrington speaking."

"It's Bryan Benson," he shouted into the link. "I'm alive and under fire."

"Er, but you're dead, sir."

"I will be if you don't pull your head out of your ass."

"I'm not reading any signal from your plant. How can we be sure you're human?"

"My fucking voice print is on file! Actually, to hell with the voice print. Do you know any Atlantians who can swear in English, you stupid son of a bitch?"

"There's no need for that kind of language, sir. I'm just doing my job."

A spear point shattered next to Benson's ankle. Kuul shouted an obscenity-laced warning at the warrior who threw it and tightened zer grip on their prisoner's neck.

"Just run the goddammed print!" Benson screamed.

An eternity later, the voice returned. "All right, we've confirmed your identity. How can I help you, Mr Benson?"

"I need you to unlock my rifle!"

"For which user?" came a patient reply.

"Any user! Just turn the damned recognition system off."

"But that's against—"

"If you say one fucking word about safety protocols and I somehow survive this shit storm, it will be very hazardous to your health. Clear?"

"OK, sir. I understand. I just need you to read me the serial number located on top of the side of the magazine well."

"Are you fucking kidding me right now?"

CHAPTER THIRTY-FOUR

"What's our girl doing now?" Korolev asked as he slid back into Theresa's office.

Theresa glanced up from her desk's screen, then spun it around so her junior constable could see the feed from inside cell number four where Hallstead was being held. "Nothing," she said. "Just sitting there cooling her heels, letting her hair dry."

"Sure isn't acting like someone facing a death sentence, is she?"

Theresa rubbed her chin. "No, she sure isn't. I think she still believes she's going to get bailed out of this somehow."

"Are we sure she isn't?"

"Yeah. I am." There was a finality in her voice that did not invite further commentary. Korolev had the good sense not to argue.

"So, what's the game? Good Cop/Bad Cop? Double Blind? Solberman's Gambit?"

"I thought I'd just go in there and hit her until she talks," Theresa said.

"By the book, chief," Korolev scolded.

"Can I hit her with the book?"

"No."

"Fine." Theresa huffed and crossed her arms. "Then let's just go talk until her ears bleed."

"That I can get behind."

As a precaution, both of them slipped back into their jerryrigged helmets before transferring Hallstead from her cramped holding cell to the interrogation room. The Sweatbox, as the constables had nicknamed it, was larger than the cells and contained an L-shaped desk and three chairs. Two of the chairs were padded and comfortable, one of which sat in the L for the backup constable to take notes, monitor recording or diagnostic equipment, or review case files. The other comfortable chair was for the interviewer. The third chair was a thin metal folding chair with a straight back and no cushioning. It was intentionally uncomfortable, and meant for the interviewee. Across from the desk was a large, one-way mirror leading into a second room, ostensibly to give the interviewee the sense that unseen people were watching the proceedings, but in practice the anteroom was almost always empty.

The walls and doors of the sweatbox, as well as the individual cells, were imbedded with a fine copper mesh that acted as a Faraday cage to block all contact prisoners had to the plant network. To make sure that no one "disappeared" while in custody, each cell was equipped with video cameras that live-streamed onto the network where anyone could check in on prisoners at any time. The sweatbox lacked the live feeds, but still employed a CCTV system that could be reviewed on demand after interrogations were over.

Korolev plopped Hallstead down in the tiny chair and locked her foot shackles into a steel loop set into the floor.

"Comfortable?" Korolev asked. "Are the cuffs loose enough?"

"Well, I'm still in them, so no."

"I think you're fine." Korolev walked around and sat in the chair behind the desk, then tapped a few icons on his tablet to start recording. "We're ready."

Theresa didn't take a seat, preferring instead to lean against the door, arms folded. "Let's make one thing clear. You found a way to make our stun-sticks inert, or at least unable to recognize you. You may have thought you were being clever, but here's the problem. If you'd left them alone and tried anything, we would've just stunned you. But, since that won't work, if you try anything, and I do mean anything, we'll just have to handle you the old-fashioned way. Which is quite a bit more painful."

Theresa nodded at the butterfly strip covering half the

woman's nose. "Sorry about the knee, needed to make sure your head was scrambled enough that you couldn't send the detonation command to that little package of yours."

"It'll make me look more distinguished."

"For all the hot dates you're going to be going on?"

Hallstead shrugged, oozing confidence. The little idiot really still believed she was going to be protected somehow.

"I don't know what you thought you were going to accomplish with that little stunt, but I really wish you hadn't done it. Now we're going to have to install chem sniffers and backscatter scanners at the spaceport, the anchor platform. Put security guards on the gates. You made a lot more work for us."

"My heart bleeds," Hallstead replied.

"I'm sure. We're fishing your bomb out of the drink now. The techs will have it apart in a few hours, and we'll be able to backtrack all of the components you used to build it, which will lead us to your accomplices and suppliers within a couple of days. But that's not what interests me right now. What I want to know is how a minimally competent programmer somehow managed to rewrite the plant source code to induce heart attacks. We already know that's how you killed Administrator Valmassoi, Captain Mahama, and I strongly suspect that's what happened to my husband."

Hallstead's eyes twitched, just a fraction, and only for the barest instant. If Theresa hadn't been intensely studying her face, it would have been very easy to miss.

"Oh, you didn't know about that one? Or you didn't think I knew? Well, whichever it is, your next thought should be whether or not you want to keep fucking around with a grieving widow who currently has no one to blame but you, or do you want to start answering her questions?"

"I want to see my lawyer," Hallstead said.

"That's hilarious. How did you insert the code? That's not supposed to be possible. You even stumped Dr Russell on that one."

"Take off that helmet and I'll show you," she snapped back.

"So you admit it. Good. Now I just need to know how."

Hallstead blinked, trying to regain her composure. "I didn't kill nobody."

"That's a double negative. So you did kill somebody."

"Anybody," she corrected. "I didn't kill anybody."

"Sorry, but someone who just threatened to blow up the goddamned beanstalk seems like the sort of person who doesn't have a whole lot of moral compunctions about taking human life."

"Look, I didn't kill anyone. But, speaking... hypothetically."

Theresa looked at Korolev. "This will be good. Please, Ms Hallstead, hypothetically..."

"*Hypothetically*, you wouldn't have to write any new code at all. You'd just have to stumble on some really old code. Legacy code, see, left over from the very first plant OS, Starfire. It's still in there, you know, buried under two centuries of tinkering and updates and bug fixes and performance upgrades and integration patches."

"And this Starfire OS had a heart attack app? Is that what you're saying?"

"No, just the opposite, see. That first generation of people on the Ark, the real pioneers, they were as close to perfect as people could get, but they still came from Earth, with all the pollution and crap food and what have you. Even if they weren't hereditary, there were still heart attacks. Hell, marathoners sometimes drop dead in the middle of races, and those people are psychotic about health."

"This is coming back around to a point, I trust?"

"I was just coming to it," Hallstead said, excitement in her voice. She was enjoying this. "The Starfire app wasn't to induce a heart attack, it was an internal defibrillator. Heart stops, the plant itself jolts it back to life right that second, minutes before a medic or doctor could administer a shock."

"But," Korolev jumped in, "if it was triggered on a heart that was beating properly."

"Yahtzee," Hallstead said triumphantly. "Instant heart attack."

Theresa nodded along with the revelation. "But if it was so effective, why did we stop using it two centuries ago?"

"Because it wasn't effective. During a heart attack, there's so much disruption in the central nervous system because of the disruption of the oxygen flow to the brain that the bioelectrical voltage to the plant gets spotty and throws up errors. The app didn't have the power it needed in a real-life situation to deliver the shock half the time, so they stopped using it. A couple of updates later, everyone forgot it was there altogether. It was one of those things that worked great on paper, just not in practice. But to throw a healthy heart into v-fib? No problem."

Hallstead beamed with pride at her cleverness. Theresa held back her sudden urge to smack the smug little bitch across the face. Instead, she picked an even tenderer target.

"Well, thank you. That was thorough and illuminating. It makes sense to me now. You weren't clever enough to write the code. Someone else did all the work, you were just lucky enough to blindly stumble onto the answer."

"Hey, now just a minute–"

"Sorry," Theresa cooed. "Hypothetically speaking."

There was a knock on the door behind her. Theresa glanced back over her shoulder to see what the issue was. One of her newer constables looked back at her through the mesh in the glass making a "phone-call" gesture with his pinky and thumb held up to his head.

Theresa opened the door a crack. "I'm kinda busy, Epstein."

"Sorry, chief, but the administrator is on the vid asking for you."

She rolled her eyes. The man had the timing of a shitty comedian. "Sorry, kids," she said to Korolev and the shackled Hallstead. "Take five. I won't be long." She returned to her office and brought the waiting call up on her display.

"Chief constable," Merick said impatiently. "I couldn't raise you on your plant."

"I was in the sweatbox." Theresa pulled off her helmet and shook out her hair. "I'm in the middle of an interrogation, which I'd like to get back to."

"I'm afraid that won't be possible."

Theresa stared blankly at the screen, not sure she'd actually heard the last sentence. "I beg your pardon?"

"You are to stop your interrogation of Ms Hallstead immediately and prepare her for transport to the Ark."

"Like hell," she snapped. "She's been arrested for assault,

terrorist threats, possession and manufacture of an improvised explosive device, and resisting arrest. And on top of that, she's under suspicion of involvement in the deaths of Administrator Valmassoi, Captain Mahama, and maybe even my husband."

"Chief, I know you're in mourning, but your husband was killed in an attack by natives."

Her eyes narrowed. "Sure, that's the official story."

Silence stretched over several heartbeats. Merick was the first to speak. "Are you questioning the official record, chief constable?"

"Not yet. But someone has been running around tugging at strings all over the place. And that someone certainly has the capability to have a few seconds of plant recording doctored. I think she's sitting in my interrogation room. And she's not going anywhere."

"Chief constable," Merick said with the weight of his position. "I've been in contact with Acting Captain Hitoshi, and we agree that Ms Hallstead should be extradited to the Ark where she will stand trial for Captain Mahama's murder."

"So, you agree it was murder now? What about Valmassoi? Our claim on him is just as strong as Hitoshi's."

"This wasn't a request or an invitation to debate, Theresa. Clean Hallstead up and get her back to the beanstalk. You did your job. Congratulations on making the arrest. She wouldn't be facing any sort of justice if not for that. But I shouldn't have to remind you that your immediate concern is getting your team assembled and in the air for Atlantis so you really can find out what happened to your husband. Surely, you haven't forgotten that?"

Theresa's jaw clenched tight. "No, sir."

"Good. Now then, I..." Merick's face froze as something off screen grabbed his attention. "Er, I have to attend to another matter. You have your orders, chief, see to them. Merick out." The connection dropped.

"Cocksucker," Theresa mumbled, then got up from her desk. After a moment's consideration, she set the helmet down in her chair and returned to the sweatbox.

"Chief!" Korolev shouted as she opened the door. "Your head!"

She waved away his warning. "Shut off the recorders, Pavel."

Korolev blanched, but did as he was told. Theresa walked right up to Hallstead's seat. "Here's your shot, kid. You want it? Take it. It's not like you could be in *more* trouble."

Hallstead stared up at her, incomprehension and fear mixing on her gaunt face. "What the hell are you doing?"

"Testing a theory. See, you don't strike me as a coldblooded killer. A leech, sure, but I don't think you have it in you to murder someone."

"I would've gotten you at the dock if it wasn't for your helmet."

"Yeah, sure. But it was that or get caught. Life and death. Now, we're just two people standing here. So, what's it going to be?"

Hallstead held her gaze for a long time. Long enough that uncertainty started to creep up Theresa's spine. What if she'd miscalculated? What if she winced and her heart suddenly stopped? Could they get her help in time?

Then, her anxiety was banished as Hallstead broke eye contact and looked at the floor. "I didn't kill nobo... anybody."

"I believe you," Theresa said. "But you did give them the tools to do it, which still makes you an accomplice."

"I haven't admitted to anything."

"No, you just walked us through an incredibly detailed hypothetical that explains the whole thing the way only someone with direct knowledge could. Just prefacing it with 'hypothetical' doesn't mean we can't use it against you at trial."

"But—"

"But nothing, Yvonne. You're sunk. And here's where it gets worse for you. I've just been ordered to extradite you up to the Ark. We're not even supposed to be having this conversation."

Hallstead's expression lightened instantly. "Well, today's my lucky day after all."

"Don't be stupid," Theresa snapped. "You were caught, Yvonne. They'll need a scapegoat, and a dishonorably discharged, pill-popping crew member fits that bill nicely. Whatever deal you had with them is out the airlock, and you'll be right behind it if you go back up there. Do you really believe the sort of people who are willing to assassinate an administrator and a captain will bat an eye over killing you?"

Theresa's words hit home, and Hallstead's attitude sank back into the depths again. "That's what I thought. Listen, Yvonne, work with me and I'll do what I can to keep you down here and away from them. I can't let you walk, you're way too deep for that now, but I can try to keep you from getting the death penalty and safely away from them. Just give me the bigger fish."

There was another knock on the door. Epstein looked in sheepishly. Theresa flung the door open. "Dammit, What now? I'm working in here."

"I'm really sorry, chief, but Mr Feng is on the line for you. He says it's urgent."

Theresa threw up her hands. "Fine!" She jabbed a finger at Hallstead's face. "You. Think about what I said. The offer's open for the next ten minutes. After that, it's out of my hands." She stormed out of the sweatbox and back into her office and answered the call. She didn't even bother to sit down.

"What?"

"Theresa," Feng's face was taunt, stressed, as if in shock. "You have to get those knuckledraggers of yours on a shuttle right now and burn for Atlantis."

"You too now?" she yelled. "I just got this shit from Merick. I'm busy with an interrogation."

"No, you don't understand." Feng grabbed the camera and drew it to him until his face took up the entire display. "Bryan's alive. He's alive and he's in a metric shit-tonne of trouble."

CHAPTER THIRTY-FIVE

The standoff collapsed with the suddenness of a sinkhole. One of the Dweller warriors, no way to know which, tried to return Kuul with a well-aimed spear. They nearly succeeded. Only a shouted warning from Mei allowed Kuul to spot the spear in flight and get zer head out of the way. In a fit of rage, Kuul plunged zer dagger into the hollow of their prisoner's shoulder, severing zer nerve streams and sending the limp body tumbling into a heap on the ground amid a spray of blood.

Now, they were running.

Fortunately, Benson had somehow managed to get zer gun working again without an eyeblink to spare. Its thunder echoed through the canyon with every shot. Without it, the entire caravan would have already been overrun, but the dweller warriors were wary of the strange weapon that boomed like lightning and killed with invisible spears, though not wary enough to end the chase.

The Black Bridge was still a quarter stone away, and Kexx knew Benson's gun would run dry eventually. So they ran among the rain of spears and sling stones, they ran until their legs and airsacks burned with the effort. Kuul led the warriors of every village as they grabbed up the stones and spears that landed at their feet, then turned around to throw them right back at their pursuers to keep at least some of the attention off Benson and zer deadly gun. They fell into a rhythm, Kuul threw a spear, then Benson shot the Dweller whose attention was fixed on trying to get out of the way.

Warriors on both sides fell to the ground, writhing in pain or motionless as they returned to Xis. Then, the Dwellers' trained injri joined the fray, diving on Kexx and the rest of them, clawing at their faces and arms. One unfortunate creature made the mistake of targeting Mei, who quickly hacked off one of its wings with zer butchering knife, but not before it left three ragged claw marks across zer cheek.

"We have to keep moving," Benson shouted between short bursts from zer gun. "I can't hold them back forever."

"Warriors wait for us on the other side of the bridge," Kexx shouted back. "We will be attacked on two sides."

"I can hold them on the bridge while you deal with the scouts." Benson wiped sweat off zer forehead with an arm. "They can't come at me more than a handful at a time."

Kexx nodded and turned back for the enormous black rock slab. But something at the top of the canyon's far side caught zer eye. Figures, fullhands of them, too far away to make out in any detail, stood at the top of the cliff.

"Benson!" Kexx shouted, then pointed at the cliff. The human detective spotted the figures and whirled zer gun around, peering through the small far-seeing tube perched on its top. Ze pulled back in disbelief, then looked again.

"It's Tuko," Benson said. "And hundreds of other warriors armed to the teeth. They're already starting down the cliff."

A thrilling jolt of hope surged through Kexx's body. Tuko must've rallied the rest of the villages on the road network. Kexx couldn't believe they'd gotten here so fast. They must've run dozens of dux'ah through the night to catch up so quickly.

They were not alone. The Dweller warriors on the other side of the bridge would be cornered on both sides as well. Now all they had to do was survive long enough for Tuko and zer forces to climb down the cliffs. Kexx saw the Black Bridge, remembered a strange, almost unbelievable conversation ze'd had with the human days before, and knew ze could save them all.

"Benson!" ze yelled across the battle. "Can your ship's light-spear destroy the bridge?"

Benson looked over zer shoulder. In a glorious moment of understanding, zer eyes grew huge and zer mouth erupted in a wide, carnivorous grin.

"Why yes. Yes it can."

CHAPTER THIRTY-SIX

Should've come up with it myself, Benson thought. As big and impressive as the Black Bridge was, the Ark's navigational lasers had been designed to knock around dino-killer sized asteroids like billiard balls. They'd slice through it like a hot knife through margarine. Now all he needed to do was convince whoever was in charge up there to pull the trigger, and make sure everyone down here was on the other side of the bridge when the hammer came down.

They continued their leapfrogging retreat toward the bridge. Sprint, stop, turn, fire, repeat. Even through the sweat, blood, and screams, Benson couldn't help but be impressed. Outnumbered ten, maybe fifteen to one, his people weren't cracking. They'd never trained together, hell, hadn't met one another before a handful of days ago. Yet here they were, fighting and moving together. Not with the rigidness of military precision, but organically, like a school of fish cutting through the water. Gaps closed almost as soon as they appeared. Everyone kept pace, taking their turns to stop and throw back whatever they could pick up at their pursuers. Nobody broke ranks to run for the bridge by themselves. They were learning and adapting at an incredible rate.

Unfortunately, so were the Dwellers. Their initial shock and fear at Benson's rifle faded. They grew bold, tested the perimeter. Benson had lost count of how many of them he'd already dropped, but they simply didn't care. They'd just pick up the fallen's spear and step over the body.

"Kexx," he shouted. "I need to reload. I'm running ahead to the bridge to get set."

"Go," Kexx yelled back. "Kuul," ze pointed at Benson and yelled something in Atlantian. Kuul flashed acknowledgment, then dropped alongside Benson, grabbed his shoulder, and started to run. Even exhausted, Benson easily outpaced the warrior in a sprint. Their omnidirectional joints were great for climbing, grappling, and a hundred other uses, but it made them unstable in a run. By the time Benson reached the middle of the bridge, Kuul was already thirty meters behind him.

Benson dropped to a knee and checked his magazine count. Three rounds left. He put the rifle up to his shoulder, cranked up the scope magnification to max, and picked a target. Kneeling gave him a much more stable and accurate firing platform. He couldn't think of it as a person, even one that was trying to kill him. He imagined it as part of a movie.

Bang.

Two hundred meters away, the stuntman fell down on cue as the special effects guy triggered the exploding blood pack taped to the side of his head. Benson moved on to the next in line.

Bang.

Another perfectly acted death.

Bang.

And he was empty. Benson ripped the dry magazine off the top of the gun and let it clatter onto the black rock and over the side. Kuul reached him then and took up a guard position, zer crests flying high and flaring bright red and purple, screaming challenges.

Benson slapped a fresh magazine home, his last, and cycled the bolt closed with a *thunk*. He exhaled. The rest of the caravan's survivors caught up with them and flowed around him and Kuul like rocks in a stream. Benson caught sight of Mei and gave her a nod. She slapped him on the back as she passed.

That was when Benson realized he'd overlooked something *really* important. He could shoot, or talk into his link and coordinate with the Ark, but not both. He looked up at Kuul. There was nothing for it.

"Kuul," he said, handing the rifle up to the confused warrior.

"Cover me." He pointed at the rapidly-closing mob. Kuul didn't understand the words, but ze didn't need to. Ze dropped zer spear and took up the gun, shouldering it in as close an approximation of Benson's stance as zer arms could manage. Benson cranked the scope magnification back down to one power. No need to confuse the alien further. He set it to single fire to make the fifty-shot mag last as long as possible. Benson pointed into the reticule, then pointed at his eye. Kuul looked inside, found the glowing crosshairs, and nodded. After the shortest firearms training session in history, Kuul lined up the muzzle and fired.

The rifle bucked in zer hands, kicking back into zer shoulder and making zer flinch badly. But the warrior tightened up zer grip, put eye to glass, and fired again. Benson slapped zer on the shoulder and walked several paces away to call the Ark.

"Bryan?!" an excitable voice jumped out from the link.

"Chao?" Benson asked. "Why the hell are you on this line?"

"Ah, I'm sort of in command at the moment."

"You're *what*?"

"Well, Acting Captain Hitoshi tried to order your rifle relocked. I objected and ordered him to submit to a BILD scan. He refused. I arrested him. There was some fighting. I stunned some people. It's been a busy few minutes up here."

Despite the gunfire and spears filling the air like a swarm of hornets, or maybe because of them, Benson couldn't stop himself from laughing. Kuul was settling into zer groove as the bottleneck at the foot of the bridge forced their pursuers to approach no more than four abreast. With less than a dozen shots under zer belt, Kuul had already dropped a half dozen Dwellers. Ze was a quick study in death. The bodies piled up, creating a temporary fence that slowed them even more and gave Kuul more time to aim zer shots.

"Chao," Benson yelled into the link. "Listen carefully. I need you to warm up a nav laser and fire on this location, full power."

"What? That's insane."

"No time, Chao. Target this link and fire as soon as you can."

"But you're right there!"

A spear sailed centimeters from Benson's face, close enough to whistle as it passed. The Dwellers were spreading out across the cliff and trying to take them out from range. "Trust me, I won't be here for long."

"I'm going to have to testify before the Cultural Contamination Committee over this, aren't I?"

"Time is money, Chao!"

"OK, sixty seconds. Get your ass moving."

"I owe you one."

"You owe me several. Leave the link open."

Benson left the line active and locked the screen, then quickly dug through his pack to his first aid kit and ripped off four long strips of medical tape. He slapped the handheld onto the hot black stone of the bridge and taped each side down in turn. His head snapped up. "Kuul, we got to mo–"

Benson spotted a spear thrown from the right side of the bridge arc through the air in a perfect parabola, spinning as it flew. He tried to shout a warning, but it was too late. The spear found its target and plunged through the warrior's lower abdomen, shredding skin, muscle, and tendons as it burrowed through zer body before its tip erupted out of zer right hip.

Kuul fell, screaming in agony and fury, yet somehow managed to stay up on one knee. Ze didn't even drop the rifle. Emboldened by zer injury, the Dwellers that had held at the foot of the bridge pushed the bodies of their fallen comrades out of the way, sending them tumbling into the raging river below to open a path to the critically wounded Kuul.

"Oh no you don't, motherfuckers." Benson was on his feet in a second, running right for Kuul. He sidestepped one spear in flight, another. Then he was on top of the fallen warrior. He tried to grab the rifle, but Kuul's grip tightened on it. Ze jabbed a finger toward the other side of the bridge, telling Benson to run.

"Not happening." Benson grabbed Kuul's left arm and dragged zer up onto his broad shoulders into a fireman carry, the spear shaft in zer waist sticking almost a meter up into the air. Kuul shouted something angry, but Benson ignored zer. Ze was heavy, but still lighter than he'd expected an adult Atlantian to be. Benson actually managed a jog even under the awkward, unbalanced weight.

Even as they bounced across the bridge, Kuul, impaled and

groaning in pain, kept firing into the advancing Dwellers. Each step sent jolts of agony through zer wounded hip, but it only fueled zer rage. Benson ran straight ahead in disbelief as Kuul sent round after round downrange from zer perch on his shoulders. He saw a flash of the future. God help anyone who faced these lunatics once they were properly trained and equipped.

They passed his link taped to the bridge, and Benson said a little prayer to the universe that nobody kicked it off before the Ark sent a seven-hundred megawatt beam of coherent light down to vaporize the rock behind it. In space, the nav lasers could boil off enough mass from a ten kilometer asteroid to subtly nudge it into a safe orbit. Down here, against an object less than seven meters across, Benson expected the reaction to be quite a bit more energetic.

How many seconds had already burned away? Twenty? Thirty? He had no idea. If his plant was still active, he'd have set a countdown. It didn't matter. Knowing how much time was left wouldn't change the fact that all of his concerns and responsibilities in the world had shrunk down to running as fast as he could right now. On the other side of the bridge, Benson could see Kexx, Mei, and the rest of the warriors of the village network holding their own against a handful of the scouts they'd spotted on the way in. The rest of them must've moved off to the cliffs to engage Tuko's forces as they climbed down.

There was a chance this was going to work.

From his shoulders, Benson heard his rifle click. Kuul shouted out in frustration as ze threw the empty rifle over the bridge and spinning into the chasm.

It didn't matter.

Only running mattered.

CHAPTER THIRTY-SEVEN

"Let's move, people. Hut, hut, hut, or whatever you gorillas say on the field," Theresa yelled at the line of men and women forming up outside the station house's armory. She and Epstein were busy handing out rifles, magazines, and riot armor as fast as they could. Thirty had already answered her call to muster, and another thirty-five had already confirmed they were en route.

It was, without a doubt, they most shabbily assembled, inadequately trained, and undisciplined military force mankind had fielded in centuries. It was also the *only* military force mankind had fielded in centuries, and despite its undeniable shortcomings, it was already the most powerful unit anywhere on the planet.

A part of Theresa felt badly about that, felt guilt at the prospect of browbeating aliens with stones and spears into line with assault rifles. That part of her had been tied up and thrown in the basement the moment Feng told her Benson was alive and in trouble. She was going to rescue him, and God help anyone or anything who got in her way.

Their shuttle was already warming up, all they needed now was to fill it.

"Don't bother putting on your gear," she shouted. "Just get out to the airfield. It's still a three-hour flight. We can kit out once we're in the air."

An alert popped up in Theresa's field of vision. A call from Korolev. She connected it.

<Chief, I've got Gregory Alexander in custody. We're on our

way back to the station house now.>

<Did you have to stun him?>

<Actually, he had the same plant mod Hallstead did. He made me take a more… proactive approach to get the cuffs on him.>

<Pity,> Theresa said, not feeling any pity at all. <We'll just have to add resisting arrest and assaulting a constable to the charges.>

<Yes ma'am.>

<Get back here as soon as you can and get him in a cell. Let one of the rookies do the paperwork. I need you on the shuttle.>

<10-4, chief. Over and out.>

Theresa smiled. Yvonne Hallstead had done the smart thing and flipped on him before her ten minutes were up. Alexander had been the one to commission Hallstead to find an untraceable assassination tool, not to mention the hijacking of the stolen drones and satellites. Theresa was sure he wasn't alone, but her questions were going to have to wait until she returned from the rescue mission.

Alexander was just going to have to languish in a cell until she got back. Theresa found the thought didn't upset her very much. Her only regret was she hadn't been able to be the one to make the arrest.

They'd commandeered a dozen of the small electric carts to ferry bodies and equipment back and forth to the airstrip. Every other minute, an empty cart returned, was loaded up with as many people and weapons as would fit, then sped away, suspension sagging under the load of linebackers. They were travelling as light and fast as they could safely manage, just the clothes on their backs, armor, canteen, and a day's worth of dried rations. The shuttle would have some additional emergency supplies, especially medical, but this was a search and rescue mission that shouldn't last more than a day. Theresa wasn't going to have them putting up tents and occupying land.

The electric whine of a cart's motor quickly grew from the right before suddenly disappearing, replaced by the sound of synthetic rubber skidding to a stop against the pavement. Theresa glanced around Epstein to see what all the commotion was about. Sure enough, Acting Administrator Merick climbed out of the cart and pushed his way past the line of Theresa's waiting soldiers, shadowed closely by Lieutenant DeSanto who, she couldn't help but notice, carried a rifle at a low ready position.

"Where's Chief Benson?" he demanded of one of the Mustang's wide receivers.

"I'm right here, Merick. What can I do for you?"

"I've just received word that you ordered Mr Alexander arrested!"

"Yes," Theresa said evenly, "I did. He'll be here shortly to be booked into the jail."

"On what charge?"

"Two counts of conspiracy to commit murder, for starters. Then there's theft, dissemination of illegal software, resisting arrest, assaulting a constable, it's a growing list."

"Gregory Alexander is a pillar of this community. His reputation is beyond reproach. What evidence could you possibly have to justify these charges?"

"I'm sorry, administrator, but you are neither his legal consul nor the magistrate, so I'm not at liberty to share that information with you at this time."

"It's that prisoner, that Hallstead. Isn't it." It was not a question.

"I can neither confirm, nor deny–"

"I ordered you to extradite her to the Ark!"

"Yes, I remember, considering it was less than ten minutes ago. But she's since requested political asylum."

"Politi... That's crazy! The woman is an accused assassin."

"Yes, but she seems to think that her life would be in danger if she were extradited."

"Of course her life's in danger, she's facing the death penalty!" Merick was starting to visibly shake with anger. He was off balance, out of his element, and he wasn't handling the stress very well. Theresa decided to keep pushing.

"She seems to be afraid that they won't get around to the trial part before the penalty part. Nevertheless, I have a duty to protect everyone under my custody, so she's going to have to stay here until her request for asylum can be decided on."

"It's denied, obviously." Merick put his hands on his hips and puffed out what little chest was available to him.

Theresa smiled. "I'm sure that will be your vote. But seeing as the next council session isn't scheduled until Monday afternoon, we won't know the full decision until then. Besides, I heard there's some upheaval in Ark Command just now. Who knows if they even still want her extradited?"

"Upheaval? You mean mutiny! Chao Feng stunned Captain Hitoshi in front of the entire bridge crew!"

"It's my understanding Acting Captain Hitoshi was interfering with Constable Feng's investigation."

Merick stuck a finger in Theresa's face. "This was your plan all along, wasn't it?"

"I'm sure I don't know what you're talking about. Now, if you'll excuse me, we have a rescue mission to organize."

"The hell you do. The operation to Atlantis is cancelled."

Theresa's eyes hardened. "You just ordered me to launch it."

"Well now I'm ordering you to halt it. The situation in Atlantis has gotten much more complicated and–"

"No, it hasn't." It was Theresa's turn to interrupt. "It has gotten really simple. One of our people is under attack, and we're going to go rescue him. This conversation is over, Mr Administrator."

"You're damned right it is, because I've heard quite enough. You're relieved. Constable DeSanto, place Mrs Benson under arrest for refusing the lawful orders of her duly elected superiors."

The crowd of reservists surrounding the argument stopped milling about and stood very, unnervingly still. Several of them made a show of tightening their grips on their rifles, although muzzles remained pointed at the ground for the moment. DeSanto, feeling the crowd's energy, took his hands off his own rifle and let it hang from his shoulder by its sling, trying not to look confrontational.

"Ma'am," he said apologetically. "If you'll come with me?"

"They arrested my husband right before Kimura tried to nuke us, too. Remember how that almost turned out?"

"I'm sorry, but..."

Just then, Korolev walked up from behind DeSanto. "Pick your next move very carefully, Ricky," he said quietly as he stuck his stun-stick to DeSanto's neck.

"C'mon, man," DeSanto said looking over his shoulder. "I've

been given an order."

"A bullshit order. It's Bryan Benson, Ricky. He's saved all of our asses. He's saved your ass twice now. They lied about him being dead, and now they're lying to stop a rescue so they'll have another chance to finish the job."

"This is too big, Pavel. Guys like us just have to do what they're told or we end up making shit worse. We got rules."

"Rules these people aren't playing by," Theresa said. "It's my husband, Ricky. Just let me go save him."

"Lieutenant," Merick said. "If you don't obey my order right now, you will be charged right along with her."

DeSanto's face twisted as he chewed over his options, none of them good. Finally, he arrived at one, carefully reached up with one hand, unsnapped his rifle from its sling, and set it on the ground. "Administrator, I regret to inform you that I have decided to resign, effective immediately."

All eyes turned to Merick, who took a big step backwards under the sudden pressure. "This is a revolt," he said angrily.

"Oh no, it's all by the book," Theresa said, shooting a smirk at Korolev.

"This isn't over, chief constable."

Theresa took a big stride forward and put a finger into Merick's chest. "That's the first thing you've gotten right since you pulled up. This isn't over, not by a long shot. I'm going to go retrieve my husband. When I get back, I'm going to have a few questions for Mr Alexander and Captain Hitoshi. And when I'm done with them, I imagine I'll have some questions for you, too. Like, what panicked you in the middle of our call before you came here just now? And why did it seem to coincide with Bryan breaking radio silence? And why was your first impulse to come here and cancel his rescue?" She straightened her back and crossed her arms. "I'm sure you'll have some very entertaining answers for me."

"You're insane," Merick half whispered.

Theresa leaned to talk into Merick's ear, matching his volume and pitch. "Count on it."

Merick half ran, half stumbled back to the cart, then peeled off in the direction of the Beehive. For a moment, everyone stood dumbfounded, staring blankly at each other trying to figure out what had happened.

"Well," DeSanto broke the silence. "Guess I'm out of a job."

"Did anyone hear Constable DeSanto resign?" Theresa asked the crowd, and was immediately answered by a chorus of "No"s and shaking heads.

DeSanto smiled. "Thanks guys, but the administrator heard it loud and clear."

"Oh, I wouldn't worry about that," Korolev handed him his rifle back. "I don't think the good administrator will be in a position to accept your resignation for very long."

"And he's got more pressing concerns on his mind," Theresa said as she watched the cart speed off down the street. She turned to the line of reservists. "Well? Don't just stand there like a bunch of cattle. Get on the damned shuttle, we have a rescue mission to fly!"

CHAPTER THIRTY-EIGHT

Kexx stole a look back at the bridge just as Benson scooped up Kuul and started running back toward what remained of the caravan on the other side. Kuul, ever the consummate warrior, continued firing from Benson's shoulders. Kexx wasn't the only one to notice. The frenetic pace of shouting and clanging spears slowed as every pair of eyes on both sides watched the two of them run and fight as a single animal. Even their pursuers stood on the far end of the bridge, transfixed, their chase momentarily forgotten.

Then, the thunder from the gun ceased, bringing an eerie stillness to the scene. With a shout, Kuul chucked the gun into the canyon. The spell broken, the dwellers realized the threat of the gun had evaporated. There was now nothing stopping them from charging over the bridge and wiping out every last member of the caravan in short order.

They needed more time. Ze'd have to improvise.

Kexx grabbed up a discarded spear in each hand and ran back for the bridge. Benson saw zer coming. "Kexx, what the hell are you doing?!"

"I'm stalling them. Go!" Kexx ran past the human and Kuul without slowing until ze could see the pupils of the charging horde. Ze skidded to a stop and crossed zer spears.

"In Varr's name, I command you to stop!"

Admittedly, it had already been a pretty weird day for everyone. The Dwellers had all seen their first humans, many of them saw their first gun. And now a solitary truth-digger armed

349

with only a pair of spears and righteous indignation had elected to face down a charging army.

It proved to be a little much.

The pursuers ground to a halt, forming a battle line six bodies across, spears out and pointed less than an arm span from Kexx's head. Yet they did not strike, more out of curiosity for what the crazy person was going to do next than any actual sense of intimidation.

"We stopped, truth-digger," the leader taunted. It was only then that Kexx noticed the bound leg. It was the first time ze'd seen the Dweller elder in the light. "What's next? Are you going to dance for us?"

The mass of warriors laughed behind their elder.

"You have broken your oaths," Kexx said, trying to keep zer growing terror out of zer voice and off zer skin. Ze needed to project absolute confidence. "You have attacked a truth-digger before zer accusations have been resolved. Did you honestly believe there would be no retribution from the gods? Has your faith fallen so far living in the dark?"

The elder, still nameless, looked back at zer fighters growing impatient for blood. "Looks like the retribution will be ours, Cuut spawn. But please, you live in the light. So *enlighten* us."

"Kexx!" Benson called from the opposite side of the bridge. "Get the fuck out of there!"

It was time, then. "Your sins have been weighed in the names of Xis, Cuut, and Varr, and now their judgment falls upon you!" Kexx uncrossed zer arms, raised zer spears high into the air, then brought their obsidian points crashing down into the black stone of the bridge, shattering them with a crack and sending the shards flying in every direction.

And that was it. Nothing else happened. Suddenly, Kexx found zerself staring down fullhands of warriors with nothing but a pair of overly long sticks. The elder warrior laughed, long and hard. The rest of the horde joined zer. "That *was* impressive, truth-digger. But I think I can do better." The elder reversed zer grip on zer spear and hauled it back, preparing to plunge it into Kexx's forehead. Then, without warning or explanation, everyone on the bridge was cast in a bright red light. Their skin tone changed, washed out until they were all glowing like the setting sun. Everywhere the light touched, their skin felt warm, like a sunburn. The elder warrior paused in mid strike to look at Kexx in alarm. "What's happening? How are you doing this?"

Kexx looked back at Benson. "What's going on?" ze shouted in the human tongue.

"It's a low power range-finding laser. They're adjusting for atmospheric distortions!"

"What does that mean?" Kexx asked in a panic.

"It means get off the fucking bridge, you idiot!"

The red light vanished as suddenly as it had appeared. Everyone on the bridge sighed in relief. Everyone except Kexx, who dropped zer broken spears, pointed to the far side of the canyon, and started scrambling as fast as zer weary legs could carry zer. "Go back!" ze implored the Dwellers still standing about. "Return to your city!"

A few of them followed zer advice and ran for the opposite end of the bridge. Many stood around dumbly, hoping in vain for clarity. But the warrior elder would not be denied.

"Stop, coward!" ze bellowed, shambling forward as quickly as zer injured leg would allow. "No more tricks. Face me like aaaAAAAHHHHHH!"

The shriek quickly changed in tone from one of anger, to panic, to fathomless pain before dissolving into a sizzling noise as the elder's body disintegrated into smoke and ash. The walls of the canyon and onlookers on the far side of the bridge were washed out in white light, brighter than the midday sun. The skin on Kexx's back, shoulders, arms, and legs felt like ze was facing away from a wildfire.

Then, it got worse. Behind Kexx, the rock wasn't melting. The amount of energy being transferred was too devastating. Instead, the bridge boiled away directly into a scalding cloud of expanding gas. Around the perimeter of the armspan-wide circle of light pouring into the black stone, rock chips shattered and flew in every direction like tiny daggers, piercing Kexx's skin in a fullhand places, yet barely distinguishable from the burn ze already felt.

A voice in zer head, growing in strength, demanded that ze drop and curl into a ball, but ze ignored it and channeled the terror into zer legs. The bridge let out a deafening *crack*, then

groaned under zer feet, violently shifting to one side so quickly
that Kexx nearly fell flat on zer face. Kexx threw out zer hands
to catch zer fall, then scrambled on all fours even as the angle of
the stone underneath zer sagged alarmingly fast. The single span
of rock had been split in two by the light spear's assault.

"Get up, Kexx!" Benson shouted. "The bridge is collapsing!"

No shit, Kexx shouted internally as ze regained zer balance and
leaped forward. Benson stood right at the foot of the bridge, an
outstretched hand promising salvation if Kexx could only reach
it. The light and heat disappeared, but the burning on Kexx's
flesh remained. *Later*, ze thought, *just move*. Ze dug deep, ignoring
the fire in zer muscles and tapping whatever tiny reserves of
strength and energy ze had remaining, then surpassing them.
Kexx surged forward like a flash flood, eating up the last few
armspans between zer and safety.

Then the bridge fell away entirely. Kexx jumped, pushing
off from the mass of falling black rock with all of zer power.
For a long, glorious moment, ze was just... floating, as though
ze'd been transported back to a childhood summer spent fishing
in the ocean. No feeling of weight pressed down on zer feet or
bones. It was, Kexx thought, a lovely final sensation for zer
return to Xis. Maybe it was a small mercy Xis was affording zer
for a life well lived. It was a pleasant thought.

And then something made of rock snatched Kexx's wrist out
of the air, crushing down on it like the jaws of an ulik. Kexx
stopped floating, and started dangling over the chasm. Ze looked
up and into Benson's waiting eyes.

"Gotcha," the human said.

Kexx looked back down just in time to see the two halves
of the Black Bridge, along with the tumbling bodies of those
Dweller warriors who'd stood their ground, plunge into the river
with an enormous splash of water and foam.

"We did it, Kexx," Benson said, zer smile bisecting zer face
as ze clamped down on Kexx's wrist with zer other hand. Kexx
realized Benson was not alone. Another fullhand of hands held
onto zer clothes, keeping them both from falling.

"Yes, we did, Benson. Now can you *fucking pull me up*, please?"

•••

By the time the Dwellers on the other side of the canyon had regrouped and their shock at the devastation had begun to fade, Tuko and the rest of zer force had made their way down the cliffs, easily dispatching the few scouts foolhardy enough to engage them.

The two armies stood on opposite sides of the chasm, throwing rocks and taunts, spoiling for a fight but lacking the physical proximity to have one. Kexx lay face down to avoid aggravating the burns on zer back, flanked by Kuul lying on zer side worrying after the spear in zer waist, and Benson standing between them, doing whatever ze could to make the two of them comfortable.

Then, in the distant air, Kexx heard an eerie whine, one ze'd only heard once before. It wasn't long before the humans' great bird circled overhead, held aloft on four powerful hurricanes. It picked a flat, open spot on Kexx's side of the canyon to settle down, then disgorged *seven fullhands* of humans holding guns.

Suddenly, everyone's enthusiasm for fighting faded.

"Wait here," Benson said as soon as the great bird touched down. "I'll bring help."

Kuul asked Kexx to translate, then laughed when ze heard what Benson had said and grasped at the spear shaft still sticking out of zer hip. Kexx laughed right along with zer.

"What did he say?" Benson asked.

"He said, 'We're not going anywhere, deadskin,'" Kexx said, chuckling.

"Oh. Right, of course not. I'm getting help."

"Can't wait."

Benson and Mei ran off to welcome their tribe members, leaving Kexx and Kuul alone.

"I was wrong," Kuul said quietly.

"Yes, I know," Kexx said sarcastically. "What about this time?"

"I'm trying to say something important, truth-digger. Don't mock me."

"I'm sorry," Kexx soothed. "What do you mean?"

"I was wrong about the humans. They are ignorant, but strong, and honest, and brave. We should trust them."

"I don't know about all of them," Kexx said. "But I know we can trust at least two of them, and that's a start."

"I dishonored myself that night I took Benson's gun," Kuul continued. "I hoped ze would die. Expected ze would, because without it, I thought ze was weak. But then ze saved me *with my own spear*. And today ze handed the gun to me, trusted me with it to defend us both. Who does that?"

"Was ze wrong, Kuul? You did fight for Benson, and Benson fought for us. And together, we won."

"We did, didn't we?" Kuul let zer head roll back to rest on the hard packed dirt. "It was a good day."

"That it was." Kexx experimented with resting zer head on zer hands, which were not as badly burnt as the rest of zer arms and back. Ze watched with a distant sort of interest as four human figures ran toward them from the great bird. Two of them were Benson and Mei; the others, Kexx didn't recognize, but one of them stayed very close to Benson. Ze was shorter than Benson, but not as short as Mei, yet shared more in build and figure with the smaller human. Ze was svelte and moved with less stiffness than Benson, despite being thicker in certain areas. Long, straight hair adorned zer scalp.

The fourth human was hunched over, burdened by a pair of large sacks with the same white circle and red crossed lines Kexx had seen before when Mei pulled Benson back from returning to wherever it was humans went after death. A healer, then.

Benson stopped just short of where Kexx and Kuul lay. "Kexx, Kuul, this is my, er, mate, Theresa." Ze held a hand toward the truth-digger before moving on to the recumbent warrior. "Esa, this is Kexx and Kuul. These are my new friends. They saved my life."

"*Our* new friends," Theresa corrected. Ze leaned down and took Kexx's hand. Zer palm was soft, yet firm, conveying the urgency present on zer face. "Thank you, Kexx. I won't forget it. And you, Kuul."

Kexx translated. Kuul made a small flourish with zer arm. Theresa stood back up, looked sternly at the healer, and pointed at the pair of them. "These two get whatever they need. Do you understand me?"

The human healer went to work on their injuries, applying a generous amount of antiseptic to Kexx's burns, cooling them immediately and bringing immense relief. Then, ze moved on to the spear in Kuul's side.

Kuul allowed the human to help zer without interference or complaint. It was the third miracle Kexx had seen in as many days.

CHAPTER THIRTY-NINE

The trip back from the Dwellers' city to Kexx's village was considerably shorter than the six-day march Theresa's husband and his new partner had endured to get there. Once everyone was secured in the shuttle, the flight took less than an hour.

"You don't look as nervous as I expected you to." Theresa squeezed Benson's wrist as the shuttle began its descent.

"I'm much too tired to care about flying."

Theresa giggled. "I'll bet. Some of our new friends don't look so good, however." She looked over her shoulder to the row of surviving Atlantians, each a little too big for the human-sized chairs they were strapped into. She'd only seen her first alien in person less than a day ago, but even she could tell from their pale skin and wide eyes that they weren't terribly happy.

"Can you blame them," Benson asked. "They're the first Atlantians to fly. Ever. I'd be shitting myself."

"Are we sure they aren't?"

"Trust me, that's not a smell you can overlook, or forget."

Theresa wrinkled her nose. "Thanks for that tidbit."

"You asked."

"I suppose I did." Theresa sighed as the seat harness pressed into her chest as the shuttle decelerated, transitioning to hover mode. They'd arrived, but wouldn't be sticking around for dinner. As soon as the Atlantian survivors of the Battle of the Black Bridge were offloaded and their goodbyes said, they'd be dusting off and headed back to Shambhala.

There was another fight to finish back home.

The warrior called Kuul was still strapped into a stretcher, owing to the spear that had traveled all the way through his hip preventing him from walking under his own power. Benson and Kexx insisted on being the ones to carry him back into the village. Typical Bryan, making new friends almost as easily as he made new enemies. People always ended up with strong opinions about him, in one direction or the other.

After making sure the survivors were settled and leaving some fresh supplies and replacement equipment for the Unbound encampment, they turned for home. Even fighting against prevailing winds, the flight would take less than three hours.

Theresa'd left Shambhala only twelve hours earlier with her shuttleful of greenhorn soldiers. Now she was returning to the city with humanity's favorite hero returned from the dead to confront two of the most powerful men alive. She distracted Bryan during the ascent phase of the flight by bringing him up to speed with the investigation on her end, Hallstead's confession, Alexander's arrest, Merick's attempted interference. Bryan listened intently, glad for something to focus on. By the end of her debrief, his eyes were drooping.

A call routed through the shuttle's com system and into her plant. It was Feng on the Ark.

<Go ahead, Chao.>

<Theresa, everything all right down there?>

<Down here? I'm fifteen thousand meters in the air.>

<And I'm forty-five thousand *kilometers* in the air.>

She smirked. <Yes, of course. All about perspective. We're fine here. Bryan is, miraculously, unharmed apart from some scrapes, bruises, and a nasty sunburn from that laser of yours.>

<I'm glad. That was an insane call to make.>

Theresa looked over at her sleeping husband and shook her head. <You're talking about a man who disarmed a nuke by shooting it.>

<True.>

<What's the story up there?>

<Things have calmed down a bit. There's still some argument among the Command staff if I had jurisdiction to arrest Hitoshi, but nobody wanted to challenge me on it in the end.>

<Have you put him through a BILD scan yet?> Theresa asked, referring to a method of direct imaging system that had replaced the polygraph but was only legal for use on crew members because of the obvious privacy concerns.

<I have,> Feng confirmed. <And you're going to love what I have to tell you.>

Theresa reclined her seat the miserly fraction it would allow, and settled in to listen in on the most rewarding gossip she'd ever heard. Much to Theresa's surprise, Bryan actually slept for most of the flight.

They landed on Shambhala's rough and tumble runway a few hours later. Theresa shook her husband awake.

"Rise and shine, sleeping beauty," she taunted. "We're home."

His eyes fluttered open, then looked out the artificial window to familiar surroundings. It was just before dusk. "I fell asleep?" He wiped a bit of drool on his shirt sleeve.

"And stayed asleep through the whole flight, descent, and the landing."

"I don't believe it."

"Believe it, and wake up, unless you want to miss Gregory Alexander's interrogation?"

That woke him up for real.

"That's what I thought." Theresa unbuckled her harness. "Let's go."

They grabbed a cart and Lindqvist and made tracks for the station house. She'd left Korolev in charge while she'd gone. He'd fought to be included in the rescue mission, but someone needed to keep watch over their prisoners, and Theresa simply didn't trust anyone but herself or Korolev to do the job.

Gregory Alexander was waiting for them inside, sitting in the same interrogation room Hallstead had occupied that morning, hands cuffed to the uncomfortable metal chair. His bespoke synthetic spidersilk suit was a bit worse for wear from his apprehension, with dirt on the knees and elbows, and even a ripped seam on the left shoulder. The man himself was in a similar state, his normally perfectly groomed and coiffed hair gone wild, his cheeks red, and his ample face sullen. He also had a rather impressive shiner over his left eye, and a slight swelling on his jawline. Mementos of a very brief fight with Korolev as he was taken into custody.

"Greg," Bryan said as he slid into the chair behind the L-shaped desk. "You look like shit."

"Thanks to the brutality and unprofessionalism of your constables. You'll answer for that, and the rest of this farce." He held his head high as he said the words, but even as he said them, they lacked a certain conviction.

"Oh, they're not my constables, Greg. They're hers."

Theresa took her seat directly in front of the prisoner. "Yes, they are. And Constable Korolev wouldn't have needed to get physical with you if you hadn't used an illegal plant mod to disable his stun-stick function. Why might someone want to do that, I wonder?"

"Fear of a fascist police force trampling our civil rights, for starters."

"Of course. Nevermind your earlier enthusiasm for drastically expanding both the size and combat power of exactly that police force," Theresa said.

"Thanks, by the way," Benson added. "They came in very handy."

"I'll save us all some time and cut right to it, Mr Alexander. Your associate, Yvonne Hallstead, has flipped on you."

"Never heard of her," he said reflexively.

"No?" Theresa stood up and flipped a switch next to the mirror that made up the back wall. It turned transparent, showing Hallstead sitting cuffed to a chair and under guard in the next room. She looked up and immediately made eye contact with Alexander.

It was not a pleasant look.

"She seems to know you," Theresa said.

"Everyone knows me."

"She worked for you. We have records of Alexander Custom Buildings hiring her to do app development."

Alexander snorted at this. "Everyone works for me, too. Or close to it. ACB employs a full sixth of the workforce down here, and again that many independent contractors. I can hardly be expected to keep track of everyone. That's why I have managers."

"So, one of your managers hired Ms Hallstead to develop illegal apps, one of which wound up inside your own head? Think a jury will believe that whopper?"

"This is ridicul–"

Theresa rolled right over his objection. "But that's not the only app she wrote, is it? Turns out she figured out a way exploit an old line of plant code to induce heart attacks. Heart attacks that killed Administrator Valmassoi, Captain Mahama, and, temporarily, a certain Zero Hero sitting to your right."

Her husband smiled and rapped his knuckles on his ribcage. "Didn't stick, in my case."

"This is simply absurd. I had nothing to do with her criminal behavior."

"Really?" Theresa said. "So you didn't work with then-First Officer Hitoshi to get Hallstead's security clearance reinstated after her dishonorable discharge, restoring her access to the plant's original source code?"

"Of course not!"

"Oh, just tell him, sweetie," Benson said.

"Tell me what?" Alexander shouted, his whole face turning red as his breathing quickened.

"Hitoshi's been arrested and subjected to a BILD scan. We know, Mr Alexander."

"From who? That traitor, Feng?"

"He's really come around," Theresa said. "Here's what I think happened, Mr Alexander. Tell me if I miss any high points. Over the course of the last few years, you've built up your own little independent reconnaissance system by paying Ms Hallstead there to hijack satellites and other colony assets like drones, rovers, and so forth. You discovered a fortune in precious metals, minerals, basically everything a new world industrialist could ask for in Atlantis. So you bribed people to change the data, replace the survey maps with fakes, and started building a network of coconspirators so that everything was in place once you were ready to cash in."

"I don't have to sit here and listen to this."

"Actually, sitting here and listening to this is all that you *can* do, presently. Anyway, you brought in Hitoshi when he was still first officer, promising him a cut and giving you access to the Ark's resources like the linguistics lab to work on the Dwellers' dialect. You brought in that little weasel Merick to handle things dirtside. And you even convinced a tribal chief that you were the voice of their god–"

"Xis," Benson added helpfully.

"Yes, thank you dear – and convinced them to start a war with the Atlantians living on the land you intended to strip-mine to either drive them off or wipe them out entirely."

"That last part is spectacularly narcissistic, by the way. Actual, legitimate god complex stuff."

"Do you have a shred of evidence for this incredibly detailed and vivid delusion, Constable Benson?" Alexander asked.

"I wasn't finished yet," Theresa said coolly. "But then, your timeline was upended by the discovery of the Unbound, alive and well–"

"Most of them, at any rate," Benson said.

"Honey, could you not for a minute?" Theresa said sweetly. "Alive and well living on Atlantis, forcing us to launch the first contact mission. But, like any savvy businessman, you saw opportunity in upheaval and threw together a plan to trigger your war between the natives by attacking our delegation, simultaneously eliminating the handful of people in positions of power who would oppose your land grab, installing your puppets in their place, and even priming public opinion for punitive measures against our new neighbors."

"It was a good plan," Benson said. "It would've worked, too, if only I'd been a little less difficult to kill. That's something like six legitimate tries people have made now. They keep coming up just a few millimeters short."

"We already have Hitoshi's confession, Mr Alexander. And now that we're fresh off the shuttle from Atlantis, we also have this." Theresa stood and opened the door. Korolev and another constable walked into the already crowded room, carrying a disabled quadcopter survey drone.

"And what is that supposed to be?"

"This," Theresa knocked on the carbon fiber fuselage, "is the hijacked drone you used to con the Dweller under chief. She–"

"Ze," Benson corrected.

"What?"

"Ze. Their genders are… they take getting used to."

"Whatever! *Zeee*… was none too happy when we explained what actually happened. Ze was only too eager to give this back so we can do a nice, deep, thorough forensic investigation of its drives. And I have a pretty good idea of what we're going to find."

"Son," her husband said, "you're in a whole reclamation vat of trouble."

"It'll be better for you if you just confess now before I have to confirm all this for myself," Theresa said. "And I *will* confirm it. Make no mistake." Theresa motioned for Korolev to take the drone back out, then returned to her seat. The seconds stretched out between them.

"Your choice, Mr Alexander. The last choice about your future you're ever going to make. Choose wisely."

The older man sighed heavily, signaling defeat. "You've got it almost entirely right, Chief Benson. Except for one detail. I was not the mastermind. That honor falls to Administrator Merick."

"Merick?" Bryan said. "That little shit couldn't find his ass if it was on fire in a dark room."

"That ability to make people underestimate him is one of his more cunning attributes. No, he had learned of the mineral and metal deposits. He was the one to have the maps altered originally."

"But he wasn't even a crew member," Theresa said. "How the hell would he know how to do that?"

"He recruited Hitoshi first. He then approached me with a proposition on how to acquire them."

"Which you only too gleefully accepted," Theresa said.

"Well of course," Alexander puffed back up a fraction. "Do you have any idea what those materials are worth, young lady? And I don't just mean monetarily."

"Then what do you mean?" Benson snapped.

"Time," Alexander said forcefully. "Those resources buy us the one thing money can't. More time. Mining them today, on the surface, saves us years off our development projections. Years we can use instead to build our new generation of ships faster, to return to space faster, to start developing the next wave of planets faster. The longer we sit here idle, the more time we give whoever destroyed Earth to adjust their aim and do it all over again."

"They don't know we're here," Theresa said. "We're taking great care with our radio signals to keep Gaia dark."

"Chief Benson, please. Don't be naïve. We announced our arrival in the system by detonating thousands of nuclear bombs. Our enemy are blackhole-spitting monsters. Do you really think anyone that technologically advanced won't figure out we're here just as soon as the gamma radiation spikes from our deceleration have the time to reach their homeworld, or one of their outposts? Don't be ridiculous. This was never going to be our home. It's a pit stop, nothing more. What Merick and Hitoshi and I did was for the good of the human race."

"With only the tangential benefit of making you fabulously wealthy in the process," Benson added. "Even if this is only a 'pit stop,' that doesn't give us the right to ransack the place and leave the natives for dead. How are we any better than the aliens who destroyed Earth in that scenario?"

"We're past morality, Mr Benson. This is about survival."

Benson's jaw clenched. Theresa had seen her husband angry before, but this was different. Colder.

"I saved the human race from a madman who believed we were monsters. Now I'm saving another race from a madman in a rush to confirm everything the first one believed about us. You disgust me."

"Bryan," Theresa stood and put a hand on his shoulder. "We're finished here. But we have to go round up Merick."

Benson flexed his fists a couple of times and tried to stare a hole straight through Gregory Alexander's head. But eventually, he relented. "Yes. Yes of course you're right."

"OK, let's go. He'll be here when we get back if you want to stare at him some more."

"No." Her husband shook his head. "I don't think I ever want to see him again."

They returned to the cart and, with Korolov and Lindqvist in tow, headed for the Beehive. On the way, a medical emergency alert popped up in Theresa's plant screen.

"Shit!"

"What's wrong," her husband asked.

"Med alert, Merick's office. He's coding. Floor it!"

Benson obliged, and within moments they were "racing" toward the Beehive at the cart's top speed of thirty kilometers an hour. But it was no use. By the time they reached Acting Administrator Merick's office, it was too late.

Merick had elected to save the good people of Shambhala the costs of a protracted and very public trial using his belt and a ceiling fan.

It was the only election he would ever win.

EPILOGUE

Three months passed.

Captain Hitoshi's courtmartial was a brief, if very public, spectacle. After being found guilty, the crew added him to the constellation of satellites he'd helped Merick and Alexander hijack by shoving him out an airlock without a suit.

He got off light.

Gregory Alexander was less fortunate. Dweller Under Chief Ryj and G'tel Chief Tuko jointly demanded that, to ease tensions and begin healing the wounds that the conspiracy caused, Alexander be sent to them to face Atlantian judgement.

After very little deliberation among Shambhala's leaders, he was extradited a week later. It was requested that, once his sentence was complete, he be returned to Shambhala to face up to his crimes against the colony, but no one was holding their breath.

Word came back through Mei, Atlantis's newly-appointed ambassador of the Earth in Exile Embassy, that the G'tel, the Dwellers, and representatives from the rest of the Free Atlantian Nations were ready for the first legitimate diplomatic meeting between all of Gaia's interested parties.

It was a four-day trip up the beanstalk. It was also the first time Benson had been a passenger in the "up" direction, but the first time Chief Tuko, Under Chief Ryj, and the two dozen representatives selected from each village on the road network, and even a shaman from one of the larger nomadic tribes, had been more than ten meters above the surface of their planet.

The first day of the ascent was... trying. But after the alternating waves of prayers, panic, and protests, their guests came to accept the danger was not as immediate as it first appeared and settled in for the rest of the journey, the first among their species to witness their planet from such an illuminating viewpoint.

Which was how Bryan Benson came to find himself floating inside the Can where he'd led the Two-Eighteen Mustangs to the Zero Championship all those long years before. A lifetime before, maybe two. It would always be his old sports stadium, where he'd spent thousands of hours sweating in training, experiencing the painful disappointment of a hard-fought loss, and the electric thrill of a crowd as he pulled out some last-second heroics that vaulted their favorite team to victory. He saw the stadium in those terms, visualizing the goal hoops suspended at the ends, the arrows flying through the air swift as birds, and the ball, always focused on the ball, ricocheting off arms, knees, and walls.

But like Benson himself, the Can had undergone some painful, yet ultimately necessary changes to keep with the times. It was no longer a place of recreation. Hopeful, energetic kids from Avalon and Shangri-La modules didn't come here any more waiting to get noticed by one of the Zero team scouts. Hell, Shangri-La had only recently been repressurized after the cataclysmic terrorist attack that had killed twenty thousand people and almost ended humanity forever. An attack Benson had only barely managed to survive three and a half years earlier. It had taken that long to ship enough nitrogen and O_2 back up the beanstalk.

Instead, after waiting almost two and a half centuries, the Can had finally fulfilled its ultimate design intention as a manufacturing and sub-assembly center. It was, after all, the largest pressurized, zero-G open volume anywhere aboard ship. Both crew members and VI assembly robots and gantries toiled away furiously on new satellites, early-warning telescopes, short-range inner-system shuttles, and much more.

If everything went to schedule, the elevator system would soon start ferrying payload and people beyond the Ark, all the way out to the Pathfinder probe that now acted as the anchor on the far side of the space elevator system, some fifteen thousand kilometers further up the line from where the Ark hung in geosynchronous orbit. From there, cargo didn't even need propellant to move deeper into the Tau Ceti system. All you had to do was wait for the appropriate moment in Gaia's orbit and just... let go. Angular momentum would do the rest. There were two other entire planets sitting at the etreme ends of the system's habitable zone just waiting to be explored and developed. The rest of the Tao Ceti system was about to open up to human and Atlantian alike.

"You look lost, Benson." Kexx floated up easily beside where Benson hung, looking out a portal. The Atlantians had trouble with the null gravity at first, but owing to their aquatic heritage, they quickly adapted. Within a handful of hours of gleeful, almost childlike play, they'd mastered how to aim for hand rails, angle off walls, and hit their targeted landing spots like professionals. Their visual/spatial centers worked in three dimensions naturally, like fish or birds. Benson felt a sudden itch to coach an all-Atlantian Zero team. It would have to wait.

"Not lost, Kexx. Not exactly. Just... displaced." Benson took a deep breath. "This place has changed from what I used to know. It meant something different to me before."

"Really?" Kexx looked longingly, desperately out of the small portal to the perfect jewel of a planet hanging in space below them. "I have no idea what that must feel like."

"Ah," Benson said. "So you've discovered sarcasm. Who taught you? Theresa, Feng? I know it wasn't Korolev. He's too much of a straight man."

"I managed by myself, thank you," Kexx said before falling silent once more. The truth-digger had suffered severe burns to zer back, shoulders, and limbs from the laser strike on the bridge. Still, zer skin had healed with superhuman speed, which was apparently normal speed for an Atlantian. Their regenerative ability was simply astounding. It had taken multiple surgeries, skin grafts, nanite treatments, and many months of recovery before Benson had looked like his old self after his fight with Kimura. But only three months after the Battle of the Black Bridge, Kuul was walking around on zer hip like nothing had happened. Chief Tuko's missing arm was already halfway to regrown, dangling as it did from zer side like a mismatched prosthesis.

But the survivors were not without their scars. Kexx in particular would bear reminders of Black Bridge for the rest of zer life. The burns on zer back had been deep. Deep enough to destroy the chromatophores and bioluminescent cells that gave zer skin its amazing glow and patterns. They did not regenerate. From then on, half of Kexx's body would be dead skin. Benson declined to acknowledge the obvious metaphor.

"What's different?" Kexx asked.

"Hmm?" Benson said, distracted by his thoughts.

"What is different about this place that makes you feel lost?"

Benson sighed. "We used to play here when I was a child. Actually, I used to play here when I was an adult, too. But then, I had to grow up for real."

"That's a hard thing," Kexx said solemnly. "Some of us believed we were grown, only to be thrown back into childhood."

Benson saw the look in his friend's eyes. Recognized it. Lamented it.

"You're no child, Kexx. And neither are the rest of your people."

Kexx smiled. "It's kind of you to say that. But look at where we are now." Ze held zer hands toward the portal framing Gaia. "We are the children. You are the elders."

"Hold that thought and follow me," Benson said as he pushed back from the small portal and grabbed a rail, pulling himself up and around the circumference of the Can.

"Where are we going, Benson?"

"You'll see, just trust me."

"I do." Kexx sighed. "Only Xis knows why."

Benson ignored the barb and flew almost a quarter of the way around the inside of the Can to a prominently marked hatch, which unsealed at his touch. On the other side of a longish tunnel, an opaque, perfect half-hemisphere awaited them.

"OK, we can't stay out here for very long because of the radiation, but there's something I want you to see."

Benson linked up with the simple controls inside the observation dome. In an instant, an electric current surged through the polymer structure of the dome, coaxing the molecules to turn in just such a way that light was allowed through. Suddenly, the black dome was a perfectly transparent crystal. Gaia hung above them. Kexx had already seen it, of course, through the small portals in the lift car, or on their "photorealistic" display screens, but nothing could compare to an unobstructed view.

With a force of will, Benson navigated the new plant interface still taking root in his frontal lobe. The one he'd been "born" with had been destroyed, shorted out and riddled with errors when Merick had tried to stop his heart. The new matrix was an upgrade, the first major overhaul of the plant wetware and OS in almost a hundred years. The bugs and backdoors that had allowed the cyber attack on his heart were closed, and both memory and processing speed were significantly enhanced.

But for now it was still weaving itself into his neural pathways. It would be months, maybe years before he achieved full integration, and it would never function at the same intuitive level his original plant had. Some scars were less obvious than others.

Still, Benson managed to link up the Ark's mainframe and route a streaming data feed to the transparent display in front of him and Kexx. Alongside Gaia, a window opened streaming real-time imaging from one of the constellation of GPS/com sats in low orbit around the planet. It showed surveillance telescope imaging of the surface down to meter resolution. Benson scrolled through coordinates until he found what he was looking for.

"See these branching lines?" He pointed at the holographic image of the planet's surface, Atlantis's surface. "That's your road network seen from orbit, Kexx. Your people built structures visible from space before we even showed up. That's incredible."

"That's nice of you to say, Benson, but–"

"And your signal towers," Benson continued, ignoring the objection. "You figured out how to use light to transmit information. We do the exact same thing up here with fiber optic cables. We move more data, but the idea is exactly the same. You were already on the path before we even left Earth, Kexx. The only difference between my people and yours is time. That's it."

Benson tried to read the emotions on his friend's face as ze looked down on zer world. Was it pride? Hope? Embarrassment? Awe? All of the above? It was probably unfair to expect any one clear thought to take precedent. There was a lot of territory to fight over inside Kexx's soul.

Instead, Benson closed the display and looked upon Gaia through the crystal clear observation dome, a perfect blue, lavender, and tan ball floating motionless in an ocean of black punctuated by starlight. He looked over at Kexx, staring wide-eyed and open mouthed like an overwhelmed child. He could relate. He'd never seen his home planet like this either. In truth, he didn't have one. This was as close as he would ever get.

"You asked me once if your world was big enough for all of us to share. But that's the wrong question. Gaia has been shrinking since the moment you started building your roads and signal towers. It was going to keep shrinking, but since we pulled into orbit, it's going to shrink a whole lot faster. We'll be on top of each other within a few generations. The truth is, it's already too small not to share."

"You really believe that, don't you?" Kexx asked earnestly. "Why? You sit on this incredible throne, with all the power in this world, but you don't want to use it. Why?"

Benson thought about the question for a long time, had been thinking about it since long before it was asked, really. "Because I gave my word a few years back to a confused woman who did all the wrong things for all the right reasons," he said finally. "Her name was Avalina da Silva, and she tried to kill all of us to save all of you."

"Why?" Kexx asked simply.

"Because she believed humans were inherently predatory. She thought we would take over your world and destroy you in the process. She thought we deserved our extinction."

"But you won't?" Kexx said. "Take over, I mean. Some of your leaders tried to do exactly that."

"I promised her I wouldn't let that happen." Benson gripped the railing tighter, fury coursing through his veins. Fury at Alexander, Hitoshi, and Merick for trying to prove da Silva right at the first available opportunity. Fury at da Silva and Kimura for almost being right. Fury at all of them for all sharing the belief that humanity hadn't learned a better way during its exile between the stars. His forearms started to burn from the tension. He relaxed. "I didn't let it happen. And I won't. Not so long as I'm breathing."

Kexx put a strange, boneless, slightly clammy hand on Benson's shoulder. He welcomed it. "I trust that is true," ze said. "And I'm not the only one. These talks, up here on your Ark, they've brought our people a new perspective. We're forging a trident, with G'tel, Dwellers, and Humans as its prongs. Three peoples, united into one weapon."

"Nice symbolism," Benson said. "Wouldn't have anything to do with the trident I used during the battle in your village, would it?"

Kexx shrugged. "It's a powerful image. Would be a shame to waste it." Kexx's eyes drifted around the rest of the observation dome, taking in the view of the Ark's giant spinning habitats before coming to rest on an object floating just off the elevator cable two kilometers further up.

"What's that?" Kexx asked.

Benson smiled and zoomed in on it with the display. Enlarged ten times, the display revealed the scaffolding of two emerging rings arranged around a central core. Something very early in the process of being born. Merely a skeleton, really.

"That," Benson said with pride, "is the future."

"A ship, like this Ark?"

"A ship, yes. But not like the Ark. Not like anything we've ever built before."

An alert dinged at the edge of Benson's vision. Another ritual ceremony was about to get underway down in Avalon module. Their attendance was not optional. "Ugh, c'mon, we're up."

"Ah, the sacrifice to Varr," Kexx said.

"I really don't like the sacrifices."

"This one will be different."

"Good," Benson said. "I'm sick of smelling like fish guts." There had been several sacrifice ceremonies over the last few days. The Atlantians had brought along mostly small, larval animals for the occasions, while the human delegation had opted for catfish, chickens still being quite expensive. The chicken Benson had called down to the surface, meanwhile, having survived its assassination attempt, had since found a comfortable niche in Kexx's village being venerated alongside the rover as a minor deity.

They left the dome behind, flew through the Can, and settled into a lift car that would take them down to the bottom floor of Avalon. During the drop, Benson noticed that here and there, light bulbs needed replacing on the axle running through the module. Not quite as many people around to swap them out, he supposed.

Stepping out onto the vast, slightly curved inner hull of the module, held in place by centrifugal force equal to one G, Benson actually found himself feeling the tiniest bit sick. He still didn't care all that much for the skies on Gaia, but now that his body had experienced real gravity, nothing else would feel quite right again. They walked down one of the old footpaths. The apple trees lining their way had grown a bit wild in the last few years, their leaves and blossoms left to clutter up the cobblestones just a bit longer than before. Not as many gardeners and arborists' around to sweep up after them, he guessed.

Soon, they reached the small park his plant had designated as the staging point for the ceremony. It was an open-air affair with benches on three sides, while the fourth was a sandy beach overlooking Avalon's large retaining lake. Benson had visited the spot many times, using it as a water stop on his morning runs around the module. Tuko was there, along with Kuul and old Chak, against zer better judgement, from the look on zer face.

Standing next to them was Miraculously-Still-Acting-Captain Feng, Ambassador Mei, and Theresa.

But most curious was who was absent. None of the other village reps were present, nor anyone from the Dweller camp. Benson sidled up alongside his wife and leaned in to whisper in her ear. "What's going on?"

"Don't ask me. I just go where I'm told."

A small pedestal with a familiar bowl was set up in the middle of the park. Tuko and Chak handled the spoken parts of the ceremony, and despite the fact his translation matrix was still shoddy, Benson managed to kneel down at the right parts this time. Then, it was time for the sacrifice. Tuko reached down to a wicker basket at the foot of the pedestal and returned with a blanket, something squirming inside.

A deep, cold dread clenched at Benson's chest. This wasn't the normal sacrificial ceremony. It was close, but subtly different. He'd seen it once before. He took to his feet and made two bounding strides for the bundle even as Tuko set it down in the bowl. Benson snatched it up and dug through the folds of cloth, dreading what he might find.

And then he found it. A small, wriggling baby Atlantian, its skin pulsing without pattern or rhythm, its tiny, tentacle fingers reaching up from the blanket, grasping for Benson's hand.

"No," he said firmly. "Absolutely not. I've already been through this with you people." Benson pointed a quaking finger at Chak. "With you in particular."

"Benson," Kexx interrupted. "Calm yourself."

"No, Kexx!" Benson snapped. "We are *not* sacrificing this baby."

"You're right," Kexx said.

"I am?" Benson said, his budding tirade cut short.

Kexx put a hand on Benson's wrist. "No. We are giving it to you."

"I'm sorry?"

Theresa stepped in. "You're what now?"

"This is the same infant that you saved from culling a month ago when you stayed Chak's hand. We know that you and your mate have not been able to have your own children. So, after much discussion, we have decided that since humans have sent Mei and her people to become part of our village, we will do the same. We give one of our own to join the family of humans in the home of the ones we trust the most. Ze will walk among you, learn from you, and one day become a bridge between our people. If you will honor us."

"I'm sorry?" Benson repeated dumbly, but Theresa had already snatched the baby up and started coddling it.

"Oh, Kexx, we say yes!" she said between coos.

"We do?" Benson asked.

"Yes. We do." There was no room for negotiation in her tone. "Ah, honey, look, she has her daddy's eyes."

Benson looked at the baby's large, yellow irises encircling pupils shaped like the number eight filled in. A glint of light reflected off the backs of them. "Does ze?"

"Good, it's settled then," Kexx said, then translated the news to the other assembled Atlantians, who greeted it with cheers.

"It is?" Benson was starting to feel lightheaded. Was there a hull breach? His new baby, er, something, turned zer head and smiled at him, then squirted a stream of water out of zer right ear.

"Is ze supposed to do that? Hello? What the hell are we supposed to feed zer?"

ACKNOWLEDGMENTS

Every author, every creative really, builds their house upon a foundation laid down by everyone who came before them. As an avid reader of sci-fi over the last twenty odd years, one of the most engaging and rewarding experiences I had was discovering new alien societies. Taken far beyond "Monsters of the Week," the best of them blended not only plausible, yet unique biology, but language, morality, technology, and culture, all perfectly blended into their environment.

As some astute readers and reviewers have already guessed, *The Ark* was not written initially as the beginning of a series. It was conceived as a standalone novel, and remained so until the third rewrite, at which point my agent wanted synopses for two more books so he could pitch it as a trilogy. A furious rewrite of the last couple chapters set the stage for *Trident's Forge* and anything that follows. As such, I was starting with a clean slate. I knew I wanted to write something very different from the locked-room mystery of *The Ark*. This novel would be more about adventure and exploration. With *Trident's Forge*, I had the unexpected opportunity to sit down and create my own alien race to add to the sci-fi canon. An opportunity I was eager to take.

For inspiration, I drew upon those aliens who had stirred my imagination in the past. The safety-obsessed Pierson's Puppeteers of Larry Niven's *Ringworld*. The enigmatic Pequeinios of Orson Scott Card's *Speaker for the Dead*. The telepathic pack-minds of the Tines from Vernor Vinge's *A Fire Upon the Deep* and *Children of the Sky*. And most recently, but perhaps most convincingly, the waterborne Ilmataran and consensus-building Sholen of James L Cambias's *A Darkling Sea*.

It is because of these captivating examples of race-building that I decided to make *Trident's Forge* a story of first contact. I set out to craft the Atlantians as much as a tribute to these authors, and countless others, as a challenge to myself. And while I'm far from convinced that they measure up to the above examples, I hope they are enjoyed, and that readers will tag along for the ride in future novels as I continue to explore their evolving culture and uneasy partnership with these strange, powerful, dangerous, yet wondrous creatures they call deadskins.

EXTRA
A new tale from
the Dead Earth

LAST LAUNCH

Our last day on Earth was the grey overcast of an approaching storm, which was appropriate.

"Don't make eye contact with them, Barbara." I put my hand on my wife's knee. "Don't do anything to provoke them."

Her head didn't turn away from the ruins of Clearwater, or the retched sea of humanity frothing just centimeters away from her face. A beer bottle filled with... an unmentionable substance, shattered against the window with a *Crack!* Barbara flinched and pulled away in shock.

"Can they get through?" she asked breathlessly.

"Don't worry, dear." I rapped a knuckle against the Class III ballistic window. "It'll take a lot more than a shit-filled Bud Light bottle to get into this car."

A resigned little sigh escaped from Barbara's lips. "I almost wish they could."

"Don't be a fatalist. We need to focus on getting through the next hour alive."

"Whatever you say, Maximillian."

I cringed. She only used my full name when she was cross, but there wasn't time for the little games that had been a hallmark of our marriage. Instead, I pressed the intercom button for the driver's compartment.

"Reggie?"

"Yes, Mr. Benson?" came the answer from the car's speakers. The fidelity was almost too good. Reggie sounded like he was sitting right next to me. I was really going to miss the car.

"Can we move any faster?"

"I'm trying, sir, but these refugees keep blocking the car."

"Persuade them."

Silence drew out on the intercom.

"Reggie?"

"Yes, sir. Of course."

Reggie gave the rabble in his path a blast from the pair of LRAD sound cannons built into the bumper. That had been a seventy-thousand dollar upgrade, but it proved to be a good investment as the crowd parted like the Red Sea. The Bentley surged forward on its four electric motors. As soon as they were clear of the deafening zone ahead of the car, the crowd turned ugly and lunged at the doors. But the Bentley had answers for them, too.

A huge, shirtless, heavily tattooed slab of beef in the rough outline of a man wrapped his fingers around the handle, and immediately regretted the decision. For his trouble, a hundred-thousand volts of rapidly-alternating current surged through his arm and down the rest of his body. He crumpled to the ground like a marionette with its strings cut.

I couldn't help but chuckle.

"That's funny to you?" Barbara barked.

"Not exactly. But you've got to admit it was impressive."

"These are people, Max. But it's like you don't even see them. They're desperate and terrified."

"We're all desperate and terrified, Barbara. The only thing separating us from them is I had the resources to do something about it."

She crossed her arms. "Resources you were born into. It's not like you earned them."

My patience for her faux-righteousness wore thin. "And that's somehow less noble than marrying into them?" Her mouth hung open in shocked fury, and for a moment I thought I'd regret the outburst, but she stayed silent.

"What do you want me to do, Barb? Take the time to look at all ten billion doomed people on this rock until I break? I'm sorry. But there's only fifty-thousand seats on that ship. That wasn't my call, okay? These people outside? I can't do anything for them. It's taken literally everything I have to keep us on this side of the glass. That's all the control I have left, so that's what I see."

She didn't argue. Instead, she gazed out the window at the blurred faces streaming by and sank deeper into her own budding survivor's guilt.

The risky car ride wouldn't have been necessary at all if it weren't for the No Fly Zone. The military had pulled back from the cities, but their drones still ruled the skies. After those Salafist idiots took out the Kuala Lumpur tether with a hijacked cargo plane, the U.N. shut down air traffic within a hundred miles of any of the tethers and launch sites in a hurry.

For not the first time, my hand absent-mindedly reached into my jacket pocket to rub the data disks tucked inside. I pulled them out, a pair of iridescent holographic memory disks little bigger than half-dollar coins encased in clear protective sleeves. They held our genomes, medical histories, and heredity going back ten generations. They were our Golden Tickets off the dying Earth.

I'd traded every last red cent of our vast family fortune on the contents of those two small disks, and I hadn't even blinked. Money was meaningless now. Tickets aboard the Ark were the only currency that had any real meaning anymore. More valuable than any coin, or piece of art, or bar of precious metal. The Ark represented the clearest line of delineation between the haves and the have-nots in the history of wealth. Yet the majority of humanity, even with mere months left to live, still fought over money like some instinctual cultural reflex they couldn't break free of.

The fools.

Maybe it had always been that way. Generals had always fought the last war. The same was true in business. Companies failed by chasing the last fad, instead of recognizing the next one. Or better yet, creating it. I'd seen the truth about money since I was a child. It was an illusion. A sleight of hand. With it, you could fool people into giving you what you really wanted. The only difference between the poor and the rich was the rich recognized real value. Still, I pitied them, but sentimentality wouldn't stop me from doing what must be done.

"Trouble coming up, Mr. Benson."

I couldn't see the windshield through the privacy screen, so instead I put the forward camera feed on the display. Some enterprising souls had set up a makeshift barricade of burned-out cars across the entrance to the Cortney Campbell Causeway. The swarms of refugees were thinner here, owing in no small measure to the motley crew of rednecks patrolling the barricade with automatic weapons.

Barbara grabbed my thigh and squeezed. "Max, they have machine guns."

"They've got squat. This car's rated up to Three Thirty-Eight Lapua."

"What does that even mean?"

"It's a type of bullet, dear. A big one. These hillbillies don't have anything bigger than a five point five—"

WHAM!

The car jumped three inches to the left with the force of the impact. At first, I was sure we'd hit an IED. The display automatically switched over to damage and threat assessment screens. The front passenger side drive motor was disabled, cutting the car's acceleration by a quarter, and braking by almost a third.

"Reggie, back up!" I shouted into the intercom as I hit the icon to deploy smoke canisters. The threat assessment software matched the acoustic signature of the attack not to a bomb, but to a Barrett fifty caliber BMG sniper rifle. Somebody's grandfather had passed down some heavy firepower. God bless America.

"What happened?" Barbara shrieked as Reggie floored it into reverse, pressing us into our seatbelts.

"We were shot."

"I thought you said this car was safe against big bullets!"

"This one was bigger than that."

Outside, bullets danced across the hood, windshield, and roof like hail as the militia opened up with their assault rifles. The car slid back to rest behind the cover of a fallen billboard. The shot to the wheel had been intentionally placed to disable us. Any normal car, it would have carried straight through both front wheels, drive motors, and their battery packs without so much as slowing down. The reinforcements had been money well spent.

"Reggie, do you think you've got enough road to bust through that barricade?"

"I'm not sure, sir. Not with this wheel knocked out."

"Do your best."

"Wait," Barbara gripped my arm tight with fear. "We're not going back out there?"

"We don't have a choice. This is the only open route since the National Guard pulled out."

She stabbed a finger at the wrecked cars blocking the road. "But it's not open, Max. We'll crash."

"Reggie can handle it."

"But they're shooting at us!"

"Shut. Up. Barbara." I didn't mean to yell. I'd never shouted at her like that before, and I could see the words hit her like fists. She shrank back into her seat. I'd smooth it over later, when we were safe.

"Reggie, floor it."

The Bentley, all sixty-seven hundred pounds of it, took off like a scalded cat. Even wounded, it had acceleration that would be a match for many gas-powered sports cars of only a few decades ago. The lead hail continued to *tink* off the car's armored paneling as the hicks manning the barricade tried ineffectually to stop it. Soon, the expanding cloud of smoke churning out of the canisters I'd dropped enveloped them.

A second sniper bullet the size of my thumb slammed into the car. Fortunately, he'd misjudged our speed. Instead of hitting the rear right drive motor, the bullet passed harmlessly through the trunk. Although the damage it did to our luggage on its way through didn't bear thinking about at the moment.

One of the amateur-hour ambushers lost in the smoke met the Bentley's grill at seventy miles an hour. His broken body snapped off the hood ornament as it rolled over the top of the car before crashing back to the pavement behind us like a garbage-bag full of ground chuck.

"Brace yourselves." Reggie said calmly as the burned car shells filled the screen. On instinct, I threw my arms around Barbara and squeezed her tight just as the car smashed headlong into the barrier. With mighty *Thump* and a cascade of sparks, the gutted cars spun out of the way like dreidels. The Bentley shook like it had been struck by a wrecking ball, but coasted onward regardless.

"Yeah!" I pumped a triumphant fist in the air, almost punching the roof liner in the process. "Good work, Reggie."

"Thank you, sir."

"Think it'll buff out?"

"I doubt it, sir."

I leaned back in my chair and let the hot rush of adrenaline suffuse through my body. The causeway on the other side of the barricade was empty. Two lanes and ten miles of vacant road. With the worst behind us, the rest of the drive to Tampa International would be peaceful.

Everything was coming apart. Frost clung to the fronds of the palm trees lining the road. In July. In Florida. The black hole coming to destroy mankind was already making its presence felt by stretching Earth's orbit into an egg shape, wreaking havoc with everything from weather patterns to the tides and tripping off earthquakes and volcanism throughout the globe.

Between the unnaturally high tides and the damage we'd already done to the ice caps, Miami and the Kennedy Space Center were already underwater most of the time. Tampa fared a little better, which was why her commercial spaceport had been commandeered for the Ark project. The Earth's network of space elevators had been working overtime for decades to move the millions of tons of material needed to build the grand ship, leaving traditional, and more dangerous, chemical rockets to act as passenger ferries.

From the crest of the Cortney Campbell's first bridge, I could just make out the gleaming white nose cone of our salvation. I nudged Barb, who hugged her knees to her chest and gently swayed in her seat. She'd never been in a gunfight before. Then again, neither had I, but we all dealt with stress differently.

"Barb, honey. Look south." I pointed towards the rocket standing on its pad, taller than all but the biggest buildings in Tampa's skyline. "That's our cab. We've made it, baby."

She followed my finger and locked eyes with the rocket, burning like a beacon in the pre-dawn darkness.

"It's over?" She relaxed a bit and unfolded her legs. "We're safe?"

"Yes, the U.N. controls the other side of the bridge, and as soon as we reach the checkpoint, we... will..."

Something was wrong. The car was slowing down. I pulled up the diagnostic screen, afraid the damage was more serious than I first thought, but it still showed only the front right motor down.

I keyed the intercom. "Reggie, why are we stopping?"

Nothing.

"Reggie? Can you hear me?"

The Bentley came to a stop at the side of the road. With growing alarm, I reached for the button to roll down the privacy screen, but it came down before I touched it. A chill ran through my body as I saw an older woman sitting in the front passenger seat beside Reggie.

"Reggie," I said gently. "Why is your wife in the car?"

As an answer, Reggie turned around, rested a handgun on the dividing wall, and pointed the barrel at my left eye. My bullet-resistant suit wouldn't do much good against a point-blank headshot.

"I'm sorry about this, Mr. Benson, but we'll have your tickets now." The safety clicked off for emphasis. "Please."

It took my mind a few moments to accept what I was seeing. Reggie had been my driver for going on twenty years. He was my most trusted employee, and he was pointing a gun at me. I'd once heard a saying, 'Every dog is two missed meals away from being a wolf.' I never knew what it meant until that moment.

I eyed the button to raise the privacy screen, but it would take far too long to roll up. Funny, I'd spent a small fortune on armor to protect us from bad people with guns. It never once occurred to me that one of them would be inside the car.

"I can't give them to you."

"Then I'll have to take them off your body, sir."

"Reggie!" Barbara gasped. "What on earth are you doing?"

"Retiring," he said flatly. "Consider this my letter of resignation."

I put up my hands in a sign of submission. "They won't work for you, Reggie. I'm sorry."

"Oh don't give me that bullshit, Maximillian. I've worked for your family for thirty years. I know you better than your own parents did, God rest their souls. I strapped you into a car seat. I dropped you off your first day at Princeton, the day you took over your father's company. And I've been keeping your secrets the whole time, from your father, the police, your girlfriends." He waved the gun in Barbara's direction. "Even her."

"From me? What secrets is he talking about, Max?" Barbara turned and stared the accusation into the side of my face, but I didn't dare take my eyes off the muzzle of Reggie's gun.

"Can we maybe table this conversation for now, dear?"

Reggie didn't have time for our domestic squabble. "I'd threaten Mrs. Benson, but for that to work, you'd have to be capable of loving someone more than yourself, and I just don't think you have that in you, Maximillian. I'll count down from five. Five."

"I can give them to you, but they're coded for me and Barbara. They won't work for anyone else."

"Four."

"Use your head, Reggie." I struggled to keep my voice even and under control, not to let the desperation I felt creep in. So long as he believed I was in control, it didn't matter who was holding the gun. "You won't get past the first checkpoint."

"I know they're faked. So change them. Three."

"Faked? What does he mean, faked?" Barbara broke in.

"Not now," I said coldly before returning to Reggie. "The disks aren't fakes, Reggie. Our genome profiles were altered to get us through the screening process, but the disks are genuine. They have quantum guillotine encryption. If I so much as try to open the case without the right equipment, the entanglement breaks and they wipe themselves automatically. That's the point of the disks in the first place. They're physically impossible to tamper with."

"Three..." Reggie's voice wavered as his eyes started to mist over.

"Besides, the cut-off for the project was forty-five. You and

Mrs. Palmer couldn't possibly pass for that age. Not that you don't look lovely, Mrs. Palmer," I hurried to add.

"Two." Tears flowed freely down Reggie's checks now as his last, desperate plan fell apart before his eyes.

"C'mon, Reggie. You and Barbara are all the family I have left. If there had been any way, any way at all to save you and your wife, I would have. But I couldn't. If you do this, you're only going to be killing all four of us. There won't be anyone left to carry the legacy."

He finally broke down. The gun sagged in his hand as Reggie threw his arm around his wife and started sobbing. "I'm sorry. I'm so sorry. I didn't know what else to do."

"It's okay, Reg." I forced soothing tones into my voice, as if I was talking to a child. "I understand. You're scared, but it's going to be alright. Just, give me the gun and everything will be alright."

Reggie looked down at the black pistol in his hand as though he'd already forgotten it was there. Still clutching his wife, he turned it around and held it out to me butt first.

"I'm sorry, Mr. Benson."

I reached for the gun and slipped my hand into the grips. The plastic was still warm and slick with sweat. "I forgive you."

I pulled the trigger.

The world exploded with noise as the overpressure echoed through the confines of the car's interior, deafening me instantly. Reggie's head snapped back from the bullet impact, then slumped against Mrs. Palmer's arm. Before she had time to scream, I put one in her head too. It was all over in less than a second.

It wasn't something I thought about, it just had to be done. I would have to drive the rest of the way. I turned around to get Barbara to help with the bodies, but she'd gone white as a sheet. Her eyes fixated on the gun, hypnotized by it.

"Barbara." I reached out to touch her shoulder to try and snap her out of it, but she started screaming like a banshee and tried to crawl backwards up the seat. When that didn't work, she ripped at the door handle trying to get out, breaking two of her nails in the process. But the doors were locked.

"Get away from me!" she shouted loud enough that I could

hear it over the ringing in my ears.

I put the gun down on the floor and held up my hands. "Barbara, stop. I'm not going to hurt you."

"He gave up! He said he was sorry and you shot him!"

"I had to, honey. He didn't give me a choice. Now, we have to focus. We're running late already and we have to get to—"

"I'm not going anywhere with you. You're a killer!"

"Barbara!" I'd had enough, so I grabbed her shoulders and tried to shake some sense into the panicked little ingrate. "I didn't kill anyone. You see these two?" I pointed at the corpses hunched over in the front seats. "They're ghosts. They were already dead. Everyone who doesn't have a ticket is already dead. Like zombies, okay? Reggie figured it out, I don't know how, but he did. If I'd let him go, he might have told someone and we'd be caught and they wouldn't let us on. And in a couple of months, we'd be just as dead as the rest of the zombies."

"You're a monster."

"I can live with that, if it means we *live*. Now, we need to get the bodies out of the car so I can drive us the rest of the way. Will you help?"

"No." She shook her head gravely. "I won't help you."

"Fine, then just stay in the car." I grabbed the gun, then unlocked the door and got out into the chill of pre-dawn. With my old college baseball arm, I pitched the gun into Old Tampa Bay. It took me three tries to get Reggie's legs out from the foot well and past the steering wheel, and another three hard jerks to get his body out of the car. He hadn't taken much time in the gym over the last ten years and it showed. His head, already hollowed out from the gunshot, hit the pavement with the sound of a dropped cantaloupe. I could see my breath in the air as I strained to drag the body to the side of the road. His wife's body was much more accommodating by comparison. She'd been that way in life, too.

The driver's compartment was coated in blood and... other unmentionable substances. I selected some cotton shirts from the trunk that had already fallen victim to the sniper's bullet to use as rags. A few minutes later the interior was as clean as it was going to get, so I threw the shirts in the water and rinsed the blood off my hands as best I could, but it left stains on the cuffs of my shirt.

By the time I sat down in the driver's seat, Barbara had already closed the privacy screen, which was fine. It took me a minute to find the "START" button, then another to figure out how to put the car in drive, but we were moving again before long. As I brought the hobbled Bentley up to speed, it occurred to me that I hadn't driven a car for myself in years, not since I wrecked that 458 Italia racing in the classics series. This would be the last time I drove anything.

"So you just left them on the side of the road for the seagulls?"

The question startled me, as if the accusatory voice had come from the sky. Then I realized it was just Barbara talking through the intercom.

"I forgot to pack a shovel."

"You can joke right now? Don't you have any remorse at all?" With the immediate shock of the ambush, Reggie's betrayal, and my first double-homicide fading, her voice was drifting back towards normal.

"Maybe later I'll make time for it."

"You didn't have to shoot them. You could have made them promise not to tell."

"I'm sorry, you want me to trust our lives to a man who'd just pointed a gun at my head?"

"They weren't zombies, Max. They were living people. Your friends."

"You think I don't know that?"

"Obviously not!"

"What's Mrs. Palmer's first name?"

"I…"

"C'mon, Barb. You don't know? It's Irene. They have two nieces, Jennifer and Iris, and a godson named Chad. They were like grandparents to me, and they just tried to kill both of us. So don't sit there pretending like they were more 'real' to you, okay?"

"But, you didn't even hesitate. You just… killed them. They weren't even armed."

"Think, Barbara! Use that poli-sci degree and think this

through. Getting on that ship is all that matters. When that's done, then we can afford the privilege, the *luxury* of agonizing over what we had to do to get there."

The intercom fell silent, the privacy screen an opaque wall between us. Maybe that was a good thing. It was helping Barbara compartmentalize, literally and figuratively.

"It's not like I feel good about it," I said quietly.

"What *do* you feel?"

"Nothing. Resolve, if that's an emotion."

"You said our genomes were altered. What did you mean?"

I took a deep breath, bracing myself for the plunge. I'd managed to keep the truth from her through the whole process. It was just easier to keep her in the dark. One fewer mouth to let it slip. But Reggie had screwed that up, damn him.

"I rigged the lottery to get our spots."

"You *what*?"

"I paid people to purge our genome records of all the knockout disease markers, then bribed some key members of the selection committee. You didn't really think that we both just happened to make it through the selection process, did you? Do you know what the odds against that would have been? They're bottlenecking the human race from ten billion to fifty thousand people. We might be the only married couple to actually board the ship together."

"Are you saying we didn't earn our spots? That I'm stealing a spot from someone who deserves it?"

I snorted. "Deserves it? Christ, Barbara, people talk about the selection process like it's the fucking Rapture. But it's not God bringing the faithful home, it's a bunch of dweebs in lab coats and tweed jackets picking through mankind like they're breeding horses. You, my dear, do you know why you don't *deserve* to survive?"

"Why?" she asked in a small voice.

"Because you have the genetic markers for Addison's disease. There's a less than five percent chance our children might be born with it."

"Well that won't be a problem, because there's no way I'm having children with you."

"It's not me, it's you. The risk will be there no matter who you're with. But you'll have that choice, thanks to me."

"My fucking hero," she said viciously. "Cheater of the system and killer of the elderly."

"You can always get out of the car if your conscience can't take the strain. No really, I'll pull over right now."

The intercom fell silent again. *That's what I thought.* I managed not to say it aloud.

Poor Barbara. She was a sheltered little girl who fancied herself an activist right up to the moment she might have to make real sacrifices. Maybe I was being too harsh, but since the black hole arrived in the Oort Cloud eighty years ago, the world had become a very harsh place indeed.

Some idiot had named it Nibiru, after a rouge planet some New Age conspiracy twit had predicted would destroy the Earth more than a hundred years ago in the early days of the internet. She'd been wrong about the type of object, the century, basically everything, but they still wanted to treat her like some kind of fucking prophet. Humans would endure any amount of self-delusion if it meant they could continue to believe that somebody was in control or knew what the hell was going on. Too bad the Ark committee hadn't selectively eliminated *that* stupid trait.

"It's not right." Barbara rejoined the conversation. "What we're doing. It's not right."

I noticed the pronoun usage, but didn't mention it. "No, what's not 'right' is the way our family was treated since this whole thing started. Ninety-percent income tax to fund construction? 'Renting' the lion's share of our elevator slots at a third of the going market rate, crippling our business. Then when father complained, the government just nationalized the whole company. That damned ship wouldn't even exist if it wasn't for the heavy-lift capacity they stole from us, and they couldn't cough up waivers for two spots onboard? That isn't right."

"Ah, so you're just restoring some justice to the universe?"

"It's more than that."

"Why were you rejected?"

"Hmm?"

"You told me why I was rejected. Why were you? What was

your knockout marker?"

I squeezed the soft Napa leather of the steering wheel, the memory of reading the email still fresh. "My psych eval. The shrink said I 'exhibited evidence of oppositional defiant disorder,' and 'lacked empathy.'"

"Ah, so they said you don't respect authority. So to prove them wrong you went around and broke all their rules." She actually laughed. "You sure showed them, honey."

"No." I clenched a fist and pounded the steering wheel. "That's not it at all. Don't you see? They're not just selecting for diseases, they're trying to reshape humanity to fit some arbitrary ideal. They think we're going to live in a crime-free fucking hippie commune in the sky where everyone's a vegan and holds hands around a damned drum circle. They're trying to select initiative and individuality right out of us. Like, I don't know, a herd of cattle."

"You just executed two people you've known your entire life without batting an eye. 'Lacks empathy' would seem to be the least of your problems. Can you honestly tell me rejecting you was bad idea?"

"Of course it's a bad idea! They're trying to pick the 'right' people to build a whole new world. But they're using the wrong paradigm. They're picking artists and poets and grief counselors and yoga instructors, but they're entirely wrong for the job. Artists and poets are a *result* of civilization, a side-effect of stability and prosperity. They don't create it. You need explorers and entrepreneurs and leaders and soldiers. They stake out the land, they take the risks, they build the settlements and hunt the game. They make the hard calls that make the rest of it possible."

"Now I see," Barbara said, sarcasm dripping from every word. "You're not doing this to save your own skin. You're doing this for the betterment of the whole species. Who else can lead us poor little lambs but a big strong wolf? How philanthropic of you."

"Don't mock me, Barbara. The people they've got up there now? How many of them would have had the balls to take the risks I did to get here, or make the tough decisions, not because I enjoyed them, but because they had to be made? No, they have this shit completely backwards. They shouldn't have been sifting through us. They should have let us all fight it out and grabbed the winners."

"Sure, an entire starship filled with fifty-thousand testosterone-poisoned narcissists and sociopaths. What could go wrong?"

Another barricade approached as we reached the end of the causeway. But unlike the last one, this one was manned with professional soldiers wearing the light blue helmets of the UN, along with a pair of marines in heavy combat exoskeletons. As soon as they saw our headlights, their recoilless anti-material rifles snapped into the ready position.

"I'd love to keep this conversation going, dear, but the checkpoint is coming up. If you want to leave, I won't stop you. But now's the time."

She didn't respond.

"Okay, I'm going to take that as you're staying. But that means we can't breathe a word of this to anyone. Not ever. In fact, we probably shouldn't talk about it between ourselves in private. Who knows what kind of surveillance they've built into that ship?"

"Feeling a little paranoid, Maximillian?"

"Covering our bases. We're about to cross the Rubicon, Barb. I'm sorry to drop all this in your lap at the eleventh hour, but I have to know if you're in, or out?"

She sighed heavily. "In, God forgive me."

"I don't think God's hanging around here anymore, my love."

The UN soldiers manning the barricade signaled me to stop short of the gate. Glancing over at the enormous cannons the exos mounted, there didn't seem to be any reason to argue the point.

One of the uniformed soldiers walked purposefully up to my window. His sidearm remained in its holster, but his brothers had him well-covered. I rolled down my window to greet him. Look friendly. Look like I belonged there.

"Good morning, soldier."

"Will you please power down and exit the vehicle, hands where I can see them."

"I have a passenger in the back. Should she get out, too?"

He nodded. "Yes, sir."

I pushed the intercom. "They want us to step out of the car. It's okay, just follow their orders." I shut down the Bentley and stepped out, hands at my sides. Act like I'm in charge, but not condescending. Soldiers obey orders. They respect status.

"Nice car," the soldier said.

"It was," I said bitterly.

"The lady's credentials, please," he said curtly.

"Our disks are in my jacket pocket. I'm going to reach for them, if that's okay."

His face tweaked in confusion. "You're not her driver?"

"No, I'm her husband," I answered, but the soldier was already looking past me into the driver's compartment. He signaled for more troops to approach.

"There's blood in here."

"Our driver was killed in an ambush. I took over."

He knocked on the windshield. "Windows are intact, care to explain that?"

"Yes, the old fool rolled down his window and they shot him." I shrugged my shoulders and let my voice ratchet up a few decibels. "Look, private?"

"Sergeant Lantz, sir."

"My apologies, Sergeant. We've been through absolute hell to get here. I just saw a man I've known for thirty years get shot in the face. I don't want to be out in the open any longer than necessary. The disks in my pocket have everything you need."

Lantz stepped up as two other soldiers with rifles took up positions behind me.

"Left or right?" he asked.

"Sorry?"

"Left or right pocket?"

"Ah, inside left."

He grabbed the disks and gave them a cursory inspection. Satisfied for the moment, he handed them back to me and nodded to the two guards behind me. "Okay, Mister?"

"Benson," I said.

"If you and your wife will follow me, we'll escort you to the processing station."

"Thank you, Sergeant. Oh, and we have some luggage in the trunk that—"

He shook his head. "Your personal items have to be searched for contraband before they can be transferred to processing. We'll handle them from here."

I handed over my keys and walked away from the car, indeed, away from the last remnants of my old life. Barbara walked beside me, but said nothing. The silence was anything but companionable. I couldn't tell if the waves of cold I felt came from the bay, or her.

The soldiers led us into a staging area. The launch tower and rocket stack was still more than a mile away, but it already loomed large. Our candle was larger than the NASA Space Launch System that had taken the first humans to Mars. Today, it would take just under two hundred people up to the largest construct in history, and mankind's home for the next two centuries.

The next few minutes would determine whether or not we were among them. I'd done everything I could to ensure our survival, made huge, mind-boggling sacrifices, done things I didn't know I was capable of, and learned some things about myself that I wasn't comfortable knowing. Now, I just had to trust that everything had been done right. There was no one else to bribe. No one else to kill. Nothing more I could do to affect the outcome. All that remained were all the ways it could go wrong.

I'd never felt so helpless in my life.

"Just, be calm. Stay collected," I whispered to Barbara, pitching my voice low enough that our escorts couldn't eavesdrop. "There'll be plenty of time to break down later."

"Are you telling me, or yourself?" Her voice had taken on a hard edge, a reflection of the wall that had been built between us over the last half hour. I didn't know if I'd ever see the other side of it. I wasn't sure I cared.

"Just act like you belong here."

"I don't."

"Yes, you do. Maybe even more than me."

"No argument here."

I let it go. We arrived at a large tent shelter serving as a command post. A short queue stood off to one side. Under guard,

I couldn't help but notice.

"What's up with them?" I asked Sergeant Lantz conversationally.

"Stand-by passengers," he said. "If one of you doesn't turn up, they're the replacements."

"Does that happen a lot?"

"More than you'd think."

A couple of the men in line shouted angrily as we passed, but most of them just sat in resigned silence as two more chances for survival evaporated. A fresh worry shot through me. It was easier to justify taking someone's spot when it was an abstract concept. But, faced with living, breathing people? I looked over at Barbara, trying to gage if her guilt was about to make her do something stupid, but her face was a mask. She wasn't looking at the alternates. Maybe that was a good sign.

"Your disk, please."

I'd been so distracted, I hadn't noticed the bald man sitting at a table. He appeared all the shorter by the tall chair he sat in. Focus, Max. You belong here. No one will question it as long as you're confident.

"Of course." I offered the disk to him. He plugged it into a complicated device that looked like one of the eye-checkers at the DMV cross-bred with an espresso machine.

"Please look into the opening and place your right hand on the scanner."

I did so. Inside the little box there was a 3D picture of a small house.

"Focus on the house and try not to blink. There will be a flash in three..."

A white light like a camera flash burned into my retinas, leaving a glowing orb floating in my vision. At the same instant, something stabbed my middle finger. I pulled back from the scanner squinting and clutching my hand.

"Your fingerprint scanner stabbed me."

"I didn't say it was a fingerprint scanner," the humorless little man said dryly. An icon on his screen turned green. "Ah, here we are. Retina and DNA are both a match to the disk. Welcome aboard, Mr. Benson." He waved me through the turnstile deeper into the compound.

"Thanks, but I'd like to wait for my wife, if that's okay."

"Your wife?" The bald man took Barbara's disk and pulled up a passenger list. "Well, that's a first. Some people have all the luck, eh?"

"Yeah. Luck," she mumbled. My jaw tensed, but I forced myself to relax. Nothing to see here. The statistically improbable happened a million times a day. She repeated the process then stood back to wait for the results, shivering like a mouse in a snake cage.

"Nervous, Mrs. Benson?" The little man asked her with a cocked eyebrow.

"I should've brought a coat is all." Her answer sounded less than convincing. Not a great liar, my wife.

"We were in a firefight on the way over here," I hurried to add. "We're still pretty shaken up."

"I can imagine," he said. Which was funny; I doubted the diminutive twerp had any imagination to speak of. A yellow icon popped up on his screen. He adjusted his glasses. "Well, that's peculiar. Her retina scan is a match, but I'm seeing some discrepancies in the DNA profile."

"Discrepancies?" I managed to say it without my voice cracking like an adolescent.

"There's some small genome variance."

"Maybe there's contamination in the scanner. This isn't exactly a clean-room out here." I could feel my hands getting clammy with nervous sweat. I put them in my pockets, trying to look unconcerned.

"Maybe..."

Dread spread through my body like an electric shock, threatening to paralyze me where I stood. Somewhere along the line, somebody had fucked up. Our lives were in the hands of this paper-pushing pipsqueak, and it was all about to come flying apart. I wanted to scream, to run straight for the rocket, to grab Sergeant Lantz's sidearm and fight our way to freedom, or go down in a blaze of glory.

Instead, I stood there, silent and immobile as a statue. Impotent.

Barbara stepped up to the table and leaned a hand on it. "I had a blood transfusion a couple months ago after a car accident. Is that what you're seeing?" I was surprised by her improvisation. Maybe she wasn't such a bad liar after all.

"I don't know. I guess it could be…"

"Is there a problem here?" Sergeant Lantz came forward with is palm not-so-discreetly resting on the handle of his pistol.

"No," I said. "No problem. This man is just having some difficulty telling if my wife is really my wife."

"Is she?" The question barely concealed the threat behind it.

"Of course." I leaned in and whispered to him. "Honestly, I'd have swapped her out already if I could've gotten away with it."

The threat hovered in the air until my heart was about to beat its way out of my chest. Finally, the tension in Lantz's shoulders relaxed and his hand dropped away from his gun.

"I saw them come in together, Doc. What's the issue with her disk?"

"Her disk is fine. It's just a small variance in the DNA match that I can't account for."

"How small?"

"Point zero zero three five percent."

Sergeant Lantz's eyes rolled like bowling balls. "That's it? C'mon, Doc. We're on a tight schedule here, and we still have to process the alternates. Green out her screen and let's go."

The little man waved an arm dismissively. "Fine, fine. Who's next?"

Behind us, four people were cut from the front of the stand-by line and brought forward. Four people had won the lottery, but didn't survive long enough to collect their reward. I saw the two people left at the front of the line. The first losers. The two whose places we'd stolen. I'd live with those faces forever.

Barbara and I walked through the turnstiles together and didn't look back. And that was it. No fireworks. No trophy. No cooler full of Gatorade poured over my head in celebration of victory. I reached over to hold Barbara's hand as we walked, like we used to down by Clearwater beach late at night to watch the sunset, but she pulled away.

I'd won, against the longest odds anyone had ever faced. So why did it still feel like I'd lost everything?

ABOUT THE AUTHOR

Patrick S. Tomlinson is the son of an ex-hippie psychologist and an ex-cowboy electrician. He lives in Milwaukee, Wisconsin, USA, with a menagerie of houseplants in varying levels of health, a Ford Mustang, and a Triumph motorcycle bought specifically to embarrass and infuriate Harley riders. When not writing sci-fi and fantasy novels and short stories, Patrick is busy developing his other passion for performing stand-up comedy.

patrickstomlinson.com • *twitter.com/stealthygeek*

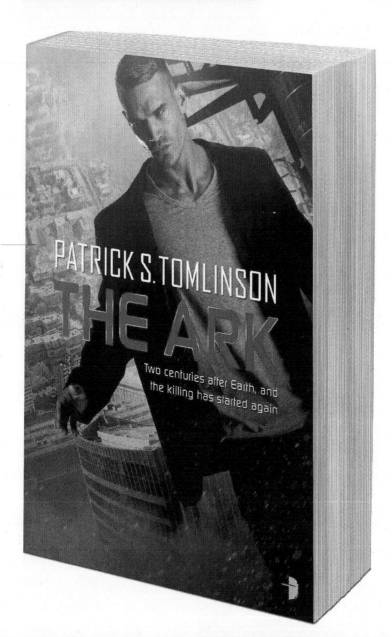

PATRICK S. TOMLINSON

THE ARK

Two centuries after Earth, and
the killing has started again